IRONHEART
The Primal Deception

Dakota Kemp

Text copyright © 2016 Dakota Kemp

First Edition Kwill Books 978-0-9905954-6-5

Kwill Books,

Plaza De La Marina 1,

Málaga 29015 Spain

www.kwillbooks.com/dakotakemp

Books by Dakota Kemp

The Arrival

The Shrike Chronicles: Goddess

This book is dedicated to the Sentinels in my life.
Dad, Kaleb – the world could not ask for better protectors.

Prologue

Freedom's gaze was unwavering.

Something was dreadfully wrong.

The Celestial Realm was a place of light and music and beauty – the visual, physical representation of paradise – but all Freedom could see was the filth of oppression. This wondrous place held no charms for her now. It all reeked of Tyranny.

Freedom's hands hardened into enraged fists.

The prisoners below trudged down the diamond-pressed streets – heads down, shoulders cringed, as if expecting some heavy blow to descend on their backs. In all likelihood, that blow would fall shortly. Order was not merciful to criminals, and Tyranny...

The bright, shining spires, columns, and statues around her glittered in the constant, golden light of the Celestial Realm. No sun sent its glaring rays down upon the white stone and hardened glass structures. The light simply *was*. Its brilliant illumination permeated the air and filled all space. No shadows existed to blight the faultless structures and landscapes with imperfection. Freedom had almost forgotten what it was like to bask in the radiant glow. Now that she had returned, the hypocrisy was enough to make her sick.

This was likely the first any of the prisoners had seen of the Celestial Realm. Myrmidons were rarely admitted, and these petty thieves and gangsters were not the sort to make such a prestigious list. The Celestial Realm was the home of the Primals. It was not intended for the mundane, pathetic existence of humanity – or, such is what traditional Primal logic would hold, even before the rise of Tyranny and his ilk.

Some of Tyranny's Primals surrounded the Myrmidons, escorting them to their assured deaths at the Court of Law. Freedom was confident they would not be taken to the Court of Justice in the heart of the Citadel – or she hoped not. If Tyranny were dealing with these personally...He would not, surely. Freedom was certain it was *far* beneath him. Regardless, she would need to act soon to prevent the procession moving farther into the city.

Freedom's eyes searched diligently over the Primal guards. She recognized Rage's black and red slashed armor immediately, and grimaced. He would make this much more difficult, as would Villain, who brought up the rear. Odium, Spite, and Bondage also accompanied the march, but Freedom liked their chances against those three. Freedom could easily pick out Bondage's black manacles splayed across his chest and Spite's venomous fangs, but Odium's sigil eluded her. Perhaps he didn't have one. Many Primals did not, such as Rage, who likely felt his purpose needed no more indication than his utterly random and brutal outbursts. She didn't need to see Villain's sigil. His black mask was well known to her.

Slight movement to her left caught Freedom's attention, and she glimpsed Sentinel sliding into position behind a nearby spire across the street, six stories up. His thick, rectangular shield and long, leaf-bladed spear were already in his hands. A glance toward the flat-topped building to Freedom's right revealed Valkyrie crawling warily into position as well.

All was ready.

Freedom summoned her weapon and felt the familiar weight of her sword drop into her hand as she stepped from behind a pillar and into the street. She grasped the hilt firmly and swung the double-edged blade into a two-handed grip – three feet of Celestial steel gleaming like a bonfire in the Realm's bright glow. Valkyrie responded to the signal just as the Primals' heads whirled at the blinding light. Rage's face twisted, and Spite's eyes widened with disbelief just before an ear-splitting BOOM exploded in the air from Valkyrie's scoped Sharps rifle. Spite took the bullet in the back, and he stumbled lamely, collapsing to a knee.

Freedom's wings burst from her back. Shimmering splayed lines of blue-tinted light spread behind her in a radiant azure wingspan. Sentinel dove from his height on green wings, spear held before him like a jousting lance. Justice and Hero roared into the street from her right and left. Hero was a blur of maniacal glee as he made a beeline for Villain, whose face twisted into a snarling rictus. Those two *hated* each other.

Freedom lowered her helm over her head and lifted off the ground. Her eyes locked on Rage. He bellowed with fury. A wicked, spiked mace appeared in his hand, and roaring wings of fire exploded behind him in gouts of flame.

The prisoners scattered.

Freedom shot forward like a bolt of light.

Rage rose up to meet her in the air.

Freedom collided with Rage in a colossal crash, their armor smashing together with the force of a falling comet. She had the greater momentum, and Rage tumbled violently back. Freedom slowed and slid into a landing, skidding across the diamond-pressed street on her armor-plated feet. She couldn't hear the metallic screech over the roar of combat around her. Justice was delivering crushing, repeated blows down on Odium's shoulders with his sword.

Hero and Villain were nothing but a grappling blur, whirling through the air over the street, ramming precariously into the buildings around them. Sentinel had pinned Bondage to the ground through his shoulder in the initial dive, but Bondage was spitting with rage, swinging about with his spiked chains. Sentinel was forced to leap back and withdraw his spear, weathering the enraged attack behind his blocky aegis.

Spite staggered up, finding his footing, and advanced unsteadily toward Sentinel's exposed back.

Another BOOM echoed throughout the street, and a second bullet connected with Spite's breastplate, flinging him back to the ground. The Primal's wings sputtered to life beneath him, but he was disinclined to rejoin the fight. He lifted off and flew down the street toward the Citadel, crashing erratically into columns as he went. *One down*, Freedom thought grimly. Spite would sound the alarm and bring back reinforcements from the Citadel soon enough. They had to finish this fast.

Rage had smashed into a beautiful spire with enough force that its front façade of diamond-pressed glass spiderwebbed from the point of impact, but he leapt to his feet with alacrity. His twisted, horned head turned toward her, eyes burning with red fire, and he charged with a ferocious roar. His wings flared behind him.

Freedom waited calmly in the center of the street. She raised her sword to catch the crushing blow that Rage aimed at her head and twisted when the weapons connected, allowing the spiked mace to slide to the side. Her counterthrust sought the weak point connecting his breastplate and fauld, but Rage anticipated the move. He stepped in close, allowing the blade to skate ineffectually off his breastplate, and grabbed her in an iron grip before bringing his horned head forward in a powerful headbutt.

Freedom's helm took the brunt of the blow, but she stumbled back, stunned, and tried desperately to retrieve her bearings. When her vision cleared, she had just enough time to recognize the flaming fist of stone flying toward her before it struck: The Fist of Rage.

Rage's unique attack connected with her breastplate like a full-speed locomotive, smashing into her Celestial Steel breastplate with enough power to cave it in toward her chest.

Freedom was lifted off her feet and thrown helplessly through the air, crashing to the street in a shower of sparks. She gasped for breath, her vision swimming. A sharp pain spiked through her chest. Beneath her, Freedom felt her wings flickering fitfully. A triumphant bellow sounded from above. Freedom summoned every shred of strength she had left and rolled, chest screaming in protest.

Rage descended not a moment later from a plummeting dive, his mace driving a divot in the hardened diamond surface to shatter the glass beneath. Freedom came up on a knee, swinging her sword in a savage arc. The blade found a gap in her opponent's plate beneath his outstretched arm and bit deeply through the chainmail beneath. A third BOOM split the air at the same moment, driving a Celestial steel .52 caliber bullet into the base of his neck, straight through the back of the gorget.

Rage doubled over her blade, but Freedom ripped her sword free and planted a foot on the side of his face that sprawled him on his back. Still ignoring her shortness of breath, Freedom leapt above him and drove her sword down through his shoulder, pinning him to the ground and forcing him to release his mace, which fell from his slackening grip and faded into mist. The bright wings of flame beneath him guttered and died.

Freedom glanced about her hurriedly, still wheezing, unable to breathe in her damaged breastplate. Bondage was flying away in fitful bursts, injured badly enough that his wings kept dying on him, but Sentinel had not pursued. Her steadfast ally had collapsed on a knee, with a hand pressed to his side. Justice was chasing Bondage towards the Citadel, but the golden warrior stopped regretfully at Valkyrie's cry of caution. The sniper was hurrying toward the fray, having abandoned her perch when the fight looked to be ending. Hero and Villain doggedly continued their vicious battle, but at Rage's fall and the flight of his companions Villain reluctantly broke away, speeding up the street on dark wings. Hero cursed after him, raging disappointedly, but allowed him to escape. Freedom motioned to him, and Hero hurried over, helping her pull off the bulk of her armor. She gasped as the breastplate peeled away, sucking in air gratefully.

Rage still hissed in anger, struggling weakly beneath her, but Freedom could see the light dying in his eyes. Finally able to breath, Freedom bent to Rage's ear, placing a foot on the wound in his side and pressing down.

"Tell me, Rage," Freedom said urgently. "What is the Instrument of Fate?"

Rage's eyes widened at this, but he just began to laugh. It was a croaking, horrible, dying sound. "The Myrmidon's champion, eh, Freedom? You're no different than Order or Tyranny. You're not here to save the rabble." He jerked his horned head toward the prisoners cowering along the edges of the street. "You're here for the power – for the Instrument."

Freedom twisted the sword in his shoulder savagely. She felt her expression distorting, and a dangerous darkness began to pass over her eyes. She forced it back.

"Fate's Instrument, Rage," Freedom insisted, twisting harder.

Rage continued laughing, his face distorting in pain. He spat back at her.

"Tell me," Freedom said again, stomping on his wound. His laughter didn't cease.

"The Instrument, Rage!" His amusements cut off into choking grunts. "Tell me!" The light flickered in his eyes. Freedom grabbed his face desperately. "TELL ME!" Rage's head fell sideways on his horns, his expression empty. Freedom ripped her sword free angrily and allowed it to dissipate, cursing with frustration.

She had failed. Again.

Chapter 1

"The Grounded Realm is located between the Celestial Realm and the Dark Realm (known in common language as The Abyss). While the Celestial Realm is the abode of our gods, the Grounded Realm has been set aside as the home for the subjects of the Primal Empire: the Myrmidons. The Dark Realm is a blasted wasteland where survival is rare, and it is the hellish destination of exiles, criminals, undesirables, and other enemies of the State.

No more will be written about the land of the banished here."

– Excerpt from *An Introduction to the Primal Empire and its Geography* by
Rubeus Bernah

Jack wasn't exceptional. He knew that. The wretched existence of an exile in The Abyss was not his fate, and neither was he the son of an aristocrat. Jack was an orphan. Just an orphan: one of thousands from the streets of Victorian. Or he had been. At eighteen he was a man, full grown and past the classification of his parents' presence or absence.

Jack leaned back in his seat, musing soberly. They called him "Dull Jack" here in Fist's gang, because he rarely spoke, but it wasn't because he couldn't think.

Jack knew all too well how to do that; he just never showed anyone how well. In fact, he was willing to bet he was a good deal more intelligent than the rest of his companions. He had put in his time on Victorian's streets, and he was a quick learner – quick enough to know that sometimes the most useful assets were the ones kept hidden.

So Jack kept his mouth shut, and let everyone think what they would. Sometimes he wished he was as dull as they imagined, then he wouldn't have to think about all the things he'd rather just leave to rest.

All of them were easy enough to fool. All except Fist himself. Sometimes Gurney would complain that Fist had no appreciation for cleverness or skill, because Jack was one of the boss's favorites and often got to lead on jobs.

"Sure, you know how to handle yourself alright, Jackie boy," Gurney had grumbled to him once. "But one o' these days

Brutality's coppers are going to catch up to us, and I'll be damned if we ain't goin' to need someone in charge who can *think*."

Jack had said nothing.

He was sure that Fist knew exactly who could think, and he was unsure if that was good or bad. On the one hand, it was always best to be on Fist's good side, but on the other, Jack's secret was compromised. Fist was a shrewd one. He used every advantage he could smell out to its fullest potential.

A gust of air howled through the peephole. Jack shifted absentmindedly to slip his thick, muscular torso into his grubby coat, covering his shirtsleeves. He pulled his bowler down tighter on his curly brown hair. The cramped look-out cavities that ran along the safe-house's brick exterior were drafty and moist this time of year, when autumn took full control from summer's lingering grasp, but he often found himself here despite the discomfort. It was the only place to go for a bit of solitude.

Jack liked to be alone, a nearly impossible state to achieve in one of Victorian's street gangs. But it was better than starving in the gutters, no matter how much more privacy he might find there. He could be in the dormitory-style bunkroom with the others – gambling, drinking, and doing all the other things men do when they're bored – but he was content to fill his belly, collect his share, and be left alone.

Jack had always liked isolation, but he could remember a time when he would have enjoyed occasional companionship. Those days were long gone, now. This was who he was. He preferred the seclusion.

Scuffling footsteps echoed behind him, and Jack grunted irritably. When he frowned, his thick jaw pulled at the skin around his eyes, emphasizing his prominent brow. He leaned back to allow Dasher to poke his head through the low entryway.

"Jack?" the boy queried, his eyes adjusting to the gloom of the lookout cubby. Jack still thought of Dasher as a lad, though the energetic young man couldn't possibly be any more than four years younger than Jack himself. Looking at the fine dark hair, sharp cheekbones, and bright eyes of Fist's most accomplished young pickpocket, Jack thought he was peering into a portal to the past.

Jack grunted sourly in affirmation, angry that he couldn't keep his memories in check. "What is it, Dasher?" he growled, more severely than he had intended.

Dasher faltered for a moment at his tone, but entered when Jack made more room. "Fist is looking for you. It's almost time."

Jack hid his surprise. Was it that late already? Time spent with his thoughts always passed more quickly than it should. "He still plans to go through with this mad scheme, then?"

Dasher shifted worriedly and looked at him with concern. "I wish you wouldn't say such things, Jack. You know Fist doesn't like it when people question him, and he's not happy about your backtalk recently."

"You let me worry about Fist," Jack replied harshly. "Just stay out of his way. Understand?"

Dasher nodded mutely, his bright eyes wide.

Jack pulled his Webley Bull Dog Pocket Revolver from the back of his waistband and flipped open the receiver. Five .44 caliber short rimfire cartridges filled the chambers. He shifted his left hand to his coat pocket and felt the handful of spare cartridges inside.

"We'll be headed out soon?"

Dasher nodded again. His eyes followed Jack's practiced hands sliding over the small handgun.

Satisfied that the weapon would be ready for use, Jack tucked it in his waistband next to the small of his back. "I'll head up to the common room, then. Run fetch my coach and a handful of shells."

Dasher leapt up enthusiastically to do his bidding. Jack stood slowly, shrugged more comfortably into his coat, gave another firm tug on the brim of his bowler, and followed him out.

Chapter 2
(Twelve Years Ago)

"Ah, Victorian! City of my birth! The smell of waste on the wind and a sense of desperation in the air! What a wonderful place it is, where the aristocracy whore themselves to the Primals and the rest of the populace wishes they could! The common man wallows in hopeless conditions amidst decrepit buildings and poverty-stricken streets. Victorian! Gem of my heart!"

– Lord Victor Rolfe, Political Wit and Social Radical

It was cloudy and rainy.

Jack stared gloomily out of the open door of the ramshackle flat into the cobblestone street, his dark brown eyes serious despite his youth. His feet were bare; too-short trousers ended at the tops of his ankles, little suspenders crisscrossed over his back and filthy shirt, and sandy-brown hair curled around his temples and neck. The rain continued to drip down off the eaves and pool in the sunken depressions of the street.

That's when Jack knew.

It had been cloudy and rainy the day his father had died too. Jack's discerning eyes flickered from the sodden street when he remembered. Strange men had knocked on the door, huddled up against the rain in their coal-caked jackets, and asked in soft voices if they might come in. His mother had let them hesitantly. He could still recall the look on her face. Fear. Fear and grief. She hadn't been afraid of the men, but she had known, somehow…

Jack had listened to the men's mumbled words as he gripped his mother's skirts. Some had been strange words, and he could only remember choppy bits.

"Boiler explosion…factory up in smoke…everything we could…so sorry, Mary." Just words. That's all. Words that had caused Mum to sink to the floor in silent shock. It had been cloudy and rainy, and Father had never come home.

Now, today, it was cloudy and rainy again.

That wasn't unusual in Victorian. The sprawling city, capital of the Grounded Realm, was often covered in thick fog, soaking in light showers, or under copious cloud cover. The days that the sun shone

9

down from a blue sky were great treats, when the streets filled with scampering children and grown-ups out for a stroll. So the clouds and the rain weren't abnormal – but something was. And Jack could tell, because it was cloudy and rainy.

Jack knew Mum was never coming home again. He didn't know how he knew. Probably the same way Mum had known about Father. It was a feeling. A heavy, dead feeling in his gut. It was as if the men in coal-caked jackets were climbing the steps to the door at that very moment.

"Jack?"

Jack didn't turn from the door.

"Jack, Harv's hungry, and me too."

Jack felt his own stomach rumble at the words. He stared out into the street with greater intensity, his little eyes narrowing. Mum brought food when she came home at night. But she wasn't coming home tonight, not ever again.

How do you get food? Jack wondered. Mum had got it from somewhere out there. Jack's mouth tightened when his stomach rumbled a second time. He would have to find out where.

"Jack?"

Jack sighed and turned. Morgan's dark hair, bright eyes, and quick smile greeted him. Harv, his youngest brother, clutched Morgan's wrist with one hand and sucked the thumb of the other, despite being nearly two and a half. Morgan bore this with a charitable, long suffering look on his face. Five was nearly too old to let your baby brother suck his thumb and hold your hand, but Morgan was too good-natured to push him away.

Jack jerked his head toward the kitchen. "I think Mum left some bread and cheese in the pantry. Go get you and Harv some."

"What about Mum?" Morgan asked, quizzically. "When is she coming back with food?"

"Go on, now," Jack shooed him away roughly. The words he had meant to say stuck in his throat. *Mum's never coming back.* "Eat your bread and cheese, and don't let Harv smash his crumbs on the table like he does."

Morgan jerked his hand from Harv's and raced for the kitchen. Harv yelled his protest at the unfair headstart and hurried after him.

Jack turned back to the clouds and the rain.

His brain raced behind the serious brown eyes. Mum was never coming home again. What did that mean?

Chapter 3

"The vast majority of the human population in the Grounded Realm is purposefully kept in abject poverty by the Emperors. Subjugation is disregarded when there is time for nothing but survival. Is it any wonder that the cities are rife with organized crime? The possibility of execution or banishment is acceptable to many a man in exchange for a full belly and a pocketful of schillings."

– Excerpt from *Freedom's Progress* by Lady Liberty (pseudonym), blacklisted author

Jack shambled up the stairs from the basement safehouse into the common room of the tavern that served as a cover. Most everyone was already there, crowding round the front, where Fist leaned against the bar. Jack brushed past Gurney, and the rest made way when they recognized his short, thick, broad-shouldered build.

Fist was waiting for him. Impatiently.

"I've been looking everywhere for you, Jack. Where the hell have you been?" The rough voice came across casual, but Jack knew a tone of warning when he heard it from Fist.

"Thinking," Jack grunted in response.

Fist chuckled, and when he did, so did everyone else in the room. "Thinking isn't a place, Jack," Fist replied, straightening.

"Dull Jack," a mutter came from behind, followed by muffled laughter. Jack ignored them.

Standing at full height, Fist was a big man. He towered a foot over Jack's compact, well-muscled frame, and was every bit as broad. His thick arms and torso had faded perhaps a little into fat with age, but he was still the largest, strongest man Jack had ever seen. His face had a blunt, stony look, with a strong brow and jaw that lent an iron quality to his gray eyes.

Jack grunted again, shrugging. "I'm here now. If we're going to kick a bloody hornet's nest, let's get to it."

The room stilled, and a wave of uneasy shuffling echoed around him. Fist displayed a considering look of mixed irritation and contemplation.

"We've already discussed this, Jack." Fist's warning was clearer this time.

Jack held his eyes for a moment before he grunted in acceptance. "Fine."

Fist nodded, but Jack could tell he had expected nothing less than compliance. It rankled him something terrible.

"Listen up," Fist addressed the room at large, though it was already silent. "The shipment is near the airdocks in a warehouse on Wilshire Street. We'll split into three groups under Harry, Jack, and myself."

A flurry of motion swept the room as the oration began. Small revolvers emerged from cheap, filthy waistcoats, knives slid into boots and belts, thick, hardwood clubs slipped up sleeves and into trouser waistbands, and brass knuckles gripped over fingers as the ragtag gangsters checked and double checked their weapons. Dasher slipped easily through the sour, unwashed crowd and handed Jack his break-over, double-barreled coach shotgun.

"Wagon teams?" Jack asked, accepting the bag of 12-gauge shells Dasher provided. He broke the coach over his left forearm and inserted two rounds before closing the barrel breech with a snap.

"Harry's group will have the wagons for pickup," Fist replied. "I'll take the front entry. Jack, you have the back alley. I don't want anyone slipping by you to the coppers, understand?"

Jack grunted, giving him a slight nod.

"I've got Dasher and his pickers working watch in a five-block radius around the warehouse," Fist continued. "I'm not expecting any copper trouble if we do this quick and clean, but they'll let us know about any problems. Jack, you'll send a man to Harry and his boys when we're ready for the wagons." Fist turned to the beefy, black-haired and whiskered man to his left. "Harry, roll it up near the Grelich Street warehouses like you're waiting for a pickup from the airdock. When you get word from Jack, split over to the back entrance to the warehouse on Wilshire through the east alley."

Harry grinned, his blocky, tobacco-stained teeth pulling tightly against his lips. "If it goes down crooked, you best save a man or three for me, Jack."

Jack's lip curled slightly, but he stayed silent, casually slipping a hand into his coat pocket.

"I don't want anything mucking this up," Fist warned. "Keep everything contained. No bloody gunshots unless we're already blown."

Harry shrugged back at him. "Sure, Fist. Just don't want to miss all the fun if Dull Jack forgets why we're there."

A few chuckles came from the other side of the room, but everyone around Jack remained silent, eyeing him uneasily. Jack said nothing. He slipped a hand into his breast pocket and pulled out a small, rolled cigar. He raised it to his lips, struck a match and lit it up, never looking at the other side of the room. Fist was watching him with a slight smile on his lips, as if indifferently curious to see his reaction. Jack blew out a cloud of smoke.

"That all, Fist?"

Fist's face still held a look of relaxed amusement, but he just placed a revolver behind his waistband in answer and grabbed his shotgun on the way to the door.

"Five minutes in and out, boys. Let's keep this tight."

Chapter 4

(Twelve Years Ago)

"Despite our lowly origins and insignificance, the gods continue to stretch out their hands in aid as a gesture of their great love. Nowhere can this be better seen than in the creation of the Illuminati. The gods gave us purpose. We aid the sick and the weary, the poor and the meek, the widow and the orphan. All of this is possible because of the Primals' great compassion for us, regardless of our unworthiness.

What else can we do but praise them and give thanks?"

– Gaius III, Victorian Illuminati Pontifex and Radical Primaphile

Harv was dead within four weeks.

Jack was lost. He didn't know whether it was his fault or not. They had all been starving – Harv, Morgan, and himself. He had taken Morgan into the streets to find food, digging in garbage piles, taking what they could when the street vendors weren't looking, asking everyone who hurried by. Sometimes they managed to get a little food. Sometimes they didn't.

The hunger had shown visibly after the first couple of weeks. Morgan and Harv looked like fragile little sticks, and Jack had no doubt his appearance was similar. Harv cried all of the time, and Morgan did often. Jack didn't. Not when anyone was around to see, anyway, especially Morgan and Harv.

A lucky find in the garbage had occurred on the day it started. Jack had found a half-eaten loaf of stale bread, and had brought the prize home triumphantly. It had been a good night. Their shrunken bellies hadn't felt full perhaps, but they didn't ache either. Harv had stopped crying, and Morgan had even laughed while they'd eaten, with that bright sparkle back in his exuberant eyes. But that was the night Jack first noticed the cough.

He hadn't thought much of it at first, but the next few days were different. Instead of crying, Harv slept and shivered. An awful, persistent hacking noise came from out of the depths of his lungs. Jack didn't know what to do except find more food, but the boy refused to eat even what little he managed to bring back.

It was over as quickly as it had started. Five days after he had found the loaf of bread, Jack had awoken to find Harv silent for the first time since Mum's disappearance. No crying. No raging cough. His little body had been stiff and cold. The thin limbs were unmoving, as were his big staring eyes, and Jack had been afraid. He knew that father was "dead," but it wasn't until looking down at his brother's lifeless body that he finally understood the concept. Harv was gone. He was still there, lying in the tiny bed, but he wasn't – not really. Harv had left them. Just like their parents.

Eventually, Jack had summoned the courage to touch Harv-but-not-Harv. He had wrapped him in a blanket and taken him out to the alley behind the flat. He didn't know what else to do.

Morgan didn't laugh anymore.

It had been a week since Jack had dragged that little bundle into the alley. Hunger forced him outside in the mornings, and it was with him when he returned home. Only in blissful sleep could he escape for a few brief hours from the constant, sucking ache in his midriff. Jack's mind was never at rest, though. Could he have done something differently? He couldn't think of anything else he might have tried. Food was the only thing he knew he could get to help, and there was never enough of it. His role was always the same. Get up – hungry – and scrounge for food in the streets. Come home, nibble on the collected morsels of the day, and collapse into an exhausted sleep. Repeat.

But the cycle had been broken today.

Jack couldn't decide if he was inconvenienced or relieved to find the two men in the flat when he returned. It was an interruption in the pattern – either a hindrance to the constant quest for food, or a boon of change. He was wary though, and scared. He knew that for certain.

The younger of the two men, a clean-shaven, bright-eyed fellow with a long nose and thin face, smiled at Jack where he had frozen in the flat's doorway. The other man, who had creased wrinkles around his eyes and cheeks, watched him over steepled fingers with a solemn expression. Jack squinted at them suspiciously, his serious eyes taking in their strange garb and kindly faces. Their hair looked odd, cut in a round bowl shape that was long on top but shaved beneath. Jack tugged unconsciously on his ragged little coat, thinking that he had never seen such queer clothes as bedecked these strangers. They didn't wear a coat or jacket over a shirt and trousers. Instead, flowing robes covered them from neck to ankle. The robes were beautiful – bright blue for one and red for the other – with golden patterns and intricate shapes scrolled across the chest, shoulders, and arms. Jack shifted doubtfully. They were very clean.

"Hello," the young man said warmly, standing from his seat at the table. His voice was pitched soft, as if he was afraid that Jack might run away. "My name is Father Kyle," he gestured toward the older man, "And this is Father Anthony."

Jack didn't move. His eyes shifted from one stranger to the other. Behind him, Morgan poked at his back impatiently, craning to see over his shoulder. Jack ignored him.

"It's all right, boy," Father Anthony said. His voice was gruff, but kind. "We've been waiting for you. Come in out of the street."

Jack remained in the doorway. "What do you want?"

"We're here to help," Father Kyle replied. "What's your name? And who is your friend?"

Jack was silent a moment before answering. "I'm Jack, and this is my brother, Morgan." He eyed the robed men with a distrustful, considering gaze. "What do you mean, help?"

"Tell me, Jack," Father Anthony leaned forward on his elbows. "Have you ever heard of the Illuminati?"

Jack shook his head, as he had never heard the term. But he had seen men like these before, in their fine robes. Jack had watched them occasionally in the past, but Mum had always hurried him away, muttering about religious madmen.

"You're from the temples." Jack stated.

"That's correct," Father Kyle answered, beaming at him. His voice was encouraging and soothing, like the dirty man from the alley who had tried to take the scrap of food he had found a few days before. Jack didn't trust him.

"Where are your parents?" Father Anthony asked after a moment's silence.

"They're gone," Morgan burst out, finally squeezing past Jack and into the flat. Jack growled at him when he pushed by, but Morgan kept speaking anyway. "Father died at the factory, and Mum left to find food but didn't come back. Harv started coughing a few days ago and then he didn't wake up." His earnest voice fell. "We took him into the alley."

17

Jack noticed the two priests exchange knowing glances. Father Kyle's face was sad. Father Anthony's was resigned.

"Tell me," Father Kyle said, crouching down to look them in the eyes. "When was the last time you ate?"

Jack's hand leapt protectively to the half-rotten vegetables in his coat pocket, and he punched Morgan in the shoulder when his brother opened his mouth to speak.

"Why?" Jack asked suspiciously.

Father Kyle smiled at him again, as if he knew what he was thinking. "Don't worry, Jack. I'm not going to steal anything. In fact, I'm going to take you where there is plenty of food. You'll never be hungry again."

Jack still didn't trust these priests, but Father Kyle had his attention at 'food.'

Chapter 5

"Some praise the ingenuity of the chevaline, a masterpiece of intricate machinery. And it is, indeed, a marvelous invention – technology that simulates life. Some laud the steam-powered jetpack; never let it be said that the power of flight is not a magnificent thing. But I say it is the airship – that simple marriage of basic steam technology and mundane transportation – that has most deeply affected the world."

– Benjamin Norton, Engineer

Jack leaned casually on the brick alley wall of a warehouse just off the airship quays, short-barreled shotgun resting against his shoulder. The warehouse was empty, so Jack didn't expect any security in the immediate area. But around the dock and warehouse districts you could never be sure, even with Dasher and the rest of his pickpockets keeping an eye out.

Jack didn't like it. This was a risky job, and Fist knew it. Airship cargo was more valuable than freight from the steam locomotives, but more value meant more security, and the coppers assigned extra patrols to the docks. Besides, Fist was getting uncomfortably close to Primal turf with this escapade, and Jack didn't think Chaos and his boys would take too kindly to anyone muscling in to their markets. Fist's gang had feuded with a few other human street gangs over the years, but getting in Chaos's way was a whole different story. Jack didn't even want to think about the attention they might attract from the authorities pulling a job like this, either. They'd had to evade a few raids and step carefully to avoid drawing too much notice, but the bolder Fist became the more risk they ran of catching Brutality's eye. Jack knew they could handle random run-ins with a copper or two, but he wasn't eager to find out what would happen if they drew the attention of Brutality and the full strength of his enforcers.

Jack didn't show any of this, of course. Not to the other men. As far as they knew, he was as solid as ever, waiting with a slow, patient air for the excitement to begin. They knew he had objected to this heist in the first place, but they didn't know how strongly. Jack had only voiced stringent objections to Fist – not that it had done any good.

So, Jack acted like this was just another job, the same as pulling cargo off the steam engines that came into Victorian from the west. He was good at hiding things. He was Dull Jack – unfazed, invincible, and too stupid to be worried.

Gurney was whispering to Black Jim and Goldilocks, so he turned with a grunt. "What is it, Gurney?"

"Well, Jack," the toothless gossiper answered. "I reckon I saw one o' them airships coming in to dock. I saw the lights coming down from the clouds. What if it lands close to this warehouse? Streets around here could get uncomfortable busy in a few minutes, if you catch my meaning."

Jack regarded the old man. Gurney was the most ancient gang member he'd ever seen, nearing sixty, to hear him tell it. Life expectancy in street gangs was normally less than half that age, but the old-timer was still here. He wasn't good with a gun, or tough, or intimidating. If Jack was any judge, Gurney was a coward, but a likeable one. This had worked to keep him alive all these years, despite gang in-fighting, feuds, and the coppers. Cowardice kept him from getting into any situations that might get him killed, and an ingratiating attitude kept him in good graces with the right people – namely Fist – or anyone else bigger and meaner, which was everyone.

Jack shrugged stupidly in response. "Docks are full around here; they'll make berth further on south. It won't be a problem."

"If you say so, Jackie boy," Gurney muttered nervously. "All the same, maybe we'd better–"

Jack cut him off, addressing Black Jim with a deadpan expression. "Don't let the old man slip away on us, Jim. Keep an eye out." Jack smiled at Gurney. "Cover his back. To make sure he continues to cover ours." Black Jim nodded and displayed big, tobacco-stained teeth in a wide smile.

Gurney scowled with a hurt expression. "Now, Jackie boy, you know I'd never abandon you boys–"

"Bullocks," Goldilocks muttered, cutting through the old timer's protests. The stark blond-haired youth was a year younger than Jack, but looked more like he still belonged with the pickpockets. His namesake was pulled back in a long ponytail, and a petulant look covered his pockmarked face. "I recall you saying something similar

20

on the last job, just before you cut out and left me in that alley all by myself."

"That was only 'cause you was going on and on about proving yourself, is all," Gurney objected. "I was just giving you the chance you deserve…"

Jack turned back to the alley's entrance, ignoring the rest of the argument. Black Jim would keep him honest. Or at least too scared to leave.

Gurney hadn't been lying about seeing an airship coming in to dock. They rarely arrived after nightfall, so Jack had assumed the wizened old man had been making that up as an excuse to sneak away, but a cargo ship was sailing from the clouds, lit up with lanterns and illuminated further by the docks high lighthouses. The docks were full near his group, however, just as he had said, and it descended further south.

Jack gazed at the airship with a mixture of longing and curiosity. He had loved to watch the airships as a boy, to see the massive wooden hulls sailing out and away over Victorian's streets. The smokestacks churning out steam into the air from the aft boiler, the zeppelin balloon filling into a long oval above the ship, the lines connected to the hull straining to lift the vessel over the highest towers and into the sky… Jack had thought he could go anywhere, if he could only board one. He could go out to the wild mystery of the west beyond Jackson, or even sail up to the Celestial Realm. On occasion he heard airships were ordered to sail down to the Abyss to unload new groups of unfortunates, but Jack thought he could live just fine without ever seeing the Dark Realm.

The gliding fins were spread out on this airship to aid its gradual descent. The horizontal sails, fanned out wide to either side, bulged with the wind they caught, and the balloon above the ship slowly deflated as the steam engine in the rear began working to help regulate the speed of the landing. Jack watched the ship until it was out of sight behind the warehouse roofs, and then shook himself disapprovingly. It wouldn't do to drift from the present tonight; the risk was too great.

Across the street and down the block, a dim light bloomed as a small lantern was uncovered. Its glow was nearly undetectable in the brighter illumination of the streetlamps, but Jack was looking for it. It was time.

21

"You're in luck, Gurney," Jack growled, turning back to the men gathered in the alley behind him. "Someone needs to tell Harry to bring the wagons around, and you got this shifty look in your eye like you're ready to bolt." He checked his coach and Bull Dog one last time as he addressed the old man. "I guess you get to keep out of the thick of it again."

"Now, Jackie boy, you know I would never–"

"Gurney, just go tell him."

"My pleasure," Gurney grinned, tipping his hat. He slipped away down the alley.

Black Jim gave him a disappointed look. Jack shrugged. "Best to send him off now, that way he doesn't disappear when we think he's got our backs."

Black Jim sighed heavily, the sound whistling through his severely broken nose, but he straightened his bowler in readiness. Jack did the same. Goldilocks had an enthusiastic light shining in his eyes and a hand gripped tight around the hardwood club in his coat. Jack regarded him doubtfully. He was glad he hadn't trusted the lad with a gun yet. He was far too eager to prove himself, and the last thing they needed tonight was an overzealous gunshot bringing every copper on the airship docks down on them.

Jack tucked the short-barreled coach under his coat and swung out into the well-lit street. His two companions followed close behind him. He moved at a brisk pace, not too hurried and not too leisurely. Just some chaps finishing up late-night business. This being the warehouse district at an exceptionally late hour, the streets remained almost entirely empty as Jack's group wound toward Wilshire Street. He kept to the alleys as much as possible and out of the incriminating light of the streetlamps. A few beggars and heroin addicts curled up against the cobblestones as they slipped by. None spoke or acknowledged their passing but for the peering of curious eyes. They reached their destination without incident.

Jack stepped down Wilshire Street, which seemed to blaze with light after the expedition through the backstreets. He crossed the gutter behind the target warehouse and stopped at the mouth to the back alley, then swept the street behind them with his eyes one last time before sliding into the dark. Jack motioned for Jim and Goldilocks to cover the alley's entrance, and they crouched in the shadows just beyond the light of the streetlamps.

Jack crept down the alley for a few moments before he saw the dim outline of a warehouse security guard pacing alertly ahead. Then Jack stumbled into the wall, kicking a bottle nearby. He chuckled bemusedly, and muttered a drunken song to himself. The security man stiffened. A holstered revolver hung from his belt in position for a cross-draw, and a club was in his hand.

"Who goes there?" The voice was sharp and carried a suspicious tone. The man stepped forward a few paces, his arm tense, poised to deliver a blow with the thick cane. Jack's blood pumped with adrenaline. He absently noted the magnificent, bushy mustache below the man's squinted eyes and flat cap.

"You don' know whereee Baker Street is, do ya, sirrr?" Jack slurred the words to make the man strain to hear. The guard took another step closer. Jack tripped and stumbled toward the man, catching himself on the wall. He chuckled again, throwing in a hiccup for good measure. "I see… seem to 'ave lost it."

There was a bit of revulsion in the man's eyes, but also a shred of amusement. His club dropped the slightest bit. "Bloody sot, get out of here before I–" The club fell nearer to his side. It was all the opening Jack needed.

Jack shot upright, bringing the butt of his shotgun from beneath his coat to smack directly on the guard's mustache. He reeled back, hands flying up to cover his face. Jack grabbed his coat and placed the barrel of his coach on the center of his chest. The man moaned and spit out a tooth, his lip smashed and bleeding. Jack ripped the revolver from the guard's holster and slipped it into his belt beside his Bull Dog.

"Don't make a sound," Jack warned calmly, "or I blow a fist-sized hole through your rib cage." An angry gleam was coming into the man's eyes as he tongued his gums gingerly. Jack decided he wasn't quite cowed enough. He reached around and grabbed the back of the guard's collar, levering him face-first into the alley's brick wall. His nose made a sharp, cracking sound. A hand rose defensively, cringing; the other covered his face. The guard slid down to his knees.

"You do as I told you, you hear?" Jack grunted. "Or it'll go badly for you." He whistled lightly down the alley, and a few moments later Black Jim and Goldilocks appeared.

"Goldi," Jack ordered brusquely, handing the lad the guard's club. "If he makes a sound or moves even the slightest bit, you cave his head in." Goldilocks nodded, face slightly green as he watched the guard hack and spit gobbets of blood between the fingers covering his brutalized face, but he gripped the club determinedly.

Jack's ears caught the sound of wagon wheels bouncing on cobblestones. He turned to the warehouse's alley door. "Jim, you're with me."

Muffled scuffling and grunted curses reached Jack's ears as he cautiously pushed open the heavy plank door. He jerked his head indicatively at Black Jim. Clearly, Fist had already arrived.

Jack hurried through a back room filled with a table, chairs, a stack of cards, and cigar butts. It was blessedly empty of guards. Just as he presumed, Jack found them in the main storage area, hands and legs splayed out against the wall, held to silence at gunpoint by Fist's men. Jack counted six of them – seven including the guard in the alley. It was a suspiciously large amount of security in Jack's experience. He wondered briefly if Fist was as surprised as he was, or if he had expected as much. Jack's eyes narrowed.

The hulking, muscular gang leader spotted him as he entered. Fist jerked his head toward the back. "Any in the alley, Jack?" His eyes flickered around at the crates and the captive guards, his shotgun resting on his shoulder.

"One," Jack said shortly. "No problems. Goldilocks has him. I heard Harry and his boys rolling up as we came in."

"Good," Fist laughed approvingly. "I'm giving us three minutes to load as much of this cargo as we can, then we get the hell out. Anymore and we'll have bloody coppers coming to investigate." He motioned to one of his group and dropped his shotgun down into a ready grip. "Jack, have Goldilocks bring the other in with this lot. Lom and I will hold 'em. You get all the others dragging these crates out back. And get Harry's ass moving. We're down to two and half minutes."

Jack nodded in confirmation and grabbed the end of one of the thick wooden crates, motioning Jim to the other side. The room filled with scuffling movement as every available man set to the task. They lifted with a grunt and struggled toward the back door. The cargo was surprisingly heavy, despite its relatively small size.

24

The first of Harry's wagons was entering the alley when Jack shuffled backwards out of the door with his load, and he set it down.

"Goldi," Jack barked. "Take him inside with the rest. Then, set to loading these crates." Harry pulled up in the wagon as the pox-faced boy complied. He grinned down at Jack sneeringly.

"How'd it go, Jack? Bugger anyone up?"

Jack didn't deign to answer as he lifted his end of the crate. "Get off that bloody wagon and start loading. Fist says we got two minutes." He grunted with exertion, pushing the freight to the front of the buckboard.

When Jack went to get another crate, the guards were all lying bound and gagged in a corner out of the way. Some looked much the worse for wear, but they would all be fine until morning. He grabbed another crate with Jim and joined the queue shuffling out to the wagons.

Jack was just heaving this second crate into a cart when it happened. Goldilocks, who was lifting the end of his own crate, slipped. The crate teetered on the edge of the wagon for a long moment, and Jack hissed.

"Watch it!"

The crate toppled off sideways and smashed into the ground. The wooden top busted loose, and the contents came spilling out, tumbling across the cobblestones.

Jack was silent for a long moment. Then, he stepped forward and bent, grasping one of the apple-sized stones in his hand. It shone with a silvery light, tinged with the slightest hint of a golden glow. Jack's teeth clenched.

Celestial Steel.

Chapter 6

(Seven Years Ago)

"It can be plainly seen that the gods love strong men, because one always sees the weak dominated by the strong."

– 'Red' Ragen, Infamous Victorian Mob Boss

"The Primals are our caretakers, our protectors, and, when deserved, the unwilling instruments of our discipline. Benevolent and wise, they desire nothing less than the best for us, and they strive always for our wellbeing, providing order, and fighting for peace."

It was a chapel day. Most of the other boys had groaned and cursed when Father Kyle had made the announcement, but not Jack. He loved chapel days. He eagerly awaited the tours through the vaulted temple with its marvelous stained glass, soaring arches, and intricately carved stone statues of the Primals over the altars. He even enjoyed the instructions on proper living as demanded by the gods, but the stories of the great deeds performed by the various Primals were his favorite.

Father Kyle opened his mouth to speak further, but Jack raised his hand, confused. "Father, what of the rogue Primals like Chaos and Freedom? Aren't they gods, too?"

"An excellent question, Jack, thank you." Father Kyle said enthusiastically. He paced in front of them where they sat in the rickety wooden pews. His golden-scrolled red robes flapped as he delivered his instruction. "Yes, Chaos, Freedom, Justice, and other rogues are all Primals. Some are aptly named, while others are clearly aliases intended as mocking heresies. But do we worship them? No! Truly great beings like our gods will always have powerful enemies – an antithesis, if you will – but the true gods will ultimately prevail over their evil counterparts."

Father Kyle smiled long-sufferingly when Jack's hand shot up again. A few pews over, Jack saw Johnny Topper glaring at him, and all the boys started muttering. The more he asked questions, the longer they had to stay here. Jack ignored them.

"Yes, Jack? Something else?"

"If the evil Primals *are* Primals, and all Primals are gods, then why don't the Illuminati worship them, too? Are there people who worship the rogue Primals?"

"There are," Father Kyle admitted. "Cults exist that worship various evil Primals, or sometimes all of them, but most of these cults are only prevalent in the West or in the Abyss. There are even a few influential insurrectionist cults here in Victorian. The largest and strongest is undoubtedly Freedom's powerful cult, but the most radical and zealous are the followers of Chaos. One of our two chief deities, the wise and benevolent Order, has outlawed these cults for encouraging rebellion. And our other great leader, the just and implacable Tyranny, has proclaimed that Myrmidons – the Primal term for humans – in any way associated with such grotesque factions be executed immediately for their disturbing crimes.

"As to your other question, we of the Illuminati do not worship the rogue Primals because, put simply, they are not *worthy* of worship. We are not devoted to our rulers just because they are gods. We revere them because they stand for what is right – order, fairness, peace, and obedience – and because they have chosen to watch over us, despite having no reason to do so. In short, they *deserve* our affection. The rogue Primals deserve nothing but our hate and steadfast opposition."

Jack's mind chewed over this slowly and steadily. He didn't ask any more questions. He was content to ponder what he had heard.

"That's enough for today," Father Kyle proclaimed, smiling widely at the sea of stupefied faces around him. "Everyone is dismissed to the yard. Dinner is at six."

A furious scuffling erupted upon this announcement, and a mad rush to the temple doors ensued despite Father Kyle's call for caution and respect of the holy place. Jack waited calmly at the back of the shoving crowd with Morgan beside him. Jack's bright-eyed brother had grown gangly over the years at the orphanage, drastically opposed to Jack's stocky frame. It worried Jack a tiny bit that Morgan might soon be taller than him, though both were quite short for their age.

"Tommy, Lem, and I are going to play toss ball, Jack." Morgan stated excitedly. "You want to come?"

Jack opened his mouth to say no. It was a response that came naturally to him, but the hopeful look in his brother's youthful eyes stopped him short. Jack sighed.

Few friends were a part of his life at the orphanage, though he never lacked for companionship with his brother around. Morgan was much more outgoing and frequently drew others in, but Jack often watched from afar. He was quiet and serious and rarely laughed, while Morgan practically burbled over with delight and enthusiasm. They could not have been more different. Morgan frequently sought to draw Jack into his circle of friends. Jack continually refused. He didn't go in much for games or mischief. He shared his thoughts and plans with no one but Morgan, and he continued to observe everything from a cautious distance.

But Morgan's eyes were pleading today, and Jack buckled reluctantly under the guilt. "All right," Jack nodded unwillingly. "I'll play for a bit."

"Yes!" Morgan whooped. "I'll go tell the others. Meet you by the fence!" He scampered off.

Jack shook his head, but walked slowly after him, exiting out of the temple doors and wandering toward the orphanage yard behind the temple proper. The wrought iron fence surrounding the entire complex was stark black and severe. Jack remembered how he had thought it intimidating and confining when he arrived five years previous, but now he found it somewhat protective and comforting. Strange how perceptions could alter. It wasn't the only change since the day Father Kyle and Father Anthony had been waiting for them at the flat.

Jack had known nothing of privacy since he and Morgan first stepped into the grey stone orphanage behind the temple. The dormitory style rooms were filled to bursting with bunks, overflowing with boys from ages three to sixteen. Despite the excess of children, the years here had been good to them. Jack and Morgan's bellies had never been distended with hunger, though the food was bland and they were rarely able to eat their fill. Jack had learned what he could, mostly in the way of trade skills, but with overcrowding and few caretakers, the majority of days were spent in the factories. The factory was hot and unpleasant and the days were long, but Jack knew nothing different or better anyway.

It was days like today, spent in the temple or out in the yard, that Jack enjoyed most. He would question Father Kyle or any of the other Illuminati priests about Primals, or wander the massive temple steps, halls, and balconies, enamored by the magnificence around him. And sometimes, he didn't do any of these things. He would find a secluded spot in the yard and think. Sometimes about the grueling days at the factory, about things the priests had said, about what he had learned during the week, about Father, or Mum, or Harv. Sometimes he didn't think at all, just watched Morgan race across the yard with his friends. Jack wondered what would have happened if the priests had never found them. They would have starved long ago.

Jack looked down at his worn shoes as he scuffed his way toward the back fence of the yard, but raised his head suspiciously when he heard derisive laughter ahead. His brows drew down into a scowl beneath his curly hair, and the hands in his trouser pockets tightened into fists. He stayed his pace, and stepped from behind the back wing of the orphanage.

Jack had known what he would see before he entered the yard. Morgan and his two friends stood in the center of a jeering circle of older boys, who shoved them this way and that, until they stumbled and fell into the dirt. Johnny Topper stood in the middle of the group, holding young Tommy with his eyes. Morgan was glaring up at him from the ground, the knees of his trousers torn and bloody, sniffling furiously to keep from crying. Lem was gingerly holding his arm as he crouched next to Morgan.

Boys, young and old, watched from around the yard. Some sniggered appreciatively; some pretended they didn't see what was happening. Many watched with a slight air of worry.

"Look at 'im *crying*!" Topper was sneering derisively. "At least Tommy's looking me in the eye, Morgan. I thought you Booker boys were supposed to be tough? Get up, pussy." He kicked at the dirt, sending a cloud of dust into Morgan's face. Morgan recoiled, frantically pawing at his eyes. Topper seemed to be growing bored. He turned back to Tommy, who still clenched the toss-ball fearfully in one hand.

"Give me that ball," Topper demanded. Tommy complied immediately. Topper chucked it as far over the fence as he could.

29

Raucous laughter erupted from Johnny's buddies at this, but the sneering mirth on the faces of those across the circle died away quickly when they noticed Jack's relaxed approach. Topper noticed their lack of amusement and turned to glower over his shoulder.

The look of uncomfortable surprise, fear, and hesitation that flashed across his face made anything that followed worth it, but it was replaced as quickly as it had come with belligerence and disdain. Jack stopped a few paces away.

"They wasn't doing nothing, Jack, honest," spindly Kricket stuttered, approaching from outside Topper's circle. Jack said nothing. He just stared at Johnny.

Johnny Topper was a big kid: one of the oldest at the orphanage and soon to be sent on his way in the world. He was taller than Jack by several inches, and was thick and beefy in a way that displayed he had already grown into his adult physique. Jack hated everything about him. His short, bristly, red hair, the overbearing brow protruding above his eyes, the way he spoke like he knew everything – and wanted everyone to know that he did – the ease with which he gathered fearful cronies to run with him. Jack had hated it all from the beginning.

He and Morgan hadn't been at the temple orphanage a month before first running afoul of Topper and his gang. They'd done nothing to draw his attention other than to be in the same room when he decided he was in a black mood. Topper had come roaring at Jack first – because he was new and looked vulnerable or lost, perhaps – and punched him in the stomach. When Jack had doubled over and offered no resistance, it had only increased the older boy's aggression, and he had beaten him mercilessly for several minutes before growing bored. Jack had been a ball of bruises and pain on the floor. He didn't know what he had done to cause such a reaction, but he knew he didn't want it to happen again.

Topper hadn't been finished, though, and he had moved on to the other newcomer. Jack hadn't struggled when he was the one being assaulted, but when Morgan took a blow, Jack was back on his feet, swinging like a madman. It hadn't gone well for him, and Topper had been furious. No one ever fought back. Everyone was afraid of Johnny Topper.

Now, everyone was afraid of Jack Booker.

He had taken a lot of beatings, spent time spitting blood in the dirt. Anyone Johnny Topper hated got it bad at the orphanage, but Jack never took it lying down again. He fought back. Every time. Jack expected the pain that came with a fight and learned to deal with it. He wasn't afraid. Soon, Johnny was hiding bruises too, and eventually he wasn't walking away at all. Jack was shoving his face into the mud with his foot.

Nobody fought Jack Booker anymore.

Jack finally broke his silence, speaking over Kricket's anxious babbling. Jack didn't take his eyes off Topper. He drawled his words quietly. "You all right, Morgan? Lem?"

Morgan nodded, still sniffling, and stood, walking out of the circle. Lem followed, continuing to clutch his arm. Tommy edged away from Johnny.

"I see Tommy's ball was accidently knocked out of the yard." Jack continued softly. "Why don't you go get it for him, Topper?"

Something was different today, though. Maybe it was because he would be leaving soon, or maybe he was simply tired of no longer doing whatever he wanted. Johnny spat and called his bluff. "Piss off, Booker."

Jack took a threatening step forward.

Kricket leapt in, chattering uneasily. "Now, Jack, they was just funnin' with–"

"Shut up, Kricket," Johnny broke in, snarling. Something had snapped this time, and Jack could tell he wasn't going to back down. "We weren't funnin' nobody. We were going to find out what it was like to see a Booker without any teeth." He grinned. "I didn't want little bitch blood anyway; I'm going to have some of the *real* Booker's teeth to wear as a necklace."

Jack grunted, removing his balled fists from his pockets. "You're going to regret this, Topper." Jack stepped up, shifting into a crouching boxer's stance. He knew as soon as Johnny didn't step up to meet him that something was wrong, but he had no chance to react.

Johnny signaled with his hands, and his whole gang collapsed upon Jack, fists swinging, feet kicking, voices screaming. Jack was buried underneath a wave of hands intent on beating, scratching, tearing him into a bloody mess.

A high-pitched, panicked voice was shrieking angrily at Topper from outside the flurry of fists. "Coward! Coward!" But it was soon silenced, and then all Jack could hear was the smack of blows connecting with his flesh, the grunts of both his attackers and himself, and Johnny furiously bellowing at him.

"Take that shit, Booker! Take it, you son of a bitch! You never did have any friends to back you up, freak! What you going to do to me now?"

The heel of a shoe caught Jack solidly on the side of the head, and the world fuzzed around him in a haze of pain and blurry fog. He couldn't see correctly. The blows rained down on his back, ribs, and legs as he attempted to cover his face and stomach. Red was beginning to color the blurry shapes in his vision. Another foot slipped through his fetal defenses and struck his face. He felt his nose crack, and hot, metallic blood washed over his lips.

Jack shook his head. Everything moved strangely, like he was floating. Something swam into sight, coming into focus between the churning feet around him. Jack reached out, heedless of the blows. He couldn't feel them anymore anyway. His hand grasped the rock.

The pain returned as soon as Jack's fingers touched the stone, as if it were a lifeline linking him to consciousness, and the sharp, sting of the blows filled him with blistering rage. He rose up to a knee through the hands trying to keep him down and roared with fury, flailing with the rock at every kneecap and shin to enter his narrowed vision.

Soon, he was alone, thrashing madly about him as the boys scattered away from his primitive weapon. Jack stumbled to his feet, intent only on Johnny Topper, who stood staring at him with eyes wide in an expression of terrified horror. Jack could feel the blood trailing down his face from cuts along his scalp and from his nose, dripping off his chin to speckle the dirt between his feet. Jack was unable to think of anything but ruining the thick, brutish face that stared at him in stunned disbelief. He roared at Johnny, faltering forward on uncooperative legs.

Johnny Topper stood transfixed for a moment at the sight of him, then let out a frightened screech and swung to keep him away. Jack ignored the fist and let it thump into his shoulder. He brought the rock down on Johnny's head as hard as he could. Topper fell. Jack climbed on top of him, enraged, and brought the rock down

32

over and over. Everything was very dim, but Jack didn't stop. Shouting voices echoed around him. Hands grasped at his arms. He battered the unrecognizable face once more. Jack was lifted away.

Father Kyle. It was Father Kyle. He was shouting frantically, and holding him back, but Jack could barely move anymore. All of his energy was gone, expended. He looked down at Johnny Topper.

Johnny's face was a mangled mess of red and pale white. A low moaning sound escaped from the brutalized flesh. Topper rolled onto his side and coughed, hacking up a great mixture of blood and chips of white.

Teeth.

Johnny had wanted some teeth, Jack remembered vaguely.

Chapter 7

"Aw, Celestial Steel – metal of gods! What a privilege it is to work such precious metal all the days of my existence! It is a marvelous substance, hard as diamond, with no trace of brittleness. Forging the arms and armor of my newly born brothers and sisters has been my life's honor. We have a strange relationship with this remarkable metal – at once both an affinity and a curse. Our weapons and plate become almost a part of us, a portion of who we are as individuals. But it is also our great weakness. No other matter can hurt us quite like our beloved steel. Like silver to a werewolf – if I may use such a base example as one of the Myrmidon's asinine superstitions – we can be grievously harmed or even killed by this substance. The answer as to why has baffled our greatest minds for millennia."

– Craft, Imperial Smith and Legendary Primal Artist

"What the hell is this, Fist?" Jack asked through clenched teeth. He held aloft a chunk of silvery metal in one hand.

"It's Celestial Steel, Jack." Fist replied casually, leaning back against the bar at the safehouse. The entire crew was shuffling about in the large common room after having unloaded the wagons' crates into the underground storage rooms. All of them were attempting to appear disinterested – and failing spectacularly. Fist grinned back at him like this was a joke. "Surely even *you* know that."

Jack growled angrily. Fist knew perfectly well what he was asking, but the gang boss was playing it off like Jack was the simpleton everyone thought him to be. Jack jerked his head in irritation but held his peace for a time. Fist got the hint, but he let the other men linger for several hours, drinking and celebrating the successful heist. Jack waited with ill-concealed impatience.

Finally, Fist descended the stairs to his private quarters and allowed Jack to follow him. The boss walked toward the small table and seated himself there, pouring a helping of amber whiskey into a glass. Jack snapped the door shut. He didn't wait for Fist to begin.

"You know what I mean, Fist." Jack said quietly, a mere moment after the door closed behind him. "You *knew* this was the cargo. We deal in illegal steam tech and goods from the West. Celestial Steel?" Jack tossed the hunk of metal on the wooden table, where it struck with a solid *thunk*, followed by a vibrant ringing, like bells.

"What are you bitching about, Jack?" Fist grumbled irritably. "We'll make more off this load than we would in a decade pulling freight off the locomotives."

"Who cares about profit when we won't be around to spend it?" Jack demanded, placing his hands on the table and leaning toward his boss. "Dealing in Celestial Steel is like holding on to a live grenade!

"We'll be careful."

"We'll be *careful*?" Jack was beside himself. "Who are we going to deal this stuff to? Chaos? The Independent Army of Liberty? Chaos is as likely to kill us and take it as he is to deal, and getting involved with Freedom's insurrectionists will set off a flare over our heads so big they'll see it in the Celestial Realm! We've had our share of trouble from the coppers before, but nothing like we're going to see if Brutality traces that cargo to us."

"What do you want from me, Jack?" Fist demanded, standing up. His immense bulk loomed threateningly. "I've spent my entire steamblown life grubbing in the shit and filth of this Primal-cursed city. I'm tired of these streets and dodging the coppers and eking a tiny profit out of the scraps Chaos and his kind leave for the rest of us 'petty criminals'." He spat the words like a bitter draught from his tongue, his mouth twisting. "And I'm steaming tired of keeping an eye over my shoulder for Tyranny's watchdogs and having nothing but piss to show for it!" He kicked his chair away angrily. It spun away, clattering against the wall. Jack leaned back cautiously, but crossed his arms in a semblance of calm. Fist stepped forward, his eyes boring into Jack's. The crime boss thrust his chin forward belligerently and continued.

"No – if I have to watch every day for Brutality coming to beat down my door, I'm going to make it worth it. I'm going to be a real threat, with the benefits that entails." Fist gestured at the walls around him scornfully. "You think Chaos's boys live like this? In a hovel?"

"I think Chaos's boys are barking mad!" Jack shot back, furious that Fist didn't see what he did. "They worship a steamblown *god of chaos*, Fist. I don't know where they live or what it's like, but they don't live there very bloody long, because they've got Tyranny gunning for them all the time!"

35

Fist's eyes were dark. "Jack..." His hands clenched. Jack plowed on angrily.

"You want to be cock of the walk, Fist? You want to say you ran with the big dogs and the Primals before you died? Because that's what will happen; you'll die. *We'll all die.* Brutality will find this place and burn it to the ground around us before you've taken a second step into that world." Fist was reaching the truly dangerous point. Jack had seen that look before, usually before he made an example for the crew. A violent one.

Jack was past caring. "Don't you get it? This isn't just about what *you* are willing to risk. This affects your entire crew, right down to the youngest picker!"

"Have you forgotten who I am, boy?" Fist roared, hurling the table out of his way. He rushed up on Jack and grabbed his coat collar, his face inches from Jack's own. "This is my crew! I've been running the streets of this quarter since you were nothing but a moan in your mother's whore mouth!" Spittle sprayed across Jack's face, and he grabbed Fist's wrist recklessly.

Fist shoved him back against the wall. "Try it!" he snarled, his eyes blazing. "You starting to believe your own steamblown legend, Jack? That you're invincible? Before you decide to test it, maybe you should remember whose reputation you'd be throwing it against. This is my city, boy!"

Jack hesitated, but didn't let his hand drop.

Fist sighed abruptly, relaxing a little, but he didn't let go of Jack's collar, and his eyes continued to burn into Jack's from a finger's length away. "Have you forgotten everything I've done for you? How I took you and your brother out of those bloody streets and gave you a chance?"

Jack's jaw was clenched hard, and he didn't drop his eyes, either, but he let go of Fist's wrist and nodded grudgingly.

"I gave a lot of boys a better life. Not a good one, damn it, but a better one than starving to death in the steamblown gutter." Fist let go and stepped back a pace, eyeing him contemplatively. "I never promised a safe life or a long one – you know that better than most – but it's a life." Fist turned away and leaned on the wall, appearing suddenly old and tired. He didn't look at Jack.

When he finally spoke, his voice was quiet, but harsh. "You've always been my favorite, Jack, since I first found you. But that

36

doesn't mean I won't kill you if you ever throw down on me again." Jack was silent. Fist rubbed a weary hand across his forehead. "I don't want to hear another word about how I operate this gang, understand?" He sighed, and his beefy shoulders slumped further. "I'll think about what you've said. Now get out."

Jack stood unmoving for a moment, considering the boss pensively. Then, he turned and slipped through the door.

Chapter 8

(Six Years Ago)

"Charitable works? True charity is not based on an agenda. The Illuminati feeds and clothes orphans, widows, and the poor, but at the cost of ignorance, pouring whispered lies into the ears of the innocent. Give me knowledge to make informed choices over a full stomach. Give me harsh liberties over false security and propaganda."

– Lord Patrick Hamilton, Orator and Anti-Primal Radical

It was a bright and sunny day in Victorian. Jack felt it shouldn't be. It was cloudy and rainy to him. A loud ringing echoed in his ears, and he could feel the blood pumping hot through his veins. "Tell me again," he said, keeping his expression calm and unworried on the outside. He was seething within. "What has Father Anthony been doing?"

Morgan's normally bright face was downcast in shame and fear, but he did as Jack said. "He takes me to the purification chamber sometimes and helps me wash myself." He hesitated again, his young face troubled. "He does...strange things. He told me it was a secret ritual of the gods, and that I'm not supposed to tell anyone because the Primals are blessing me. He says they'll be angry if I tell the secret, but..." He was looked around fearfully, then leaned back toward Jack. "It *feels* wrong."

Jack understood little else of what Morgan told him, but he was old enough to know that, whatever it was, it *was* wrong. Very wrong. He had no doubts on that count.

And Father Anthony was doing it to Morgan.

When Morgan finished his explanation, he stopped awkwardly, unsure what else to say. Jack laid a hand on his shoulder. "You don't worry about it anymore, Morgan. You hear me? I'm going to take care of it. If he comes to you again, don't go with him. All right?"

Morgan nodded. The relief he felt was evident on his trusting face. Jack gave him a calm smile, then stood up and walked outside into the yard.

Jack didn't think he had ever been this angry in his life. Blood thundered in his ears. A hot roiling in his belly made him think for a moment he might vomit. He and Morgan had trusted them, the

Illuminati priests, and Father Anthony had rewarded that trust with something grotesque that Jack didn't understand.

No. He understood. He didn't have to know what all of it meant. He knew what it was.

It was betrayal of the worst kind.

Jack wanted to punch something. He wanted to scream at the bright blue sky until he was hoarse. He wanted to tear something beautiful apart with his bare hands. He wanted to…

Jack peered beyond the yard's wrought iron fence. His thoughts leapt to the gunshots they sometimes heard at night, echoing from far off beyond the temple's thin, metal boundary. He thought of the stories he had heard of rough men in the West far away from Victorian's streets, who rode horses and carried revolvers. He scuffed a toe broodingly across the yard's packed dirt. Unfortunately, Jack didn't have a revolver like the bandits in the wilds that robbed from the steam locomotives. His worn shoe kicked at a small stone. It clattered across the yard.

Jack hesitated, staring at the stone. He strode over slowly and picked up the jagged rock. He turned it over contemplatively in his fingers. His mind churned at an alarming speed.

Memories flashed through Jack's mind: The feet rising and falling; the hot tang of blood in his mouth and coursing down his chin; the rage that burned in him when he grasped the rock; Johnny Topper's disbelieving expression; the crushing, ripping sensation as Jack smashed the stone down on his face.

Jack hadn't been caned after that fight, because he was too badly beaten already. It had taken several weeks for him to recover sufficiently to get out of bed, but he was confined to a small, solitary closet for another month after that. Jack didn't mind, except that he didn't get to see Morgan. After he had finally been allowed to rejoin the others, no one talked to him anyway. Even Morgan's friends were too scared to sit with him at mealtimes. But it wasn't all bad. Johnny Topper had never bothered anyone again. When Jack entered the room Topper would huddle down, as if to avoid being seen, his mouth clamped down firmly in a perpetual grimace to hide his toothless gums. There was no hiding the scars though. His face was a mishmash of discolored strips of imperfectly healed flesh, and remained that way until he was released from the orphanage a few months later.

Jack wheeled suddenly, and hurled the stone in his hand with as much force as he could muster. It sailed over the orphanage fence. He didn't know how to find a gun, but he knew he could get his hands on a rock. Johnny Topper hadn't bothered anyone ever again.

Father Anthony would never bother Morgan again, either, if Jack's rock had anything to say about it. Father Anthony was much bigger than Johnny Topper. Jack was going to need a bigger rock.

***

It was rather light for the dead of night, thanks to a bright full moon and cloudless sky.

Jack slipped into the priests' sleeping quarters.

Getting past the priests on vigil hadn't been difficult, and the priest on watch over the dormitories had drifted to sleep quickly, despite the small prayer book in his lap. Finding Father Anthony's sleeping cell had been far more difficult, but finally Jack crouched beside the bed of the sleeping priest.

Jack looked down at the man for several moments. Anthony's face was as he remembered from the first time he had met the man. Creased wrinkles covered the leathery face, caused by his frequent laughter, but in sleep, the same somber expression was present that he had worn that day at the flat.

Jack had lost the blazing fire of fury in his breast as the hours had passed, but it had simply settled into hot, smoldering coals, and his resolve had not lessened. Jack gripped the large cobblestone he had pried up out of the street dispassionately. He might have thought Father Anthony a friend all these years, but he knew better now than to trust in indefinite impressions. The priest was hurting Morgan. Jack felt the sting of betrayal as much as the rage of righteous protection.

Jack raised the cobblestone over his head with both hands. He didn't think he was afraid, but his arms almost refused to obey him. They jerked, trying to drop the stone. Jack stood, hands raised to deliver the blow for several minutes.

Then, with a decisive grunt, Jack forced his arms to comply, and the cobble descended with as much strength as he could manage. The stone smashed into Father Anthony's temple with an awful squelching sound. Blood squirted onto the bed's headboard.

Father Anthony grunted and jerked.

Suddenly, Jack was terribly afraid. Butterflies exploded throughout his stomach and chest. What if Father Anthony woke and beat *him* with the rock? Or did the strange things to him that he had done to Morgan? Jack brought the rock down frantically over and over, as hard and fast as his terrified arms would allow. Blood continued to spatter the bed and walls, and much sprayed on Jack. But he didn't stop. Not until the last of his strength was spent and he collapsed, gasping, to the floor.

Jack didn't know how long he sat there – eyes glazed, chest heaving – but eventually it occurred to him that Anthony was not breathing. He had never seen so much blood in his life, even after all of Johnny's teeth fell out. Jack climbed unsteadily to his feet and stumbled back to the dormitories. He was shaking so badly he was sure he would be caught, but no one saw him, and the priest near the dormitories was still asleep with the book on his lap.

Jack shook Morgan roughly, and stifled his cry with a hand when his brother woke to the sight of him covered in blood.

"Get up, Morgan, and grab your things. Bring whatever you can carry. We've got to leave." Morgan's eyes were as wide as the full moon outside, but he nodded mutely and did as he was told. Jack gathered his meager possessions in his pillowcase.

Five minutes later, Jack and Morgan slipped through the protection of the orphanage's wrought iron fence and back into the streets of Victorian.

Chapter 9

"Mob politics is a messy affair – brutal and uncivilized. The lower city gangs live by one, overarching law: The strongest always rules."

– This Interminable Affliction: A Study of the Underworld Gangs and the Danger They Pose, Mother Gertrude, Illuminati Scholar

"Fist was so pleased he said I might get to leave the pickers soon," Dasher boasted proudly, his face positively beaming. Jack thought the boy might even thump his chest for a moment. "Just a few more weeks. Probably."

Jack grunted absently for an answer. The small bit of his conscious self that was listening to Dasher's chatter knew Fist's admonishment to be a lie. There was no way the gang leader was promoting his best pickpocket anytime soon. Dasher was too good at what he did, and Jack didn't figure him for the unflappable sort able to handle the violent confrontations that might crop up in riskier jobs.

"Of course," Dasher continued, his expression falling a tiny bit. "Fist's been saying stuff like that for a year and I *still* haven't..."

Jack barely heard him. He'd done very little listening since the boy interrupted his solitary contemplations in his customary lookout cubby. There were a lot of things on his mind.

In the few days since the successful heist, Jack had been on tenterhooks, just waiting for the coppers to kick down the door. It hadn't happened yet, but Jack knew he wouldn't be at ease until they'd offloaded the steamblown Celestial Steel to someone else. None of the others seemed to share his reservations. Fist's confidence had filled them with a dangerous sense of accomplishment and a lack of healthy caution. Worse, many had overheard bits and pieces of Jack's objections to Fist and were muttering amongst themselves, whispering that he was dragging them down or a threat of turning informant. Jack didn't necessarily mind; he'd always intentionally estranged himself from the others. Some, like Harry, had been waiting a long time for him to fall out of favor with Fist, though, and the mutterings he had overheard were hinting at hostility. Jack was keeping as close an eye on the rest of the gang as he was on the safehouse door.

"Jack? Are you all right?"

"Yeah," Jack mumbled automatically, shaking out of his thoughts and glancing at Dasher. The boy was regarding him with a strange expression.

"Are you sure? I mean, it's not like you're *talking* any less than usual, but you've been kind of, I don't know, distant..."

"Got a lot on my mind, boy," Jack growled sharply, cutting him off. "You been keeping your head down, like I told you?"

Dasher nodded earnestly, his eyes bright. "Uh huh. I've been staying out of Fist's way and the others, especially Harry, and I don't pick marks with any bodyguards, just like you said."

"Good," Jack grunted. "You best keep it that way. I don't want to hear about any bloody heroics." Dasher scowled at this, but nodded sullenly.

Jack watched Dasher for a moment, his eyes running over the fine black hair and cheerful grin that was present even now, while sulking. Jack cursed himself for a fool. He didn't know why he bothered trying to protect the lad while he was in Fist's gang. Danger was a part of the business, even – no, *especially* – for the youngsters. He knew that all too well. Worrying was pointless, but the boy looked just like...

Jack shook his head angrily, growling to himself. *Stop that.* Dasher wasn't that ghost, and it didn't matter anyway. No good ever came out of dredging up those memories.

Dasher didn't say anything about the odd silence, but he did speak up again after a few moments.

"Some of the others have been saying stuff, Jack," Dasher said quietly, giving him a sidelong glance. "Harry and Switch, even Goldilocks is muttering that you're holding the gang down, talking back to Fist all the time like you do. They're saying that Fist isn't taking care of you himself because he wants one of them to step up and do it. To see who is worthy of being a new second."

Jack didn't say anything. He'd heard all of this himself. It was funny, but it seemed that when people knew you didn't talk much, they assumed you couldn't hear very well either. Or maybe they just thought he was too stupid to catch on to the whispers.

43

"Black Jim told them they're all cracked, though," Dasher continued. "He says everyone knows you're invincible. He says there ain't nothing that can kill you, and that's why Fist won't try to take you down, because he's scared. 'Course," Dasher admitted. "He didn't say that last part very loud, because he doesn't want Fist thinking he's a turncoat."

Jack chuckled darkly. "Jim's as big a fool as the rest of them. I've lived through some shit, but I'm not invincible. And if he thinks Fist is scared of me, he hasn't been paying attention."

Dasher just shrugged. Jack scowled. He didn't think the damned boy believed him.

"Anyway," Dasher persisted. "Gurney didn't say much. He's probably trying to stay on everyone's good side. But I think he agrees with Black Jim. Every time the others start conspiring, he gets real scarce, real fast."

A chill wind blew with a ragged shriek through the peepholes, and Jack pulled his coat more snugly around himself. Dasher was looking at him expectantly, like he was waiting for an answer. Jack decided to oblige him.

"Doesn't matter what any of those bastards think," he grunted, pulling his bowler down over his eyes. "They can all go jump off a steamblown airship."

***

Tensions with the rest of the gang came to a head sooner than Jack expected.

The drinking was heavy in the safe-house common room. Fist wouldn't let anyone go out, despite there being little to do before the cargo exchange. It was the first smart decision the boss had made in the past week, in Jack's opinion. They couldn't risk one of the men bragging in his cups or trying to impress a whore. All it might take was one whisper to land them all at the end of a hangman's rope.

Jack wasn't one to join in the fun, usually, so he had expected to stay well clear of the celebrations this evening as well.

Fist had other plans.

Jack found himself climbing the stairs after a summons was delivered by Dasher. Contact had been made with some of Chaos's people, and the drop had been scheduled for Thursday night, two

44

days from now. Fist would want to lay out his thoughts for a plan. The last thing they needed was for an exchange with Chaos to go poorly.

The common room was abuzz with raucous laughter and cloudy with smoke. The hazy scent of burning tobacco mingled with the odor of sweat and dirt and drink. Jack lit a cigar of his own methodically. His entrance didn't dampen the lively atmosphere. Instead, amused muttering filled the room, followed by the snorts of suppressed mirth. The table on the far side went back to gambling after a few moments, but those at the long table to the left continued to follow him with glittering, almost anticipatory, eyes. Jack pretended to ignore them, but he strained his ears for the scrape of stools on splintery wood as he walked toward Fist.

The gang boss was at a small table by himself, puffing contentedly on a thick, black pipe and sipping from a tankard. Fist had some papers with crude drawings spread out before him, but he looked up expectantly at Jack's arrival. He kicked a chair out roughly as an invitation. Jack grasped the chair's rickety frame and settled into the seat, his eyes already taking in the rudimentary diagrams on the table. It looked like a layout of streets and alleys.

"You received a confirmation from Chaos on the location for the drop, I see," Jack grunted, gesturing. "I–"

"Well, look who it is." A drunken voice broke through the rest of the noise in the room. "Dull Jack's finally come to join the rest of the crew."

The long table erupted with laughter as Goldilocks stood up from his seat and walked toward him, but the rest of the room grew very quiet.

Jack turned to face the long-haired boy expressionlessly. He didn't stand, but leaned back in his seat and took a long draw on his cigar.

"Glad you could finally deign to celebrate with us, your Invincibleness." Goldilocks slurred his words, and his gait wasn't entirely steady. "You're too good for us, isn't that right? You're the invincible Jack Booker. Unkillable. Even a steamblown Primal couldn't finish you! You think you're better than the rest of us, don't you, you turncoat son of a bitch?"

Black Jim spoke up in his deep, slow voice from the gambling table. "That's enough, Goldi." He was red-faced from drink, but he

45

looked wary, and his voice was sharp. "He just can't hold his liquor, Jack. That's all." Jim addressed Jack quietly, but he wouldn't meet his eyes.

Goldilocks ignored the big, bearded man. "Or maybe you're just so stupid you don't know what we're on about most of the time, eh Dull Jack? I bet it hurts your poor head, all the confusing stuff going on up here."

"I like that theory better," Harry boomed from the long table. Switch and the rest of his cronies whooped with laughter and yelled encouragement at Goldilocks. Jack glanced at Harry, who shrugged minutely and grinned back at him. The steamblown man knew what would happen if Goldi tried to take him; this was just an amusement. Jack ground his teeth. He took another long pull on his cigar.

"Everyone knows you're dragging us down, Jack," Goldilocks continued, coming to a halt a mere three paces from Jack's chair. "We're tired of you back-talking Fist. He's going to lead us to riches!"

Jack looked sidelong at Fist, but the boss was sitting back in his seat, his eyes glittering with amusement and curiosity. He wasn't going to stop this. The boss usually let quarrels play themselves out, because he thought it made for a stronger band. The toughest were always on top. Jack let out a frustrated stream of cigar smoke.

Fine.

Fist wanted to see if he was still committed? Jack would show him; he'd show all of the bastards.

It was too bad it was Goldilocks.

"I'm going to prove you're not invincible," Goldi was saying. "Fist's waiting for someone to take your place. That's going to be me." A sheen of sweat covered his pockmarked face, and his eyes carried an excited gleam behind the glaze from drink. The idiot boy had been dying to prove himself for weeks now, and he thought he was going to do it in spectacular fashion.

Jack slowly stood.

Goldilocks took an involuntary step back, but peered over his shoulder, thought better of it, and steeled himself. Jack stubbed out his cigar and kicked his chair out of the way. Goldi flinched.

"Go sit back down, Goldi," Jack said quietly. "Finish your ale and sleep it off. You'll think better of this in the morning." He put both hands in his coat pockets in a relaxed, casual pose.

46

Goldilocks wavered again, but the drink had done its work. The long table whooped at him. He smiled confidently – and pulled a small revolver from underneath his coat, pointing it at Jack's chest. The common room abruptly became silent.

Jack stared at the barrel, his mind churning. Which of those bastards had given Goldi a bloody gun?

"Goldilocks," Jack said slowly, carefully taking a step forward. "You put that away. You want to fight? We'll fight. But we don't have to do this." Jack could feel the handle of his Bull Dog pressed against his back. He itched to grab for it.

Goldi's gun didn't drop.

"If you don't put that gun away, I'm going to kill you," Jack snarled, his voice harsh. "Understand? Not bleeding, not hurting. I'm going to put a bullet through your head."

Goldilocks had made up his mind. He shook his head and sneered. "Piss off, Jack." His trigger finger tightened noticeably.

"So, your first kill is going to be someone who's invincible?" Jack said softly. "You aim too high." Goldi hesitated for the briefest of moments as Jack spoke, trying to catch what he said.

Jack struck.

He stepped forward and his left hand shot out, grasping the revolver and twisting the barrel toward the roof. Goldilocks reflexively pulled the trigger and the gun went off with a roar, sending a bullet into the planks of the ceiling. Jack's right hand emerged from his coat pocket, brass knuckles curled around his fist. He smashed the metal grips into Goldi's face, and the boy's nose exploded in a spray of red.

Goldilocks reeled back, firing a second shot that followed the first. Blood from his nose scattered behind him in a crimson curtain. Jack drew back his fist a subsequent time and jabbed forward sharply. The brass knuckles crushed into Goldi's windpipe. More blood spurted from his mouth an instant later.

The boy released his grip on the revolver and collapsed to the floor, both hands holding his throat as he struggled for breath. When he did manage to get a gasp of air, it came back out a hacking cough that dribbled blood down his chin and pooled on the floor.

Jack watched with a deadpan expression. He noted the strange mixture of red on gold in the tangles of long blond hair. The room was silent but for Goldi's tortured wheezing and the burbling,

47

sucking sounds issuing from his nose and throat. Jack flicked open the revolver's receiver and pushed the remaining cartridges out into his hand.

"Someone clean him up and move him to his bunk. He's not going to be doing much for some time, but he probably won't die." Jack tossed the revolver onto the long table, and searched its occupants' faces dispassionately. Then, he turned, picked up his chair, and sat back down across from Fist. Gurney, Jim, and a few others moved to do as he said. Harry watched him with a sneering, amused expression on his face. He grinned again when he saw Jack looking at him, and gave a slight tip of his hat.

Fist was silent until Goldilocks had been removed downstairs.

"Why didn't you kill him?" the boss asked, puffing on his pipe. He didn't look at Jack.

Jack shrugged and grunted. "He didn't deserve it. He was drunk and probably talked into it by one of those other bastards."

"I've seen you kill others for much less."

"Yeah," Jack agreed, lighting up another cigar. "But they deserved to die."

Chapter 10

(Six Years Ago)

"Picking a pocket is just like slipping a pretty lass out of her dress. If you know what you're about, there ain't nothing easier in all the world. If you don't, you're like to end up with nothing but bruises to show for your efforts."

– Jasker "Flickerfinger" Macomb, Victorian Pickpocket

Jack peered out into the busy streets running along the airship wharves. His eyes narrowed to thin slits. Wagons rumbled, dockworkers heaved and cursed, and everyone bustled. Ladies in fine lace petticoats moved delicately through the crowds on the arms of men in fine coats and top hats; dirty, screaming urchins raced through the throngs, ignoring the angry shouts that followed them; laymen bore their loads with heads tilted down and tipped their caps sullenly at the aristocrats; foremen bellowed and pointed importantly, and even a mechanical chevaline or two trotted past with gears whirring and grinding and steam puffing intermittently from artificial nostrils.

Jack took all of this in carefully, assessing. There was no room for mistakes today. He and Morgan hadn't eaten in three days but for a mouthful of stale bread.

Jack had almost forgotten the terrible hunger after so long in the orphanage, but it was what they had returned to after their nighttime escape. Jack hated it. But he was older now, and smarter. He was shrewd enough to watch and listen, and he learned many interesting things from careful observation, like the value of money, who had it and who didn't.

The second day after their flight, Jack observed a curious incident. A grubby boy in patched trousers and a soot-covered shirt – perhaps a few years older than he – stumbled into a man wearing a fine black coat and glancing at a silver watch. The boy apologized quickly and scampered away, but a suspicious look flashed over the man's face, and he shouted angrily, hurrying after the boy. Jack had been puzzled, but he witnessed similar incidents as the days passed, until he noticed the finely dressed people checking their pockets afterwards. He finally understood. The boys were rifling through coats in the collisions.

Jack had tried his hand several times, to no avail. He wasn't very good at it, and all he procured were a few panicked flights from furious gentlemen, who waved threateningly after him with dueling canes. One had even shot at him with a revolver. Jack hadn't been expecting that, and the incident scared him badly enough that he had ceased his efforts for a time.

Those had been tough days. The hunger had returned in full strength, and Jack and Morgan had gone back to scrounging in the waste, as they had before the orphanage. They slept in the alleyways in every kind of weather, covered only by a thin, tattered blanket Jack had discovered in the garbage. They stayed well clear of the alleys' other residents. Jack knew they would steal food in a heartbeat, if they saw it before Jack and Morgan crammed it eagerly into their mouths. They might even try to do the things Father Anthony had done. Jack always kept a broken cobblestone in his coat pocket and a splintered shovel handle looped to his trousers.

Jack had gotten better at picking marks, though, and he grew quicker the more he practiced. He still rarely managed a successful getaway with any more than his skin, but, on occasion, the reward of a trinket or clinking coins could be found in his clenched fists.

But not lately. The last two marks had known what he was up to before he even managed to reach them. Jack had only just slipped away. If he didn't score on a mark today, they would be back to scrounging for rotten vegetables in the gutters. His stomach rumbled at the thought.

Jack shrank back instinctively when two constables strode past, clubs swinging from their belts next to black revolvers. They wore the blue uniforms, and hard, conical helmets, with the silver badges of Brutality's police force. Neither paid him any mind, and Jack shook himself roughly, breathing a sigh of relief. Acting suspicious was sure to draw unwanted attention. He was just an urchin, Jack reminded himself. Another urchin resting in the shade of an alley and watching the airships take off.

All the same, he couldn't help shivering. Very little was as the Illuminati priests had told him at the orphanage. He had never heard of the Primal known as Brutality there, only that the coppers were the arm of Order, benevolently providing protection and stability in

Victorian. Outside the temple walls was nothing but the fear of Brutality and his enforcers. No one thought the coppers were providing protection, but everyone seemed to be afraid.

Jack waited until the coppers were far beyond his sight before continuing his search. Picking a mark was a delicate business. Rich women rarely carried money, their valuables were never in a pocket or some other easily reached place, and they were hardly ever alone. Young, athletic men were definitely to be avoided, as their pride was easily wounded. And if they decided to give chase they would almost certainly catch you. Jack tended to pick fat men, who were often confident enough to walk the streets alone, but too overweight to catch him even if they realized his intent. Fat and elderly was ideal, but the man who shot at him had been elderly, so Jack was leery of drawing similar attention.

There! Jack's searching eyes picked out an ideal mark. He was a big man, with a golden watch chain dangling from his vest pocket. His wide girth pushed the fine fabric of his shirt and vest over the confines of his waistband. A top hat sat precariously on his black curls, and his eyes squinted through wire-framed spectacles. Most importantly, he didn't appear to be holding a dueling cane, and he was alone.

Jack slipped out of the alley. "Come on, Morgan." His younger brother followed, weaving skillfully behind him through the thick crowd.

"The fat one with the glasses?" he muttered after Jack.

"Yeah," Jack grunted quietly. They were only a few paces from the man, and Jack raised his voice in an excited yell. "You can't catch me!" He started running, pushing his way through the gaps in the throng. Morgan shouted after him, keeping up the ruse, and followed.

The fat man's head turned when he heard Jack, as did everyone else in the immediate area, but it was important that the mark heard the game. That way, he would think it a bothersome accident when Jack crashed into him in a few moments.

Everything went as expected. Jack feigned like he was searching over his shoulder for Morgan as he pushed through the crowd, before he ran slap-bang into the fat man. The mark grunted as Jack collided with his belly, and Jack stumbled. He grasped at the man's coat with his left hand to steady himself, and slipped his right into a pocket.

Success! Jack's fingers closed around metal and he withdrew his hand with the prize, stuffing it into his own coat as he staggered back.

"Sorry, good master," Jack gasped, shaking his head as if stunned by the collision.

The fat man eyed him angrily. "Watch yourself, filthy brat!" When the man snarled, his fat lips peeled back in a revolted scowl. He brushed at his coat and vest with a disgusted air. "You steamblown urchins are becoming–" He cut off suddenly, and his eyes squinted behind his glasses. He pawed at his pockets, but Jack was already gone, sprinting as fast as he could for the nearest alley, Morgan on his heels.

"Thief!" The shout rang after him. Then, Jack heard something far more chilling. "Bruce, after them!"

Jack looked back over his shoulder anxiously. He had been *certain* the man was alone. His heart leapt into his throat.

A bodyguard. The man was tall and muscular and dressed in layman's clothing. Only now, as the man shoved unapologetically after them, did Jack see the revolver hanging from his belt and the thick club in his hand. He was far too clean for a real layman. Jack cursed as he pushed himself for more speed and urged Morgan to run faster. Workers were never that clean. He should have seen it.

The alley split three ways ahead, and Jack shoved Morgan to the right. He waved his right hand in the air for their pursuer to see – the coins still clutched in his hand – and split left. He glanced over his shoulder quickly, his breaths coming in frantic gasps. The bodyguard followed. Jack put on another spurt of speed, relieved that Morgan had escaped. His legs were churning with panicked adrenalin. Another fork was ahead. Jack tore around the corner to the right…

And ran straight into a dead end. He spun to backtrack, but the bodyguard already stood behind him. The man wore a satisfied grin, and Jack didn't like what he saw in his eyes. The bodyguard advanced slowly, cane in hand.

Jack's breathing shortened. He saw no escape. He dropped the shillings to the alley floor and backed up further until his shoulders hit the brick wall behind him. It did little good. The bodyguard scooped up the coins and kept coming.

Images flashed in front of Jack's eyes: The stomp of feet and burst of red, the rock in his hand above Johnny Topper's broken face, Father Anthony's unmoving form on the bed.

Jack drew the shovel handle from his waistband in one hand and pulled the cobblestone from his pocket with the other.

The bodyguard halted for a moment, a look of surprise replacing that of pleasure. Then, the alley boomed with his laughter. "You got balls, kid. I'll give you that."

He grabbed at the scruff of Jack's shirt casually, and Jack cracked him in the wrist with the shovel handle. The man bellowed, his face contorting with rage, and he backhanded viciously with the club. The hardened wood crashed into Jack's head.

Pain exploded across his skull, and he fell limply to the cobblestones. His head rang like tiny bells. His arms felt numb, and his weapons clattered to the ground beside him.

"You little bastard," the man snarled above him, flexing his hand and wrist. He raised the cane above his head. Jack's head throbbed, and he struggled to move. The club fell savagely.

The bodyguard grunted and jerked. His head snapped forward, and he fell face first to the ground, half landing on Jack. Jack struggled, kicking his legs out from beneath the man. The back of the guard's head was bloody.

Jack looked up, shaking his head to try to clear away the pain and the ringing. The biggest man he had ever seen was towering over him. Eyes of a smoky grey peered down from a blunt, stony face. The man's arms and legs seemed as thick as three normal men's combined. He leaned down, and a huge barrel chest seemed to block out the sky. Jack realized the stranger was offering him his hand.

Jack took it warily and was pulled him to his feet. He saw that the man had a revolver tucked in his waistband beneath his coat. Luckily, he was smiling.

"Never steal from someone with a bodyguard, lad!" The man's tone was joking, but he seemed to mean what he said. "Always plan your escape routes before a pick, too. Otherwise you could end up stuck in a dead end." He raised an eyebrow at their surroundings indicatively.

Jack nodded because he didn't know what else to do. He stopped quickly, though, because his head was aching like thunder.

"How do you know so much about pickpocketing?" The man was so big he could probably just take whatever he wanted.

"A lot of pickers work for me," the man admitted, tucking the club up his coat sleeve. "But I didn't always have people to steal for me either." He looked down at Jack with considering eyes, weighing him. "What's your name, boy?"

Jack didn't want to say, but the man *had* just saved him from a beating. "Jack."

The man grunted. "Well, Jack, you've got a pair o' brass ones. I'll say that much. I ain't ever seen a boy draw down on a bodyguard like that." He spat on the guard's back. "You're nothing but skin and bone. You hungry?"

Jack nodded, suspicious.

"I tell you what. You come work for me, and you'll never be hungry again." Jack opened his mouth to say no. He'd heard that before. The man raised a finger, forestalling him. "I'll teach you everything there is to know about pickpocketing. Plus, you won't have to sleep in the street anymore. You'll have a roof over your head, at any rate."

Jack looked at the limp bodyguard, then back at the huge man. "Morgan, too?"

"That other kid you were running with?"

Jack grunted. "My brother."

The blunt head moved up and down. "Him, too." The man bent over the bodyguard, pulled the revolver out of his belt, and tucked it into his coat. He offered Jack the guard's club. "What do you say?"

In answer, Jack spat on the back of the bodyguard's head, then took the proffered club. "Yes, sir."

The man grinned.

"My name's Fist, boy. Welcome to the gang."

Chapter 11

"Organized crime is the prevalent plague of this Primalforsaken city. It is the worst kind of epidemic, and I WILL root it out. Starting with that steamblown madman, Chaos, and his crazed mobsters."

– Brutality, Victorian's Chief of Enforcement

Fist was nervous.

Good, Jack thought. Maybe the boss was finally realizing just how deep in the shit he'd gotten himself – and the rest of them. Not only was Chaos a Primal, but he was *crazy*. Dealing with the fickle, psychopathic god of mayhem wasn't Jack's idea of a sound business move, no matter how lucrative it might be.

Fist fidgeted to Jack's left, drawing his revolver and checking the receiver again. Jack tried to remember the last time he'd seen the man this edgy. He came up blank.

Jack chewed on the end of an unlit cigar, trying, and, akin to Fist, likely failing, to appear nonchalant. He rubbed a thumb up and down the barrel of his coach, held under the crook of his arm beneath his coat. Black Jim and Switch were with them, crouching in the shadows and breathing rapidly. No one spoke. Black Jim looked as if he might vomit, and Switch's thin face didn't appear much more confident. Jack swallowed carefully. He hoped the others in the cover team were ready for anything, because with Chaos, there really was no way of knowing.

Fist spoke up suddenly, his eyes trained on a cheap pocket watch. "It's time." His voice was curt. Jack swore he could hear him grinding his teeth.

Fist started to the east, picking his way around the puddles in the alley from the evening rain. Jack followed just behind his right shoulder, pulling out his shotgun from beneath his coat and resting it against his collarbone. Jim and Switch brought up the rear.

It was three blocks to the meeting place, but Jack could see the contacts lounging against tumbled crates before he was within one hundred paces. They didn't seem to be very worried about subtlety. Raucous laughter drifted to Jack's ears, and he could both smell the smoke and see the lights of flaring cigars and pipes. Jack counted five.

"No bravado, boys," Fist muttered as they closed with Chaos's men. "This needs to stay brief, friendly, and professional. Understand?" Switch gave a strangled grunt in confirmation, and Black Jim kept his lips locked tight. Jack almost laughed. There had never been instructions less needed. Bravado was the furthest thing from his companions' minds, replaced by a furious battle with bowel control.

Their contacts straightened up casually and formed a loose line as Jack and the rest came closer. All but one, who remained perched atop a stack of crates behind his fellows. Jack gaped. The man had a *lever-action rifle*. Jack had only ever heard of those.

Those in front of Jack were armed in a more traditional fashion, with shotguns or revolvers in their hands. None of them looked different from gangsters Jack had met from human run gangs. Bowlers, patched coats, trousers held up with suspenders, and cracked leather shoes covered unwashed bodies. Bearded faces peered at them in the alley's murk. But the eyes…the eyes were different. Jack didn't know if he should call it fervor or lunacy, but there was something distinctly frenzied in the way the pupils shifted about.

At least they were all human. Or he hoped they were. Jack was well aware how ordinary Primals could appear when they wanted to.

"You must be Fist," drawled a man in the middle of the line. He had dirty blond hair curling around the edges of his bowler, and a spiteful grin was displayed behind two or three days' worth of stubble. "Reckon I've heard of you, once or twice when I had nothing better to do than sit on the shitter."

Jack noticed Fist's shoulders stiffen, but he didn't reply.

The blond man turned. "And you brought your prize dog. Jack Booker, eh? I might have heard a mutter on the street that you were *invincible*." His grin grew wider, like he thought something exceedingly amusing. A stream of tobacco juice squirted from his mouth to the cobblestones between them, almost hitting Jack's shoe. "Horseshit, I say. It's mighty easy for a runt pup to win out in a den of rodents. Look at those other two with them filling their shoes with terror-piss!" The alley boomed as his companions' laughter rebounded off the alley walls. Jim and Switch ducked their heads, faces red.

"You trying to bring every copper in the city down here?" Jack grunted, after their mirth had faded.

"What do we care about coppers?" the blond man scoffed. "You're dealing with Chaos now, boy. We fight those bastards every Primal-damned day." He smirked. "But I forgot what you Myrmidon gangs do when the enforcers are sniffing around: bolt down your rabbit holes. We ain't afraid of steaming coppers."

Jack snorted. "I'd like to hear you say that to Brutality's face."

The leader's face twisted, and he spat on the ground again. The others followed suit. "There's for Brutality, boy. I'd drop a shit right here for him to find if I had the time. We got Primals of our own, and we know how to deal with Tyranny's bloody animals." It didn't seem possible, but the man's grin came back even wider than before. "You hear about that factory explosion on Downy Street the other day? That was us. Blew that place to the Abyss with everyone inside it. Then we had us a big ol' brawl with the enforcers."

Their shifting eyes made more sense to Jack now. They really *weren't* afraid. At all.

Steamblown Primal fanatics.

"You got our payment?" Fist demanded, cutting through the idle chatter. His voice was short and cold.

"Sure, we got it." The leader pulled an immense bag of sovereigns from the breast of his coat. "But the real question is, you got our C-steel? We got some Primal killing work needs doing with that shit."

In answer, Jack dug the rock of Celestial Steel out of his pocket. He tossed it to the man. It sang with a long, reverberating hum as it went on its short flight. The leader caught the rock in one hand and tapped it delicately with a knuckle. A deep golden note filled the air.

The man sighed contentedly, tucking the steel away. "*That's* what I like to hear. Genuine, grade-A C-steel is what that is." He quirked an eyebrow. "Where's the rest?"

"A block west," Fist growled, jerking his head indicatively. "All loaded in wagons and ready to go. In the interest of time, we'll give you the wagons and the mules. Just hop up and drive out of here, but once you leave it's not our responsibility anymore."

"You boys *are* frightened of the coppers, aren't you?" The leader chuckled. "Take us to it."

Jack glanced at Fist with surprise. They were willing to walk straight to the wagons in the middle of Fist's entire crew? Obviously they weren't worried Fist would try anything. Of course, he would be mad to even entertain the idea. Chaos would turn their safehouse into a crater.

"Jack, you go on ahead and let Harry know we're coming." Fist said calmly. "I don't want him shooting anyone because of the change of plans."

Jack nodded, glancing one last time at Chaos's men. The leader grinned back with contemptuous amusement at their caution. Jack growled irritably, but hurried away.

***

He knew something was wrong as soon as he saw the wagons. Most of the men had their handguns out, and Harry was speaking in a rough, excited voice.

"We have a problem?" Jack asked as soon as he was within earshot. Harry turned toward him, surprised, and an irritated scowl crossed his face. Jack noticed Dasher standing behind the big man, his youthful face worried. If Dasher was here in the middle of the operation, it could only mean one thing: trouble was headed their way.

"Dasher says we got a pair of coppers headed straight for us by way of Tawny Street," Harry explained as Jack joined the circle. He waved indicatively at the boy as he spoke. "The pickers are keeping an eye on their movements, but it doesn't look like their straying at all. They're just strolling straight ahead. They'll be on us in a couple minutes."

Jack cursed, thinking quickly. The last thing they needed were inquisitive coppers while dealing with Chaos. He made up his mind decisively and shoved his shotgun into Dasher's hands. "Hold that. I won't be able to keep it concealed." Jack turned to Harry. "I'll go head them off before they get close. Fist is on his way, and he's got Chaos's boys with him. *Don't* shoot anybody. They'll take the wagons, then we'll get the hell out of here before we run into more company."

Harry blocked his way. "This is *my* group, Jack. We'll deal with the coppers. What are you going to do? Take on two enforcers alone?"

"No, idiot," Jack said, shouldering past him. "There's no time to argue. The coppers are going to be here any minute now. Get these wagons transferred to the contacts, and make it fast."

Jack took off at a dead sprint toward Tawny Street, thinking hastily. *Come on. Think, Jack. A plan, you need a plan.* He could feel his Bull Dog pressing against his back, but he pushed aside his desire to draw it.

When he hit Tawny Street, Jack raced around the corner, the beginnings of a plan manifesting in his brain. He cast his eyes wildly behind him, and nearly collided with the two coppers sauntering up the boulevard.

"Halt!" The first shouted, as Jack tried to barrel past. They grabbed his coat and laid hands on their clubs warily. "This is the police. Calm yourself, man! What's your hurry?"

"Let me go! Let me–" Jack shouted, spreading panic liberally through his words. Then he made a show of recognizing their uniforms. "Oh, constables!" He grasped at their coats desperately. "I've only just escaped! There was Chaos and screaming and I ran for *miles–*"

"Wait, *Chaos*?" The coppers shook him roughly. "You *saw* him? Where? What did you see?"

"Please, sirs," Jack gasped. "I was catching me a breath o' midnight air near the docks, see, having a smoke. And I saw *him*. Chaos! He was with a bunch o' men with guns, moving through the alleys all quiet like–"

"How did you know it was Chaos?"

"Primals got wings, right?" Jack continued desperately. "I seen 'em flickering behind his coat, sirs, as bright as my shiny white arse! Then, he lifted off the ground! Flew right up toward the rooftops. I was scared spitless, I tell you true, but I heard a couple of those boys who had been walking with 'im talking about making another example. 'Like the factory on Downy the other day.' He said that clear as crystal. But then one o' 'em saw me skulking and he shouted and I took off like my arse was afire. I was expecting a bullet in the back or Chaos 'imself to come screaming down at me outta the sky. I kept running, didn't make no mind where I was going. I just kept running."

The two coppers shared a glance. One spoke quietly in the other's ear. "Sounds like a Primal. Probably not Chaos, but definitely one of his supporters. I'll head for the docks, while you run it in. *Make bloody sure* you get some Primal backup."

Jack hid a grin behind a frightened face. It was working. They were in the clear.

Two subsequent gunshots split the night. Hot blood sprayed across Jack's face. He stood unmoving for a second, too stunned by the unexpected, ear-splitting booms and the coppers' subsequent collapse to react.

Harry stepped from the shadows of the alley from his right, grinning from ear to ear. Tiny tendrils of smoke drifted from his shotgun's double barrels. One of the enforcers was still alive, scrabbling ineffectually at the cobblestones. His intestines were slopping through a hole in his midriff. Harry walked forward, drew his revolver and put a bullet through his skull, then put one in the other copper for good measure.

Jack looked at the bodies in the street. He raised a hand up to his face and wiped at the gore, then stared at his red-slathered hand. His fingers closed into a fist. He glared at Harry.

The black bearded man grinned back at him. "I said I'd handle it, Jack." He kicked at a limp boot. "It's handled."

He turned, walking back toward the wagons, and left Jack standing over two silent corpses.

Chapter 12

(Five Years Ago)

"The Narrows is a wretched pit of misery and crime. If I had to point to one, irredeemable source of all Victorian's woes, it would be that villainous hive of twisting alleys.

Every inhabitant should be shipped off to The Abyss."

– Lord Theodore Walter, Imperial Tory and Politician

"Breathe out slowly," Fist instructed from close to his ear. "Keep your eyes sighted down the length of the barrel. Always make sure the muzzle is in line with both your target and the back sights."

Jack held the shotgun up to his shoulder, arms shaking slightly with the weight. He did as Fist instructed, and carefully attempted to situate the muzzle in a straight line from his eye to the target. It was more difficult than he'd thought. His hands kept swaying ever so slightly, making it complicated to keep the weapon directed where he wished. Jack let out a long, slow breath.

"That a boy, Jack. Your first reaction when you fire will be to close your eyes, but I want you to try to keep them open and focused on your target. Now, *squeeze.* Don't jerk back on the trigger; squeeze it lightly, *gently.* It's your lover, not your whore. Don't go being rough and abrupt with her. Every shot should be smooth."

Jack continued his efforts determinedly, trying to incorporate everything Fist said. He reached the end of his breath, and squeezed as lightly as he knew how.

BOOM.

The shotgun discharged with a thunderous roar, slamming back against Jack's shoulder and leaping in his hands. Fire spouted from the barrel in a cloud of billowy smoke. Jack stumbled back a bit before regaining his balance. His shoulder ached a bit from the recoil, but he hardly felt it as he searched down the alley excitedly with his eyes.

Fist was whooping beside him. "That's my boy, Jack!" He laid a hand on Jack's shoulder and pointed toward the alley's dead end.

Jack peered down range, still a little disoriented from the explosion in his hands. The bottle was gone. Shattered. Jack grinned happily.

"Now what do you do, boy?"

Jack kept the barrel pointed down the alley, just as Fist had told him. He pushed the small catch near the front of the shotgun's stock, and its barrel broke forward, exposing the loading breech. Jack pulled the spent shot casing free with excited, shaking hands, and inserted another round. He snapped the shotgun closed again with difficulty, then pushed the small safety pin in place to lock the trigger.

"It's like you've been doing it for years," Fist praised, holding out his hands. Jack passed over the weapon stock first, careful to keep the muzzle pointed away from both of them. Fist accepted it with a grin.

"You shot better your first time than most of the fools working jobs with me." Fist said, clapping Jack on the back. "Hitting a bottle at thirty paces..." he shook his head. "Most of those bastards are doing well by not shooting themselves in the foot."

Jack continued to grin, but frowned when a troubling thought crossed his mind. "Won't the coppers come to investigate gunshots, sir?"

Fist snorted. "Not likely. Not here, at any rate. Not in The Narrows. Coppers only come here if something big happens, or if they're on a raid. There's very little of value for anyone to steal or destroy down here, so they don't care much what happens, and it's dangerous for small groups of enforcers in this area. The Narrows is where most of the gangs' safehouses are located, hidden beneath the poverty. It's rumored that even the big Primal gangs are based somewhere in The Narrows."

Fist turned to Morgan, who stood watching from nearby. His hands still hovered over his ears from the noise. "You want to try, Morgan?"

The gangly youth shook his head quickly, but he grinned in congratulations at Jack. "I think it would probably knock me over," the boy confessed.

Fist laughed, his voice ringing loud and harsh against the brick walls. "It might, at that. You're going to have to learn sometime in this gang, though." Morgan nodded, and he smiled tremulously. Fist gave Morgan an appraising look. "How'd the picking go yesterday? Bring back anything?"

Jack watched, smiling, when Morgan's eyes lit up at the question. Both Jack and Morgan had been taught everything there was to know about pickpocketing when they entered Fist's force of urchin pickers: what marks were the least risky or carried the best payoffs, the street layout of several of Victorian's busiest districts, how to lie effectively, the techniques for engaging a mark, how best to slip trinkets and coins from hard-to-reach pockets. They had grown fleeter of foot and quicker of eye and hand, and their dexterity only continued to increase as they practiced and grew older. Jack was good – one of the best. Morgan was better. His younger brother had an uncanny propensity for thievery, with hands quicker than a striking snake and subtler than a shadow. Jack was amazed at his talent, and a tiny bit jealous.

"I snatched a *gold* pocket watch off a gentleman by the docks," Morgan reeled off excitedly, enthused that Fist had asked. Jack couldn't help chuckling. Morgan had already told everyone else who would listen. Jack had heard the story near on fifty times. "It even had little jewels inlaid on the face!"

Fist boomed another laugh. "You put it in the lock box?" Morgan nodded eagerly, and Fist gave him an approving slap on the back. "I'll take a look at it when we get back to the safehouse."

Jack grinned at Morgan, and his brother smiled back. His slim face was full of happiness. This was how things were supposed to be. They were important in Fist's gang. They weren't hungry, they were happy. And they *mattered*.

Fist tousled their hair, his big hands dwarfing their heads. He grinned down at them. "Now that's what I expect out of you two! Where would I be without my Booker boys?"

Chapter 13

"Once, I killed a man because he looked at me funny. What do you think happens when someone seriously pisses me off?"

— 'Red' Ragen, Infamous Victorian Mob Boss

"Do you have any idea what you've *done*?"

Jack had held his peace until the gang had arrived back at the safehouse. Chaos's men had taken the wagons and rumbled away with the Celestial Steel. They should have left with the rest of Jack's worries as well, but two dead coppers in the street insured that those would be around for some time.

Jack hadn't said anything when he arrived back at the wagons, wiping blood from his face with his sleeve, and Fist hadn't either. Jack had seen the skin around his eyes tighten, though, and he knew that his boss was either worried or angry. It didn't matter. Jack knew how he felt.

He was furious.

The gang was excitedly discussing what they would do with all their money. All trace of the evening's earlier terror had been replaced by the thrill of success. Jack had to admit he never knew that much money *existed*, but, at the moment, he could have cared less about the heavy bag in Fist's coat pocket.

Harry turned slowly from his group of cronies, his usual grin pasted across his face. Jack noticed it looked a bit thin.

"What's that, Dull Jack?" Harry asked. "What've I done? I'll explain it slowly so you'll understand." He made slow, wide hand motions as he continued. "I killed those coppers," his hands made a shooting gesture, "just like I told you I would. I didn't want them having any chance of stumbling on our operation." His tone told Jack he was quite pleased with himself. "What were you going to do, talk them to death?" He chuckled, shaking his head. "It had been a long while since I killed me a copper or two, so there was that as well."

"You witless, bloodthirsty bastard!" Jack roared, lunging forward. His hands grasped Harry's collar and yanked him to within an inch of his enraged face. The intense anger pumped through his

64

veins like molten liquid, urging him recklessly on. He hadn't felt like this since...

A red-stained yard. A rock rising and falling in his fist. The priest's face as he lay sleeping peacefully. A flicker of light rising from the back of the mark's coat. Morgan slipping forward on silent feet. Jack raising his revolver as he ran, screaming at Morgan to wait – too late, TOO LATE...

Jack jerked viciously out of the memories and back to the present. Harry's whiskered face was a breath away from his own. The man's eyes were wide with surprise and panic.

"You've endangered this entire crew. Fist, the gang, me, even the bloody pickpockets with your steamblown stunt," Jack breathed venomously. The room had grown deathly quiet, and everyone shuffled away a few paces. Jack noticed Switch moving slowly to position himself behind him, but Fist grunted and jerked his head to the side. Switch retreated reluctantly.

Harry's shock wore off and he threw off Jack's arms. He stepped back a pace. An ugly glower had replaced his customary grin. "What are you on about, Booker? You pissed off because you didn't get your way?"

"You don't get it, do you?" Jack snarled. "You killed those bloody coppers *during an exchange with Chaos*. If we didn't have Brutality and the force on our tails already, we sure as hell do now. There are two dead enforcers in the bloody street!"

"So what?" Harry asked, half scathing, half uneasy. Jack could tell he was starting to get through with his extreme agitation. "This gang has had to off enforcers before–"

"Those were isolated run-ins in the alleys!" Jack bellowed, cutting him off. He could see the fear in Harry's eyes, and the rest of crew had backed off several paces. Jack never raised his voice above a low growl. Now, he couldn't seem to stop shouting. *So angry...*

"The coppers knew us for what we were," Jack continued, his voice thunderous and harsh. "A Myrmidon gang dealing in stolen goods and steam tech. We were worth a certain amount of trouble, and no more than that. Now, we're dealing in *Celestial Steel*, the most illegal substance in all the steaming three realms, with *Chaos*, who might very well be public enemy number one."

65

Harry was clearly shaken. His eyes flickered from Jack to Fist and back. "But…they might not know…I mean, there's no guarantee that they'll find out it was us–"

"This is Brutality we're talking about," Jack's voice had grown quite again. Deadly. "He'll find out. When they find dead enforcers near a mysterious drop just after a shipment of Celestial Steel has gone missing, the force isn't going to delegate the investigation to some human detectives; there are going to be Primal enforcers involved. All we can do is pray to steamblown *something* they don't find a bloody connection to us."

Everyone was silent as they considered this with growing dismay. Harry looked around desperately for support. Even Switch and Gurney avoided his eyes.

"I'm going to kill you, Harry," Jack said into the silence. His voice sounded strange even to his ears. Flat. Deadpan. "You've compromised everyone here, and I'm going to kill you for it."

Harry's eyes bulged. He turned to Fist in desperation. "Fist, he's overacting, right? I–"

Fist was leaning back with a relaxed air against the bar, but his voice was ice cold. "Harry, if Jack wasn't so inclined to kill you, I would probably do it myself."

Jack glanced to his left, where Dasher held his coach. The boy was watching fearfully, but he looked ready help. Jack gave him a stern look, and Dasher moved further away with reluctance.

Harry found no help from the others either, as if any would have been willing to help a man doomed by Fist's own admonition. Harry turned to face Jack, attempting to replace the shock and anxiety that had overtaken him with an unconcerned grin.

"You wouldn't throw down on me, would you, Jack?" Harry queried, putting as much camaraderie into his voice as he could muster, but his hand drifted toward his waist, and Jack could see him glancing toward his shotgun where it rested on the bar. "After all we've been through? All the years we been running this gang under Fist? Hell, I can remember when you first joined, a young pickpocket with–"

"Piss off, Harry," Jack said emotionlessly. "We've always hated each other. You've wanted me out of the way for years."

The friendly tone dropped, but the grin didn't. "Invincible Jack Booker," Harry snarled. His hand went for his waistband. "Well, I don't bloody believe it..."

Jack drew his Webley Bull Dog revolver.

Time seemed to slow.

The gang members scattered away from the line of fire. Jack's pistol rose as if in water, and his thumb pulled back the hammer as he strafed to his right. Harry's own revolver was coming up, and Jack heard the report of a gunshot as if muffled behind a thick timbered door. The bark of Harry's handgun coincided with its muzzle flash, and Jack felt the boards beneath his feet vibrate as the bullet tore a gouge through the wood. Even at three paces, Jack remembered to keep his fear distant. Apart. He couldn't let it affect his reactions.

He wasn't afraid.

Jack lined up the sights on the short-barreled pocket pistol in his hand with Harry's sweat stained chest – and fired.

The .44 caliber rimfire cartridge struck in the center of Harry's sternum, and red exploded out behind his back. The big man jerked, and an overwhelmingly loud bang exploded as Harry fired a second time only a millisecond later, his pistol jolting to the right as Jack's bullet tore a ragged swath through bone, tissue, and organs.

Jack grunted as a blunt, burning hammer punched into the meaty part of his left thigh, and he stumbled to a knee, firing off two more rounds that smashed into his rival's shoulder and skull. Harry's body wrenched violently with the impacts and he toppled back. His pistol barrel slumped toward the floor, where a third blast was triggered by a final twitch of his finger, sending up a scattering of splinters.

The revolver slipped from his hand.

Jack straightened slowly, *painfully*, rising from his knees. He hobbled toward Harry and put a final bullet into his head. He kicked the pistol a few paces away. The chest no longer rose and fell. Harry was still.

Smoke drifted in lazy swirls above his head, curling from his Bull Dog's barrel. The room was quiet.

Jack flipped open the receiver and replaced the spent casings with fresh cartridges.

He tucked the Webley back into his waistband.

Chapter 14

(Four Years Ago)

"You might think the persistent rumble that can be heard in Victorian is thunder, but you would be wrong."

— Mother Gertrude, Illuminati Scholar

The leather soles on Jack's shoes flitted quietly over the cobblestones, skirting loose garbage, stones, and the pools of water in the alley's sunken depressions, just like he'd been taught. He moved at a brisk pace; swift, but not sacrificing stealth for speed. He avoided the routes illuminated by streetlamps, passing with sure-footed confidence in the shadows.

Soon, Fist and his team appeared ahead, moving with hushed, furtive movements. Jack slipped behind them and tapped on Fist's shoulder. Fist cut off from murmuring instructions and turned with surprise.

"Jack! You're getting a little too good at sneaking, boy. Is something wrong?"

The news Jack brought wasn't good, but he kept his voice and demeanor calm. "We've run into some other picker scouts, Fist. It looks like another gang is headed this way. I think they're after the cargo, too."

Fist growled in frustration. He gave Jack a sharp look. "Do you know who it is?"

Jack nodded grimly. "Bolters."

Fist groaned. "Damn it! This is going to complicate things. How many?"

"Six. Headed this way from the east."

"I knew I shouldn't have tried to pull two jobs in one night," Fist muttered angrily. "Shit like this always happens when you spread yourself too thin." His eyes flicked around the alley. Jack could practically see his brain working overtime. "Are their pickers still active?"

"Bolt's men know you're here," Jack admitted. "But we came out on top in the scuffle. All their pickers have pulled back a ways. Morgan's got the rest of our scouts spread along the streets ahead to make sure they stay back behind their gang members."

"Good," Fist muttered, his eyes still moving. He turned. "Harry, Buckley! Get over here. We're going to have company."

The two other members of the gang with Fist – the others were trying to pull in a haul off the locomotives under Splitter – set down their loads and hurried over.

"What's the news, boss?" Harry asked, grinning at Fist. Then he noticed Jack. His grin grew wider and nastier.

Jack eyed the big, black-bearded man with distaste. He was a foul sort, and he smiled too much. Jack didn't trust anyone that smiled all the time. Except Morgan. But Morgan's smile was different. Harry's was just…malicious.

"Steamblown Bolters are headed this way. Six of them," Fist reeled off quickly, clipping his words the way he did when things got deadly serious. Buckley was a usually affable man with a thin build and quiet, reckless manner, but his face drained of color at the news. Harry blanched as well.

"*Six*?" Buckley said. "The three of us can't take six here. There's no cover!"

"You have a better idea?" Fist demanded. "Even with our pickers screening, their scouts are going to know if we try to leave. They already know we're here."

"We can take 'em," Harry snarled, his grin widening, but Jack thought he could hear the forced bravado in his voice.

"We can," Fist agreed grimly. "But I don't like anybody's chances getting out of here unscathed." He turned to Jack, his brow drawn down and face troubled. "Jack, run back to Morgan and…" Fist's eyes narrowed, and he stood up straight suddenly, glancing at his shotgun where it rested against the alley wall.

"How old are you now, Jack?" Fist asked slowly.

"Fourteen."

"You remember what I taught you about shooting and fighting?"

Jack nodded. "Yes, sir."

"Good," Fist grabbed up the shotgun and tossed it toward him. Jack caught it, surprised. "You're officially part of the gang now. We'll call it a field promotion out of sheer damned desperation." Fist smiled at him in jest. "Morgan was always better at picking anyway."

Jack grinned back, gripping the shotgun tightly.

69

"Welcome to the gang, kid," Harry sneered. "I hope to the steamblown Primals you don't piss your pants and run away."

"Shut up, Harry," Fist drawled. "You and Buckley check your weapons. They'll be on us in a moment." Fist drew his revolver and checked it expertly. He gave Jack a considering look. "Check your shotgun, Jack. You all right?"

Jack did as he was told, breaking open the shotgun breach, and noted the shells. He nodded. "Yes, sir."

"You're not scared?"

Jack thought about this for a moment. A hundred fights flashed through his mind from the orphanage. Many had ended with him lying in the dirt. If he lost this fight, though, the result would be deadly. A blood-soaked memory arose next. A rock was raised in his fist. Jack shook his head. He had learned how to fight long ago. Once he had conquered the fear that naturally accompanied the violence, he had begun to win.

Jack snapped the shotgun closed and shook his head. "No."

Fist looked surprised, but he didn't press him. He held his revolver in an easy grip by his side. "You ever killed a man before?"

Jack was silent for a brief moment. "Yes."

This time, Fist's head jerked up, and he gave him a hard look. He opened his mouth, but closed it after a moment. Then he nodded with a sort of acquiescence. "I guess we don't have to worry about you freezing up on us, then." Fist muttered bemusedly. "Killing a man with a gun is the simplest thing in the world if you've done it any other way, Jack," Fist said, clapping him on the shoulder. "Come on, Booker. Shoot that thing like I taught you."

Shadowy silhouettes darkened the alley's mouth, and the scrape of feet was followed by a motley group of men in dirty coats and bowler hats. They didn't look much different than the men from Fist's own gang. Jack thought absently that if he was in Bolt's mob he might be trying to kill Fist, Harry, and Buckley right now. But he wasn't. It was Fist who had given him a chance, who meant something to Jack. He'd taken a gamble on the Booker boys, and Jack was ready, and willing, to repay him.

Fist, Harry, and Buckley spread out in a thin line, and Jack joined them, stepping up beside Buckley at the left edge. Buckley was clutching a revolver, like Fist, while Harry held a double-barreled shotgun. Jack emulated him with his borrowed coach, holding the weapon loosely across his chest.

The men approaching followed their example, but with six men, they stretched from wall to wall of the alley. Jack grunted grimly. At least he wouldn't be able to miss.

A gap-toothed fellow in the center was obviously the leader. He held a shotgun loosely in the hand hanging by his side. The eyes glittering from beneath his overbearing brow were filled with a predatory gleam. He knew he had Fist and the others cornered. *And me, too.*

Jack focused intently on the two men closest to him. One was bareheaded, with a wispy mustache creeping over his thin, tense face. The other was stocky and had a swarthy complexion beneath his black bowler. Both carried revolvers. Jack had two shots. He had to make them count.

The gap-toothed leader was smirking openly when he and his men drew to a halt five paces from Fist, Harry, Buckley, and Jack. He sneered, spitting a stream of tobacco juice from twisted lips, and opened his mouth mockingly, addressing Fist.

Fist shot him in the forehead.

Jack was as stunned as everyone else. In the briefest of moments after the opening gunshot, everyone – Harry, Buckley, the Bolters, Jack – stood frozen in a shared moment of astounded alarm. Jack didn't know what he had been expecting. Some little bit of fanfare, perhaps, before they killed each other, or a tense, anticipatory exchange. But he was left with ringing ears and slack-jawed surprise for the fraction of a second following the revolver's report. Then, everyone exploded into action all at once.

Fist was still moving during the crucial instant of collective astonishment, and his second shot followed his first before anyone else half-raised a firearm, blowing a ragged hole in the man directly to the collapsing leader's left.

Jack turned the barrels of his shotgun toward his opponents urgently. Despite his earlier insistence, panic flooded through his chest. He had to forcibly push Fist's training through the fear threatening to overwhelm his entire body, and his memories and instincts took over. Jack's shotgun rose in his hands. The sheer terror on the thin man's face swam into his vision through a haze. Jack squeezed the trigger.

71

A thunderous roar engulfed Jack's senses as every firearm in the alley discharged in the space of second.

The shotgun leapt in his hands. Jack saw his shot take the thin man above the right calf, taking his leg off at the knee, just as Buckley's revolver cartridge simultaneously blew through his vital organs. The colossal noise and extreme stress was overloading Jack's senses. His vision had narrowed to a thin tunnel, and he watched the thin man fall in excruciating slow motion.

A bullet slammed into Jack's chest.

A scream erupted from his throat as the metal projectile crashed into one of his ribs at short-range and high-velocity, shattering the bone. Abruptly, he realized he was on the ground, slumped against the cold alley wall. He couldn't recall falling. All he knew or remembered was waves of searing, jagged pain.

But it was only pain – horrible and excruciating – but still merely pain. He had felt pain before; he had *beaten* pain before. The red staining his shirt and coat was just blood. He had lost a lot of that in the past too.

Somehow, the shotgun was still clutched in his fists. Jack raised his eyes. The swarthy man with the bowler was pointing the revolver at him, and Jack could see the muscles tensing in his hand, about to release another bullet to finish him.

Jack rose to a knee.

Everything in his body screamed at him to stop moving, to lie still forever. Jack ignored it. He raised the shotgun.

The swarthy man's revolver exploded again. Jack heard the round whistle by his left ear and strike the alley's wall, throwing chips of brick against the back of his neck. Jack lined up his shot and fired.

His enemy's body jerked as if struck by a sledgehammer when the buckshot blew a fist-sized hole in his midriff.

Jack collapsed back against the alley wall as his opponent did the same. Every gasp was unimaginable agony, so he breathed as lightly as he could. Fist was leaning over him.

"Jack? You hang in there, boy. We already lost Buckley; don't you die on me too." Fist's blunt, gruff face was peering down at him with concern. His arm was bloody and hung strangely at his side. He left Jack's sight for a moment before returning with the swarthy man's bowler in his hands. He grinned as he pushed it gently over

Jack's head. "There you go, boy. It's a bit bloody, but it'll fit. Your first trophy."

Jack tried to protest. He didn't want a trophy. The words came out as pained mumbles from his throat, however, so the bowler remained. Jack reached up with difficulty and pulled it down tighter on his dark curls. Fist beamed approvingly and turned away again.

"Harry! Get over here and help me carry Jack back to the safehouse. He's in a bad way, and Buckley ain't going to care where we leave him."

Fist picked him up clumsily with one arm, while Harry hobbled over and grabbed his legs. Fist was gentle, but the motion still sent a blaze of pain throughout his chest.

"He's a goner, Fist," Jack heard Harry saying, as if from far away. "He's not even going to make it back to the safehouse. We ought to put him out of his misery."

"He'll make it," Fist replied. "You hear me, Jack? I'm going to be pissed if I lose one of my Booker boys. Hang in there, or I'll bloody find you in Hell and kill you myself."

Chapter 15

"Reputation is the most potent tool a mobster can utilize.
Cultivate the right impression, and nobody gets in your way."

– 'Red' Ragen, Infamous Victorian Mob Boss

Jack was laid up in his bunk for two weeks.

Fortunately, the bullet had passed through the muscle in his thigh and out the other side. A clean exit wound was easy enough to deal with: no digging around in his insides to find the elusive instigator of all the damage. Jack still shuddered when he thought about the first time he'd been shot. *That* bullet had hit a rib, shattering part of the bone into miniscule splinters and the bullet into multiple shrapnel shreds. He still carried a metal sliver they were unable to reach somewhere in his chest. This wound was nothing compared to that first experience.

He had pulled through from that first bullet four years ago, to the amazement of Fist's crew. That was when they'd initially started calling him invincible, jokingly at first. Then as the years wore on and Jack suffered more wounds – gunshot and knife mostly – the sarcasm had shifted into awe, culminating with the Primal…

Jack grunted and sat up in his bunk, leaning against the headboard. Was he invincible? No. He had seen the edge of death too many times to believe it. Street crews were a suspicious lot, and if there was anything they liked doing more than drinking, gambling, and whoring, it was creating reputations out of superstition.

Jack shifted uncomfortably, moving his leg with a grimace. It was healing nicely, and the only risk now was infection. Fist had poured whiskey into the wound to keep it clean, but Jack was still being extra cautious. The last thing he needed was gangrene to deprive him of a leg.

Jack was just lighting a cigar when Fist stepped into the dormitory, followed by Dasher. Jack hadn't been alone up to that point, by any means. The bunkroom was never empty. But the crew seemed almost unwilling to disturb him. They had been staying crowded up in the common area or whispering in hushed voices at

74

the other end of the room. Jack could swear he'd even seen them throwing furtive looks his way.

Fist stopped at the foot of the bed, and Dasher sat on the bunk opposite. The boy was grinning happily, as usual. "How's it coming along, Jack?" Fist asked. He wouldn't meet Jack's eyes.

"Decent," Jack replied, shifting his leg again. "I'll be up and around in a day or two, though I won't be moving well for a while."

Fist grunted. "You take your time. It's not like we're going out anytime soon."

Jack nodded sourly, giving Fist a significant look. The burly man cut his eyes away as if he hadn't noticed. "How are the rest of the boys taking the confinement?"

"As well as can be expected," Fist admitted. "Everyone's on edge, expecting Brutality to hammer down the door at any moment; that's not helping anyone's mood. But they *are* all scared shitless, so I haven't had trouble convincing them to keep their heads down."

"I haven't seen many of them down here, except to sleep. Where's Black Jim and Gurney?"

Fist shifted uncomfortably. "I think you've gone and blown your stupidity act. They don't believe it anymore, not after all the stuff you were screaming at Harry."

Jack grunted irritably. He had been afraid of that.

"And, well…"

Jack gave Fist a suspicious look when he didn't continue. "Well, what?"

"They all think you're a Primal in disguise!" Dasher burst out, snorting with laughter. He ignored the glares Fist was throwing at him.

"*What?*"

Fist picked up where Dasher left off, though he still gave the boy an irritated look that indicated he had wanted to keep that information unsaid. "It's just another rumor about how you should be dead by now, with all the stuff that's happened to you. You know how they are, superstitious and all. Gurney got this idea in his head and had to open his fool mouth. Now they all think you're half Primal or something."

"Gurney says that you're too tough to be human, but too wingless to be a Primal, which means the only explanation is that

75

you're both." Dasher chimed in excitedly. Jack groaned. The idiot boy *believed* it. He could see it in his eyes.

"That is the stupidest thing I've ever heard," Jack said bluntly. He sucked greedily on his cigar, trying to release some of the knotted tension in his muscles. This news wasn't helping.

Dasher ignored him. "Goldilocks says…well, whispers anyway. His voice isn't coming back so good after you crushed his windpipe. He says that you're too dangerous to be a normal man. Black Jim agreed, and said that no mere Myrmidon could survive everything you have."

"Since when did Jim start calling us Myrmidons?" Jack growled crossly. "Did he join the bloody Illuminati or something?"

Dasher was finding all this highly amusing. "He knows that's what Primals call humans, and he thinks you're a Primal now, remember? Or at least half Primal." He grinned, shrugging. "He probably thinks he's being respectful."

Jack rubbed his temples in disbelief.

"Dasher, I need to speak with Jack. Alone." Fist said abruptly. Dasher gave him a curious look, but complied with the command. He shut the door as he left.

Jack watched the boss carefully. Fist stared back for a long moment.

"We're in a bit of a corner, Jack," Fist finally said. "I've seen the signs before. The coppers are in The Narrows in force, and even a few rocketeers and Primals are swooping through the area. They're looking for something."

"It doesn't take more than one guess to figure out what," Jack grunted.

Fist nodded. He continued reluctantly. "Chaos is already putting the Celestial Steel to use. His people have been ambushing coppers and Primal enforcers in the streets. Two low-level Primals have been killed. It's a bloody warzone out there."

Jack shook his head. "Much more of that and Tyranny will start sending in the troops." He glared at Fist. "This is your fault."

Fist's eyes narrowed. "This is Harry's fault, if the fool–"

"We both knew something like this could happen," Jack cut him off. "When you play with fire, there's a good chance you'll get burned. Was it worth it, Fist? Was the money worth it?"

76

Fist didn't answer for a long time. His eyes were piercing daggers. Finally, he spoke. "This will all blow over eventually. We'll be sitting on a fortune when that day comes. We can go where we want. Anywhere we want. The West, maybe. Somewhere far away from Tyranny and Order, away from all steamblown Primals–"

"*If* that day comes, Fist," Jack interrupted quietly. "Not when. If." Jack laid his head back against the wall and closed his eyes. "And you'd never leave Victorian, even if you could. These streets are all you know. They're all you've ever known. Just like me."

Jack kept his eyes closed, and Fist was silent. Jack wondered if he'd finally gone too far, if Fist would kill him and be done. But when he opened his eyes, Fist was gone.

Chapter 16

(Three Years Ago)

"There is a better world out there. Somewhere."
— Captain Peter Pantucket, Explorer

Jack watched Morgan covertly and smiled. His younger brother was sprawled against the crates beside him, watching the swarms of people scurrying about their business on the docks. Jack had never seen such self-assurance as he now saw in the bright-eyed pickpocket. The boy was content, strong and confident in himself and his abilities.

Jack could hardly recall a time when he had been this happy. He had felt a weight for as long as he could remember. It had always been his burden to keep Morgan safe, to help him be something more than the frightened child the world had tried to force him to become. Jack had failed often, but looking at the contentment of the boy beside him, Jack felt a certain peace.

It was an unusual day in Victorian. The sun was a bright yellow ball shining down through empty skies of vivid blue. It seemed every Victorian resident was determined to take advantage of the wonderful weather, and the wharves were packed to bursting. Everyone was enjoying the shunshine: beggars and lords, dock-laborers, merchants. Even fine ladies with parasols descended from the ramps of airships with retinues of suitors and servants. The sunlight on Jack's skin provided the perfect amount of warmth to banish autumn's chill, and the smell of roasting meat, baking bread, and grilled vegetables issuing from the taverns delighted his senses. He could remember a time when those smells would have been torture to his empty belly, but now they simply made his mouth water. He was satisfied in the knowledge that he could purchase food at any time he wished.

"You ever seen such a fine day, Jack?" Morgan exclaimed. He lifted his eyes to the sky and grinned, spreading his arms out as if he would catch it all and keep it forever. "I feel like I could pickpocket the world, buy me my own airship, and sail away into the blue infinity."

Jack laughed. "Where would you go out there? If you missed the Celestial Realm, you might drift until you ran out of supplies and starved. They say the sky goes on forever in every direction."

"Gloomy ol' Jack, always jumping to the worst conclusion first," Morgan teased. "I bet you I'd sail right up and up until I found an island in the stars, just like that young explorer fellow, Captain Peter Pan."

Jack blushed at the statement. He *did* always consider the worst possibility first, and it just wouldn't do on a day as fine as this. So Jack held his tongue and didn't venture the opinion that Captain Peter Pantucket's expedition had never returned because he had gotten lost somewhere in the sky and died of thirst. The legend that he had found an island of paradise amongst the stars was just some myth that parents told children.

"We'd make berth on a star-island filled with beautiful mermaids," Jack offered instead, playing along. "Any island with no mermaid lagoon isn't good enough for us."

"And trees folding over with Celestial fruit, just like the Primals and aristocrats eat," Morgan said excitedly. "With forests filled with wild boar, rocks of piping hot bread, and mountains made of sugar candy."

"That would be a proper star-island for us," Jack agreed. "We'd live there forever and never grow old."

"If any sky pirates stumbled upon our home by chance," Morgan declared, thrusting his fist into the air. "I'd take the helm of our airship, you'd take the guns, and we'd shoot 'em down!"

"Our ship would have twelve-pounders," Jack put in. "Just like the Imperial Navy. The pirate vessel would fall right out of the stars when we hit their boiler."

Morgan's face grew a little red before his next input, but both he and Jack were to the age now that girls were almost always on their minds. "The mermaids would be so grateful we saved them that they would beg us to stay. We'd probably get four or five apiece."

"At least that many," Jack laughed. "Unless I stole some of yours, then you'd only have one or two."

Morgan grinned and punched him. "They wouldn't go with you anyway. Your nose is all crooked. Girls like a man with a straight nose."

"They like something straight on a man, but I don't think it's the nose."

Morgan blushed bright red, but he sniggered appreciatively. He laid a hand on Jack's coat collar and hopped down from his crate. "Neither of us is going to get to see our star-island *or* what mermaid girls like if I don't get some work done today."

"Fist giving out some good perks for going over quota lately?"

"Uh huh," Morgan nodded, his eyes scanning the crowds expertly. "I bet I get a few pounds this week for my extra haul."

Jack whistled admiringly. "We might be able to buy that airship sooner than we thought."

"Only a hundred years or so at this rate," Morgan agreed, laughing. He clapped suddenly, delighted. "He's *perfect*! See the dandy in the top hat? There – no, there! He's got that look like he's discovered dung on his upper lip. See him? With the monocle?"

Jack searched through the throng. It wasn't too hard to spot the man in his current surroundings. He had the finest suit Jack had ever seen, and Morgan was right about the look. He was deliberate and precise in his movements, obviously attempting to avoid touching anything around him. "Yeah, I see him. You see his suit? He's got some coin. I can't believe he doesn't have any bodyguards."

"He's very fit," Morgan admitted. "But with no bodyguards, he won't chase me if I slip anything away from him. That might make him get *dirty*."

He was the perfect target, but Jack had a slight feeling of unease. The man had a certain poise, a confidence of movement and purpose that Jack couldn't place.

Jack shook his head irritably, banishing the feeling. Morgan was right; he was pessimistic to the bone. Today was not a day for worst possibilities.

"Go get him, then," Jack grinned, somewhat uneasily, but Morgan was already gone, slipping into the crowd with a mischievous wink.

Jack followed slowly, letting the crowd carry him in its confining, jostling flow. He smiled again, observing Morgan's skillful traverse of the street, despite the veritable wall of people. His brother was a wraith, slipping between everyone with barely a touch and hardly a glance. His fleet feet swerved expertly into the gaps and through the crevices.

Jack's sight of Morgan's approach was cut off for a short moment as a wagon rumbled between them, scattering those in the way with shouts and curses. When it had moved past, Morgan was no longer visible, but the mark was.

It was the first good look Jack had gotten of the gentleman from up close, and the more Jack saw, the stronger the agitation in his belly became. The mark was in his mid-twenties by Jack's judgment and had an astonishingly handsome face. Perfect, actually – like a chiseled marble bust. He had become unnaturally alert in the few moments that Jack had lost sight of him. It was almost as if the man had sensed something.

Jack's unease reached an unbearable point. The mark had eyes that appeared almost *golden* in the bright sunlight. Jack reached beneath his coat and grasped the handle of the Webley Bull Dog revolver Fist had given him. *Something is wrong…*

The man twisted away, still scanning the crowd with his extraordinary eyes, and Jack saw it as the gentleman turned.

A flicker of golden light flashed from the back of his waistcoat.

Horror flooded Jack's veins, and he opened his mouth to shout a warning. Just before the sound left his throat, Morgan materialized from the crowd.

"MORGAN, NO!"

Every head in the crowd turned towards him. All except Morgan and the mark. His brother was struggling to free himself from the man's casual grip on his coat collar. He'd never even collided with the man.

Not the man.

The Primal.

Jack was running, crashing into those too slow to step aside. His revolver was in his hand; he didn't remember drawing it. The crowd was too thick. Jack bellowed in sheer panicked desperation and fired into the air.

At the deafening roar of the revolver, everyone in the crowd started running or ducking. Some started screaming. But Jack's path cleared. He fired off another shot, and those nearest him scrambled away in terror. TOO LATE…

The Primal ignored all of this, as if he didn't hear the screaming and the gunshots or could care less. Morgan had stopped struggling in his grip, and he stared up at the perfect face and golden eyes with a mixture of terror and open-mouthed awe.

Jack ran harder and faster than he had in all his life, but despite his speed and fear, a small part of him considered the Primal. The god's eyes were curiously wide, and Jack was astounded by the expression on his flawless face.

It was disdain.

That wasn't strange in itself. Jack had seen such an expression many times on the face of aristocratic marks as they beheld the thieves who dared rob them. Jack knew it well. But what he normally saw was the contempt of one level of human existence for that of an almost meaningless, but still human, life.

This was not.

The Primal's disdain was pure and boundless. He wasn't regarding an equal in even the most stretched of terms. Those golden eyes pierced a rodent, an insect, a bit of dirt. Morgan's face told Jack that he understood. He was the focus of the attention of a god, a being so infinitely greater as to defy comprehension.

Jack roared his refusal to believe the situation. His legs pumped. His lungs burned. His voice was a raw scream.

The Primal casually backhanded Morgan across the face.

Jack heard the resounding crack over the sound of his thumping feet, ragged breath, and beating heart. Morgan's head spun awkwardly, facing backward on his neck in a grotesque fashion, and he slumped slowly to the ground.

A loud ringing filled Jack's ears, and all breath died in his chest. It took an eternity for Morgan to sag to the cobblestones. The Primal pulled a handkerchief from his breast pocket and brushed lightly at his hands with a disgusted air.

Jack found his voice.

He didn't know what he meant to yell, but all that emerged was a harsh, animalistic bellow. Jack slid to a halt in front of the murderer.

He emptied his pistol into the Primal's chest and face at point-blank range.

The Primal jerked as each bullet made contact, but aside from a few small drops of shining silver blood on his pristine brow, a look of mild surprise in his eyes, and holes in his waistcoat, Jack saw no indication that he'd even fired his weapon.

The Primal fingered the ragged tears in his clothing and looked him in the eye. Jack saw annoyance there and intense fury.

Abruptly, the man's back exploded into twin waves of crackling strands of sunlight. He rose up into the air and hovered just off the grimy cobblestones. Jack stumbled back a step, utterly awestruck.

A flail of blazing, golden rays appeared in the god's right hand. It rose imperiously above the majestic head and descended.

Burning strands of fiery pain imploded down into Jack's chest. He felt his feet leave the ground for several moments until he struck the ground with incredible force.

***

When Jack woke, everything was darkness and pain. He groaned and tried to sit up, but the blistering sensation that lanced through his chest stopped his movement. He was lying on the street, slumped against a tavern wall. Jack turned his head slightly. The soft glow of streetlamps grew in his vision until he could discern the hulking shapes of airships resting in their docks on the water. He was at the wharves.

Then Jack remembered.

It didn't bring instant horror and grief, and Jack dimly wondered why. He managed to force himself past the pain and sit up, gritting his teeth. The docks were deserted and the street as well. Nothing shared Jack's solitude but the dark, crumpled lump lying in the center of the roadway.

Morgan.

Jack crawled, ignoring the pain, ignoring his thoughts. He was lifeless in mind and body. Silence reigned but for his scuffling, incompliant limbs. He absently wondered why the cobblestones were so icy on his hands. *Because it's nighttime and cold, you dolt. There's no sun...* Jack shrank from the thought. He didn't want to consider the sun.

His sluggish brain wondered next why no one was about. Why would they be left lying in the street? The answer was simple, but it was still slow in coming. He had reached the small form before it had fully coalesced in his mind.

Because they are afraid...

Jack turned over Morgan with hesitant fingers. His brother was still and stiff as a block of wood. The eyes…the ever-sparkling eyes were wide and open, but now dull and empty. Like windows that had once depicted the warmth of lit candles shattered by the force of wind and hail.

Jack's sat weakly next to the cold body. His hand rested on Morgan's face. He turned his face to the sky, avoiding the unnatural, twisted sight that was not his brother. Not anymore. The glimmer of a few stars infiltrated Victorian's streetlamp glow, and a single thought passed through Jack's traumatized mind.

Star-islands…

Chapter 17

"Let us be frank, at least. I do not condone the criminal elements of this city, but Victorian's Enforcement arm is not a protective service. It is an occupation force. It is a military division intent only on eradicating resistance to the regime, not protecting Imperial citizens."

— Lord Damian Devalere, Political Moderate

Jack almost felt relief when they came. If nothing else, the tense anxiety of the wait was over. The feeling didn't last long. In the space of a moment it had been replaced by sickening, oily fear.

"They're coming!" Gurney exclaimed as he burst through the door into the dormitory. His voice was a warbling, high-pitched yelp, barely audible and unnatural as a result of the terror constricting his throat. "It's a raid! They're coming!"

Stunned silence followed for a brief second. The living quarters exploded into a panicked flurry of activity. Jack swung his legs off his bunk and grabbed the loaded coach resting next to his bed. He grimaced slightly as his booted feet connected with the floor and sent a sharp sensation of pain up to his still tender thigh. "RAID!" Jack bellowed at the top of his voice as he strode out of the door and down the bunker hallways with determination, dragging his uncooperative leg. He had no time for injuries. "UP AND ABOUT, LADS!"

Fist burst out of his quarters with a shotgun in hand and his suspenders hanging half off. The boss marched purposefully up the hall toward the stairs to the common room, taking up the cry in a tone filled with command. "RAID! STIR ABOUT, YOU LAZY SONS OF WHORES! THERE'S COPPERS OUTSIDE WHO AIM TO RAPE YOUR CORPSES! RAID, DAMN YOU ALL!"

Jack hobbled up the stairs as quickly as his leg would allow, and helped Black Jim flip over one of the heavy wooden tables as a barricade. Fist and the others followed suit around the room, positioning themselves to fire towards the door. More gang members poured into the common room, squeezing in behind the flipped tables. Those who arrived last moved reluctantly forward to the tables closest to the door, and the space behind the bar was quickly filled. Black Jim's eyes were wide and frantic to Jack's left, but he

85

held steady. Jack could hear Gurney whispering fervently to his right, clutching at a small, rusty totem of a seven-pointed star that hung around his neck.

It's too late for that, Jack thought sourly. *Promises to deaf gods won't save us from our sins now.*

"Jack!" Morgan slid in beside him. His face was earnest but slick with panicky sweat. A shaky hand held out Jack's specialty ammunition pouch.

Celestial Steel bullets, we might need those. Jack scooped the pouch up hurriedly but glared at Morgan. *No, not Morgan*, Jack shook his head. *Dasher.*

"What are you doing here?" Jack hissed. "Get to the back exit and slip out with the rest of the pickers!"

"The back exit is covered," Dasher panted. His voice was just shy of hysterical. "There are coppers swarming the back alley!"

"Then hide in the smuggling rooms," Jack commanded desperately. "Maybe they won't find…"

"Jack, they brought *Primal* enforcers too!" Dasher squealed, interrupting him. "There's one in the alley! I saw him!"

Black Jim turned wide terrified eyes on them. "Oh, sh–"

The common room door exploded into a flurry of wooden slivers.

A Primal leapt through the door, carried on wings of hellish flame. His right hand was curled into a massive fist of glowing, red stone, but as Jack watched it faded back into an armored hand. A wicked, spiked mace materialized in its grip. Jack gasped. The Primal was like something from a nightmare. Flaring yellow eyes blazed out a of twisted devil's face, and great, sharp horns rose from either side of the evil head.

The common room erupted in gunfire, but bullets deflected harmlessly off of the black and red Celestial Steel plate armor covering the demon from neck to toe. Those few that connected with the face did little more but enrage the Primal. He swung his mace into the nearest barricade. It smashed into flying chunks, and the men behind it screamed and died.

True pandemonium ensued.

Jack, Fist, Black Jim, and a few others managed to stay behind cover. The rest leapt from their barricades in a mass. All discipline was forgotten in the urgent need to escape the common room and the maniacal god of death.

The enforcers stormed through the breach from behind their living battering ram.

The gang members scrambling for the exit screamed and died as the coppers peppered the room with small arms fire. Jack lifted above cover long enough to unload both barrels of buckshot. Between his own fire and that of Fist and Jim, they managed to stop up the gap momentarily as the enforcers' momentum slowed on the dead and wounded filling up the breach. The coppers forced through after an inconclusive moment, however, and they rushed through the room, answering the gang's fire with salvos of shotgun slugs and revolver rounds.

Jack huddled behind the thick table as he reloaded his shotgun, wincing when several bullets smacked into the planks near his head. He broke over the coach breech and slipped in two thick, silvery slugs. Beside him, Black Jim peeked above cover and fired off three rounds from his revolver before jerking back, holding his throat and choking. He stumbled to a knee before another bullet took him in the eye.

Gurney suddenly screamed in terror, and Jack looked up to see the demon Primal bearing down on them at incredible speed. Jack's overstressed mind noted that the Primal wasn't running, but floating forward, propelled by the massive wings of fire. Jack dived on top of Dasher.

The Primal smashed into the table, tossing it over Jack's head and across the room as if it were no more than a brittle twig. Jack scrambled up, grabbing Dasher and forcing him toward the back stairs. Behind him, Gurney's scream cut off abruptly when the red god's mace descended on his head.

Dasher's churning legs faltered, and he shouted in agony, grasping at his back. Jack kept his grip on the lad's arm, ignoring the bullets whizzing by him, and thrust the boy down the stairs. The staircase was a mass of men scrambling to escape the certain death that had overtaken the common room. Jack hurried with the rest of them, keeping a tight hold on Dasher.

"Jack!" Fist was beside him. He was holding a hand to his side. Blood seeped through his thick fingers. "Over here!" Fist steered him and a few others into his private quarters.

They burst into the small room, and Jack helped Dasher lie down while Fist, Switch, and Duncan overturned tables, beds, and dressers for cover. The boy's face was ashen. Jack noted the bullet hole in his back and the exit wound in his stomach.

"Jack?" Dasher's voice was pained and weak. "I'm cold, Jack. Did we get away?" He shivered visibly. "Did we get away from that monster? He was so dark, Jack. Dark and red and cold. Even with the fire all about him."

"Hush, now," Jack said, laying a trembling hand on the lad's brow. A dim street flashed through his mind, a crumpled form lying beneath the cold light of star-islands. *This can't be happening. Not again.* "We're going to get out of here."

"Jack!" Fist grabbed his shoulder. His right hand held out a few silvery shotgun slugs. "I've got a small stockpile of Celestial Steel in here. It's not much, but it might be enough to stop one of those Primal bastards."

Jack waved him away. "Give it to Switch and Duncan. I made some of my own." He indicated his shotgun lying next to him.

"Come on then, Jack," Fist urged. "We've got the lad covered as best we can. All that can be done for him now is to hold this room."

Jack nodded reluctantly. He scooped up his shotgun and settled behind a dresser with Fist. Duncan and Switch crouched behind the overturned table. Jack pulled out his Bull Dog, opened the receiver, and let the cartridges fall to the floor. He methodically selected the Celestial Steel .44 rimfire cartridges from his pouch and inserted those instead.

Something thumped hard into the door outside, but it held. Several more blows followed, shivering the thick wood until the bar over the entry splintered and cracked.

The door crashed open.

Jack fired his Bull Dog simultaneously with his three companions, and the first enforcer to leap through the doorway collapsed in a heap, riddled with bullets and buckshot. The second fared no better.

Return shots answered, ripping through the breech and smacking into the walls, floor, and dresser. Fist grunted, blood oozing from two fresh punctures in his left shoulder. Jack's revolver was empty, and he grabbed up his shotgun, blasting another copper in the chest as he tried to shoulder his way past the bodies of his comrades. A bullet winged his shoulder as he ducked back down; he gritted his teeth at the sting.

Fist fired both barrels of his coach as the coppers attempted another entry, killing the leading man, but a round whizzed through the door and slammed into the boss's chest. He sagged back, bleeding profusely from four wounds. Duncan took a bullet in the temple, and he slumped over the table. Jack and Switch fired in a frenetic frenzy, narrowly forcing the coppers back again.

"Switch, cover me!" Jack shouted. "I'm reloading!" The pinch-faced man nodded and dropped his empty shotgun, pulling out a revolver.

Jack broke open his shotgun and Bull Dog desperately, inserting the casings as quickly as his fumbling fingers would allow. He glanced at Dasher and Fist. Dasher's head was lolling to the side. Jack thought he might have passed out. Fist was barely conscious, struggling to breathe. Jack saw with amazement that he was still groping at his shotgun and trying to reload.

"Jack?" The boss's voice was barely audible over the incessant discharge of firearms, but the big man leaned forward and grasped his arm. "You were right, Jack. All my fault. All of it...my fault." Fist's eyes searched upward, but Jack was unsure if Fist could see him anymore. "I – just so tired, Jack. So tired of grubbing in the filth and the shit in the alleys of this damned city. I wanted *something*...Morgan killed by that steamblown Primal...wanted it to be worth something. *Anything*." The big man's words were fading; his eyes stopped flitting about. "Don't let them get you, Jack." A small smile twitched at the corners of his mouth. "Invincible...don't let...them–"

Fist's eyes stared ahead, and the empty shotgun dropped from his limp grip.

"Booker!" Switch's shout was hysterical with fear. "They've stopped trying to force a way in, and they're barely firing anymore. Something is coming..."

Jack knew what was coming.

He spun back toward the door, centering both shotgun barrels over the doorway. It was barely visible behind the thick smoke from their firearms.

The Primal burst through the gap.

Jack let loose with both barrels.

89

The devil roared with rage, but was stopped cold by the twin blasts of Celestial Steel slugs, which punctured his armor and spun him about. The demon's fiery wings flickered for the briefest of moments.

The Primal turned a baleful eye on Jack.

Jack swallowed. He might have wounded the god slightly, but it was more enraged than hurt. Jack could see his death in that yellow eye.

Abruptly, another Primal slid through the door before the demon could pounce. In the brief moment it took for the newcomer to cross the room, Jack saw a black mask painted on a red breastplate.

An armored fist crashed down.

Chapter 18

"The moments that define our existence often sneak up on us. Many do not recognize destiny when it walks up and spits on their boots. Of course, sometimes it slaps you in the face like a dueling gauntlet. Good luck ignoring that."

– Lord Victor Rolfe, Political Wit and Social Radical

A swaying sense of motion crept into Jack's mind, and he groaned. His ears popped and his head throbbed. He stirred unwillingly, feeling the rough texture of wooden planks under his cheek.

"Look who's awake," a thin voice muttered near him. Jack opened his eyes to murky darkness. "I should've known you'd survive. Invincible and all. I wonder if it will kill you when they stretch our necks? Or will you just flop forever on the end of the rope?"

Jack moved his arms and legs experimentally, wincing at their soreness, and sat up. He found a wall next to him with a fumbling hand and leaned against it, resting his aching head as he surveyed the gloom with his eyes. Faint light filtered into the darkness around him, dimly illuminating Jack's surroundings.

He was in some sort of cell, made of wood and metal, but Jack distinctly felt a moving sensation beneath him. Shadowy figures crouched in the murk. He could see their eyes gleaming in the weak light that entered through some sort of grate in the ceiling.

"Where are we?" Jack ventured. His voice was raw and weak, and the dry tissue of his throat grated irritably upon his speech.

"We are in a lovely cabin aboard the Imperial Navy's *HMS Titanfall*," the voice answered. The words were said in jest, but irony sounded strange coming off a bitter tongue. Jack knew the voice. It was almost back to its normal pitch.

"Goldilocks?" Jack croaked.

"One and the same," Goldi stated grimly, and Jack recognized the muted sheen of his long, yellow hair. "We are not in a cabin, as I'm sure you've realized, but the brig. As a lad, I always wanted to sail aboard one of the Imperial Navy's airships. Now that I'm here, I find that a man-o'-war isn't quite up to my imagination."

Jack grunted. "I hear you." His thoughts were coalescing slowly into memory, and he struggled to make sense of them. "There was a raid…"

"Yes."

"Dasher!" Jack remembered suddenly. "He was hit, bleeding–"

"He's here, Booker," Goldilocks answered. His voice carried assurance, but it was also filled with doubt. "Whether he survives much longer…" Goldi's shadowy form shrugged. "I'm betting he doesn't stay alive long enough to be executed."

"Executed?"

"Where do you think they're taking us? Paradise?" Goldilocks chuckled without humor. "Well, you'd be right. We're bound for the Celestial Realm, Jack, but I doubt we'll be finding much once we get there besides a traitor's trial, a conviction of treason, and the gallows' rope."

Jack's head spun, but the stupidity of unconsciousness was fading, and everything started to fall into place. "Trafficking Celestial Steel isn't going to land us anywhere else." Jack agreed. He ran a tentative hand across his scalp, but stopped when he felt a bloody lump. "Where's Dasher?"

"In the other cell with Switch and a few of the others," Goldilocks jerked his head indicatively. "Don't worry. They're keeping him as comfortable as possible." He glanced at Jack for a moment, and then ducked his eyes away. "We're the lucky ones, Jack. You know that?"

"By 'lucky' you mean 'alive'?" Jack grunted.

"Uh huh. Most of the boys got slaughtered at the safehouse. But those Primals said we were going to be made examples." Goldilocks laughed nervously. Jack thought he might be holding back some tears. "At least we get a few more days, though, eh?"

"Fist and the others might be the lucky ones."

Goldilocks fell silent at this, and Jack was left with a sense of guilt. These were likely their final days, and here he was making them as unbearable as possible.

"We'll get to see the Celestial Realm before we die," Jack muttered. "How many people get to say that?"

Goldilocks brightened considerably, and Jack realized the lad's sanity was hanging by a thread. "Damn right," Goldi agreed.

Jack left it at that, not trusting himself to say more. He never was one for cheering others.

Goldilocks will get to see the Celestial Realm, Jack thought bleakly, *but he won't see his eighteenth birthday.*

***

The journey to the Celestial Realm lasted several days, by Jack's judgment. It made him queasy to think about how high over Victorian and the rest of the Grounded Realm they were by now. But queasy was a constant state here in the brig.

Their jailors rarely fed them, though Jack couldn't care less. He could keep nothing down anyway. At least their privy buckets were emptied, infrequent as it might be. The Emperors' Imperial Marines were a closed-mouthed lot, and brutal, even by his estimation. Coppers considered themselves opponents of the gangs, more or less. These Marines of the Imperial Navy did not. They perceived Jack and the rest of the prisoners far beneath their notice, and the fact that they were tasked with guard duty clearly ruffled their pride. Of course, Jack had no doubt that much of the hate came from their being traitors as well. They were as good as convicted for treason already. Why else would street filth be shipped to the home of gods?

Jack fingered his head wound pensively, wincing at its tenderness. The swelling had gone down, but he was still dubious that he could fit his bowler on his head, wherever his cap had gone. He didn't miss the hat. It was nothing more than a grotesque trophy, and Jack had never wanted it anyway. It stood for something else in his mind, though. It was Harv, Morgan, even Fist – anything he'd ever lost.

Steamblown Primals. Jack gritted his teeth angrily. The world was unforgiving, and he knew better than to shift blame. But by his reckoning, the existence of the Primals was what had brought it all about. *We live under their thumb, and they take to rule as if it is their natural right. Perhaps it is, but I don't have to stand for it.*

Jack laughed to himself quietly. *What are you going to do, Dull Jack? What's left of your pathetic existence is about to be finished. Your life belongs to the Primals' whims as much as any other. Maybe more.*

He was Jack Booker, plaything of the gods, even if they didn't realize it. His whole life had been one gigantic struggle to protect both others and himself. And he had failed spectacularly.

Jack punched the wooden planks in a surge of unrestrained savagery, ripping open new wounds on his knuckles. He hardly even noticed. *Bloody invincible. You didn't save Harv or Morgan or Fist or Dasher. In the end you can't even save the one person you're known for never failing: yourself.*

Abruptly, loud calls filtered from the above decks, and the pounding of feet echoed on the planks. Jack peered up through the grate and caught a glimpse of canvas sails spreading beneath the rapidly deflating balloon that kept them aloft. A deep, vibrating hum reverberated through the boards beneath his feet as the steam engines in the aft boiler room chugged to life.

We're preparing to land, Jack realized.

Their descent was almost unnoticeable in the bowels of the *Titanfall* but for the painful popping in Jack's ears. The others stirred around him, realizing they had reached their destination. He frowned. *More like the end of the line. I wonder what awaits us beyond these cells?*

It wasn't long before the vessel came to a halt with an abrupt lurch, and Jack almost lost his feet. He stood up straight and grasped the bars just as the thumping of boots began on the stairs. In the next moment, the brig hallways were filled with Marines in resplendent, deep red uniforms, cursing and shouting at the prisoners to get to their feet. Jack waited patiently with the others until his cell was unlocked, then he shuffled out behind Goldilocks. He allowed himself to be herded toward the upper decks with the others.

A sudden commotion to his right drew his attention. An officer in a blue uniform – a sergeant, maybe, Jack didn't fully understand the significance of the individual uniforms – was shouting at a bewildered shape on the floor. With a sudden jolt, Jack realized it was Dasher, too injured to move or understand what was happening.

"Get up, dog!" The officer screamed, kicking at Dasher. The boy moaned painfully, curling up in a ball to cover his stomach. "Get up!" The officer's boot descended again. The man threw up his hands, turning to one of the Marines. "This one's too far gone to make it to the gallows anyway. Shoot him."

Jack bulled out of the line, ignoring the shouts and threats directed toward him. Several Marines pulled sabers free from their scabbards or pointed shortened naval carbines at his chest.

The officer drew a Webley sidearm and shoved it in his face. "Halt!" The man's mustache and high officer's hat quivered when he shouted, and spittle flew from his lips. Jack stopped and put up his hands. "Back in line, treasonous bastard, or I shoot you now."

"Let me carry him," Jack said calmly, keeping his voice quiet in an attempt to defuse the situation. "He's badly wounded. I'll carry the boy."

"He's going to die soon anyway, fool," the officer said, then brandished his pistol again. "If he can't walk, better to die now and save us some trouble. I told you to get back in line!"

"I'll carry him," Jack continued stubbornly. "He won't be any trouble. You're to bring us to trial, yes? The Emperors will want us all for examples."

"You're here for execution, not trial," the officer snorted, but he jerked his head indicatively. "You want to carry him? Fine. You'll both be dead soon anyway. Get this piece of shit from my sight, and your own filth too."

Jack knelt beside Dasher's huddled form and slung him over a shoulder, trying to ignore the lad's whimpers. Then, he shuffled with his burden back into the crowd of prisoners moving slowly toward the upper deck.

As Jack's head broke the surface of the hatch, bright light nearly blinded him. He squinted and covered his eyes with his left hand, though it did little good. The light didn't seem to be coming from any particular direction. It just *was*. Water squeezed from his eyelids, but eventually he grew accustomed to the bright glow. He dropped his hand to venture a look at their destination.

Jack's jaw dropped open, and his pained eyes widened with astonishment.

This was…paradise.

Jack still had dim memories from long ago when his mother would tell him of Heaven. The afterlife, she'd called it – where father was – a place of wonder and beauty and perfection. Jack couldn't think of anything else to describe what spread around him.

The *HMS Titanfall* had made berth on the shores of a crystal sea that spread away and beyond Jack's left as far as the eye could see.

The calm, listless waves glittered like uncounted diamonds, roiling softly in a vast expanse of white splendor. To the man-of-war's right spread a magnificent city, so alien to the brick chimneys and muddy, cobblestone streets of Victorian as to defy adequate description. Its white and silver spires of pale stone and glittering glass sparkled in an ambient glow, marred by no glare of a traditional sun. Somewhere in Jack's awestruck mind, he imagined fields of spring green or colorful autumn rolling forever past the glorious city's far edge. Fields and trees and mountains and valleys the likes of which he had only heard stories.

"Dasher," Jack found his voice in the midst of his reverie. "Look; you won't want to have missed this." The boy stirred on his shoulder, peering about, and together they shared the moment of visual marvel.

"Move, filth!" The shouts of the Marines echoed along the line of captives, ripping Jack brusquely out of his trance.

"This beauty isn't for the likes of you, traitorous scum!" The officer from below bawled, marching along the line of prisoners. "It's not even for the likes of me, who has served the Primal Empire faithfully and with honor! You are witnessing the glory of our gods and your Emperors, Order and Tyranny, whom you betrayed! If it were up to me, you'd never have had the privilege. I'd have had you shot in the squalor your whore mothers birthed you in. It's only by the good grace of those infinitely your better that you have this privilege before execution."

The cabin doors to Jack's left opened slowly, and a Primal emerged. Jack's eyes narrowed. He wore blood red armor, and a black mask was splayed across his breastplate.

"On your knees, maggots!" The officer roared, drawing his saber and laying about with the flat of the blade on those too slow to comply. When he was certain all the prisoners were properly bowed, the officer himself went to a knee.

"My lord, these scum are unfit to walk the shores of this holy realm," the officer protested. "But I obey both the Emperors' and your command. Captain Bracken and I relinquish these prisoners into your custody."

Jack held Dasher carefully, so as not to drop him as he knelt, but risked a careful glance up at the Primal who had subdued him. He appeared a perfect specimen of humanity, just like the Primal who

96

had killed Morgan. Close-cropped, jet-black hair was slicked back over his head, and sharp cheekbones protruded from a thin, unblemished face. He regarded the officer with mischievous grey eyes.

"Very well, lieutenant," the Primal answered indifferently. "We'll take them to the Court of Law for public execution." His voice was so silky and smooth that Jack could have listened to him speak all day, even if it was about his impending death. "Give my regards to Captain Bracken."

"Of course, my lord."

Four more Primals emerged from the cabin doors. Jack quickly ducked his head, not daring to even breathe for fear that he might be recognized and singled out. The red demon from the safehouse was in the lead. Jack noticed two substantial holes in the Primal's breastplate with absurd satisfaction. Jack didn't get a good look at the other three, intent as he was on his boots, though he noted their human-like appearance and shining Celestial Steel plate armor.

"Ah," the black mask Primal's voice greeted the rest with a satisfied sigh. The Marines stood forgotten around them. "It's good to be back. Stints in that shithole of a realm are a bloody nightmare."

A deep chuckle rumbled above Jack's head, and he knew it was the demon answering. "Pine after this luxury all you wish, Villain. The fight is below, and as long as Tyranny gives me enemies to kill, that's where I'll be."

"You're so barbaric, Rage," the original Primal, who Jack assumed was Villain, answered lightly.

"I, for one, am glad to be clear of the Myrmidon's stench," a new voice put in. Jack risked a quick glance up to see a Primal whose armor bore a pair of dripping fangs. The Primal kicked at one of the prisoners nearest him distastefully. "Though as long as we're running Tyranny's waste detail, I have to put up with their disgusting odor even here. At least this entire realm doesn't reek of their kind."

"The sooner we get them to the Court of Law the sooner we can rid ourselves of them," Villain, who seemed to be the leader, answered calmly. "Get them to their feet," he commanded.

Jack stumbled up, still grasping Dasher firmly. The Marines went roaring down the line of prisoners, flailing with their blades and carbine butts at those who struggled up too slowly. Villain strode to the back of the group, while Rage stalked to the front. He turned his devil's eyes on them. Revulsion was evident on his twisted face.

"Wingless Myrmidons move slower than shit traveling uphill," he growled simply. "Anyone who holds us up doesn't get the mercy of execution; you get the pleasure of my attention."

It wasn't the most vehement or disturbing threat Jack had ever heard. In fact, it was laughably straightforward, but coming from the maw of the red monster, it was perhaps the most terrifying thing every uttered.

"Move," Rage grunted.

They went single file down the *Titanfall*'s gangway to a dock of strange silver stone, but that was the last opportunity Jack had to gawk at his surroundings. The Primals set a brutal pace made all the more unbearable by the weakness, hunger, and thirst brought on by the journey in the brig. Dasher's added weight threatened to drag Jack to his knees, but he gritted his teeth and kept moving, placing one foot in front of the other. He concentrated on moving over the sparkling streets. They were like glass, with brilliant, crystalline jewels beneath the transparent surface. He heard a few of the prisoners stumble and fall, but no one stayed down. The demon's threat was clear in all of their minds.

Jack wondered dully why he didn't just stop. Refuse to run. His legs were wobbly and weak, and his breaths came in harsh gasps. They were only hastening to their own execution. Why make it easy for the Primals? He wasn't afraid of dying. It might be better to die a few minutes early in a display of defiance than to go meekly to the slaughter. The Primals were just using them as examples.

You are responsible for Dasher. You must press on. Jack cursed himself for an idiot. *When has your responsibility ever helped those you swore to protect? Your efforts, your determination, your* very existence *has been futile. Dasher is going to die anyway, as are you.*

His mind waged a ferocious war. Jack's legs kept churning, regardless.

Eventually, it became apparent that none of the prisoners would be capable of maintaining such a pace to their ultimate destination, and the Primals reluctantly allowed them to falter into a trudging walk. Jack's feet slowed to a resigned plodding pace, but his embattled mind continued its inner struggle despite his exhaustion.

Jack checked on Dasher, who was utterly silent. He wondered if the lad had expired during their forced march. Light, irregular breathing greeted him, and a tiny sense of relief penetrated his fatigue.

As Jack dropped his eyes back to the glassy surface of the street, a flicker of movement caught his eye from a silver spire ahead, and he squinted curiously.

A glint of sunlight off of the tower, Jack decided. Then, he frowned. *There's no sun here…*

A brilliant glow as dazzling as a newborn star burst suddenly into being to Jack's left, spraying the bright world around him with intense drops of searing light. He stumbled to a knee and shielded his eyes, bewildered at the radiant explosion.

A deafening BOOM shattered the Celestial air. One of their captors stumbled. The center of the brilliant blaze faded into the shape of the most beautiful woman Jack had ever seen.

She stood on a dais atop white stone steps with arms upraised. Her hands bore a glowing, double-edged sword. Silvery blue, Celestial Steel armor fit to her form as if it were a part of her body, and gleaming, silver-white hair flowed behind her in a luminescent stream. Eyes of shocking blue pierced the air from a face that Jack could describe only as perfection. She was a regal manifestation of power, like a force of nature: beautiful, dangerous, and terrifying.

Waves of shifting light burst from her back in refracting lines of crackling cerulean, and she rose slowly off her feet to hover above the steps. She placed a shining helm over her head.

A dreadful roar of fury echoed to Jack's right. Rage's wings of flame exploded behind him as he bellowed his defiance. A spiked mace coalesced in his hand.

Jack's wits abruptly returned to him. This street was about to become the arena for a gigantic god death-match.

"RUN!" Jack shouted. He followed his own advice, sprinting with for the cover of a nearby building. The other prisoners scattered in every direction.

From the corner of his eye, Jack saw the goddess take off as a blurring bolt of light. Behind him, a colossal crash resounded like the head-on collision of two locomotives. The street became chaos.

More armored Primals converged on the street. Weapons of Celestial Steel sang behind the force of powerful wings. Jack abandoned his search for shelter as Primals smashed together around him in grappling tangles of combat. He hunkered on the edge of the street next to white stone steps and covered Dasher desperately.

A second, echoing BOOM split the ringing of metallic weapons on Celestial Steel, and Jack saw the Primal with dripping fangs on his breastplate take the hit on the center of his sigil. He jerked and fell for a moment before his wings sputtered to life and carried him haphazardly away. Jack cast about wildly with his eyes and found the sniper atop a flat-roofed tower in the distance.

Villain spun by overhead, grappling with a white armored Primal. Jack ducked, but the two combatants pulled up anyway. Their reckless flight sent them careening into a column of nearby pillars. Another Primal bedecked in gold armor was hacking down on one of Jack's captors with a massive doublehanded executioner's sword, and a Primal in green and gold armor fended off another of the guards with an enormous shield.

Jack witnessed this in a confused daze, but his attention settled on the ferocious struggle in the middle of the street, where Rage and the radiant lady were exchanging inhuman blows. Rage smashed his horned head into her helmeted face, and she staggered back. Then, Rage's fist came up, and it lit with fire, hardening into a thick ram of stone before smashing into the woman's breastplate.

Villain and the white knight crashed suddenly into the street at Jack's feet, and he scrambled back, losing sight of the lady and the demon in his haste to escape the bitter battle before him. Villain and his adversary rolled over and over the glass road, weapons forgotten as they pummeled each other with armored fists. Grunted curses flew from the wrestling combatants in a steady stream. Jack dragged Dasher back as they rolled closer, but the two Primals broke apart and leapt up. Their weapons flickered back into their hands. He observed their continued combat in awe. They moved with such alien grace. Swords swiped, thrust, and parried as their armored feet moved over the ground, more like a beautiful dance than the previous violent brawl. Even when their wings once again lifted them into flight the deadly ballet continued unabated, and the Primals whirled like dervish pinwheels as their blades flickered back and forth. Jack hardly even noticed the sniper's third shot, intent as he was on the mythic contest above him. The air sang with the ringing chime of Celestial Steel and the metallic crash of deflections.

White and red armor blurred together into a perfect storm of skill and havoc.

Abruptly, the airborne duel ended as the blood red of Villain's armor spun away from a blow and retreated, leaving his adversary behind. A raging cry echoed from the white knight, but he did not follow, and Jack realized with a start that the other guards had fled.

Not all the other guards. The Primal woman stood over Rage. Her sword was planted in his shoulder and her armored boot on his side. The white knight approached and helped the woman remove her breastplate, and Jack noted the extensive damage to the silvery blue masterpiece. The demon was laughing, but a horrible gurgling sound was rising in his throat as well. The woman twisted savagely on the sword, shouting at the defeated Primal. Whatever she wanted from him, it would do little good. Jack knew death well, and the red devil had no more than a few moments left to live.

Good riddance, Jack thought maliciously. It was the first coherent thought to pass through his mind since the appearance of the Primal lady in her burst of light. The second quickly followed. *Now is the time to run, escape this city, execution, and these insane Primals.*

Jack looked down at Dasher, the boy's eyes were open, but his breaths came in short gasps. *He won't survive more than a few hours.* Jack knew he wouldn't be able to carry him while on the run in this city anyway.

Jack's feet shifted, carrying him toward escape. He stopped himself, cursing vehemently. He was a steamblown fool. In all likelihood, Dasher would be dead soon, and he knew how well his efforts to protect had ended in the past.

Best to leave him behind – he's dead anyway. Jack's feet didn't obey. He turned, growling angrily at his own weakness, and scooped the lad into his arms. He didn't want to do it, but as long as there was still a way to save Dasher, he wouldn't leave. He *couldn't* leave.

"Hey!" Jack's voice was hoarse and raspy, and his legs were weak with fatigue. But he continued to stumble toward the gathering group of Primals.

The Primal woman was raging, cursing bitterly, but she stopped and turned to look at him when he shouted. Her brilliant blue eyes seemed to pierce his soul, and Jack almost halted at the intensity in her expression. He willed his legs forward.

"This lad needs help!" Jack continued. He approached the group warily. "He's going to die without immediate medical attention!"

The white knight turned his helmed head and shared a glance with the woman. Jack continued forward, noting that he was alone. The rest of the prisoners had vanished into the surrounding streets. The huge, golden warrior pushed into the gathering circle.

"Out of the question," a deep, rich voice laced with disdain emerged from the slits of his helm. The firm tone was addressed toward the lady, and seemed to be answering some unsaid question.

"What do you propose, Justice?" the white Primal answered. "That we leave the boy to die?"

"Yes," the deep voice answered, unmoved. "What care should we have for Myrmidon gangsters? Their fate is sealed, and well deserved."

"Look at the lad, Justice!" The white knight pointed at Dasher with obvious exasperation. "It's a boy, not a gangster! What–"

"Are you proposing that one cannot be both young and a criminal?" the golden warrior's voice answered with logical calm. "Boys younger than he have caused much sorrow. Leave them, I say. The realms are better off without our prolonging their kind."

Jack looked around as the conversation unfolded, noting the participants of the ambush. The lady, who he had turned to first, was unreadable. She continued to stare at him as if thinking, but her eyes seemed far away. The gold and green armored Primal was leaning on his massive shield and holding his side. Jack could see shining silver drops oozing between his fingers, but he didn't speak up or complain. The white warrior stood next to the Primal woman, and seemed to be arguing on Dasher's behalf. The golden knight was Justice, Jack presumed, based on what had been said.

Not THE Justice, Jack told himself. *But who else could attack Tyranny and Order's Primals with such impunity? If it is the real Justice, then that would mean the lady…*

"This bickering is pointless," the lady suddenly spoke up, cutting off a retort from the white knight. Her voice rang like clear bells and exuded command. "Tyranny's forces are converging on this location as we speak." She turned to the silent knight with the shield. "Sentinel, how bad is it?"

"I'll live," Sentinel replied. He chuckled lightly and leaned on his shield. "Bondage got a lucky swipe by me, but I can manage."

"Good," the lady replied. "Valkyrie, lead on."

The sniper, whom Jack had not seen approach, nodded a black helmed head. Jack barely noticed the newcomer, so intent was he on the lady.

"What about Dasher?" Jack demanded desperately. "You can't leave him like this. He's going to die!"

The woman turned her eyes back to Jack, and he wilted under the piercing gaze. She was silent for a long moment, and when she finally spoke, her voice was soft. "We'll take him with us for medical care."

Relief flooded Jack's veins, then alarm. "I'm coming too!" Jack found his voice finally. "I'm not leaving him alone with you and yours."

The woman's eyes searched his own, and Jack found himself wishing he had never spoken. He struggled to remain standing upright and not cringe beneath the weight of her stare.

"Freedom, you can't possibly be considering–"

"I can, and am," Freedom cut off Justice's interruption. Jack's jaw dropped open.

So it *was* Freedom.

This was the Emperors' most hated enemy. This was their ultimate nemesis, leader of the IAL, right here in the flesh. Jack really did cringe at this revelation. He hunched his shoulders protectively. *She's said to be as insane as Chaos, and infinitely more intelligent.* All the atrocious things the Illuminati had ever taught him about the anti-god raced through his mind. *You left the Illuminati,* Jack reminded his shocked mind, *because you couldn't trust them, remember? You don't know that those things are true. You realized long ago that those delusional priests are nothing but propaganda criers for the Empire.*

Freedom's mind seemed to be made up, but she turned with a quizzical look on her face. "Justice?"

The golden warrior shook his head emphatically. "He is what he is, Freedom, but…" The assurance in his voice faded somewhat, and his next words emerged reluctantly from his mouth, as if forced unwillingly. "He is, perhaps, not the basest of his kind. There is strength, great courage, and a kind of primitive nobility." As if to provide context for his previous statement, Justice continued on.

103

Acid returned to his tone. "I still find him a repugnant, vile creature, deserving of little but death."

"But not *wholly* deserving of death?" The white knight's tone was both mocking and amused. "That's new. He must be a saint!"

Jack squirmed uncomfortably under Freedom's continued gaze. He had never been so thoroughly examined.

"Tyranny's forces are coming," she said simply, addressing Jack after an eternally long pause. "Choose, Myrmidon. If you come with us, you will not be allowed to leave again without my permission. You may never be released. The risk is too great that you might, willingly or unwittingly, betray our secrets. Do you wish to accompany the boy? He will be well cared for, whether you are there or not. You have my word."

Indeed, real or imagined, Jack thought he could hear a winged horde approaching from the Celestial city's center, and his decision was quick.

"I do not trust Primals," he stated simply. He forced himself to stand firm under Freedom's penetrating eyes. "There is little I can do against the likes of you, but while I still draw breath, I intend to insure that he is safe. Besides," Jack gestured away, allowing a small, humorless smile to cross his face. "Going with you is the only way I escape this place alive."

Freedom nodded almost before he was finished, as if she had already known his answer. She turned away. "So be it. Hero, take the boy. Justice, you have the other. I'll take Valkyrie."

Before Jack had time to react, the white knight plucked Dasher from his arms and lifted off on pale wings. Jack opened his mouth, and then let out a surprised shout as the golden warrior scooped him up roughly and shot into the air. His stomach dropped through his feet, and one of Justice's armored hands clamped over his mouth. The other gripped tightly around his waist.

"Fool Myrmidon," he growled. "We are attempting to evade pursuit, not draw it to us."

Jack was too terrified to answer. The world sped by at an alarming speed as they flew through the glowing streets, staying well beneath the tops of the buildings to avoid being seen. Several times Jack cringed, expecting his golden chariot to smash into upcoming walls and towers, only to turn at the last moment with incredible alacrity and soar down yet another street of sparkling glass. Right, left, straight, right, straight, right, left, left: he lost count of their blazing maneuvers, but Justice seemed to know where he was going. Occasionally Jack would catch a glimpse of white or blue or green flashing ahead. His eyes were wide and unblinking. They watered continuously because he dared not squeeze his eyes shut even for a moment.

Abruptly, Justice cut right, leaving much of Jack's stomach behind, and flew toward a mansion fronted by huge pillars. Jack expected him to swerve into the street running perpendicular, but they shot through the open door before Jack even had time to yell his alarm. The mansion's interior blurred as their breakneck pace continued. Jack vaguely noted traversing a long, curving staircase in the space of a moment, and they were suddenly speeding through a long hallway toward…nothing. There was no window or door. No exit of any kind. Only an open wardrobe, filled with hanging clothes and thick coats.

Jack flailed wildly as Justice bore him toward the dead end at high speed. He could only imagine hitting the wardrobe and wall at this velocity. There would be nothing left of him but an unrecognizable, bloody pulp.

The wardrobe continued to streak toward him. Jack struggled vainly. The armored hands wrapped around him were clamped in an iron grip. The wardrobe filled his vision.

Jack screamed.

Chapter 19

"Is the IAL evil? That depends on who you ask. Illuminati, Tories, conservatives, and even many moderates label it a terrorist organization, while political liberals conceal their support for Freedom's revolt behind poorly maintained protests. As for the commoners, they believe whatever they are instructed to believe."

— Lord Damian Devalere, Political Moderate

Jack squeezed his eyes shut at the last moment. Inexplicably, he wasn't squashed into nothing. He felt Justice come to an abrupt, gut-wrenching halt, and they were finally still. He cracked open one eye and gasped. He was lost for words.

He didn't recognize this place, and he wasn't certain how he had gotten here, because this was definitely not the hallway of the mansion.

It was a completely empty room of stone with one door that appeared to be made of thick, black iron. It was dimly lit by lanterns in the corners, which made visible a space perhaps twenty by ten paces. Justice dumped him unceremoniously to the floor. Jack attempted to climb to his feet. His legs were shaking so badly that he had trouble regaining his footing, and he stumbled over to one of the walls to support himself.

Jack leaned against the cold stone, his breaths coming in short gasps caused by the sheer terror and exhilaration of their harried flight. He focused on getting his nerves under control, forcing himself to take long, measured breaths. When he had stopped shaking, he looked around the room more intently. Justice was waiting for something, studiously ignoring him. Jack looked past the golden Primal, and saw something he had not noticed before.

There was some sort of strange altar in the back wall. A frame made of twisted wood encircled a bizarre, smoky mirror. Long, carved shutters on the frame were opened wide, allowing the mirror to replicate the room. But the reflection was wrong. It was covered in a swirling fog that distorted the image, permitting only glimpses to gleam through.

Unexpectedly, an indistinct shape materialized in the mirror's haze, and Jack pressed back against the wall. A moment later, a form of green and gold emerged through the glass and came to an abrupt halt. Jack beheld the Primal called Sentinel, who still pressed a hand to his side. The newcomer gave a pleased nod. Jack's mind scrambled to rationalize what he'd just seen, and he irrationally wondered what had become of the Primal's shield.

Sentinel moved to the side, and two more shapes followed him, one after the other, from the mirror's depths. The first materialized into the white armored knight whom Freedom had called Hero. Jack saw with relief that he still bore Dasher in his arms. Freedom came out behind them, and she released a black clad figure.

"Everyone accounted for?" Freedom asked immediately. She turned to swing closed the shutters on the altar, hiding the mirror from view.

Hero performed a short head-count, and nodded his dented helm. "Five plus two extras. Mission success, boss."

"Mission failure," Freedom replied bitterly in response; then she sighed. "But you're right. 'No casualties' always counts as a win." She tossed her silvery hair back from her face with a slim hand. "Sentinel, get yourself over to Morthal immediately and take the wounded one with you."

"His name is Dasher," Jack growled angrily, finding his voice. "And I'm going wherever he goes."

"You are in my home now, Myrmidon." Freedom responded in an even tone, but her voice brooked no argument. "So you will not presume to make more demands of me or my people. I realize you have many questions, and I know you wish to stay with the boy. But you are not in a position to press the issue." Something in her tone forced Jack to step back and be silent, but he fought the reaction stubbornly and opened his mouth to speak. Freedom, however, had already returned her attention to Sentinel, and Jack missed his chance to respond. "Check to see if Champion has returned as well," she commanded. "If he has, tell him to meet me for an operation report."

"Yes, ma'am." Sentinel took Dasher gently from Hero and exited through the iron door.

Jack itched to follow, and he craned his head in an attempt to see what lay beyond the room's only exit. The door was quickly shut. "Now," Freedom said, as if getting down to business. She skewered Jack again with her piercing, blue eyes. "What are we to do with you?"

Jack didn't like the sound of that at all, but he kept silent, observing the rest of the group arrayed around him. They seemed to be relaxing somewhat, and the remaining Primals pulled off their helms with pleased sighs.

The white knight's helmet removed first, revealing yet another flawless Primal face. The first thought that leapt to Jack's mind was that Hero appeared to be the exact opposite of Villain. Locks of long blond hair were pulled back by leather cords, counter to Villain's close, black hair. Hero's jaw was an iron anvil, and his face – cheekbones, brow, and nose – was strong and thick, completely at odds with the slim features of Villain's countenance. But there was one feature exactly the same: the eyes. They were the same precise hue of grey and even held a mischievous glint, tinged with a gleam of confidence and pride. He winked one of those eyes at Jack when his helmet came off, then shook back his hair.

Justice removed his helm next, revealing a bald, ebony head and a stern, shaved face. Jack was immediately arrested by his bright, golden irises, which virtually glowed in the room's dim illumination. The brilliance of his eyes juxtaposed starkly with his dark skin. Jack had seen a few people in Victorian with similar complexions, mostly traders from the isles far to the south of Victorian and the mainland. It did not surprise him to find that Primals were as equally diverse as humans. Justice regarded him flatly. His mouth was set in a hard, unyielding line, and his posture was straight and rigid. Jack didn't like the way the dark Primal eyed him, and he turned his eyes toward the sniper to avoid his gaze.

It was the first time Jack had given the sniper his full attention, and he was immediately surprised. The black suit was not Celestial Steel, as the rest of the Primals wore, but a tight leather combat suit with plates of armor woven into the fabric over only the most vital areas. It was built for flexibility. Even the helmet was more of a reconnaissance hood than an actual helm. Some things Jack observed didn't add up. The way the sniper held himself was somewhat odd, and the separated armor plates bulged across the chest. A long-barreled rifle and a strange, metal contraption that Jack couldn't place rested on the sniper's back. Then it came to him with a jolt. It was a steam-powered jetpack like the rocketeer enforcers sometimes used! But if he needed a jetpack, he must not have wings, which meant…

"You're human!" Jack blurted unintentionally, so thoroughly surprised that he shouted the revelation. Suddenly, the second oddity clicked in his brain, as he understood the prominence of the black armored chest. "And a *girl!*"

The sniper pulled off her helmet a short second later, and Jack was staring, open-mouthed, at a slim face framed by tangles of brunette hair. Her pretty mouth twisted into a smirk. "You don't say? At least we know you have a firm grasp of the obvious."

Jack stared. She appeared plain and unassuming next to the perfection of her Primal companions, but if he blocked the others from his vision, he saw an attractive young woman, perhaps three years his senior. His mind went blank, and he stammered unintelligibly as he tried to think of anything besides how long it had been since he'd last talked to a pretty girl. Jack was suddenly aware of how badly he smelled after days with no chance to wash.

Hero erupted with laughter, his voice ringing like silver trumpets, full and loud and cheerful. "You've got the poor boy all out of sorts, Val! Look at him blushing!"

Jack furiously attempted to control the blood rising in his cheeks. He was unsuccessful. "You called her 'Valkyrie'," he turned to Freedom accusingly. "That's a Primal name if I've ever heard one."

"Valkyrie is Valen's codename," Freedom answered. Jack angrily noted the amusement in her voice. "It's her alias when on assignment."

The girl gave him a look half derisive, half mischievous, and her green eyes sparkled in the lantern light. "I assume by your chauvinistic outburst that you're not accustomed to being rescued by girls?"

Jack opened his mouth to retort, but thought better of it and reigned himself into a short, terse answer. "Girls or Primals," he muttered.

Hero roared with laughter, and even Freedom's lips twitched a bit. Justice's face was a block of expressionless stone.

"Who are you, Myrmidon?" The dark-skinned man interrupted the laughter brusquely. "How is it that you and your fellows were headed for the executioners block in the Celestial Realm? Freedom may have brought you here, but that doesn't mean you should be allowed to remain alive."

"Forgive my judgmental companion," Hero broke in with an amicable grin. He extended an armored hand. "We'll not kill you in cold blood, no matter what he says, but we would like a few answers. No doubt you would like some as well."

Jack didn't take his proffered hand. "I don't take too kindly, sir," Jack said coldly.

"Be careful, boy," Hero replied with sudden, equal frigidity. "Or you might alienate the only allies you have here. My goodwill is not something to be flippantly cast aside." He continued despite his chill words, slipping back into an almost welcoming tone. "You've said you don't trust Primals, something I can understand, I suppose. We'll start with introductions instead." Hero gestured around at his companions. "As you've likely already discerned, I am Hero, and my severe friend is Justice. You've just met Valen, and this is our illustrious leader, Freedom."

Jack nodded grudgingly. "My name's Jack. Jack Booker."

"Well met, Jack," Hero replied, and a puzzled look crossed his face. "That name is somewhat familiar…"

"Freedom," Justice interrupted Hero's musings. "This Myrmidon will prove to be a burden and an exorbitant drain on our people's time, energy, and resources, all of which are in short supply. Bringing him here was a mistake," the Primal concluded bluntly.

"Perhaps," Freedom replied, and Jack struggled to read those calculating blue eyes. "But what's done is done."

Justice snorted loudly and glared at Jack as if his very presence was offensive. Jack glared back. The Primal sneered and turned away from the group, leaning against the stone wall with an air of finality. Apparently, he had said his piece and couldn't be bothered with the rest of the conversation.

Jack glanced at Freedom. "Am I a captive here?"

Hero immediately answered with a "no," just as Freedom said "yes." Freedom turned a cool gaze on Hero, who shrugged at Jack and grinned again, all trace of his earlier coldness gone.

"Freedom is all about the empty half of the glass," Hero joked. "Whereas I'm the opposite. It all depends on your perspective,

110

Jack." Jack flinched in surprise at Hero's familiarity, and he gave the white armored Primal a suspicious look.

"We have brought you to the base of the IAL, the Independent Army of Liberty." Freedom explained. She gave a small, rueful shrug. "Not my first choice, but, under the circumstances, it was the only option." She gave him another piercing look. "I cannot allow you to endanger my people by giving Tyranny information, Mr. Booker, so you will remain our guest here for the time being."

Jack kept his face impassive. "That makes me your prisoner, not your guest."

"If you wish to see it that way, you are free to do so," Freedom answered coolly. "But you will not live like a prisoner. You will be treated the same as anyone else. I only ask that you do not attempt to escape. Your efforts to do so would be futile, I assure you, and you will not find your stay so pleasant if you attempt to take advantage of our leniency."

Jack relapsed into silence at this, his mind whirling. Hero picked up in a cheery tone where Freedom had left off.

"We can only hope that in time you will come to see the value in what we are doing here, Jack." Hero said. "Perhaps, someday, you'll find that you *wish* to be here, fighting the good fight."

"The good fight?" Jack queried scathingly. "I'd rather be dead than help Primals wage their endless wars."

"That can be arranged," Justice rumbled from his corner. Jack cut him a sneering look and opened his mouth to answer, but the human girl, Valen, cut him off.

"That's enough," she interjected angrily. "I don't know who you are or what nonsense you've got lodged in your thick skull, but The Resistance is fighting for everyone, everywhere, both Primal and human. The least you can do is show a little respect. That's to say nothing of the fact that we just saved your life and the life of your friend, you ungrateful sot."

Jack crossed his arms, weathering the short tirade. "Don't get righteous with me, girl. You weren't there to do Dasher a favor; you had your own agenda. Primals are nothing but a blight on human existence with their incessant infighting and power struggles. Humans always get caught in the middle. I don't owe these *gods* anything," Jack snarled. "And I don't have the time or stomach for human zealots stupid enough to worship them, the Imperials or the rebels."

The girl's mouth twisted into a nasty sneer. "You prove your ignorance with your own mouth, *boy*. Freedom and–"

"Valen," Freedom said quietly. "It's all right. He speaks from what he has seen and knows. I am not offended." The girl subsided, but her face was still red with anger. She glowered at Jack.

There was a moment of terse silence, but Hero didn't seem perturbed. He continued to grin, and he spoke up, breaking the tense standoff.

"I can't say I find your views highly appealing, Jack, but I have to assume you're a bright fellow. You'll come around," Hero stated with conviction. He nodded confidently. "Do you have any questions?"

Jack scowled mutely for a few moments, but his mind was still whirling from the last hour's events. His curiosity got the better of his dislike.

"What is *that*?" Jack asked, pointing at the altar and the hidden mirror behind the shutters. "Is that how we got here? And where are we? This place doesn't look anything like the rest of the Celestial Realm."

"That," Hero answered, "is a portal mirror. They provide–"

"The boy just proclaimed his hatred for us and our cause," Justice interposed dryly. "Perhaps we should not supply him with all of our secrets, yes?"

"He's going to have the run of this place soon anyway," Hero waved him down, but Jack noticed that he glanced at Freedom. She gave the tiniest of nods, granting some kind of permission. Hero continued. "And Freedom already said he's going to be with us for some time. Best get friendly, Justice. He's one of us now."

"That he is not," Justice growled, but said nothing more.

"If I can avoid any more interruptions," Hero harrumphed pointedly, shooting Justice a look. "As I said, it's a portal mirror. There are two mirrors in every set. They provide an instantaneous link to their twin's location. We use this one for secret travel to and from the Celestial Realm."

"And we are...?"

"Safely back at our base in Victorian in the Grounded Realm."

Jack gaped at him. "You can just–? *Instantly*?"

"That's correct."

"It took us *days* to sail to the Celestial Realm on the *Titanfall*," Jack gasped, trying to wrap his mind around the implications.

"Most Primals know of the mirrors," Freedom explained. "But their existence is a carefully guarded secret of Tyranny's regime. Those Myrmidons who are allowed such top secret knowledge are sworn to secrecy and threatened with the harshest of punishments."

"So there are more than just the mirrors we traveled through?"

"Oh, yes," Hero nodded. "Most of the pairs are under the Empire's control. It's how Tyranny moves his agents so quickly between realms."

Jack's mind was spinning. Teleportation? It seemed like something out of a fairy tale, like Captain Peter Pan's journey to a star-island.

"In the Celestial Realm we passed through a wardrobe," Jack muttered. "I thought we had entered into a secret room behind it."

Hero laughed. "We've got a few Primal supporters still living among Imperial society in the Celestial Realm. The owner of that particular mansion agreed to conceal this mirror's twin in the back of a wardrobe." He continued to chuckle appreciatively. "I thought it was bloody brilliant, but *he* claims he got the idea off an old professor from another dimension ages ago."

"You look exhausted," Freedom said abruptly. She looked at Jack with a critical eye. "And you look like you could use some food and a bath."

At her words, the weakness in his legs and the rumble in his belly returned, but Jack forced back his fatigue.

"I want to see Dasher first," Jack insisted stubbornly. "I can wash and eat afterwards."

"Your friend has only just arrived. There will have been little change in his condition at this stage. I assure you, our medic is highly capable. Morthal will do everything in his power to make sure he recovers." Freedom replied dismissively. Her voice carried that same air of command Jack had noticed before. It seemed to come to her as naturally as breathing. "Get something to eat and clean yourself up, then you may visit the sick bay." Jack wanted to object, but Freedom continued without waiting for confirmation, expecting her will to be followed without question. "Valen will accompany you to make sure your get settled in."

113

The girl scowled at Jack, but she nodded grudgingly.

Freedom gave him a cursory look. "You may go."

Jack glanced around the room at the Primals once more, and Valen jerked her head indicatively. He followed her lead toward the heavy, iron door. His mind was whirling all the while.

He wasn't dead, and neither was Dasher. It was more than he had dared to expect at the day's end. But as Jack looked over his shoulder at the three Primals standing in the dim light, he couldn't help but wonder apprehensively.

What have I got us into now?

***

Freedom had already forgotten Jack Booker before the door shut behind him. Her mind was preoccupied with the last hour's events. With their failure.

Her two companions were not about to let her disregard their controversial new resident, however.

"He is a liability," Justice said the instant the door clanged shut behind Valen and the newcomer. The huge Primal had lost his disinterested pose. He stood upright, and his shoulders were tense beneath his golden armor. Freedom retreated out of her thoughts.

"You vouched for him yourself," Hero laughed.

"I told you what I saw," Justice snapped. "I *did not* vouch for him. Regardless of any primitive, Myrmidon virtues he might possess, he is nothing more than a petty street thug."

"You read that he wasn't like the rest of his fellows!" Hero argued.

"But he's still a Myrmidon!" Justice snarled. "Weak, conflicted, selfish. He is a gangster and an opportunist. He has no interest in our cause, only what we can do for him."

Hero opened his mouth to retort, but Freedom cut him off.

"Our cause is to make a better world for Myrmidon and Primal alike," Freedom addressed Justice quietly, holding his eyes. "We cannot claim to stand for the Myrmidons if we are not willing to follow that assertion with our actions. The boy was dying, just as Mr. Booker attested. We had the means and ability to help him."

"We do not have the time or resources to care for those uninterested in what we are about," Justice disagreed. "The realms

114

are better off without the existence of criminals. We could have left them in the Celestial Realm where they would have received what they justly deserve."

"Perhaps they have some part yet to play," Hero stated, crossing his arms. "A gangster with a sense of honor? That is rare enough in a criminal to warrant my curiosity."

"A part for ill can be well conceived," Justice growled. "What good will come of taking a chance on a known degenerate?"

"We may yet see," Freedom said in a soft voice, staring at the closed door pensively. "Fate is an unpredictable force."

Chapter 20

"When ignorance cannot be claimed, resistance to despotism is no longer a choice. It is a duty."

– Freedom, Primal Leader of the Independent Army of Liberty

The hallway beyond the portal room was made of the same stone and timber, but was lit by gas lamps along its length. No other doors were present along the walls until the narrow hall ran into a perpendicular passage.

A human guardsman in combat armor similar to the girl's, and bearing an unfamiliar carbine, was posted just outside the door. He nodded to Valen when she emerged.

Valen nodded back wearily, but she noticed Jack's curious gaze. "Day and night, we always have someone posted to guard the portal mirror," she explained with clipped, impatient words as she strode down the hall. Jack's fatigued legs struggled to keep up. "Just in case the empire's forces somehow discover its twin and make an entry into the back of our base. The iron door was made to be impenetrable for humans. It would even give a Primal difficulty, which would allow us time to either prepare a defense or evacuate the base."

"Wouldn't Celestial Steel be better?" Jack asked.

The girl seemed to notice the exhaustion in his voice and she grudgingly slowed her steps. "Of course, but Celestial Steel is too rare and expensive to use in such quantities. Thick iron will have to do."

"Where are we?" Jack wondered aloud, eyeing the stone corridor around him. They met a T in the hallway, and Valen took a left. "Are we underground?" Just like the gang's old safehouse, Jack hadn't noticed any windows. This was clearly no mere hideout, however. Judging just by the length of the corridors, this place was massive.

"Yes," Valen replied, and she came to an abrupt halt. Her eyes considered him. She turned and headed back the way they had come. "There's something you should see."

Jack followed her past the passage that led back to the portal mirror and down yet another corridor until they reached a set of steep, sandstone steps. They continued up these stairs until Jack's legs burned, and the climb came to a halt at what appeared to be a gigantic sandstone slab. He watched curiously as the girl put a gloved hand on a small indention in the slab's corner and pushed with her thumb. At once a grinding noise like the turning of large gears sounded around them, and Jack flinched when the enormous stone block above their heads began to move. The slab rolled back, and Valen clambered over the stair's lip.

Jack began to follow, and when his head emerged, he realized he was climbing out of the inside of a sandstone altar. He slid from its confines and stared at his surroundings.

They stood amidst the ruins of an ancient cathedral. The soft glow of twilight was filtering through the gaps in the crumbling stone and what was left of the stained glass windows. The entirety of the enormous temple stretched before him from where he stood on the dais. High stone arches supported the remains of a peaked roof far above his head. Behind him, the crumbling remnants of a beautiful façade surrounded immense metal pipes in the back wall. Jack had never been here before, but he knew this place.

"This is Blackgate Cathedral!" Jack exclaimed. "I've been able to see the bell towers of this place my whole life. I've probably passed by it thousands of times in the Narrows!"

Valen nodded in confirmation.

"This place is supposed to be haunted," Jack said doubtfully, eyeing the building around him. A gust of wind blew abruptly through the ruinous, deserted hall, and the pipes in the wall behind him let out an eerie shriek. He nearly leapt out of his skin.

A quiet snigger came from his left, and he scowled when he realized the girl was laughing at him.

"Yes," she admonished, clearly amused. "Haunted, cursed, and ruled by the Old Gods. Don't forget the pestilence. This place is a hotbed of plague."

Jack glared at her.

"The Resistance has been spreading those rumors as long as we've existed. Blackgate's reputation does all the rest."

"Surely some people still come here."

"Oh, yes," Valen agreed. "Mostly children on a dare, but they never stay long. We use the bell towers as a lookout."

Despite himself, Jack found he was impressed with the setup. "How long did it take to build the tunnels?"

She shrugged. "I wasn't here when they were built, but not as long as you might think. Much of it wasn't built by the IAL. Freedom just expanded Blackgate's catacombs."

Jack shifted uneasily. "Catacombs?"

Valen snorted. "Most of the remains have been removed, and everything has been converted into livable accommodations. I thought gangsters weren't supposed to be afraid of anything?"

"I'm brave enough when need be," Jack muttered sourly.

She sniggered again. His face went red. He clenched his teeth.

"Come on, then, Ironheart," she quipped mockingly. She climbed back into the altar. Her face twisted with disgust as she passed him. "I've no doubt you're eager to see your friend, but you *badly* need a bath. You smell like a rodent that's been dead for days."

Jack scowled, but followed her back into the altar. *What a steaming bitch.*

Valen allowed Jack to move past her back down the steps, and she closed the sandstone slab behind him by pressing on another section of stone. After descending the stairs, she led him through a number of passageways, most of which were composed of either smooth sandstone or grey stone and timber. The room to which he was directed was filled with warm, moist steam, though it contained only a small bench. A second door was set into the room's opposite wall.

"Leave your clothes here," Valen commanded when they entered. "I'll have someone take them."

"To wash?"

The girl grimaced at him. "To burn, most likely. Fresh clothes will be waiting for you when you return. Baths are in the next room."

Jack scowled at her back as she pulled the door shut behind her, but when he removed his clothing he could feel the stiffness in the fabric from accumulated sweat and grime. He did as he had been bid, and left his garments in a pile on the bench.

When he pushed open the next door, a cloud of hot steam billowed into his face. The washroom was made of the same reddish sandstone as many of the tunnels. Copper tubs filled with blistering water were connected by tubes to a giant metal contraption that periodically released jets of steam with a whistling hiss. He had never seen anything like it in his life, and he studied the machine with interest for several minutes until he determined he would never discover how it worked.

Nevertheless, Jack decided it was quite wonderful as he slid into the hot water, which began to sooth his cramped muscles. The device kept the water's temperature just bearable enough to relax without becoming uncomfortable. He would have loved to soak forever, but he was eager to check on Dasher. After he had washed the filth of his captivity away with the soap on the tub's edge, he forced himself to leave. He opened the door to the outer room to find his old clothes gone. A towel and change of clothing waited on the bench.

Jack dried off and dressed, and he was pleased to find that the shirt and trousers fit well. They had taken his cracked, leather shoes and replaced them with a pair of boots. He pulled them on with awe. He had never owned a new pair of boots before, and they had just *given* him some. They were of fine quality, and even the trousers and shirt were soft fabric, not the scratchy wool that he was used to. The boots were a bit snug and the clothes were a mite too big, but he took them gratefully. And suspiciously.

When Jack exited the dressing room, Valen was waiting for him. She had washed and changed as well. The jetpack, combat suit, and rifle were gone, replaced by tan riding pants tucked into brown, knee-high buckled boots and a tight, blue top with buttons running down the left side. The outfit struck him as militaristic, but oddly feminine at the same time. Without the Primals around to overshadow her, he immediately noted how striking she looked.

"Much better," she said airily as he emerged. "You clean up nicely, Mr. Booker. Or, at least, you don't look like a demented beggar anymore."

Jack grunted. "And I would not now mistake you for a man."

She gave him a sneering look and turned, marching away. He followed.

As they walked, Valen pointed out areas of interest in terse, clipped words.

"The living quarters for humans are down that corridor," she pointed. "Freedom and most of the Primal members of The

119

Resistance prefer to stay closer to the surface, and their rooms are in the upper reaches of The Crypt."

"Upper reaches of the what?"

Valen ignored him. "The kitchen is through that door, and food is served in The Crypt, which acts as a center of operations of sorts. It's the common area. You've seen where the bathing rooms are located, and the medical wing is down the hall on the opposite side of The Crypt."

"The Crypt?"

"Here we are," Valen said, leading him through a wide archway.

They were in a huge, open area covered by a dome far above their heads. The barest trickle of light from the evening sun filtered through a circular hole in the center of the dome. The red tinge of surrounding sandstone was illuminated more thoroughly by the gas lamps spaced along the walls. Several long tables filled the space closest to them, but the opposite half of the room was completely bare. What Jack guessed to be nearly fifty people sat in groups at the tables, and they shouted greetings at Valen when she appeared. Some few left their meals and approached, questioning her about her mission, but she waved them away.

"We didn't lose anyone," she assured them, smiling comfortably, and the faces around displayed relief. "I've got other duties to attend to now," she added, jerking her head at Jack, and all eyes turned on him with interest. "But Freedom will fill you in soon, I've no doubt."

Heads nodded agreeably. Many curious eyes followed him, but Jack kept himself distant to discourage any questions. He didn't feel like talking to these strangers right now, and with all the food spread about the tables, his rumbling stomach was at the forefront of his mind.

After the last of her welcoming party had retreated back to their meals, Valen led him to a window cut into the wall near the tables. The most delicious smells drifted from the opening, and Jack's mouth watered ravenously.

But all thought of food was immediately forgotten when Jack approached the window. A young woman dressed in rough woolens and wearing a cooking apron was smiling at Valen. She was *beautiful*, and Jack thought he had never seen such warm, welcoming eyes in all his life. Her hair was a bright gold that carried

120

a tinge of silver, and her delicate face bore an innocence and kindness Jack couldn't quite place. His tongue stuck to the roof of his mouth while he waited for either Valen or the woman to speak.

"Valen," the woman greeted her with a smile that was both radiant and anxious at the same time. "I'm so relieved you've returned safely. Sentinel passed by earlier, but he was headed for the medical wing with someone in his arms. We all feared the worst. The others, are they–?"

"Sentinel received a minor wound," Valen said, smiling back, and she grasped the woman's hand with her own. "Nothing to be alarmed about. He'll be back to full strength in no time."

"But who was he carrying in such haste?"

"A newcomer," Valen replied. "A boy who is gravely injured. Freedom brought him back for medical care."

"I pray he recovers," the woman breathed tremulously. She turned her eyes on Jack. "It seems you've returned with more than one young man, Valen. Who is our new friend?"

Jack struggled to say something. His throat wouldn't work properly, and he tripped over his tongue. "J-Jack, ma'am. I'm Jack Booker." He could feel his face going red, and he longed to hide from those warm, blue eyes.

Valen laughed uproariously at his discomfort, but the woman didn't. She just favored him with a kind smile. "Well met, Jack. I'm sure that we are going be good friends, and any day that brings a new friend is a fine one. My name is Liberty."

Jack's jaw dropped open, and the meaning behind her unearthly beauty finally made sense. Part of his brain still struggled with the revelation. She was a *Primal*? No Primal would be so warm, so genuine. She wore rough woolens and worked in the kitchen, *cooking for humans*.

"Close your mouth, Booker." Valen muttered out of the corner of her mouth. "Don't be rude. You look like you've swallowed a bug."

Jack closed his mouth with a snap. If his face grew any warmer, he thought it might catch on fire.

Liberty didn't seem offended, though. Instead, she gave him a mothering look that was half pity, half scolding. "You look starved, Jack. How much have you been eating? Never mind, I've got a platter ready to go, and you're to eat every bite. Understood?"

Jack nodded dumbly, even more embarrassed, if that was possible, at her fussy tone.

"What's on the menu today, Liberty?" Valen asked.

"Steamed fish with sautéed peppers and onions on a bed of rice, dear," she replied. "If you'll give me just a moment, I'll go fetch two platters from George." She disappeared from the window.

"You all right, Booker?" Valen said after a short silence.

"I don't know," Jack admitted. "I just...I've never seen anything like that in my life. She's a *Primal*, and she *serves you dinner?*"

Valen snorted at his incredulity, but she shrugged. "Liberty's always been like that. She's the most sweet, accepting individual you'll ever meet, human or Primal." She glanced at Jack deviously. "Freedom's not much like her sister."

If she was expecting another flabbergasted reaction, she got one.

"Liberty and Freedom are *sisters?*" Jack gasped.

"How could you not tell?" Valen asked with exasperated amusement. "They look very similar but for the difference in hair color."

"I–" Jack mumbled. All of this was too much to handle in one day. Everything he'd thought he'd known about the Empire, Primals, *the rules of the steamblown universe* – nothing was as he'd thought. This morning he had been certain he would be dead at the day's end. Instead, he was very much alive and thoroughly confused about everything he'd ever known. "They're just so...so different." Jack finished lamely. "Everything is different..."

Liberty returned carrying platters heaped with steaming mounds of vegetables that covered fish and rice beneath. She smiled at them.

"Here you are," she handed them the plates. "And Valen, dear, I'm very happy you've returned safely. Jack," she turned her warm eyes on him. "I'm so pleased to have met you. You eat all of that. No more starving yourself on my watch."

Jack accepted the food and stumbled through an expression of thanks. Valen turned toward the tables, but he balked when she headed toward a large, boisterous group of people.

"What now, Ironheart?" she asked acerbically, noting his hesitation.

Jack scowled at her. He hoped her nickname didn't remain permanent. "I don't like...I don't do well. With people," he muttered. "I like to be alone."

Valen sighed long-sufferingly. "*Fine*. But after I'm through with my babysitting duties, don't expect me stay with you in your weird, unsociable isolation."

"Who said I wanted your company?" Jack muttered under his breath. She ignored him.

Valen followed Jack reluctantly, and he sat down at a secluded end of one of the long tables, for all the good it did. He had no sooner picked up his fork than a bulky man with graying, close-cropped hair and a scarred, grizzled face pushed out of his seat and walked over. The man pulled up a stool across the table. He looked Jack over with blunt eyes. Jack returned his gaze suspiciously.

"Rook," Valen said by way of greeting. Jack thought he detected a hint of wariness in her voice.

"I see Freedom got you back in one piece, Valkyrie," the man growled. His voice was gravely and terse, and Jack detected little in the way of kindness in his tone. "First time we've brought in a new recruit in a while." His eyes scanned Jack with detached calculation.

Jack opened his mouth to respond, but Valen beat him to it. "Prisoner, more like," she said, giving him another vindictive verbal jab. He studiously disregarded her, digging into his food with a gusto brought about by starvation. It was *delicious*.

Rook grunted. "Prisoner, eh? That's too bad. We could use him. This one's a fighter."

Valen snorted, nearly losing her mouthful of fish in her amusement. "Booker? A fighter? You're sadly mistaken, Rook. Ironheart is afraid of his own shadow."

Rook chuckled. It was a grating, cold sound, and bore a tone of disdain. "You think you're some kind of hotshot 'cause you're handy with that scoped Sharps, Valkyrie, but sometimes you can't see shit that's plain as day." Valen glared at him, but the gray haired man wasn't looking at her. His eyes continued to run over Jack's hands and face, sizing him up. "I know a soldier when I see one, girl. This boy's no stranger to bloodshed. He's a killer, a fighter."

Jack said nothing.

"The name's Talon Rook," the blunt, graying man said as he extended a rough hand across the table.

Jack dropped his fork and returned the handshake warily. "Jack Booker."

"Well met, Booker," Rook growled. "Under most circumstances I'd be obliged to kill you, but if Freedom brought you here, she must have her reasons." He cocked his head to the left. "Marines or Imperial Troopers?"

Jack shook his head doubtfully. "Neither. Narrow's criminal outfit. Fist's gang."

"Aw," Rook grunted, nodding. "Gangster, eh? When Valkyrie said you were a prisoner I assumed they must have run afoul of some Imperial military."

"He was kind of a bystander," Valen put in. "Rage, Villain, and a few others were taking Booker and some of his fellows to be executed." She turned to Jack. "Rook used to be an Imperial Trooper," she explained.

"Ninth Imperial Fusiliers," Rook clarified.

"How does an Imperial Fusilier end up fighting with the IAL?" Jack asked, confused. He shoveled another bite of rice into his mouth.

"Long story," Rook said brusquely, but he shrugged. "I got tired of all the bowing and scraping. The short of it is, after the shit I saw and did in the service of the Empire, even a dumb grunt like me eventually realized I was fighting for the wrong side."

Jack scraped at the remaining morsels on his platter. "So you defected?"

"Well, I bloody well wasn't going to resign," Rook snorted. "Soldiering is all I know. I'd be useless at anything else." He shook his head. "Nah, I'm a fighter, boy, and I will be until the day it kills me."

Half of Valen's platter was still full, but she pushed it toward Rook with a sigh when Jack shot her an impatient look. He was anxious to make certain Dasher was okay, and these "Resistance" members, Primal and human alike, had stalled him long enough.

"For a prisoner, you're sure in a hurry," Rook drawled as Jack stood up, but he shrugged, digging into Valen's fish without so much as a farewell. Valen didn't offer any parting words either. Her mouth was set in a ridged line.

They hadn't yet reached the opposite side of the massive room when a flash of red light caught Jack's eye, and he noticed with interest the alcoves along the top of The Crypt's high wall. A Primal stood at the opening of one of these alcoves. He was garbed in silver armor with red slashes like bloody wounds across the left shoulder. His wings were outstretched in shimmering red tendrils that spread behind him in a giant fan. He floated down to The Crypt's floor, and his wings flickered away.

"Who's that?" Jack asked.

"Champion," Valen said, stopping as well. "He's Hero's brother, and Freedom's second in command, though that could be Justice or Hero maybe. The Primals don't seem to have much in the way of an official command structure, but Freedom always puts a lot of stock in what he says." She grunted as if amused at her own thoughts. "*If* he says anything, that is."

Jack could see the resemblance to the white knight in the Primal's face. They had the same golden hair, though Champion's was cut shorter and fell in snarled tangles as opposed to Hero's smooth, flowing locks. Champion had a thick, strong jaw as Hero did, and even their prominent brows were similar. But the mouth and eyes were totally different. The Primal before him bore a solemn expression, serious and brooding. It seemed strange to see a visage like Hero's without a beaming grin. Jack felt that something was off about him, and, after a moment, he understood. Champion was the first Primal he had seen that didn't appear *flawless*. He was like a painting masterpiece with small, regrettable smudges. The imperfections were more prominent when compared to Hero, who acted as a visible example of what Champion would be if everything about him were just a tiny bit better. If he were perfect.

The Primal strode past the gathering of humans and through one of the archways, slowing only to nod tersely at those few at the tables who called out in greeting.

"Come on," Jack turned, clearing the grim, somber Primal from his mind. "I want to see Dasher."

Valen led him down a corridor similar to those on the opposite side of The Crypt, heading toward an unmarked door at the passage's end. Before they reached it, however, it opened, and a shirtless individual with a white bandage around his torso stepped out.

"Sentinel," Valen called, approaching the Primal. "All patched up?"

"Stitches," The Primal replied, nodding. "Nothing to worry about." He turned a kind smile on Jack. "You either, son. Your friend is still unconscious, but do not fret. Morthal's the best physician in the business."

Jack eyed Sentinel critically. It was the first time he had seen the Primal without his armor or helm. His physique was lean but refined, with distinct, sculpted muscles that Jack was certain came naturally to all Primals. Shoulder-length, dark brown hair was pushed away from his face to show tough, rugged features, like a rock that had weathered fierce storms. Short stubble tinged with hints of gray covered the lower half of his face and brought out a patient, contemplative look in his eyes.

"I don't think we've yet been introduced," Sentinel continued when Jack did not respond. "My name is Sentinel." He didn't extend his hand in welcome, for which Jack was grateful.

"Jack Booker."

"I'll admit," Sentinel stated. "I don't know you, Jack. I don't know who you are or what you've done. Justice was quite adamant in his insistence that you be left to die in the Celestial Realm, but I want you to know, you've got an ally in me."

Jack blinked. "Look, I need to see Dasher, he–"

Sentinel reached out and laid a hand on his shoulder. At the motion, Jack cut off and flinched, reaching instinctively for his waistband. But, of course, his Bull Dog wasn't there.

Sentinel noted the reaction with a sad smile. He didn't remove his hand.

"Jack," Sentinel said soothingly. "Your friend is going to be *fine*. I promise you. And I also promise that we'll not harm either of you while you are guests in this place." He stepped back, and Jack relaxed slightly. "Look around you. This is a place of beauty: humans and Primals working together toward a common goal, living in harmony for symbiotic benefit! If you were nothing more than the lowliest of humans, you would have nothing to fear here. But you are not. You are clearly something more, and you have my respect."

Jack was silent for a long moment. "Why?"

Sentinel laughed. "My name is *Sentinel*, Jack. I can recognize a fellow protector when I see one. You have an innate instinct to guard those who need protection, and there will always be people who are worth defending." Jack didn't answer, but Sentinel didn't seem to care. He smiled at him one more time. Then, he strode away, but his voice echoed back down the corridor. "You are a paladin, Jack

126

Booker. I don't know what all you've done, and I don't care, because you've done right by that boy in the medical ward. We will speak again."

Jack watched the Primal's silhouette recede, utterly confused. His mind churned with an overload of thoughts and emotions brought about by the day's events. Dasher waited inside. He shook off the feelings and buried them for a later time. He turned toward the medical wing.

Valen was watching him with a strange expression, and he grunted, reaching for the door.

"What?"

She dropped her eyes and shook her head in response, then gestured inside. "Nothing."

When Jack pulled open the door, the smell and sight of sterility greeted him. Several beds occupied the left side of the room, and two operating tables were situated in the center. Strange, bronze machines sat everywhere, letting out small jets of steam with high-pitched whistling noises.

Jack's eyes immediately latched on to Dasher's prostrate form, which was lying beneath the covers of the bed furthest from the door. A man dressed in a white lab coat leaned over one of the bizarre machines next to Dasher's bed, tapping on its metal tubes and muttering to himself. At their entry, the man straightened, He hurried toward them.

"Ah, you must be the new visitor I was told to expect," the doctor said. His words flew from his mouth at incredible speed, and Jack struggled to keep up. "Valen, always good to see you too. Glad everyone made it back alive. Champion's squad had no casualties? No, no, don't answer that. Your face is not long with sorrow, though not particularly flushed with joy. Hmm, why, I wonder? No apparent injuries, no evident mission objectives failed unless briefed otherwise by Freedom. Don't like new companion, perhaps? Hmm, yes, yes, on the right track. Slight twitch in corner of mouth at my assumption. Newcomer's stance has a suspicious tone. Dislike evident in body language from both parties. But I digress. Forget my manners. I am Dr. Morthal, expert steam tech engineer, part-time botanist, part-time physicist, part-time mortician, part-time physician."

Jack was slack-jawed, and his mind struggled to catch up with everything that had been said. As his brain frantically scrambled to process the influx of dialogue, his eyes beheld the most eccentric individual he had ever seen. Dr. Morthal's hair was an uneven mat of patchy, rumpled gray on top of an abnormally thin face. Bulging eyes appeared to be actively popping from their sockets. They were casting about in twitching, wild leaps that bounced from Jack to Valen to one chugging machine then another with dizzying speed. Every feature was long, slim, and narrow, from his slightly crooked nose to his lengthy fingers to the flat, flapping shoes on his feet.

Jack's mind finally latched onto something from the flood of words. "Part-time physician?" he said worriedly, glancing at Dasher.

"By part-time, he means it's not his preferred field," Valen said dryly. "He still knows more about sickness and injuries than any doctor of medicine alive."

"Kind words, Valen," Dr. Morthal shot off, "and most likely true." A look of pride was on the man's face, but he seemed only to be stating a fact. "My field of genius is steam tech, but working for Freedom provides for regrettably large amounts of practice on my medicinal skills. Fighting Tyranny's empire can be messy. Problematic for both humans and Primals. Lots of gunfire, swords, axes, maces, etc. Save who I can. But," he raised one of his long fingers, and a huge smile spread across his face from ear to ear, "your friend will be fine. No loss here. Removed bullet, cut away dead tissue – wound had begun to fester – sterilized, provided stitches, introduced fluids to counteract blood loss. Patient will come around shortly. Did not recognize catastrophic internal damage. He is a strong lad. Haven't met him in a conscious state, as of yet, but looking forward to it." He stared severely at Jack for a moment, and Jack shifted nervously under the gaze. "You may speak with him briefly when he awakes, but then let him sleep. Patient needs rest. Understand you are concerned, but uninterrupted sleep will be best for him. Now, I forget my manners again. Silly things, manners. Take up time that could be better spent doing more productive things. You know my name. May I inquire as to yours?"

Jack shuffled through the information rapidly again. "Jack Booker."

"Pleasure, Mr. Booker. And patient's name?"

"Dasher."

"Ah, Dasher. Must be orphan – not a given name – and quick-footed. Also quick-handed, as well? Pickpocket, I would guess, based on previously observed evidence and name. I'll be sure to lock away all small valuables in the lab. Good boy, I'm sure. Still best not to tempt old habits with easily acquired plunder. Ah! Patient is waking! Go on, go on!"

Jack shuffled over and grabbed Dasher's hand in his own. Just as the doctor had guessed, the boy stirred a moment later, and his bright eyes fluttered open. They looked about in dazed confusion for a brief moment, and then settled on Jack's face. He smiled.

"Jack?" Dasher asked in a weak voice. "Are we…are we dead?"

Jack laughed. "No, we're not dead."

Dasher closed his eyes again. "I knew you'd save us. I knew it…invincible."

Jack frowned and held his hand tighter. "It wasn't me, boy, but it's good to have you back."

Dasher smiled, and his eyes fluttered. "Are we safe?"

Jack glanced at Dr. Morthal and Valen. They watched impassively. His mind flashed to Freedom and all the Primals around them. He didn't know…he just couldn't be sure. But he smiled again anyway.

"Yeah, boy. We're safe."

Chapter 21

"The Children of the Sun shall battle their own brethren amongst the Children of the Earth. There will be turmoil and strife and much sorrow, and a great war will tear the Realms asunder."

– Excerpt from The Prophecy of Fate, uttered by Omen

Champion was waiting for her in the command center.

Freedom alighted on her toes outside the alcove that she had repurposed into her center of operations. She strode into the room purposefully, and allowed her wings to fade away. Justice and Hero followed behind her. Champion's gaze lifted from his brooding contemplation of the massive, oak tabletop upon her entrance. His eyes narrowed, flickering across her face for the briefest of moments.

"Another dead end," he noted flatly. He shook his head in disappointment, leaning against the round table.

Freedom no longer wondered how he managed to read her. It simply seemed to come to him. She thought she had kept her expression blank.

"Good to see you in one piece," Hero said. He grinned at his brother. "No casualties on your end, I hope?"

"None," Champion confirmed.

"That, at least, is a blessing," Freedom sighed, placing her palms on the tabletop. "We must count them where we can, for we are no closer to the Instrument or our goal."

"Not true, boss," Hero chided, wagging a finger at her. "Rage's elimination is a boon for us, and it carried no price."

"Rage is dead?" Champion's voice carried the slightest hint of hope, and Freedom thought she saw the shadow of a smile beneath his somber features. For Champion, it was the equivalent of a beaming grin.

"Dead as a doornail," Hero crowed. "Where does that expression come from, I wonder? Such an odd saying…"

"That news will enrage Tyranny, no doubt," Justice surmised in his deep voice. "He's not fond of losing such powerful allies."

"If anyone among Tyranny's captains knows where the Instrument is, it would be just such 'powerful allies'," Freedom said.

"Rage was not forthcoming about any knowledge he might have had, but I detected nothing to suspect he was privy to the Instrument's location."

"Villain knows," Hero scowled. "He has to. You can see it on the bastard's smug, satisfied face. A few more minutes and I would have drug it kicking and screaming from that piece of–"

"Hero," Freedom interrupted with amusement. "Focus, please."

"Sorry."

"The diversion worked as planned," Champion continued. "My team didn't inflict any Primal casualties, but Myrmidon losses were high among Brutality's enforcers." He paused for a moment. "It is unfortunate that nothing clear was accomplished by a day of such success."

"Agreed," Freedom sighed. Everyone was silent for some time, each lost in their own thoughts. Even Hero was strangely reflective.

"What comes next, then?" Justice finally voiced what they were all thinking. "Despite eliminating Rage we are no closer to finding the Instrument or discovering the Emperors' purpose in using it. We are no nearer to this unjust empire's destruction."

"I have no plan of action," Freedom admitted. "Without knowledge of a location or Tyranny's design for the Instrument, we cannot strike an effective blow." She shrugged helplessly. "We could be back where we started, but guerrilla resistance against Imperial forces is useless and disheartening to our fighters without a purpose behind it. The empire is too powerful for such action to be more than an annoyance. We *need* a clear goal of substance."

"I don't know," Hero interjected. "Sheer, violent insurrection has been productive of late for Chaos."

"And equally alienating to the bulk of the Myrmidon population," Champion growled. His voice was angry. "Chaos is indifferent to the civilian casualties caused."

"It is not right that noncombatants be targeted," Justice agreed. "But the Myrmidons, as a whole, are sheep. Their slaughter is an injustice, but not altogether lamentable. They are an entire population of weak cowards, unwilling to stand up even against their own exploitation."

"I have seen much strength in the Myrmidons," Champion stated. Freedom could hear a hint of a challenge in his voice.

"*And* much fear," Hero intervened. "There is both courage and trepidation among the masses, my friends. One has only to look at those who fight for our cause to see the one and the empire's squalid populace to see the other." He raised a finger. "Might I propose that we are attempting revolution in the wrong manner? The way to a true chance at overthrow is not in the chasing of fables, but through the hearts of the people."

Freedom gave him a sharp look. "The prophecy states that–"

"Listen, Freedom," Champion interrupted quietly. "He may be on to something. I do not doubt the prophecy or any meaning behind it, but the future is always in flux. It is possible, however unlikely, that the Emperors *have not* acquired the Instrument."

Freedom scowled at him, but consented. "It *is* possible, but with the resources of the empire…"

"You've said yourself that we have no clear goal at which to aim," Champion pressed. "We would be firing blindly at shadows. We don't have to abandon the search for the Instrument, but in the meantime we should prepare an alternate course of action."

Freedom nodded grudgingly. None of them realized the peril of the prophecy, but she could not deny that they *were* wandering in the dark. "Very well."

"Ahem," Hero cleared his throat, giving Freedom a hurt look for having cut him off. "As I was saying, I believe our only hope of success rests in getting the people to sympathize with The Resistance. If we can prove to the Myrmidons that revolt is possible, and that we are fighting for their benefit, they will flock to the cause. With the bulk of the population behind us, a true rebellion would begin, one in which the Myrmidon's would fight. As for now, most deem our efforts to be just another Primal power struggle. We need to convince them that their lives will change radically for the better. Otherwise, they will simply assume that our victory would be nothing but exchanging one ruler for another."

"Putting our cause and faith in the hands of Myrmidons would be a ghastly mistake," Justice argued. His hand chopped down in an expression of his vehemence. "They are fickle, weak, and treacherous. Do not doubt me on this issue. I have seen it more times than you can imagine."

"Honor and wickedness are present in all beings," Freedom rebuked him calmly. "Both Myrmidons and Primals struggle in this regard."

"But–"

"That will be all," Freedom concluded. She was tired and disappointed with the day's failure. This bickering was fraying at her temper. "I will consider what has been said by all. Justice, Hero, you may go."

Justice cut off with a glower and stalked out.

Hero gave her a wink. "Aye, Freedom. It will be good to get out of this armor and clean away Villain's stink." He nodded at Champion and released his wings, floating from the room.

There was silence for several minutes. Freedom stared down at the polished rings in the oaken table, lost in thought. Champion approached respectfully.

"Freedom?" His voice was hesitant and considerate. "Are you all right? You are taking the mission's result too hard. We always knew that acquiring information on the Instrument would be nigh on impossible."

"The Celestial Realm was as bright as ever, Champion," she whispered. "Just as it was before...all this. Do you remember those days? It was so long ago."

Champion laid an armored hand on her shoulder. "I know."

"All I could feel there was Tyranny's taint," Freedom continued. "It is everywhere. His rule has spread like a plague from the Celestial Realm to the Grounded Realm's furthest shores."

Champion stood beside her, unmoving, solid as a rock. "We'll find something to stop him," he said simply, "And it will end."

Freedom straightened at his words, angry at herself. She changed the subject abruptly.

"Some newcomers arrived with us. Justice is displeased with my decision, and, I admit, I may yet rue allowing them into our sanctuary."

"Anything I should know?"

Freedom shook her head. "Have Valen fill you in later. She will have had more contact with the conscious one than anybody else – something for which she is no doubt cursing me at this very moment. She did not take to the assignment with much enthusiasm."

"I will do so." Champion nodded formally. "If there is nothing else, then I will retire."

Freedom nodded. "Of course. Go get cleaned up. I will join you for dinner."

Champion walked out, and Freedom heard the soft whoosh of his wings expanding. With no one around, she allowed herself to slump into one of the many seats surrounding the oaken table. She winced a bit at the soreness in her chest. Rage's fury had left its mark as a massive bruise covering most of her torso.

Freedom sat in silence for a long time. Her mind whirled, considering their discussion. *We delude ourselves with this struggle. Without some greater edge, we are doomed to continue as nothing more than biting, bothersome flies to the great beast of the empire...until we are smashed, one by one.*

She was no closer to any conclusions when Sentinel arrived, shirtless, from the medical bay. He patted the bandage around his midriff indicatively. "All patched up, ma'am. You wanted to see me?"

Freedom scowled at him. "Don't call me that, Sentinel. The longer we're in this fight the further I feel from those days when were just a bunch of idealistic friends instead of a steamblown command structure. I don't need formality in private, especially from you."

"Yes, ma'am." Sentinel's face was a mask of innocence.

Freedom rolled her eyes.

"What did I miss in the debriefing?" Sentinel continued.

"Very little," Freedom admitted, gesturing for him to sit. He did so. "In short, we suffered no casualties in either group. Everything went exactly according to plan, and yet, despite such success, nothing of substance was achieved."

Sentinel gave her a hurt look, gesturing at his bandage with mock outrage. "I don't know that *everything* went according to plan. Look," he pointed at the covered wound. "I got *stabbed*. Right here."

Freedom snorted. "Oh, stop it. You're so melodramatic. I got the bad end of Rage's fist, but you don't see me crying. Have you *seen* my chest?"

Sentinel perked up, and a sly grin spread across his face. "Are you going to show it to me?"

Freedom blushed furiously. "Of course not," she muttered.

134

"You're saying I have to take your word on this monstrous injury, then?" Sentinel asked airily. "I'll not believe it. You're just trying to cheapen my battle wounds."

Freedom laughed but gave him a flat look. "You're going to milk that for everything it's worth, aren't you?"

"Naturally."

"Good," Freedom stated, as if some issue were settled. "Then I have just the job for you. Nice, light duties to allow you to recover."

"Copious bed rest and a beautiful maid to tend to my every need?"

"You're to keep an eye on our new houseguests."

"Oh," Sentinel replied. He waved a dismissive hand. "Not what I was hoping for, but I had planned on doing that anyway."

"From what we've seen so far, I don't believe we will have any issue keeping Mr. Booker close, not until his friend is fully healed. After that, however, he may wish to leave. I'm afraid that is out of the question."

"Agreed," Sentinel nodded.

"We spent many long years making this place the bastion it is today," Freedom said. "Its location must remain anonymous. Our operations would be greatly hampered, or stopped entirely, if we were ever forced to relocate."

"Of course," Sentinel assured her. "I'll watch Mr. Booker. He is…an intriguing human. I find myself somewhat fascinated by him."

Freedom gave him a long, considering look. Sentinel weathered her piercing gaze with his usual calm. "You find his presence here agreeable?"

"Indeed," Sentinel said. "I do not have Justice's insight, but I recognize in him much of myself. The lad is a protector. That much I know for certain. It is rare for humans to show such selflessness."

"Do not assume too much," Freedom cautioned. "It seems unlikely that you will find in the long run what you think you see now. He is a criminal, after all."

"No," Sentinel shook his head. "Not anymore."

Freedom hesitated, and then nodded pensively. "Well, neither he nor his friend is going anywhere in the near future. I've no doubt that time will show their true natures."

"Yes, ma'am."

Chapter 22

"The price of exceptionality is solitude."

– Helmi, Philosopher

"There he is, all by himself again. Should we talk to him?"

"I don't know. Freedom would have told us if he was dangerous, wouldn't she?"

"*Of course*. She wouldn't let him wander about if she thought he'd hurt anyone."

"He always looks sad and lonely roving the corridors on his own. Devalere said he spoke with him and that he seemed a quiet, polite sort."

"See? We should extend a welcome…"

It was the fourth day of Jack's captivity in this enormous labyrinth, and he still didn't know his way around. At the moment, he was investigating a staircase that appeared to lead deeper even than the living areas, and he deduced that reconstruction had not yet reached this point.

Two middle-aged women whom Jack had seen cleaning from time to time were gossiping in the corridor behind him. It was pattern that had become familiar in the past several days. He had heard little else but curious whispers wherever he went. As usual, these people assumed that his quiet seclusion meant he could not hear well. Thus, Jack discerned every word spoken on the other end of the passage. He continued to ignore them. They would decide to speak to him, or they would not. He had met numerous individuals in a short period of time: humans and Primals, men and women, young and old. Those who had approached him were friendly and welcoming, but the constant attention was irritating in the extreme, like a fork dragged repeatedly across stone.

"Don't bother," a new voice joined the chattering gossipers. Jack recognized this voice and hunched his shoulders. He growled sourly to himself. "He wants to be left alone," the voice continued dryly. "You'd just be wasting your breath. Stones speak more than that one."

Steamblown woman.

Nervous tittering accompanied this statement, followed by the sound of receding feet. Jack breathed in relief, checking over his shoulder to make certain Valen had left with them. She had. He was blessedly alone.

Jack struggled to remember the passages he had taken to reach this point. On the rare occasions when he did approach someone, it was normally to ask for directions. The old soldier, Talon Rook, seemed to be around frequently, and he displayed an understanding indifference to Jack's presence that assured he wouldn't be stuck conversing for hours. By Jack's estimation, no more than a couple hundred people were living under Blackgate, but he still found himself struggling to remember most of the names offered. He often saw Valen passing in the halls, but, true to her word, she kept a measured distance after the first day, for which Jack was eternally grateful.

On one occasion, she had been dragged back into Jack's presence by one of her frequent companions. The man was in his mid-twenties and had a stiff, formal posture that seemed more a natural bearing than a conscious decision. His black hair was styled, his features poised, and his smile precise. Through their entire exchange Jack could think of nothing but the rich dandies he used to rob.

"Devalere," the man had introduced himself, and Jack had returned his handshake reluctantly.

"Jack."

Valen had been standing with arms crossed and an expression of tedium on her face. Her foot had tapped impatiently all during the brief conversation that followed, as if he wasn't worth the time.

What few moments he didn't spend exploring, Jack spent in the medical wing, which doubled as Morthal's lab. Dasher had been either sleeping or heavily sedated since their arrival, so Jack spent most of his time watching the hyperactive doctor at work. Morthal would bustle past the beds, tinkering with the metallic devices that chugged, steamed, and clanked in all corners of the room. He was like a hummingbird on heroin. He flitted about the lab, switching projects and tapping on machines and chattering away in an enthusiastic, excited hum. Jack didn't even try to follow the flood of speech spilling unimpeded from the doctor's thin lips, but he was unsure that the words were meant for him anyway. They seemed to be more a verbal affirmation of the doctor's thought process.

Jack even spent a large amount of time peering at the machines himself. He hadn't the slightest idea what most of them were supposed to do, but he tried to discern their purposes anyway. Much of the time Morthal seemed pleased by Jack's interest in his work. The doctor would happily inform him about each machine at an incomprehensible speed and with words he didn't understand. Only rarely would Morthal garble something indistinct in a high-pitched voice and wag a finger at Jack's inquisitiveness. He would shoo him away from a steam machine, muttering things like "unfinished" or "potential square kilometer explosion if activated incorrectly."

Jack recognized a steam-powered jetpack on one occasion, like those worn by Valen and the rocketeer enforcers he had seen. He had approached it excitedly and looked it over with a critical eye, attempting to discern its secrets. As usual, Morthal had approached eagerly at his curiosity.

"Steam-powered jetpack. Allows humans the power of flight! Perhaps my greatest achievement, and one of my more practical inventions," Morthal had burbled at the speed of light.

"You *invented* these?" Jack asked, surprised.

"Yes, in my younger days," Morthal continued. "Time spent in the Imperial R&D department. Top Secret clearance. Incredible assistant support. Steam tech laboratories with the most advanced equipment. Extraordinary funding and facilities." He sighed contentedly, looking away with faraway eyes. "Best time of my life."

"You worked for the empire?"

"Oh, yes. For many years. Very exciting. But eventually became morally problematic. Jetpack was one of my crowning achievements."

"Morally problematic?" Jack said slowly. "You felt bad about what you did there?"

"Simply put, but yes." Morthal nodded. "My inventions were extraordinary, but misused. Put to...evil uses. Convinced myself for a long time that the empire was rightfully in authority. Had either godly right or god-given right to rule." His lips quirked downward. "Couldn't keep eyes shut forever. Jetpack was created to give humans the power of a Primal: flight. Meant to be a means of granting a semblance of equality and mutual interest. Humans could fly on airships already, but…not the same as individual flight. Tyranny took my work. Twisted it. Produced on large scale for enforcers, troopers, Marines. Not unexpected, of course. I just wasn't prepared for the results. Empire's forces kept the technology for themselves. Punishable by death. Used increased abilities for heightened brutality, greater control of citizens, harsher crackdowns. Not how I want my work to be remembered."

It was a common theme from what Jack had observed of the other IAL members around him. Talon Rook and Morthal were far from the only defectors, and the rest seemed to have been aggrieved by Imperial personnel in some way.

Jack was peering into the gloom of the dank tunnel ahead when he heard the light swish of quiet footsteps behind him. He glanced over his shoulder to see the Primal, Sentinel, approaching. He grunted irritably and turned, crossing his arms.

"Everywhere I go in this maze I seem to notice you nearby," Jack grumbled in a low, drawling voice. "What are you, my minder?"

"Yes," Sentinel replied in an agreeable, pleased voice. Jack started in surprise. He hadn't expected the weathered Primal to admit it so easily. "You are new, you know, and didn't come to us with the intention of joining the cause. So, naturally, there's some suspicion. Don't worry. I don't intend to intrude upon your isolation too often; I also find solitude a precious thing."

"You?" Jack grunted. "I wouldn't have guessed."

"Why?" Sentinel asked with amusement. "Because I'm so cheery? Just because I'm not an impersonal rock like you and Champion doesn't mean I don't enjoy privacy. There's a difference between the friendliness of courtesy and the merry sociality of, say, Hero, who can't get enough of the limelight. Being amiable and enjoying the company of friends is a choice I've made, even when I would prefer to be alone."

Jack was silent, thinking this over. He grunted. "Fair enough. Dasher's always told me I could stand to be a bit more personable."

"Dasher's been asleep too much for me to know from experience, but he sounds like a wise lad."

Jack's eyes narrowed, but he couldn't decide if the statement was intended as an insult. "What do you want?"

140

"You've rather lost track of time, I'd say," Sentinel answered, leaning against the wall next to him. "Otherwise you'd have noticed that you're about to miss dinner. I thought you might need a guide getting back to The Crypt. You've been doing a good bit of exploring down here recently, but I'm well aware how confusing this place can be for newcomers. It's a bloody maze."

Jack's stomach rumbled at the mere mention of food, and Sentinel's eyebrows rose. Jack frowned at his midriff's betrayal. He *had* lost track of time. And he wasn't about to admit it, but he could have wandered for hours before finding his way back to The Crypt.

"Well," Jack muttered. "Dinner calls."

Sentinel laughed in agreement and led him on a twisting route back through the underground corridors. Unexpectedly, Sentinel didn't continue their conversation or attempt to engage him in any way as they walked. He hummed a little, but seemed lost in his own thoughts. Jack was mildly surprised to find the silence comfortable; it didn't feel at all forced. He grunted to himself in satisfaction. Perhaps the steamblown Primal *did* understand solitude.

The tables in The Crypt held a clattering mass of chatting, laughing humans and Primals when they arrived. Jack noted that no natural light filtered from the dome's high cylindrical skylight. Sentinel acquired two bowls filled with a hearty beef and vegetable stew at the kitchen window and exchanged some merry pleasantries with Liberty. Jack ducked his head. He was still uncomfortable around the stunning Primal and her distinctly unprimalish servitude.

Sentinel deposited Jack's bowl at an isolated portion of the long, wooden tables, and Jack sat gratefully. He was somewhat surprised that he didn't feel a twinge of annoyance when Sentinel pulled up a stool across from him. Jack listened to gossiping conversations, boisterous laughter, and tall tales drifting from the groups of diners. Sentinel ate in silence, and Jack was pleased to join the endeavor.

It didn't last. Hero, who had just finished an animated anecdote that left a nearby table clapping and laughing, found their quiet isolation appalling and soon led a troop of others to sit around them. Sentinel gave him an apologetic look, and Jack shrugged back regretfully.

Jack noticed Valen had accompanied his unwanted companions, although her face said she'd been forced against her will by her high-class companion. Rook had come over as well, but his curious expression told Jack he was more interested in seeing his reaction to this impromptu gathering than in participating.

"Jack!" Hero exclaimed loudly upon approaching. He pulled up a seat directly to Jack's left. "You've been a rare sight since your arrival." His tone was that of jovial pity. He was clearly trying his damndest to make sure he felt included. Jack found it exceedingly bothersome. "You've roused the curiosity of many of my friends," he gestured around at the others. "They've heard you were a gangster in the undercity. Why did you join the mobs?"

Jack looked around expressionlessly at the faces around him. Most were male, as was the case with the majority of IAL members he had seen. Fighting a rebellion didn't seem to be held proper for women. With the exception of Valen and particular others, what few women were present cleaned, cooked, and minded the needs of the male fighters. This didn't apply to the Primals as far as Jack had seen. Gender roles didn't appear relevant. Liberty was an anomaly in the extreme.

The presence of women, regardless of their role, was somewhat disturbing to Jack. He'd had very little contact with the opposite sex. His mother had died early. The orphanage had been exclusively for boys. The streets hadn't provided for casual interaction with anyone, and Fist's gang, like all the undercity gangs Jack had seen, was comprised entirely of males. What few females he had spoken with over the years were either barmaids or whores attending the taverns his fellow gang members had frequented.

He knew there was some kind of custom, a difference in interaction expected with women, but he was ignorant of what that might be. This led to Jack's speaking even less than usual when women were present for fear of saying something he ought naught say.

The expectant faces around the table, both male and female, were waiting for an answer. There was no staying silent in the background this time.

Jack settled a flat gaze on Hero. "I joined because they promised steady food and a place to sleep," he grunted. "I was starving in the bloody gutter, so I joined a gang."

There was an uncomfortable silence at this blunt explanation. Devalere, the dandy with Valen, appeared appalled that the conversation had turned unpleasant so quickly. Rook was leaning back in his seat. He sported an amused grin; Jack thought the man might have been expecting something like this.

Sentinel chuckled quietly and muttered for Jack's ears alone. "Not much one for charisma, are you, Jack?"

Valen shook her head hopelessly. She gave Jack another signature sneer.

"I learned that gangsters are bad men," a boy with sandy blond hair of perhaps Dasher's age said with wide-eyed trepidation. "Have you…murdered people?" Jack looked at the boy in surprise, not at the question, but because he had yet to see much in the way of youngsters here.

Valen snorted, and all eyes turned toward her. "Ironheart?" she scoffed. Her voice dripped sarcasm. "He'd killed a dozen men by fourteen, I'm sure."

Rook barked a laugh, but a knowing gleam shone from his eyes. "Girl, you think you're funny, but you're not going to like your answer."

Jack was tired of this girl's mockery. He dropped his spoon into his bowl and looked the young boy in the eye. "Twelve," he grunted.

Devalere still had a nervous grin pasted to his face. He looked desperate to turn the conversation in a more palatable direction, but he started in surprise as Jack's admonishment.

"*What?*"

"Twelve," Jack repeated emotionlessly. "I murdered my first man at twelve."

Jack could have thrown an apple through the boy's mouth. The wide, blue eyes beneath his sandy blonde hair filled with something akin to terror. Most of the others stared at him with expressions of alarm and revulsion, except Valen, who gave him a skeptical look.

Talon Rook appeared to be enjoying himself immensely. He shot Jack a pleased grin.

Hero was as thunderstruck as anyone. "Uh, I–"

"Go away, Primal," Jack interrupted him wearily, "and take your worshipers with you. I didn't ask for your inclusion." He regretted his rash revelation, regardless, and indeed, because of its truth. He regretted this entire conversation.

The humans looked as if they had never heard a more appalling exchange in their lives, but Hero just regarded him with a flat look.

He stood and walked away without another word. His admirers followed him.

Except for the steamblown woman. Devalere looked back over his shoulder and stopped uncertainly to wait when Valen held her ground at the table. Rook had declined to leave as well, and continued chuckling to himself.

"Well," Sentinel said quietly, shattering the silence that now hung over the tables like an oppressive shroud. "That went well." He went back to his stew.

"You've tricked all the others into thinking you're the big bad gangster," Valen said, staring him down. He held her eyes defiantly. "But you're not fooling me, Ironheart. Justice has you pegged. You're just a petty opportunist who came here because it helped you."

Jack picked up his spoon and went back to his stew. "You don't know me, girl."

Chapter 23

"Resistance to change cannot be explained as a refusal to acknowledge others are right, but an inability to admit we were wrong."

– Lord Victor Rolfe, Political Wit and Social Radical

Dasher was awake the next time Jack stopped by the lab, but the boy wasn't alone.

Jack scowled.

A large group of people lined the bedsides, including that bloody woman. Valen shot him a dismissive glance when he entered, but continued speaking to Dasher, whose beaming face displayed enthusiasm for the attention.

Morthal hurried over. His thin lips were stretched into a wide smile.

"Ah, Jack! Excellent, excellent. Young Dasher has recently woken, and I believe the worst is past, though he may be weak for the next several weeks. Some of the others organized a welcoming party for him, and he appears very pleased. He's been asking for you." He nodded in a satisfied manner and blinked rapidly. "Go and see him! Go and see him!" He shooed at Jack excitedly with his long, slender hands.

"What's *she* doing here?" Jack asked the doctor quietly. He gestured at Valen, who was favoring Dasher with a flood of motherly smiles. The boy was happily drowning in it. "And the others?" he added as an afterthought.

"As I said: welcoming party." Morthal's words clipped briskly from his speeding lips. "Valen organized it, I believe. Boy looks quite pleased. Don't you agree?"

"Mm," Jack grunted. Dasher was glowing amidst all the attention. "She's got to be up to something," he muttered.

"Nonsense, nonsense," Morthal wagged a reproving finger at him. "Valen is a wonderful girl with a kind heart. Give her a chance."

Jack snorted.

"Don't ruin this for him," Morthal warned amiably. "He'll be so thrilled to see you. The lad has spoken of little else."

145

Jack shifted uncomfortably, but did as he was bid, shuffling towards the circle as Morthal's hands propelled him forward.

The men and women around the boy's bedside parted when Jack approached and motioned him to the fore with encouraging expressions. He wished they wouldn't. It was making him nervous to be in the center of attention again, but he nodded around vaguely in thanks anyway.

Dasher's face lit up like a street lamp. "Jack!"

Jack smiled minutely at the excitement on the boy's face. He grasped the hand that Dasher extended in a firm, arm-wrestling grip. "Dasher, how are you feeling, lad?" He glanced at Valen for a brief moment, unsure if he wanted to sit close to where she was perched at Dasher's side. She gave him a cool look, but shifted to create more room.

"Great!" Dasher gushed. "My stomach is still sore, and Dr. Morthal says I need to be careful so I don't rip my stitches. But he says I'll be up in no time!"

"That's good, Dasher."

"Do you know where we are, Jack?" Dasher asked excitedly. He continued before Jack could open his mouth to answer. "We're in the Independent Army of Liberty's secret base! With *Freedom*! *The Freedom*!"

Jack grunted flatly. "We sure are."

"Look at all of our new friends, Jack!" He gestured around his bed. "That's Dr. Morthal, and there's Rook. That's Devalere; he's a *lord*! From the aristocracy! Only he believes that Tyranny is evil, so he's with Freedom now."

The dandy held up his hands and grinned. "My father's a lord, Dasher, not me."

Dasher ignored the admonishment and plowed on without slowing. "That's Mrs. Winsley. She says she has a daughter and son close to my age."

The dumpy woman Dasher pointed out gave the boy a kind smile, but frowned when Jack turned. He avoided her stare. Her son was likely the boy from dinner yesterday.

"That's James and Damon and Heb," Dasher rattled around the circle. Jack tried to follow. "Bannen, Sara, Tad, Elizabeth, and–oh!" Dasher turned to Valen happily, giving her a sappy grin. "I don't want to forget Valen! She's so nice and prett–" Dasher cut off, and

146

his face grew a dark shade of scarlet. "I...I mean, she's just really nice."

"Oh, we wouldn't want to forget Valen," Jack muttered. She cut him a smug look; her smile could have been used to sugarcoat candy.

"Anyway," Dasher continued somewhat shyly after his slip up. "There are a lot of others. I'd tell you about them, but you probably know them all already."

Jack cleared his throat. He thought he could hear Rook chuckling.

"And there are *Primals* here, Jack!" Dasher picked up steam again. "Loads of them! I *met* one earlier! I was scared at first because of all the stuff that we used to hear on the street and in the gang, but he was really nice. Can you believe that? He just walked up, sat down, and *talked* to me!"

Jack grunted.

"There was a Lady Primal too. Jack, she was so beautiful! She made me think of pure snow and the way that sparkly sea glittered in the Celestial Realm. Do you remember, Jack? That's what her eyes were like. She was like a princess out of the stories, kind and dazzling and lovely, but she was wearing *kitchen clothes*!"

"Calm down, calm down," Morthal chortled. "We don't want you to rip your stitches out, do we? Out everyone! Out!" He flapped his arms emphatically. "Dasher is still weak and needs to *rest*."

"But–"

"No, no," Morthal's voice brooked no nonsense. "Enough excitement for one day. No arguments, young man. Say your goodbyes for now."

Jack stood by Morthal as the gathering of people filed out. They each stopped before Dasher's bed and delivered little gifts of candy or baubles. The lad couldn't have been more delighted.

"Your friend is an exuberant one," Morthal zinged to Jack. "Reminds me of myself. Curious. Energetic. Excitable. Very friendly. Very accepting. Good boy."

"Yes, he is," Jack agreed. "He's always been like that. Drives me to distraction sometimes."

"It would," Morthal chuckled. "Multiple instances of childhood trauma, trust issues, self-imposed solitude. All hard to reconcile with easy acceptance, emotional freedom, etc. Counterproductive to your

147

considerable survival instincts. Creates psychological protective bond. Think he needs you to survive."

Jack stared, trying to follow. "What?"

"Never mind. Unimportant. Musing thoughts and hypotheses out loud again. Helps to formulate coherent theories. Pay it no mind." He smiled widely at Jack, patted him on the shoulder, and buzzed off to tinker with a machine that had started whistling ominously.

Valen was the last to leave the bedside, accompanied by her highborn hanger-on. Jack eyed her as she gave Dasher a kiss on the cheek and a warm smile. He thought the lad's face might melt with delight and embarrassment. The boy gave him a joyful wave, and Jack nodded back before exiting the lab behind the others.

"What a delightful young man," Valen was waiting for him in the corridor. She addressed him as he shut the door. "It's a shame that he hasn't rubbed off on you a bit more, Ironheart."

Jack ignored her.

"Of course," her voice followed him as he passed down the hall. "I suppose I should just be grateful that *you* haven't rubbed off on *him*." Jack stopped and turned. She shuddered with a mocking expression. "Imagine having only *you* for company for steam knows how long."

Jack's eyes narrowed. "What are you playing at, girl?" He jerked his head toward the lab. "With Dasher. What's your angle?"

"My *angle*?" she shook her head, as if she couldn't believe what he was saying. "You are a sad, sad man. He is a boy, with a good heart despite your influence, who was gravely injured and is new unto our company. I am but showing him he has a home here. Are you always so distrustful?"

"Yes," Jack replied bluntly.

Devalere, who stood by Valen's side, looked to be growing more uncomfortable by the moment. After a tense silence in which Jack and Valen glared at each other, he intervened with a nervous laugh.

"We are not your enemies, Jack," the man stated. He cut a disapproving look at Valen. "You and Dasher are with us now. We simply want to make you both feel welcome."

Jack ignored him. He didn't have the patience to deal with this aristocratic fool or his infuriating bitch. "You're trying something," he muttered. He struggled to find a tangible purpose behind these people's kindness to a boy they hardly knew. "Nobody just gives a damn like that. I...Primals and their daft worshippers..." He felt a fool, stuttering as he was. The acceptance, the loyalty, the bond these people had...*it made no sense.* Jack had witnessed arguments in his time here, but he had yet to see one end in gunshots. *What is wrong with these people? Don't they know that their blind trust is dangerous?* "If you or your bloody masters harm one hair on that boy's head–"

"Oh, wake up!" Valen snapped. Her eyes were on fire, and Jack could tell he had greatly angered her. "What have you seen of worship here? What have you seen of backstabbing and harm? I don't know where you've come from or what you've seen, and steam help me, I don't care. You're a distrustful, bitter fool who will likely go to his grave without ever having known hope or friendship or love. I feel *sorry* for you." She glared daggers at him, and she shoved a finger into his chest. "You've had your problems with Primals in the past. I get that. But what have you seen of Freedom or Sentinel or Hero or any of the rest to make you think all Primals are alike? They fight for us and us for them. Don't compare us to those sick cults who have lost themselves looking for something powerful to cling to. We are here because we believe there is goodness and decency to be found in this world. *And it's worth fighting for.*" Her enraged face was inches from his, so close that Jack could see the flecks of blue in her green eyes. She pointed toward the lab with her hand, leaving the other jabbing into his sternum. "That boy in there is part of that goodness, and I'll be damned to The Abyss before I give up trying to help and protect people like him. *That's* what we're fighting for, Booker." She cut off, breathing hard, and leaned away from him.

She calmed down enough to give him a cold sneer. "But I waste my words on you. You're nothing but a gangster lost in the scramble for your own gratification. That's all you'll ever be. A thug. Full of resentment and fear."

The last word shook Jack out of his dazed shock from the verbal onslaught. "I am not afraid," he objected, growling.

"You are," Valen shot back nearly before the words had left his mouth. "You're afraid of what you see around you. The reliance and friendship. You're afraid because you don't know how to trust your life to the care of others. This company, this family, frightens you more than you care to admit."

Jack struggled to retort, but he had no answer. Valen shoved by him and stalked down the hall. Devalere followed hastily behind. She wasn't finished yet, however. "Will you continue to struggle with your fear forever, Ironheart?" her voice called scathingly. Jack watched her retreating back. "Or will you finally learn from what you see? We fight for something greater than ourselves, and that fact makes all difference."

Jack stood alone in the corridor for a long time, but solitude was not enough to clear the pervasive whispers waging war amidst his thoughts.

The stillness of isolation failed him. Jack's mind was still a nest of incessant brooding long after Valen's angry footsteps had faded away.

Chapter 24

"Chaos is often considered the greatest threat to the Empire because of his organization's wanton destructiveness, but I am not certain. Freedom's quiet resistance is far more disturbing.

If Imperial forces were ever deployed against a large-scale insurrection, I would prefer that Chaos was the instigator. He is unpredictable, yes, but Freedom is considerably more devious. Her IAL is organized, disciplined, and alarmingly efficient. Brutality must deal with Grounded Realm revolts for now, but if their rebellions ever get out of hand, I do not relish learning of Freedom's competence first hand."

– Victory, Supreme Commander of the Imperial Armed Forces

The vibrant ring of Celestial Steel echoed like faraway bells. Freedom examined the sparring match with calculating eyes. Hero and Champion clashed again. Their swords flickered together and apart. Each searched for an opening. Hero's movements were elegant and light; he fought with a grace and precision that was as beautiful as it was effective. He appeared to be taking part more in a stunning dance than a physical brawl.

Champion countered his brother's fluidity with brutal force. Hero's whirling blade was met with methodical proficiency. Whereas Hero was a display of flashy skill, Champion was controlled power.

"You're guard is too low," Freedom observed as Champion made a direct thrust that Hero narrowly countered. The white knight adjusted to the attack and responded with a flurried riposte.

"Good, good," Freedom muttered, observing Hero's impeccable footwork. He danced away from Champion, who responded with another aggressive thrust. Nothing about Champion's form was showy: he attacked and parried with a simple efficiency that eschewed all embellishment.

Satisfied, Freedom left Justice and Sentinel to oversee the remainder of the match and turned to survey the rest of her forces.

The Crypt was a beehive of activity. Most of the Primals were taking turns sparring in a space where the tables had been cleared away. At a safe distance from the duels, Bannen was presiding over hand-to-hand sessions with many of the Myrmidons, while still further on Devalere instructed a smaller group in a fencing lesson. At the other end of the domed room, Rook was supervising the initial stages of firearm practice, where a row of Resistance members prepared to fire at targets arrayed against a wall of sandbags.

A solitary figure watching impassively from the sidelines caught her attention: the gangster Jack Booker. She had noticed him studying the Primals' duel with inscrutable eyes. Now, he wandered from group to group, noting instructions and remaining in the background. When he reached the end of The Crypt he paused to survey the Resistance members as they loaded their weapons on the firing line. Freedom drifted toward him nonchalantly to observe. She stopped far enough away to remain unnoticed by the brooding Myrmidon but close enough that her heightened Primal senses could still hear what was being said.

"Right, you lot," Rook bellowed to the room at large. "Shooting is about to begin. So please, stop your training and get to your other duties. Or, if you prefer, join us over here and prepare to cover your ears."

With his warning finished, the old Imperial sergeant returned his attention to his trainees. Most of The Crypt's occupants left the common room, but a small few, including Valen, Devalere, Bannen, and the rest of Freedom's Primal compatriots trickled over to watch the firearm training.

Rook strutted down the line of students, a soldier in his element. He eyed each individual critically, though most ignored him. Damon, Heb, Tad, and James were familiar with firearm training. Oliver Winsley occupied the end of the line, and Freedom thought she'd never seen the lad more excited. It seemed he had finally talked his mother into letting him begin training with the resistance fighters.

"What you hold in your hands," Rook barked down the line. "Is a Lee-Metford bolt-action carbine, courtesy of an Imperial Marine supply depot." Freedom was unfamiliar with small arms, but she knew this information to be purely for Oliver's benefit; the others had extensive experience using the weapons. To Rook's credit, the gruff ex-Fusilier didn't single out the boy. He addressed everyone as if it were their first time to handle the weapons. Freedom noted that the gangster was watching closely.

"This carbine fires a hefty .303 cartridge from an eight-round detachable magazine," Rook continued knowledgably, standing with an authoritative posture. His feet were shoulder-width apart and his hands clasped behind his back. "A skilled Marine or Imperial Trooper can deliver accurate, controlled fire of over twenty rounds per minute. In short, what I'm trying to impress upon the lot of you is that this weapon is a deadly son of a bitch in the hands of a skilled soldier."

Rook stepped off to the side to clear the line of fire. "Load your weapons." While the others did as they were bid, Rook crouched beside Oliver, demonstrating how to insert the magazine into the loading breech before cycling the bolt to feed a round into the firing chamber. Freedom continued to follow Booker with her eyes. The mobster's serious gaze took in everything with careful precision.

"When I give the order," Rook stated. "Aim and fire at your target's center mass. Once you've fired, cycle the bolt and fire again. Continue until your weapon is empty." He nodded at Oliver, who excitedly followed the others in raising his carbine to his shoulder. Freedom covered her ears with the rest of the spectators. "Fire!"

Even with her hands clamped tightly, the discharge from the carbines was thunderous in the domed room, and the shots left a ringing echo. The trainees fired and worked the bolts and fired again, over and over, until the room settled into silence.

Freedom's enhanced Primal eyesight surveyed the range. Some few shots had struck the body-shaped targets, while the rest had plowed into the surrounding sandbags. Damon had struck his target with five of his eight cartridges. They were improving.

"Check your weapons!" Rook shouted. "Make sure they're empty. Clear? Lay your carbines down in front of you." The trainees did as ordered.

"Not bad," Rook mused. He walked to each target and inspected the damage. "You're getting better, but a company of Imperial troopers would chew through the lot of you like a holiday ham. Heb, all your shots are high. Keep the butt of your carbine pressed firmly to your shoulder to keep recoil under control. Tad, you're still drifting left, which means you're probably flinching a tiny bit just before you pull the trigger. Keep her steady. James, you're firing action should be smooth and instinctive. Your shots are sporadic, all of over the steamblown place." He passed over Damon's wordlessly, and Freedom smiled to herself. It wasn't extraordinary shooting, but Rook obviously couldn't find anything critical to say. The soldier reached Oliver's target. "Look here, Oliver," Rook pointed. He grinned at the lad, who beamed back. "You got one, right here, down on the leg. A good beginning! We'll continue to practice, all right?

"Now," Rook continued. He stepped back off the range. "Prepare to load again—"

He cut off as Booker approached the firing line and stopped next to Oliver, who stared at him nervously. Rook cut a look at Freedom, and Valen stepped up suspiciously, as if she was about to interfere.

Freedom considered the gangster. He gave Oliver a strange look, somewhat like a grimace. She realized that he was smiling, quite unsuccessfully, in a way meant to be reassuring. She nodded to Rook, who backed off and laid a hand on Valen to restrain her. Freedom gave Sentinel an almost imperceptible look, and he sauntered over to stand just behind the gangster's shoulder. The other trainees left their weapons where they lay, forgotten, as they watched the newcomer.

"You ever handled a Lee-Metford before, Booker?" Rook asked gruffly.

The gangster shook his head. His voice was a rough, uncomfortable growl. "No, but it looked pretty straightforward." He picked up Oliver's carbine and inserted a magazine, stumbling a bit on the bolt before racking in a cartridge. "Coppers carry these a bit, so I've been shot at by them a few times, but I've never used one before."

"You mobsters like your coach shotguns and revolvers, if I recall correctly," Rook stated.

Jack grunted. "Both are easy to conceal." He turned to Oliver, and the boy flinched. The gangster simply handed the carbine to him. He was careful to keep the barrel pointed downrange. Oliver took it cautiously, and his eyes flickered anxiously about when the gangster leaned over his shoulder. He repositioned the boy's grip with firm but gentle hands. Booker then pressed the butt of the carbine to Oliver's shoulder.

The gangster began to talk in the lad's ear, quietly enough that Freedom was sure none but she and her fellow Primals could hear.

"Exhale before every shot," Jack said softly. "Sight your eye down the length of the gun. Make sure to keep that front post on the end of the barrel lined up inside this notch at the rear. The target should center directly in line with the notch and barrel tip." Freedom could see Oliver shaking, but he did as he was bid. "You'll want to blink your eyes when you fire, but try to keep them open and on target. Control recoil with this hand by keeping steady, firm pressure against your shoulder."

The room was silent for a moment before the carbine let out a deafening bang. Freedom peered forward. A new hole had ripped through the shoulder portion of the target.

Oliver stared with awe. He turned his eyes toward the gangster and grinned from ear to ear. Booker gave him a pleased grimace in return.

"See? You can do it."

Valen was scowling, but Rook chuckled knowingly. He exchanged a look with Sentinel, who let out a quiet laugh.

"Now," The gangster continued in a gravelly voice as he turned Oliver back toward the target. "This time, squeeze the trigger with a slow, steady pull. Don't jerk back on it, all right?" Oliver nodded with determination. "Your weapon is your lover, boy, not your whore. Fire with smooth, deliberate, gentle precision; don't be rough and abrupt with her."

A loud, disbelieving snort erupted from Valen, who strode forward and drug Jack away angrily. Rook exploded with laughter.

"What kind of thing is that to say to a boy?" Valen hissed scathingly. "*What's wrong with you?*"

Jack's face had grown a deep shade of red, and he shrugged her hand off. "I–I'm sorry. I didn't think...I mean, I was just trying to help–"

"Well, you're not," Valen snapped. "You–"

A gunshot roared, and Freedom leapt a foot into the air. Her wings flickered to life behind her in the space of a heartbeat and lifted her into a nervous hover. She dispelled them quickly, hoping no one had noticed.

Oliver lowered his carbine and peered toward the target. A ragged hole rested in the center of the chest. "I got it," the lad said with surprise. "*Did you see that*? I did just what he said. I exhaled and held it firm and squeezed slow on the trigger, and–"

Valen was glaring and Booker was still mumbling apologetically, but Rook, Sentinel, and Hero were gasping with laughter. Justice scowled, but Freedom couldn't help a small smile spreading across her face at the lad's excitement.

"You got it, just like he said," Rook agreed, holding back another round of hearty guffaws. "Now unload that carbine before you get too wound up."

Oliver did so with careful seriousness, but once the carbine was empty and lying in front of him the lad scampered over to Hero with renewed enthusiasm. "Did you see, Hero?"

"You're a marksman and no mistake," Hero agreed, ruffling Oliver's hair.

"Now," Rook stated, picking up the carbine. He glanced at Booker, who was still red-faced, and tossed the weapon at him. The gangster caught it with surprise and snatched the magazine that followed. "I'm curious to see what you can do with that thing."

Valen opened her mouth angrily, but cut off when Rook motioned Booker forward and gave her a look.

"I've never shot much in the way of rifles before," the gangster admitted. "Just shotguns and revolvers."

"Carbine, Booker," Rook corrected. "This is a Lee-Metford Carbine. That basically means it's shortened to be easier to handle. The downside is that it's not as accurate at long range as a standard Lee-Metford Rifle. Of course, that isn't much of an issue if you're an Imperial Marine or a Shock Trooper since most of their fighting is close in." He gestured downrange. "Give it a go. Clearly you've already figured out how to work it."

Booker nodded thoughtfully. He slammed the magazine into its entry port, and worked the bolt with an experimental air. Freedom noted the practiced efficiency of his hands as they moved over the weapon. His face held a look of concentration, and he looked over the barrel, trigger, and loading mechanism like a master craftsman discovering a new technique in his trade.

The gangster raised the carbine to his shoulder carefully, aimed, and fired. He lowered his weapon and looked downrange in consideration, cycled the bolt, then repeated the process with slow, methodical motions that appeared strangely lumbering and sluggish after the previous moment's efficiency.

After eight shots rang out in succession and the carbine was empty, the mobster lowered the weapon. Rook approached the targets to investigate. Freedom noted the hits before he got there. It was decent marksmanship, by all she had seen, but hardly impressive. She was a bit disappointed after his effective teaching session.

"Fine, accurate shooting," the grizzled trooper observed. "With the exception of a stray shot or two over the shoulders, the hits are tightly grouped and in the torso area."

"These are nice guns," the gangster grunted in answer, motioning along the line.

"Imperial standard issue," Rook agreed. He strode back to the line, but stopped next to Booker and glanced around mischievously. "You're a good shot, Booker." He said slyly, with an innocent look that was, nonetheless, filled with wicked intent. "Only myself or Valen might be able to outshoot you."

The gangster didn't rise to the bait. He simply shrugged and nodded.

Valen, however, squawked incredulously. "Ironheart? Outshoot us? *Please*."

"All right," Rook exclaimed happily and tossed her a carbine. She caught it with surprise. "That sounds like a challenge to me!" Freedom shook her head as Valen scowled. The girl had walked right into it.

"Thirty paces?" Valen scoffed as she looked at the targets. "Child's play. At least give Ironheart the chance to shoot from a *respectable* distance."

Rook raised an eyebrow at the gangster, who shrugged uneasily in return. The sergeant took that as an affirmative. "We'll back it up to the other end of The Crypt. That's over a hundred paces." He gave Valen a mocking glance. "Respectable enough for you, Valkyrie?"

"It's the furthest we have," Valen sniffed. "It'll do."

Of course, as soon as a challenge had been uttered, Oliver ran off excitedly to notify everyone in the underground bastion. In no time The Crypt was loud and raucous with spectators, who pressed up against the wall behind the two competitors. Freedom didn't think she'd ever seen anyone more uncomfortable than the gangster. His features had grown progressively uneasy as the number of people in the audience increased.

After much jostling by the crowd and arguing as to the rules – it was to be standing shots only, each participant would fire one magazine of bullets – the contest finally to begin.

"This is a great way to ensure Jack will never socialize again," Sentinel muttered in her ear from the left. "Making him the center of attention of a competitive contest in front of strangers…"

"Oh, it's fun," Hero answered him cheerfully from Freedom's right. "By the way, I'll bet you that Valen beats him handily. He's a decent shot and all, but Valen's fire support has backed me up too many times to bet against her."

"I'll take that bet," Sentinel replied after a moment of contemplative silence. Freedom cut him an incredulous look.

"Did see him shoot earlier?" Freedom asked dubiously. "He's no beginner, but it was hardly exemplary. Valen's proved her skill time and again."

Sentinel shrugged and smiled. "We might be surprised." He chuckled. "Funny, how we're betting on a firearm contest, eh? We're probably the least qualified people in the room to make such judgments. None of us have even *held* a gun."

Hero opened his mouth to reply, but Freedom hushed him. Valen had moved up to the makeshift firing line. Whistles and shouts of support came from behind her. She waved and grinned at the surrounding faces.

The room grew quiet when Valen inserted the magazine. She cycled the bolt with a relaxed, confident look on her face and raised the carbine to her shoulder. Several seconds passed while she sighted down the target – feet spread shoulder width, left foot slightly ahead of the right. The carbine discharged with a thunderous boom. Smoke poured from its barrel. She cycled the bolt with methodical calm and continued firing, pausing in short, incremental periods of a few seconds to line up her subsequent shots. When the last bullet roared from the weapon, Valen worked the bolt one last time to eject the casing and marched back to present the firearm to the gangster with a smug, self-assured expression. The crowd was cheering wildly, and with good reason. They couldn't see the grouping of holes spread across the target's torso as Freedom could. Only one had clipped over the left shoulder. But Valen had put on a professional display, and they all knew it.

Hero squinted at the target. "One slight miss and the rest spread around the torso from one hundred paces with *ironsights*. There's no way the gangster can win. This contest is already over."

Freedom was inclined to agree.

Oliver had been sent down to retrieve the target, which was being paraded in front of the onlookers to show the results that Hero had observed. It was obvious that the crowd felt the same as Hero, but they shouted encouragement anyway as the gangster stepped up to the line. He held the carbine loosely in his hands.

Freedom considered his relaxed posture and tense face. The young man almost appeared to be arguing with himself. His body displayed all the confidence of an expert gunman, the same as Valen, but the expression on his face was one of indecision. He loaded a magazine with a kind of unwilling reluctance.

"He's considering blowing this on purpose," Sentinel muttered, and Freedom raised an eyebrow. "He doesn't trust us," Sentinel explained. "He's gone his whole life hiding what is valuable, and he's hiding the only thing of value he has left: his skill."

Hero snorted in amusement at the statement. "You're just trying to save face because you're going to lose the bet."

Booker cycled the bolt carefully and raised the carbine to his shoulder.

In that moment, Freedom barely heard Valen mutter from behind Booker's back.

"This is already over, Ironheart, and you know it."

Everything changed. The gangster's face took on a stony, determined quality that matched the firm grip he had on the Lee-Metford. He dropped the carbine from his shoulder at the mocking statement and closed his eyes in exasperation. He stood this way for a brief moment – then the firearm blurred up to his shoulder.

BANG!

Smoke rolled from the barrel and the gun leapt in his hands. Without removing the stock from his shoulder, Booker racked the bolt more quickly than Freedom would have thought possible. The carbine roared a second time before the ejected shell casing had even hit the ground.

It became immediately clear that the sluggish shots from earlier had been the gangster getting a feel for a new weapon. Either that, or he had simply been faking difficulty with the carbine the whole time. The bolt was worked and fired more rapidly than the whirring pistons on a steam locomotive.

BANG – cycle – BANG –cycle – BANG – cycle…

A last report resonated throughout The Crypt. Perhaps as little as fifteen seconds had passed from the moment the first shot had ripped through the air. The crowd was utterly silent. The gangster racked the bolt with a lethargic motion that seemed unnatural after the blur of action his hands had been but moments before. The round casing fell to the floor with an audible, metallic *ping*. It echoed bizarrely in the room's stunned hush.

Freedom recovered from her astonishment and peered downrange at the target. She counted the holes in the paper.

One, two, three...

Eight. All eight shots were tightly grouped in an area no larger than her two fists pressed together – directly in the center of the paper chest.

Freedom leaned back on her heels and crossed her arms. She studied the young gangster as he handed the carbine to a gaping Valen and strode quickly from the room. The crowd parted quietly.

Freedom turned to Hero and Sentinel. "I don't care how you do it, but I want Mr. Booker willing to fight for The Resistance." She turned and walked away.

"This is a priority, you two. I want that boy invested."

Chapter 25

"There is but one, universal characteristic that is unequivocally true of all governments: The most reliable records are the tax records."

– Lord Victor Rolfe, Political Wit and Social Radical

Freedom couldn't sleep.

She never could when a team was out on assignment. It was one of the burdens of authority. The command center was adjacent to her sparse quarters in the upper levels of The Crypt, so she sat at the large oak table, unable to bear the confines of her room while her mind hummed with unwanted apprehension.

Champion insisted that her restlessness was concern for her people's safety, but Freedom didn't believe him. It was anxiety that she might lose the precious few assets she had. Soldiers in wartime – and the IAL *was* at war – were, by definition, expendable. She understood that. By day, these Myrmidons and Primals were her friends and comrades. When on operation, however, they were troops. They were resources. Freedom had been a commander for a long time. She understood that a general had to have such a view to remain sane. Each death the Resistance suffered was a blow, yes, because each soldier lost was a severe drop in fighting strength. It was a balancing act of affordable casualties with the rewards of a mission's success.

She had been dispassionate for so long that she scarcely remembered the last time she had allowed a death to truly crush her. It was yet another of Tyranny's crimes, making this war necessary. Someday he would fall. With each passing day, Freedom felt her belief fade that she would live to see that moment. But maybe, just maybe…

If she survived to see the day of victory, *then* she would permit herself to feel. Let the weight of dead souls settle heavy on her shoulders. She would revel in the pain. She would deal with the grief. And she would rejoice because she had the luxury of allowing herself to feel again.

The sound of bustling feet in The Crypt below interrupted her thoughts. Freedom leapt from her seat and hurried to the alcove's edge before stepping into midair. She allowed her wings to unfold behind her to slow her fall, and she touched down softly amidst an exhausted reconnaissance team.

"Freedom," Champion nodded. His armor was painted with the red of Myrmidon blood, and his voice was haggard. "No casualties to report. I was just about to dismiss the team and send for you."

"You were supposed to run recon only," Freedom said.

"Situation changed, Freedom." Champion admonished frankly. "I had a feeling something was off in the report, but…" Champion's eyes flickered to the fighters surrounding him. "I'll brief you in a moment."

"Champion made a solid call," Rook stated gruffly from Champion's side. The other participants nodded in support. "It was a clean ambush, ma'am."

Freedom tilted her head in acknowledgment. "Very well." She turned to Champion. "Clean yourself up and meet me for an operation report. The rest of you are dismissed. A job well done."

The Myrmidon's nodded gratefully and trudged toward their quarters. Champion strode away to remove his armor, and Freedom flitted back to the command center.

Champion didn't keep her waiting long. He landed lightly on the command center's ledge a few minutes later, his armor replaced by a loose fitting tunic and trousers.

"What were you thinking?" Freedom asked bluntly as he entered. The lateness of the hour contributed to her use of the less tactful approach. "You initiated an engagement with only one Primal in your team and no backup in the immediate area." She gave him a severe look. "Explain."

Champion wasn't disturbed by her critical assessment, nor did he show any offense. "Intelligence dropped the ball on this one," he stated directly. Her gruff second pulled out a chair and collapsed with a fatigued air. "It wasn't a shipment of weapons at all. I could tell as soon as we arrived."

"What do you mean?"

Champion shrugged. "The shipment was lightly guarded. No Primals, a few coppers for security. Nothing more. I checked and

162

triple checked to make sure it wasn't a trap before engaging, Freedom. I promise you."

Freedom sighed wearily. "I apologize, Champion. You know I trust your judgment. I...it's been a long night." She cocked an eyebrow at him. "You covered your tracks, I assume?"

"We tossed the whole area," Champion nodded. "Made it look like a random hit by Chaos."

"Good. And the cargo? You said it wasn't a weapons shipment. What did you find?"

A baffled look crossed Champion's iron face. "Paperwork, if you'll believe it. Boxes and boxes of tax records."

"No wonder it was so lightly manned," Freedom nearly smiled in amusement. "Who'd want a load of dry old tax reports?"

"Why did Courage think it was weapons? He was the contact, yes?"

"No," Freedom replied. "Newer contact, Charm, in the Empire's Intelligence Ministry. All of her information has been good before, but you know the pressure our spies are under. They have to make what inferences they can with the information they have. If they get caught..."

"The emperors don't hold with traitors," Champion finished softly.

They sat in silence for a few moments until she addressed him in tone of finality. "Anything else to report?"

Champion shook his head.

Freedom stood, and he followed suit. "Good work, Champion. Get some rest. You look like you need it."

He smiled gratefully. "All teams are in, Freedom. It's time you got some rest as well."

"I will."

"Good." Champion strode out.

***

It was still the middle of the night when it hit her.

Freedom sat bolt upright in her bed. That wondrous place between consciousness and sleep where thoughts and dreams comingle in a floating daze of nonsense had brought the unformed idea at the back of her mind to the forefront. Suddenly, it all made sense. She finally had another plan.

Freedom leapt from her bed in a state of excitement. She rushed to the door of her room, hurled it open, took two steps outside, and realized she was clad only in her smallclothes. She thought better of this and impatiently retreated inside to throw a blanket over her bare shoulders before hastening back to her task.

Hero's room was the nearest, and she wasted no time with propriety. She barged in, grasped his shoulder, and shook him insistently. The striking Primal's eyes flickered open, and the golden locks that had been spread about him like a fan fell over his face as he sat up and peered at Freedom in the darkness.

"Freedom?" Hero muttered. He pushed his hair back out of his face. "Wha…what a pleasant surprise."

Freedom blushed heavily and drew the blanket tighter around her shoulders. "That's not why I'm… Oh, never mind." She glared at him, but he likely couldn't tell in the darkness. "Get dressed and meet me in the command center. I'll be there in a few moments."

"Is something–?"

Freedom left the room hastily.

She encountered Sentinel before reaching his quarters. The weathered Primal sat on the alcoves' edge, reading by the light of the surrounding gas lamps. He shut his book and stood at her appearance. His eyes shifted about quickly, and his spear coalesced in his hands.

"Freedom!" Sentinel said in alarm. His eyes lingered on her. "What's the matter? Are we under attack?"

"We're not," Freedom assured him. "What are you doing awake at this hour?"

"Couldn't sleep," Sentinel replied. He grinned and nodded his head toward The Crypt floor. Jack Booker paced back and forth below. "Or, at least, my charge couldn't, so, naturally, I'm not allowed to either." He cocked his head to the side and raised an eyebrow. His eyes ran over her blanket wrapped figure. "Uh, so, why are *you* awake at this hour? Or, perhaps a better question is: Why are you dressed the way you normally do in my dreams? I didn't nod off did I?" He gave her a teasing smile as his eyes flickered to the surrounding alcoves. Freedom blushed again. This hurried approach was proving to have not been the best idea.

164

"I'm calling everyone together in the command center. Help me gather the others and meet me there."

"Trouble?"

"A plan. I'll explain when everyone is gathered."

"Yes, ma'am."

Freedom moved on to Champion's room, allowing Sentinel to take flight to The Crypt's opposite alcoves. She pushed open the door lightly.

Champion jerked awake and bolted upright, rolling from his bed. He landed lightly on the balls of his feet and settled into a dueling stance – legs bent, chest squared toward the target, hands raised beside his head. His sword materialized vertically in his fists in a two-handed grip.

"Freedom?" Champion said. He immediately started for clothes and armor. "We're under attack?"

"No," Freedom placed a hand on his arm to stop his frenzied attempts to equip himself. "Help Sentinel gather all operation leaders in the command center. I've come up with a plan."

"In the middle of the night?"

Freedom scowled. "I can't help when a plan comes to me."

Champion cracked a bemused smile, but he just shook his head. "I'll have everyone gathered in two minutes."

***

All the Primals were assembled by the time she emerged from her room, now sufficiently clothed in her buttoned, blue IAL uniform, tanned pants, and buckled boots. The Myrmidon leaders – Rook, Valen, Bannen, Dr. Morthal, and Devalere – were gathered as well. An air of speculation hung heavy over the room, but the whispered conversations faded when Freedom entered the command center.

"I liked her previous attire better," Sentinel muttered from across the table. He favored her with a smile that was too professional and a wink that was decidedly not.

"Hear, hear," Hero agreed.

"Gentlemen," Champion growled reprovingly. "Can we keep our minds on the task at hand?"

165

"Oh, don't lie, Champion," Sentinel quipped. "You enjoyed it too."

"I..." a red flush crept up her second's neck and cheeks. He cleared his throat roughly and addressed Freedom. He avoided her eyes. "What's this sudden meeting about, then?

Freedom took her seat at the table, pointedly ignoring the previous conversation. She looked around the table at each individual, marking each with an iron stare.

"Taxes," she stated simply.

The word hung in silence for several moments, dangling from a thread of confusion and uncertainty.

"Yes, taxes," Hero nodded authoritatively. "I've not paid mine in quite some time. They are the fuel that keeps a government running and the means by which an empire can be brought to its knees." He smiled lazily. "I am making all of this up, of course, pretending like I know what's going on. I think I speak for everyone when I say that the word 'taxes' is a very vague way to start a conversation. What about taxes?"

"Records," Freedom continued. "Can be destroyed, omitted, or removed." She ran her gaze around the table. "A government, especially one as vile as the empire, has no need for records or accountability. Any ill action is covered up, and any secret is easily concealed. Why? Because there is no need for surviving witnesses and no paper trail. Any action or knowledge that the emperors wish kept secret simply does not exist."

Justice's rich voice finished the thought she left hanging in the air. "Except when it comes to taxes."

Freedom nodded. She allowed a pleased smile to creep over her face. "In any government, the most thorough, complete records are the *tax* records." Dr. Morthal was nodding vigorously to her right. "Ladies and Gentlemen, I ask that you allow me one more chance to find the Instrument. The answer lies in the finances."

"The Instrument *again*?" Hero groaned.

"She has a point," Morthal's words burbled from his lips. "Financial records easily the best possibility for finding clues of the Instrument's existence. If the right records were found, we could search for anomalies in expenses. Unnamed projects. Strangely allocated wages. Unspecified expenditures. Gaps in official records would be exposed when compared to the fiscal reports. Best chance to determine for certain if the Instrument is in the empire's hands, and, if it is, where it is located."

The council mused over this for several moments, and Freedom settled back in her seat to observe. Most were mulling it over thoughtfully and approving expressions settled on their faces.

"So, what, we break into wherever the records are kept, grab a load of expense accounts, and sift through it all for answers?" Hero asked. The idea of working through piles of paperwork seemed to pain him physically.

"We could," Morthal answered before Freedom could reply. "Approach chancy at best. Records would be lightly guarded initially. After one attempt that would quickly change. With the volume of records it is unlikely we would find relevant data in the first effort."

"Do you have a suggestion, doctor?" Freedom asked hopefully.

"Original strategy of targeting personnel was correct but flawed." Dr. Morthal answered with controlled excitement. "Martial lieutenants unnecessary concerning sensitive information. Need-to-know only when specifically in contact with secrets. Organizational staff, however, absolutely crucial."

"We need to find imperial personnel in clerical or managerial positions." Champion clarified slowly.

"Specifically financial personnel essential to economic organization and resources," Morthal corrected. "Say, the Minister of the Treasury? Such an individual would be familiar with all funds received and issued to ensure Imperial financial stability."

Freedom surprised herself, and everyone else, by laughing out loud.

Now, they were getting somewhere.

Chapter 26

"The feet of clay will abandon their dusty pits and trample the sunlight, but remnants of the Sun shall be swayed."

– Excerpt from the Prophecy of Fate, uttered by Omen

"She asked me how I was feeling and if my injuries were healing up nicely!" Dasher beamed. "Can you *believe* that? Freedom. *The* Freedom sitting at my bedside and worried about *me*." The boy slumped back on his bed. He appeared to have worn himself out with his own enthusiasm. Jack watched him expressionlessly.

"She is so, so…" Dasher waved about vaguely with his hand. "I don't know." He cocked his head at Jack. "What's a word that sums up beautiful, fascinating, intimidating, and terrifying all at once?"

Jack gave a noncommittal grunt, shrugging his bulky shoulders. "Freedom."

Dasher laughed, his eyes sparkling. Jack found himself thinking of Morgan again.

"What do you think of her, Jack? You've probably seen her loads of times."

Jack snapped out of his thoughts. "Who?"

Dasher gave him a teasing grin. "You're doing that brooding thing again. Freedom, Jack. What do you think about Freedom?"

"I don't brood," Jack scowled, but he considered the question carefully. What *did* he think of Freedom? He was unsure. In fact, he was uncertain about a great number of things since his arrival at Blackgate. Only a few weeks ago Jack would have insisted that all Primals were evil, but now…

Was it a trick? Some elaborate scam? Jack couldn't see any advantage for the Primals in deceiving him. They had him in their power and could kill him with ease. Perhaps they were as genuine as they appeared.

"She's a Primal," Jack stated bluntly. "But I'm not sure I know what that means anymore, Dash. I–" Jack stopped for a moment to consider his answer. "I suppose I would describe her as passionate. I've never seen someone so driven. So focused on a goal."

"Intense!" Dasher exclaimed triumphantly. He'd grown tired of waiting on Jack to reply and hadn't been listening. "That's what she is, Jack. Intense! Her eyes just seem to burn through you."

Jack held back an amused smile at the boy's enthusiasm, but he nodded knowingly. "Morthal says you'll be released from the medical wing soon." he said.

Dasher nodded exuberantly. "I'm ready to get out of this bed, Jack. Even with Dr. Morthal and visitors all the time, it's *boring.*" The boy seemed to catch the look in Jack's eye, and he grew suddenly serious, giving him a strange glance. "What are we going to do once I'm well?"

Jack shook his head and grimaced at his own indecision. "We could try to escape, I suppose, but I've no doubt that would be as futile as Freedom has claimed. Besides, Fist is dead, the gang is destroyed, I–" he frowned somewhat helplessly. It was an odd feeling. One that he hoped remained foreign to him. "I don't know, Dasher."

"Jack," Dasher said softly. His eyes were almost desperate. "We could join–"

"No."

"Jack–"

"Dasher, *no.*" Jack said firmly. "I'm not helping the Primals kill each other. They fight and they fight. It's always a power struggle with them, and humans get caught in the middle."

"It's not like that!" Dasher shouted suddenly. Frustration was clear in his voice. "Not all Primals are the same, Jack! The Primal *Empire* is exploiting humans. These people are trying to stop it!"

Jack sat dumbstruck for several moments. He was utterly taken aback. Dasher had never shouted at him before. The boy had always listened to his every word.

"Dasher, you don't know that. Primals…If Freedom were to win, it is likely she would–"

"No, Jack." Dasher cut him off quietly, and Jack was struck by the vehemence in his voice. "She wouldn't." Dasher sat up in his bed and gave him an avid look. "I understand now, Jack. Before, in Fist's gang, I didn't know any better. I knew all the Primals were evil because that's what everyone in the slums thought. That was just the way life was supposed to be. We were *meant* to live under the Primals." The lad smiled at him. "But we were wrong, Jack. They

169

fight for a better world here. They, humans *and Primals*, fight for us to be free."

Jack rubbed a hand across his brow. He remained silent.

"Jack," Dasher continued hesitantly when he didn't answer. "You can help them win. Nobody can help them like you can. You're *invincible–*"

"*I'm not invincible!*" Jack snapped, irrationally furious at Dasher's naivety. He stood up, knocking over his chair in his haste. He kicked it out of the way for good measure. It didn't make him feel any better.

Dasher was looking at him with downcast eyes. Jack thought for a moment he might cry, but the lad sat up straighter after a moment and favored him with a tremulous smile.

Jack immediately felt ashamed of his outburst. He didn't know what he believed anymore, and the frustration was eating at him inside. The boy didn't deserve his anger. Jack took a few long, deep breaths. "You're wrong, Dasher," he said, putting as much certainty into his tone as he could muster. "The people here have gotten to you. *Primals cannot be trusted.*"

Jack turned away and walked stiffly toward the door.

It didn't matter what the boy said or what he saw around him. He was right about this. Primals could not be trusted.

And they could never be forgiven.

***

"Invincible..." Freedom mused. "And you're certain you heard everything?"

"I repeated the entire conversation as I heard it," Sentinel replied. "Word for word, ma'am."

"There's more, Freedom," Hero stated. He stepped up beside Sentinel at the oaken table. "I knew Jack's name sounded familiar when he first arrived, so I had Heb talk to some of our Myrmidon contacts spread throughout the city. It turns out our guest is a bit of a legend in Victorian's underworld. He was the right-hand man of a crime boss called Fist, who ran one of the city's most notorious, all-Myrmidon gangs."

"Right-hand man?" Freedom raised an eyebrow.

"That's not all, ma'am." Sentinel replied, gesturing at Hero.

170

The golden-haired Primal nodded. "Apparently he was rumored to be invincible, Freedom, just as we heard Dasher say. He's been shot and stabbed over a half dozen times, and there are eyewitnesses that say he even survived a confrontation with a Primal several years ago. Judging by the accounts Heb has heard, it wasn't idle gossip. In fact, I believe he was attacked by a High Primal." Hero's eyes flicked from Freedom to Sentinel and back. "Possibly Pride."

Freedom nodded slowly. She was careful to mask her surprise. "What do you think, Sentinel?"

Sentinel smiled. "I think that the more I find out about our guest, the more remarkable he becomes."

"He's certainly the most intriguing Myrmidon I've yet encountered," Freedom agreed.

"What do you think about his alleged...vitality?" Hero quipped. He failed to keep the sarcasm from his voice.

"Do I think he's invincible?" Freedom asked. She allowed some of her amusement to cross her face in a smile. "Don't be ridiculous." She tapped a finger on the table thoughtfully. "The whole story warrants some investigation, however. Have Heb do some more digging with our contacts in the slums and the underground. If anything seems even slightly connected to our surly guest, I want to hear about it."

Chapter 27

"The worship of Primals represents primitive theology. The Primals are elemental ideas. They represent fire and water, reason and hate. They are not a divine whole; they are the splintered fragments of existence."

– Excerpt from *Dilemma of Divinity: The Primal* by Tairie

Jack strained his eyes. He was determined to makes sense of the frustrating puzzle before him. It didn't matter how hard he struggled, however. The markings on the page meant no more to him than a hen's inane scratchings in the dirt.

Jack slammed the book closed.

He'd found the library early in his stay here, a mere hallway from his small room. The shelves and shelves of bound books still fascinated him. Useless to him though the contents were, Jack found the contemplative silence of the large, sandstone room to be peaceful. Except for today. Today he was ill-tempered and discouraged. Try as he might, the books themselves remained a mystery.

A soft knock sounded on the door. It opened to reveal Liberty's smiling face.

Jack bolted upright in his chair and blushed furiously. It was stupid, really, and he growled at himself for acting like a fool. But he didn't slouch back down.

"Hello, Jack," Liberty said lightly, gliding over to sit near him at the small table he occupied. Jack shifted awkwardly and cleared his throat in an attempt to appear nonchalant.

He knew why she made him uncomfortable. She didn't fit. She shattered the molds Jack had constructed to contain all Primals, and no matter how he reasoned, he couldn't force her into the box in which he'd lumped the others.

She was also *gorgeous*. And sitting beside him.

"I've been looking for you, Jack," Liberty beamed and laid a hand on his arm. He nearly bolted out of his seat at her touch.

"M-Me?" Jack stuttered stupidly, then struggled not to cover his face with his hands.

"I was walking to your room when I heard a loud sound in here," Liberty explained.

Jack quickly removed his hand from the cover of his book.

"Getting a bit frustrated?" Liberty laughed. Her voice sounded like beautiful bells. "Can you read, Jack?"

He shook his head. His face was on fire. "You probably think it's stupid that I'm in here when I can't even read," he muttered.

"I think that seeking to expand one's mind is a worthy goal no matter our limitations," Liberty said kindly; she picked up the book with gentle hands. Her eyes ran over the leather cover, then widened in surprise. She quirked an eyebrow at him, and the edges of her mouth flitted upward with amusement. *"Dilemma of Divinity: The Primal* by Tairie. You certainly aren't one to shy from a challenge, are you, Mr. Booker? This is a remarkably deep work on which to begin learning your letters."

Jack felt even more embarrassed at the amusement in her voice, but he could think of little besides how she reminded him of Freedom when she called him Mr. Booker. "It looked interesting."

"It *is* interesting," Liberty agreed. "And heretical. It is banned in every Realm under the authority of the Primal Empire. The emperors consider the ideas expressed inside too dangerous for even Primals to consume."

Jack eyed the tome doubtfully. "Why?"

Liberty's lips pressed together as if she were trying to hide a smile. "Because it questions the divinity of my race. Tairie held that Primals are anomalies. The product of a merging of cosmic energies and the abstract thoughts of intelligent beings." She inclined her golden-haired head toward him. "Specifically humans."

Jack struggled to wrap his mind around what she had said, but the words did not lead to understanding. Talking to Morthal often produced similar results. Instead, he eyed her warily and asked what he wanted to know.

"Are you gods?"

The library pealed with Liberty's laughter again. "That depends on your definition of divinity, Jack. If a god is simply something more powerful than the relative ability of the believer, then I suppose Primals are gods. If a god is a being that in some way influenced the creation of this world, we certainly are not. We enter a whole new discussion altogether if we assume that a god is an infallible being."

173

She stood and placed the large book where he had found it on the shelf. "I do not in any way consider myself to be divine. Nor do any of the other Primals here, except for Justice, perhaps. Unfortunately, believing we are less than divine is not a...popular view in this empire.

"In the future," Liberty continued as she walked back to him, "when I'm teaching you to read, we'll use books with words like "run" and "cat," not terms like "transmutation" and "epistemology"."

Jack leapt out of his seat, thoroughly embarrassed. "No, I don't really...What I mean to say is, you've likely got better things–"

"You wish to read, don't you?" Liberty cut him off. Her eyes twinkled at him playfully.

"I...yes," Jack mumbled.

"I will be more than happy to teach you," Liberty nodded her head. She appeared satisfied that the conversation was over. He supposed she was right.

"Now," Liberty said, taking his arm. Jack struggled to swallow his panic at the gesture. "Would you come join me and a few others for some refreshment? That's why I was looking for you in the first place, after all."

"In The Crypt?"

"In my chambers," Liberty said. "On occasion, some few of us like to gather and enjoy each other's company with food and drink."

Jack balked as they exited the library. "I don't really..."

"We would be glad of your company," Liberty stated. She continued to walk down the nearest corridor toward The Crypt. He found himself following despite himself. Her eyes and smile seemed to pull him along more than the gentle hand on his arm.

Jack hid his misgivings as they entered The Crypt. He *hated* social gatherings.

When they began to ascend the stairs that wound around the walls of The Crypt, Jack asked with surprise. "Aren't you going to fly up?"

"And leave my guest behind?" Liberty raised a delicate eyebrow at him. "I don't like flying much, anyway. It's too...flashy."

Jack thought back. He had been here for several weeks now, and he had yet to see her release her wings. He idly wondered what color they were. *White. Definitely white. It would be nice to see her spread her wings.*

"You don't like to fly at all?" Jack asked. "To be able to fly... That would be incredible, it seems to me."

She made a teasing face at him, but just squeezed his arm. "I have my moments, Mr. Booker."

They arrived rather suddenly at the landing of Liberty's alcove. She pushed the door ajar and slipped inside while gesturing for him to enter. Then, she excused herself, saying she needed to check on the food and drinks.

Jack stood uncertainly outside the door for a moment, listening to the hum of conversation. It sounded like more than a few people were inside, a thought that made him uncomfortable. The idea of entering to forced conversation wearied him.

Laughter suddenly drifted through the door. Jack listened to it for a moment. It was light laughter. Happy. Not raucous or crude or drunken like the laughter from the gang's safehouse. It was the sound of people genuinely enjoying themselves. Very strange.

Jack placed a hesitant hand on the doorframe.

Mirth burst forth from inside once again. He hesitated, and then stepped back quietly. He didn't belong here. His time among these revolutionaries had done nothing but bring confusion. He didn't understand these people, nor they him.

The door suddenly opened wide, and Jack started with surprise. Sentinel stood in the entrance, a slight smile on his lips. He jerked his head inside indicatively.

"I would ask if you planned on coming in or just standing in the hall all night," the weathered Primal joked as he ushered Jack inside despite his protests. "But I believe I already know the answer."

Liberty's rooms were brightly lit by gas lamps and had a homey feel. A rather large group of people sat around a circular table in the corner. Other groups of two or three were dispersed over the rest of the area, chatting lightly and holding drinks in their hands. Most noted his entrance with a smile or nod and carried on with their conversations, but they all appeared mildly surprised to see him there. Valen just scowled at him from her seat at the table.

Jack realized with astonishment that he knew nearly everyone in the room. Liberty was scurrying about setting out drinks and food, Justice sat in a corner drinking with Champion, and Devalere was

175

pouring a dark red liquid into a small glass. Valen, Rook, Bannen, Hero, Morthal, a younger girl whose name he thought was Sara, and a female Primal he didn't recognize were all sitting around the table. A lively conversation had ensued. Freedom was leaning against the wall with a glass in her hand, not participating but near enough to listen. She was staring at Jack with an unreadable gaze, but when she realized he was looking at her as well, she gave him a cold nod.

Jack couldn't figure out the Resistance leader. She was a living myth, after all. He thought he might describe everything she did as cold, but it didn't seem intentional, only calculated. Rigid. She shared her sister's beauty, which was set off even more, perhaps, by her stark silver hair. But a distance separated her emotionally and physically from any notion of a person in his mind. She was the rebel-god of legend, and it was a struggle to think of her in any other way.

Sentinel was prodding him toward the table. He moved forward reluctantly.

"Who is the Primal beside Hero?" Jack asked quietly as they approached.

"Tempest," Sentinel whispered. "She's been away on assignment for the past several months. She only arrived yesterday after Freedom called her back. She's a fierce warrior, Jack, and a good friend, but a bit...volatile." There was amusement in his tone, as if he were remembering something specific.

Tempest was astoundingly attractive, just as every Primal Jack had ever seen, but her beauty was different from that of Freedom or Liberty. Less angelic and more *wild*. Her features were angular to an extreme. Her hair and eyes seemed to alter sporadically. The first shifted from a deep, burnished brown to a fiery red and the second changed from sparkling blue to bright green and back. She gave him an appraising look as he approached but smiled pleasantly and gave a slight nod. Jack scowled, but nodded in return. Steaming Primals. Now he had another to keep an eye on.

The conversation at the table did not slow when Jack sat down hesitantly in a chair. Sentinel poured him a drink that turned out to be a nutty brown ale. Jack accepted it silence. He sat back in his chair in the hopes of avoiding any more attention, but he listened intently as the conversation around him continued. It seemed to be a good-natured argument.

"Magic *does not exist*," Morthal was insisting. He chopped down with his hand for emphasis. "The portal mirrors are not magic. They are science. There must be some way that teleportation is connected to the same source as Primals."

"Exactly!" Valen said with genial exasperation. "That source being *magic*."

"No, no, no," Morthal shook his head rapidly. "Abilities of Primals and the effects they produce must follow some physical law of our world. We simply are not yet advanced enough technologically to detect and measure—"

"Because it's magic," Tempest put in with amusement. Her voice was surprisingly husky and had an untamed tinge to it, as if it could hardly be controlled. "There is no way to predict or gauge our abilities precisely because they are not bound by any law of nature."

Morthal's scoff was released with incredible speed. "The very idea of a being that doesn't follow some pattern of the world in which they live is ludicrous. Primal agility, toughness, and reflex are universal traits of your species. The abilities you carry must have some similar basis as well. It comes down to some form of science." He snorted sarcastically. "Magical beings. *Indeed*."

"I'm as magical as they come," Sentinel drawled. He took a sip of his wine. "Just ask the ladies." He gave Tempest a wink over his glass.

The table burst out with laughter at this statement, but Jack noticed Tempest blushing.

"Sentinel," Freedom's voice cut through the merriment from where she leaned nonchalantly against the wall. "Shut up."

"Yes, ma'am."

"I'll see you in my chambers at the regular time tonight."

"Yes, ma'am."

Everyone laughed even harder at this. Jack turned incredulously in his seat and glanced at the Primal leader. Had Freedom just made a *joke*?

"Rook, you're a blunt, no-nonsense soldier." Morthal said to the gruff veteran seated next to him. "Back me up."

Rook chuckled roughly and took a long pull on his drink. "Sorry, Doc. Soldiers are superstitious folk. You're telling me you've never seen anything you just couldn't explain?"

"Just because I can't explain something at one moment in time doesn't mean it can't be explained at all–"

"I'll put it this way," Rook pulled a metal medallion on a chain around his neck from underneath his shirt. It was made of iron and fashioned in the shape of a dragon. There was a sizeable dent in the dragon's chest. "I've worn this medallion into every fight I've ever been in. Now, believe me, I've been in a lot of bloody battles. Somehow, I'm still alive. Explain that."

Morthal rolled his eyes. "Coincidence or skill-at-arms."

Rook shook his head authoritatively. "Luck. This is my lucky medallion. You can't explain luck, Doc. It just is. And it affects everybody in ways that can't be explained." He nodded as if he'd just won some sort of contest. "Just like magic."

"The world bows before the reasoning of your fiery intellect," Morthal said dryly.

"I took a bullet to the chest," Rook stated, poking himself in the sternum. "This baby stopped it. That's downright mystical."

Morthal threw up his hands in mock despair, but there was a smile creeping across his face. "Savages. I'm surrounded by fire worshippers and snake eaters."

"This particular conversation is a bit of a staple around here," Sentinel said quietly to Jack. "It's the only argument we can win against Morthal." He chuckled. "Or, at least, the only argument we don't necessarily lose."

"What are these Primal abilities that everyone keeps talking about?" Jack asked with confusion.

"Every Primal has an extraordinary ability," Sentinel explained to Jack while the argument moved on without them, "Sometimes powerful Primals have more than one. You've seen a few already."

Jack gave him a questioning glance.

"Rage," Sentinel prodded. "He was able to transform his fist into a juggernaut of rock that caught fire and delivered incredible amounts of force." Jack nodded. He remembered Freedom's badly crushed breastplate after the ambush in the Celestial Realm. "And Justice can peer into a person's soul. It allows him to get a feel for who a person really is."

Jack's eyes widened. "He can read minds?"

"No," Sentinel shook his head. "Nothing quite so simple. It's more a glimpse at their overall moral outlook. He gets vague

178

impressions of people's desires and ethics. In essence, he can obtain a general sense of an individual's morality."

"That's what Freedom asked him about when she took me with you!" Jack realized.

Sentinel nodded.

"Is that why he's so critical?" Jack asked curiously. He glanced at the big Primal in the corner, who was still conversing quietly with Champion. "Why he avoids everyone?"

Sentinel raised an eyebrow at him. Jack blushed, but the weathered Primal didn't comment further. Instead, he answered Jack's question.

"Yes," Sentinel admitted. "I think it is difficult for him to accept others when he so intimately knows their faults. On the other hand, people often keep Justice away as much as he does himself. It is discomfiting to be around someone who, by their very presence, is a reminder of your failings."

Jack digested this information methodically. Then, he gave Sentinel a curious glance. "What's your ability? And Freedom's?"

Sentinel laughed. "Freedom plays things pretty close to the chest, Jack."

"And you?"

"Oh, my ability is hardly worth mentioning, I assure you," Sentinel said amicably, avoiding the question. "It is of no use to me."

Jack let it go. After all, it was likely a very personal subject. He turned his attention back to the surrounding conversation.

The banter had come to an inconclusive end, however. Magic, it seemed, was the popular explanation for Primals and portal mirrors. Morthal summarily declared that the room was populated by hopeless primitives. He pushed out of his chair with a good-natured wave and went to join Champion and Justice. Most of the others drifted away as well, breaking off to chat with Liberty. All except that steamblown girl. She stared at him with a flat expression. Jack gave it right back.

Valen sneered at him silently for a moment, and then, with an enormously dramatic sigh, dragged herself out of her chair, circled the table, and sat next to him. Jack scowled suspiciously.

"Liberty said we were supposed to make you feel welcome," Valen explained. She gestured at herself. "So, this is me making you feel welcome. *Do* you feel welcome?" Her eyes sparkled mischievously.

Jack didn't know what gave this girl such pleasure in needling him.

Valen had been less derisive since their contest in The Crypt and her tone had become less contemptuous. But it had been replaced by wariness. Even when she mockingly called him "Ironheart" it now sounded more like guarded prodding than outright scorn.

"Well, Ironheart?"

Jack grunted noncommittally.

"Are you enjoying yourself?"

Jack nodded, genuinely surprised. "Yes."

"Except now that I'm here talking to you?"

"Yes."

"Tell me, Ironheart," Valen continued. Her face was a mask of innocence. "Do you practice your one word sentences in a mirror?"

"No."

"How about your vague grunts? Because your grunts are pretty spectacular."

Jack grunted and shrugged his shoulders brusquely.

"See?" She said, clapping her hands in applause. "You're the *best* at those!"

He downed the remainder of his drink in irritation.

Liberty was there immediately, handing him another cup. Jack accepted it with surprise, unsure where she'd come from. He watched her glide over to Justice and Champion, where she began chatting with them.

"You like her," Valen whispered slyly.

Jack jerked, turning to look at the irksome girl. He didn't like the grin on her face.

"No, I don't."

"Ha! Got you to say more than one word!" Valen jeered. Then, her voice dropped to a low pitch again. "But you *do* like her. I've seen you looking at her, Ironheart. You like her, and she's a *Primal*."

"*No*," Jack growled. "*I don't.*"

"It's all right," Valen scoffed. "Every male at the base – Primal or not, *married* or not – is bloody in love with her."

Jack didn't answer. He just ignored her. A thought popped into his head. "Why do you care?" He asked slowly. That had almost sounded like envy in her tone. "Are you jealous?"

A slight look of panic flashed across her face. "*What*? No! I–"

"You are!" Jack accused. It felt good to be the one doing the needling for a change. "You're jealous because that poncy lordling likes her or something. No! Because *Hero* does. That's probably it. You've got a big thing going for Hero, and he's always looking at Liberty."

The panic drained from her face, but the look of irritation didn't.

"I would do some dallying with Hero in a heartbeat," she said airily. "*Or* Champion *or* Sentinel *or* even Justice, despite the self-righteousness. I mean, have you seen that Primal physique? Gorgeous. Regardless, Primals don't mix romantically with humans, at least as far as I know. So you'd best quit working on that crush you have going." She sniffed rather forcefully. "And I am *not* jealous of Liberty."

Jack frowned. He'd had her on the ropes for a second. What had he missed?

"Explain something to me, Ironheart." Valen continued after a moment. Jack noticed she was casting sidelong glances at Freedom. "Everyone thinks Freedom is as beautiful as her sister, but no one seems to want her like they do Liberty. Why is that?"

Jack considered for a moment. He stared contemplatively Freedom, who was standing in a secluded corner observing the people around her.

"Because she's...Freedom," Jack said truthfully. He struggled to put it into words. "She's...I don't know, more like a force of nature than a person. Hard. Implacable."

Freedom seemed to sense him looking at her. She turned and met his eyes. Her gaze drilled into him. He resisted the urge to break the deadlock. Then, the edges of her mouth twitched into a small smile, and she motioned for him to join her.

Jack glanced at Valen, who shrugged at him. "You'd best go," she said. "It's best not to keep the boss waiting."

Jack found himself smiling. He turned back to Valen. "That right there," he said. "That's why." He stood and approached the rebel god.

Chapter 28

"The art of manipulation is a subtle affair. It is a game that can be played by those who say the right things, but it is mastered by those who learn when it is best to say nothing at all."

          – Deceit, Imperial Ambassador

The gangster walked towards her. His eyes flickered over her face and body, and then traveled to the sides, as if he suspected some sort of trap.

Freedom regarded him with interest, but was careful to keep her face impassive. He was a short, stocky, muscular man. Freedom was struck yet again by how *solid* he looked. He never appeared to just occupy space; he *owned* it. "Mr. Booker," she greeted formally as the man stepped up beside her. She noted the stiffness in his thick, powerful shoulders. Tense as a stretched wire. He nodded in greeting. "You've been with us for some time now," she said. "What do you think of our operation?"

He was silent for a long time, frowning into his drink. Freedom watched him closely in an attempt to read his expressions.

"It's smaller than I imagined," the gangster finally growled. "I wasn't expecting the Independent Army of Liberty to be an actual *army*, but I expected a larger force than a few strike teams."

Freedom nodded in understanding. It was a fair assessment. "We have only a small standing force, true," she admitted, "but there are many that can be called to fight if the time is ever right for full-blown rebellion."

Booker raised a questioning eyebrow. "Not here there isn't. You've got maybe a few hundred, counting women, children, cooks, and other non-combatants."

"That's because the bulk of our supporters do not live here," Freedom explained. "Only those in hiding from the empire or essential to our military operations. The vast majority are spread throughout the cities and the countryside living everyday lives. They have no idea where this base is, or even that it exists." She smiled, but not with mirth. "And who is to say women and cooks are not combatants? When what is good and right in this world is threatened, everyone should be willing to fight for what they believe."

"Not again, Freedom," Liberty broke in chidingly as she passed by. "Don't you ever put thoughts of the war to rest?"

"Not until this empire is in ashes," Freedom growled. She immediately grimaced at her brusque words. Liberty was just trying to help. She was always trying to help.

"Just remember this is a party," Liberty laughed, disregarding her tone. She pitched her voice low and said softly. "Try to relax, sister. It will do you good." Liberty squeezed her shoulder gently, smiled at Booker, and moved to leave.

Freedom kept a small smile affixed on her face until Liberty turned away. Then, she allowed it drop. Some burdens could never be put aside.

The gangster was regarding her with an unreadable expression. Freedom didn't like it when she couldn't tell what someone was thinking.

"What is it that drives you?" he asked suddenly. "Power? Revenge? Whatever it is, it is clearly…potent."

Freedom hid her surprise. She hadn't expected him to initiate further conversation, let alone anything so personal. She considered him for a moment and wondered, not for the first time, what was lying behind those dark eyes. That impenetrable mask. "Follow me," she commanded simply. She set her drink on the table and strode for the door, not looking back to see if he complied.

***

Freedom looked out over the city.

Night had fallen on Victorian, and the lights of the metropolis twinkled like thousands of fallen stars. Freedom stood at the apex of the cathedral bell tower. It was a still night. A whisper of a breeze could hardly be felt, even at this height.

The gangster stood beside her. His face was impassive, but he stood a careful distance from the edge. She thought she could detect a hint of uneasiness in his posture. He'd grown increasingly wary as she led him from the catacombs. Perhaps he thought she'd brought him all the way here just to throw him over the edge.

That was exactly what she was going to do.

"Beautiful," Freedom whispered. "Isn't it?"

Booker's only verbal response was a grunt, but he nodded in agreement.

"At night, and at this height, it's easy to either miss or ignore the squalor and poverty of The Narrows and focus on the beautiful towers," Freedom said as she swept an arm out at the city skyline beyond. "Or watch the airships as they glide out from the docks."

Booker was silent, but a faraway look was in his brooding eyes.

"You asked what drove me," Freedom said. "I can put it into words if you wish, but it is difficult and ineffective when compared to the dreams that burn like a fire in my chest. Instead," she stepped to the edge and held out a hand to him, "let me show you."

The gangsters eyes widened as he understood, and Freedom let her wings unfurl, consciously dimming them so that their radiance would not draw unwanted attention. Booker's mouth was set in a hard line. "What's the matter?" she prodded, though she knew what held him back. "You've flown with Justice. We are not intent on escape, and this flight will not be the harried affair you experienced before." She did not address the real issue.

It was not fear that held him back. At least, not fear of the height or the sky or the fall.

It was a matter of trust.

She did not urge or attempt to persuade him. She simply held out her hand. This was a struggle he had to resolve on his own.

They stood in the darkness for a long time. Booker's eyes were windows behind iron shutters, blocking everything within. Then, slowly, he stepped forward. She could see his fear in the way he moved. His meager faith was like that of a blind man on a stranger's arm. She urged him forward in her thoughts. In a life of conflict, this was likely the greatest battle he'd ever waged. The greatest struggle was to let go.

To trust another.

His fingers fell hesitantly into her hand.

Freedom pulled him into her grasp and leapt from the tower. He had made his decision; she was determined not to let him back out. They plummeted toward the ground at incredible speed. To his credit, the gangster did not scream. Freedom opened her wings and curved upwards, letting their momentum take them higher and higher, until they were far above even the bell tower. She settled into an easy glide. Booker hung solidly in her arms, a stone as firm and

184

unyielding in the air as he was on the ground. He was quiet, and Freedom held her peace as well. He did not need to hear anything she would say. She knew, somehow, that silence was the answer.

Freedom went into another small dive, picking up speed before shooting skyward again. She climbed higher, pushing toward the silver moon in the distance. At the apex of her ascent, she drifted for a moment, allowing them to hang thousands of feet above all they knew. Then, she tucked her wings and plunged back toward the city.

The wind screamed in her ears. Booker's thick muscles were tense beneath her grip, but he did not struggle in panic. The cobblestone streets grew in her vision. At this speed they would create a small crater at impact. A yell burst loose from both her lips and her passenger's, born of sheer adrenaline.

Freedom snapped open her wings at the last moment, slowing their descent and pulling them out of the dive. She skimmed the streets, recovering a few feet from the cobblestones. She pulled up further, still flying at blurring speeds, and weaved precariously back and forth through Victorian's chimneys. One of the city's highest towers loomed ahead, and she pulled away from the thoroughfares of the Diamond District, circling the high spire to its top before landing lightly on its sloping summit.

Booker's breathing was as fast as her own, but he didn't say anything. After a brief rest, Freedom spread her wings again, this time settling into a drifting glide over the city.

They coasted this way for several minutes before he finally spoke. When he did, he was characteristically to the point.

"Your answer?"

Freedom smiled. He had finally initiated an exchange. He was nearly hers, now.

"Look below you, Mr. Booker." Freedom said. "What do you see?"

The gangster was silent for a moment. He knew it was a loaded question. "Victorian."

"Victorian," she agreed. "Capital city of the Grounded Realm, the abode of Myrmidons. A city of culture to some. A pit of poverty to others. The industrial capital of the world, a center of criminal activity, a fashionable destination for balls and parties to the aristocracy, and a garbage heap to be scrounged over to the rest. It is the beating heart of this Realm. None of this matters to me."

"Why?"

"Because it is a city in chains," Freedom replied. "A city enslaved to my people for generations. All these things that Victorian is, they are just symptoms. Results inevitable because your people are dominated by mine."

Freedom angled around the tops of the towers, gliding so close that her passenger was able to stretch out a hand a brush the stone with his fingers. He seemed to be enjoying himself.

"My people live lives of irresponsible frivolity and waste, as do the sycophantic aristocrats who feed off our society. All of it is made possible by the heavy burden placed on the Myrmidons. You are told when to work, how much, and what that work will be. Then, you are sent home to wretched hovels. Those who resist such a life are brutally reminded of what they are: inferior beings. The rest accept it as the way things have always been and always will be. They are told by the Illuminati and the government that it is divine right that keeps them in subjugation. Primals are authority. We are divine.

"But it is not the poverty or the religion I detest. It is the lack of choice. Poverty is acceptable to me if chosen by lack of motivation or laziness. Worship of false divinities is not my concern if chosen freely. But freedom…with true freedom a man can drag himself from the depths of poverty if he chooses. He can decide to search for enlightenment and a true god. He can become the man he desires, not the one he is told he will be."

Freedom fell silent, and they drifted on gentle wind currents, peering at the tiny structures below. The air was cool. She hardly noticed the chill, but she was glad Booker had worn his coat. The ears poking from beneath his curly hair were red from the brisk autumn air.

"Why do you care?" Booker asked after a time. "Your people have these things."

"I *am* Freedom," she replied as honestly as she knew how. "I am the avatar of free will. From the most powerful Primal to the weakest child, the richest lord to the most pathetic beggar, and from the most charismatic leader to the lowliest follower, I would have freedom for all. I would see them given the power to choose their own path, to become who they wish to be, for good or ill. And they will each be judged as they, alone, deserve. Not as their father deserved, not as

186

their ancestors deserved, not as their profession or station or race deserves."

"And why should I care about your goals?" the gangster asked bluntly. "You profess fine sentiments, but that is why I am up here, now, with you. Is it not? You want me to follow you, to believe in these ideals as you do."

And so, he'd reached the heart of the matter.

"Every being should believe in freedom," she said softly.

"That's not an answer," the gangster's voice was brusque. "You want me to believe in these things. To be willing to fight and die for them. Why should I?"

"You've been willing to fight and die before," Freedom pointed out. "And for what? Money? Power?"

"Survival." the gangster growled, his voice harsh.

"Ah, yes," she smiled. "But whose?"

There was a long silence. All Freedom heard was the wind whistling past her ears. "You have acquired quite a reputation, Mr. Booker," she said carefully. Her passenger became abnormally rigid beneath her hands. "You may be the only Myrmidon alive to challenge a Primal and live to tell the tale." His silence could have frozen water. It was frigid and potent. "That's who you are to most people, isn't it? Your reputation is built upon that truth. Many Victorians would say it defines you. The Myrmidon who faced a Primal and survived."

Booker's voice was strained with pain and anger when he finally managed to utter a sound. "Stop."

"But you don't care about that, do you?" Freedom pressed on. "The feat is meaningless. It's a trophy unwanted and unimportant compared to the true defining moment of your life. The moment just before your rise to infamy."

"Please, don't..."

"The murder of your brother at the hands of a Primal," she finished softly.

"*Stop.*"

The raw emotion in Booker's voice was so alien that it fell like a cannon blast on Freedom's ears. She complied respectfully and carried him on their moonlit flight in utter silence. Blackgate Cathedral loomed in the distance before she spoke again.

"You can protect that boy in the medical ward all you want, but someday you will have to let go. Safety is a wonderful thing, Mr. Booker, but it's meaningless without freedom. The greatest thing you can do for anyone is to let them be free. The first, and hardest, step to protecting someone is to let them make their own choices. In this world, the Empire's world, that is not possible." Freedom alighted on the bell tower's surface. Booker pushed out of her grip, and she let him leave her grasp. He took two hesitant steps and rested his hand on the tower's cool stones, as if he needed their support to stand.

"We fight to bring down this society of slavery," Freedom declared ardently. "We fight to bring justice to those who are untouchable. There *will* be consequences again." She could no more contain her fervor than she could control a storm. "All these things can be accomplished by ending this Primal oppression. *That* is what drives me, Mr. Booker: the hope that all this will come to pass. Hope is a powerful force." She stepped forward. Intensity infused her every word. "It is a long road, and we are weak where the enemy is strong. But all of us, together, can achieve the impossible. Join us. Join us and fight for Dasher. Fight for your brother. Fight for the thousands of others like them in this Realm."

The gangster slowly began to descend the stairs, head bowed, back bent. He never looked back at her. "We can liberate humanity, Mr. Booker," Freedom called. "We can save them."

There was no reply.

***

It was nearly dawn when the knock came at the door.

A thrill traveled up Freedom's spine, and she bolted from her perch on the edge of the bed.

She had been expecting this. She had been hopeful, but she had also been uncertain.

Freedom composed herself, smoothing her rumpled clothes. She strode to the door, took a deep breath, and opened it wide.

Jack Booker stood before her. He had never looked more imposing. Despite his lack of height, the gangster seemed to loom in the doorway. The dimmed gas lamps outside glowed around his daunting outline, but shrouded his face in shadow. His brows were

188

drawn down and his brooding eyes flashed. He was quiet, but stared at her with an intensity that was overwhelming.

"I will fight." His voice was deep and calm, but strangely detached, as if holding back great emotion.

Freedom watched him impassively. Then, she nodded her head in acceptance. Inside, a sense of satisfaction swept through her, but she said nothing. He didn't need any confirmation from her. He had made his simple statement, and it was enough.

Booker's eyes met hers. Without another word, he turned and walked away. He was once again nothing more than a man, but now he was one of *her* men.

Sentinel appeared beside her in the doorway a few moments later, ever vigilant in his charge to keep watch. Freedom ignored him for a moment. She watched the young man until he left her sight.

"He was in the medical wing all night," Sentinel said finally. "Not sleeping. Not pacing. Not doing anything. Just sitting at the boy's bedside and watching him while he slept."

She nodded, unsurprised.

"Freedom," Sentinel asked. "What just happened?"

She allowed herself a rare smile. "We gained a new soldier for the war."

Chapter 29

"I'm going to tell you a secret that I've never told anyone before: I love shooting things."

— 'Red' Ragen, Infamous Victorian Mob Boss

"I can't *believe* Freedom is taking you."

Jack tried very, very hard not to shout. It was extremely difficult.

It had been two weeks since Jack had told Freedom he would fight for her cause, but he *still* couldn't believe he was a member of the steamblown IAL.

He'd spent most of his days in a kind of basic training, learning small group tactics that appeared remarkably similar to the jobs in Fist's gang. Strike teams were made up of members with varying responsibilities. Some secured a perimeter. Some executed the objective, whether that was an ambush, a snatch and grab, or raid. Normally the Primals in each group filled this role. It was all a bit more complicated than his work with the gang – what with the addition of snipers for fire support, Primal juggernauts to take the majority of the risks, and the ability of flight for quick escapes – but the concepts were the same.

Tomorrow an important operation was taking place. Apparently, Freedom was intent on capturing a high-ranking Primal. It sounded bloody insane to Jack.

Surprisingly, Freedom wanted Jack to be with the strike team, despite his inexperience with their operations. It seemed risky to take along an untested recruit on such a significant mission, but he didn't question the Primal leader on the issue. If he was going to fight for the IAL, then that's what he should do. He hadn't joined to sit around on his hands.

Now, he was walking with Valen to meet Rook in the armory. It was time for him to be issued his weapons.

"I mean, I can't believe she let you join in the first place, but taking you on *this* job?" Valen's voice was incredulous. "This is important!"

"Aren't all the assignments important?"

"Well, yes," she admitted. "But this is about finding the Instrument. Nothing is more vital to the war effort."

"What is this instrument?" Jack asked. He'd heard bits and pieces in his time here, but nothing anyone said seemed to clear up what it was or why it was important.

"The empire is too large to be defeated through traditional means," Valen stated matter-of-factly. "We could fight a guerrilla war forever and it would do little more than irritate the emperors. They have too many Primals and resources, and the whole system is too firmly entrenched. It's the foundation of every facet of both human and Primal society."

Jack glanced at her in confusion. "What does that have to do with an instrument?"

"Apparently, it's the key to bringing down the empire," Valen shrugged. "Centuries ago there was a Primal called Omen. She was one of the oldest and most revered of the Primal hierarchy. Just days before her passing, Omen made a final foretelling that predicted a challenge to the Primal Empire in the form of a great war. This war, it was said, would be decided by Fate's Instrument." Valen shook her head. "We only know the bits of the prophecy that Freedom has told us. It's all very vague. Only a few Primals, including Freedom, witnessed the foretelling. But most of them are dead now, and Freedom was very young."

Jack's head whirled. Primals fighting for the good of others, portal mirrors, and now ancient prophecies. What other mysteries would he discover that he never dreamed existed?

"But what *is* it?"

Valen shook her head. "Nobody knows. Maybe Freedom does. I think it's some kind of weapon."

Jack thought for a moment. "And capturing this Primal will help how?"

"Greed is the Minister of the Empire's treasury," Valen answered, though she rolled her eyes. She appeared to be growing tired of questions. "Freedom believes that with his knowledge of the allocation of the empire's funds she can pinpoint where Tyranny has hidden the Instrument."

"She thinks the empire has the Instrument?"

Valen nodded. "With the empire's resources, how could they not? Tyranny has been obsessed with finding the Instrument, just

191

like Freedom. They've been on, like, the most competitive treasure hunt of all time for decades."

"Why does she think Tyranny has it, then? Wouldn't the rebellion have already been defeated if he had?"

Valen sighed with exasperation. "Most of the time I can't get you to say anything. Now, I can't get you to shut up."

Jack scowled. "I like to be prepared. If I'm going to be prepared, I need to know what's going on."

"I don't know if you've noticed," Valen said, "but this isn't exactly the "great war" mentioned in the prophecy. The empire isn't threatened by us at all. The only reason they bother with Freedom or Chaos is because Tyranny and Order can't stand for their authority to be challenged. Freedom thinks the empire is virtually invulnerable *because* they have the Instrument, and it might be keeping the rebellion contained somehow. Once the Instrument is out of the empire's hands she thinks the human population will rise up, and civil war will erupt across the Realms on a massive scale."

Jack was quiet for a long time, stewing over what she'd said. "It's too mystical for me." He shook his head. "I don't know anything about prophecies and magic, but shouldn't we be trying to figure out a plan to topple the empire instead of chasing fantasies?"

"Do you have any ideas to accomplish that, Ironheart?" Valen demanded. "I *told* you. The empire is too–"

"What about assassinating the emperors?" Jack suggested.

Valen scoffed at him. "Impossible. We've considered this stuff, Ironheart. Besides, who's going to take down Tyranny? He's powerful enough to take on any of our Primals, even Justice or Freedom. And there's nowhere that we could pin him down long enough to kill him without legions of Primals and troopers descending on us within moments."

"But–"

"How do we know we can trust you?" Valen barreled right over his next question. Obviously she had finished with the topic, and was ready to return to her favorite pastime of galling him. "How do we know you won't go running to the empire as soon as you step out of this base?"

"Weren't you the one lecturing me about trust a few weeks ago?" Jack growled.

"Yeah, but I was saying you should trust *us*. Not necessarily that we should trust you." Valen sniffed.

"That's hypocritical."

"No, it's not! I mean, *we* are fighting for the freedom of humanity. You...well, you're a–"

"A criminal," Jack finished for her bluntly. "That's what you were going to say. Just say it."

At least she had the grace to look embarrassed. "No! I–"

"You're all in open rebellion to the empire," Jack pointed out. "That's treason. If that doesn't count as being a criminal, I don't know what does."

"*We* are in open rebellion to the empire." She glared at him.

"Then I guess we're all criminals together."

"It's not the same."

"I've still got little enough reason to trust all of you," Jack said. "But I've accepted your cause. I've agreed to fight. What else do you want from me, girl?"

They'd arrived at the armory, and Valen reached out a hand to swing open the door. "I want you to be less aggravating," she snapped.

"Well, that makes two of us," Jack muttered under his breath.

"What did you say, Ironheart?"

"Nothing. Just talking to myself. Being aggravating."

Jack stepped into his own personal fantasy land.

There were guns *everywhere*. Big guns, little guns, tiny guns, monster-sized guns. They hung on racks, sat in boxes, and rested on tables for display. Jack didn't know where to turn first. For a moment he almost leapt up and down and clapped his hands. Valen's presence to his immediate left kept this impulse in check.

"This...this is–"

"Like a steamblown candy shop," Valen finished in agreement, favoring him with an uncharacteristic grin. "This just might be my favorite place in the world."

He tore his eyes away from the beauties around him to look at her quizzically. "A candy shop?"

"Um, sure," Valen said. She was looking at him strangely.

"They *have* those? That's a real thing?"

Valen just shook her head and waved him away. "Never mind. Go knock yourself out, Ironheart."

Jack turned to do so with gusto, but Rook appeared a moment later from behind a row of shelves. A huge grin split his blunt, craggy face.

"Jack Booker," he said by way of greeting. "Boy, have I got some treats for you." He gestured at the room at large. "What do you think?"

"Rook organizes and maintains the armory here," Valen explained.

"Valkyrie," Rook acknowledged. "Come by to sight in your scope? You said it was a bit off since the last mission."

"Just showing the steaming new guy around," Valen shrugged. "But I do need that done before we head out."

"Bring your Sharps down after the briefing this evening and we'll make sure it's properly calibrated.

"Now," Rook said gleefully, clapping Jack on the shoulder. "What'll it be for the gangster turned freedom fighter?

Jack was a bit overwhelmed with the selection. "What do you have?"

"You'll not be disappointed with your options," Rook chuckled. "Seeing as the empire's depots supply us with most of our weapons, it's a good rule of thumb that if the empire stocks it, we've got it. Any firearm that's standard issue for the Imperial Marines, Troopers, Enforcers – even the elite Fusiliers, Grenadiers, Rocketeers, or Celestial Guard – can be found here." ·

There were so many choices. Jack had no idea where to start his search. So, he fell back on what was familiar.

"You wouldn't happen to have any coach shotguns?"

"Ah, the street howitzer," Rook laughed gruffly. "I should have known. You mobsters like your violence gritty, up-close, and personal. Good man." He steered Jack down one of the aisles. Valen followed behind.

"Now," Rook raised a finger for emphasis, "I've got loads of shotguns, and coaches are solid, but you shouldn't be settling for the same old thing." He continued talking while he pulled one of the cases from the wall. He flipped open the top like a vendor at a fair, adding a touch of a flourish to every motion.

"Feast your eyes on the shotgun pistol, commonly known as the Ranger," Rook urged. He pulled one of the two identical weapons from the case. "Double-barreled, single-handed, break-over shotguns

– standard issue to Rocketeer Enforcers for riot control and close-quarters combat. They use these so they can keep one hand free to steer their jetpacks, or, if in a tight spot, dualwield for maximum close-range firepower. One can be holstered on each hip."

Jack took the proffered weapon from Rook with glee. The Ranger was like a miniature version of his coach, but missing the stock and with an even shorter, sawed-off barrel. The whole weapon was a foot in length from tip to tip, and broke open past the grip to load the shells.

"What's the range on these?" Jack asked doubtfully.

"You lose a little distance and power compared to the coach," Rook admitted. "These are tight-quarters weapons, but you get a lovely area effect from the shortened barrels. You can fill an entire hallway with buckshot. At fifteen paces, the spread is ten paces across and just as high. Much further than that and Rangers become ineffective."

"Not bad," Jack grunted. "It would be perfect for dealing with groups of enforcers at short range. A whole squad could be eliminated with a well-placed shot." Jack popped open the breech and eyed the barrel slots. "Shells?"

"12-Gauge," Rook answered. He grinned. "Maximum power while still maintaining control. 8-Gauge would probably break your wrist if you fired single-handed."

Jack nodded to himself, pleased. "I'll take them."

Valen snorted. "*Please.*"

Jack turned. "What?"

"What are you going to do if someone is beyond fifteen paces?" she sniffed. "Or if you need to make a precision shot?"

"That's what other guns are for," Jack smirked.

"Well said!" Rook laughed. He gave Valen a sardonic look of disappointment. "Steaming snipers, eh, Booker?"

"You've never complained about my fire support on assignment!" Valen scowled at the grizzled veteran.

"Nor will I," Rook said. "*On assignment.* But off duty, I will continue to be saddened by your lack of appreciation for up-close, personal carnage."

Valen folded her arms with disgust. "So barbaric."

Rook laughed harshly, but he didn't appear offended.

"As much as I hate to say it," Jack admitted. "She has a point. What's good for some decent range around here?"

Rook looked thoughtful for a moment, and then snapped a finger. "I've got just the thing."

The grizzled soldier took them around a few shelves to an aisle lined with rifles. Jack gave him a hopeful look.

"Lee-Metford?"

"Nah," Rook said absently. "Good weapon, but that's for the common troops. We train the majority of our people here with them because they're reliable and in no short supply. But those of us on the strike teams get the best of the best." He stopped at a row of four long, bolt-action rifles.

"These beauties just went into production a year or two ago. They haven't caught on yet with Imperial troops, but I can already tell these are going to make an impact in a big way." He gestured proudly. "Meet the Lee-Enfield bolt-action rifle, your new best friend. It's like the Lee-Metford, but more robust, taking a ten-round detachable box magazine of .303 caliber ammunition. It comes fitted with a fixed post front sight and a sliding rear sight."

Rook considered the four rifles for a moment, then lifted one down that was shorter than the other three.

"At the end of the day you're still a short range fighter, so the carbine will serve you better. Its barrel is shortened by four inches, allowing for better maneuverability, but this still leaves you with a firearm with effective range. The rifle version is pretty reliable up to 500 meters, but you'll have to shorten your expectations with the carbine. Normally, I'd say a good rifleman could fire twenty accurate rounds per minute, but I've seen you shoot. I bet you could lay a solid thirty per minute down while providing covering fire." He grinned contemptuously at Valen over Jack's shoulder. "Satisfied?"

She shrugged, as if she couldn't bother to be too interested. "It'll do. At least he won't be combat-ineffective past rock-throwing distance."

Jack was careful to keep his face empty. He knew it would bother her more. "This weapon is far more versatile than a Sharps," he pointed out innocently. He ran his hands over the Lee-Enfield to get a better feel for it. "What happens if someone gets in close to your position?"

196

She snorted with disbelief at his gall, but impersonated his earlier statement in a high-pitched, mocking tone. *"That's what other guns are for."*

Jack chuckled before turning back to Rook

I'm going to need a handgun as a backup," he stated. "I always used a Webley Bull Dog pocket revolver with the gang – incredibly easy to conceal. But I assume that won't be as much of an issue here?"

"Right you are," Rook agreed. He moved down the aisle. "That's not to say concealment is never needed, but usually when strike teams move we already have enough firepower to make a blind man suspicious of our intentions. An extra handgun is just what you need."

"Suggestions?"

"I've got a few models in mind," Rook said. "It's mostly a matter of what you prefer." He stopped at a bench arrayed with every pistol imaginable, from miniature derringers to long barreled pistols unlike anything Jack had seen before.

"What are these, here?" Jack pointed curiously at the strange, long revolvers.

"Designs from out in the West past Jackson," Rook said. "The Empire orders some of them for special use." He pointed at two models side by side, nearly identical but for the length. "Here, you've got the Colt Dragoon and the Baby Dragoon, and this," he pointed further along to an even longer-barreled weapon, "is the Navy Colt."

"I've never seen anything like those before," Jack said doubtfully.

"Say what you will about those crazies out west," Rook replied. "They make good handguns, and the empire has a tough time enforcing their ban on firearms out there. These Colt and Remington models aren't very common in Victorian, but beyond Jackson you can't take two steps without having one shoved in your face."

"They're awfully...large," Jack shook his head, eyeing the smallest of the group, the "Baby" Dragoon. There was nothing baby-sized about it. "Unwieldy."

"But steaming powerful," Rook held up a finger. "If you'd rather go with something more familiar, however, you should take the Webley Mark IV. It's tough and reliable, with a six-shot cylinder

197

firing .455 caliber bullets. It's the same weapon the enforcers have been putting to use for years."

"That's what I'll do," Jack confirmed.

Rook grinned and handed him a Webley, along with several boxes of ammunition. "The Empire feels the same way you do. I keep expecting them to make the switch to the new Colt when it's released, but so far they've seemed loath to trust anything but Webleys and Enfields."

Jack turned to Valen, who'd been listening with interest. "What do you use to back up your Sharps?"

She nodded at the pistol in his hand. "Webley Mark IV. That's what all of us use, even Rook. They're good guns, and they're almost universal in Victorian."

Jack nodded, satisfied. He turned back to Rook.

Then, something large beneath a set of white sheets caught his eye.

"What's that?"

Rook turned to see where he was pointing. When he turned back, there was a delighted glimmer in his eye.

"Oh, Booker, you wouldn't be interested in that!"

Rook led the way and tore the sheet off with a flair of surprising showmanship. Jack wasn't sure what to make of the contraption beneath.

"Meet my lover," Rook declared affectionately, stroking what Jack assumed was the barrel with a tender hand. The action was slightly disturbing. "The Gatling Gun. It was invented a year ago in Jackson. The empire's military forces just received their first shipment a few months ago. We think they're going to start outfitting their airships with these. They'll probably attach them along the rails of the forecastle, quarterdeck, and on the stern."

Jack considered the machine with confusion. It was massive; likely several hundred pounds, with what looked like ten barrels arrayed in a circular pattern around a solid metal base. A strange crank rested beside the loading ports. He doubted it could be moved without some sort of cart.

"Uh, what does it do?"

"What does it do?" Rook scoffed. "Hands out death faster than a legion of angry Primals, Booker." He pointed toward the back of the contraption. "Magazines of forty rounds each are inserted here." He stepped up beside the crank and began to turn it. The barrels started moving in a clockwise motion. "Then you run this crank, and it spits out bullets from each consecutive barrel as it turns." He patted the Gatling proudly. "Hundreds of rounds a minute. You could take on an army by yourself."

Jack cocked his head sideways.

"So…when do we get to use it?"

Rook roared with laughter. "Soon, Booker. If I get my way."

***

Rook had set him up well. By the time he left the armory, Jack was loaded down with two single-handed shotguns, a Lee-Enfield Carbine, Webley Mark IV, a small, single-shot Derringer, several grenades, and ammunition pertaining to each. After dropping most of the weapons off in his room, Jack had loaded the Webley and stuck it in the back of his waistband before heading to the briefing with Valen. She had raised her eyebrows but not said anything, for which he was relieved. It had been far too long since he'd been armed. For the first time in weeks, he no longer felt like he was walking around with one boot missing.

"Valen," Jack asked as they ascended the stairs to the command center. "What was the Derringer for?" It had puzzled him when Rook had added it to the pile. It had *one shot*, after all, with a low-powered cartridge. What use could it possibly be?"

"You slip it in the top of your boot for emergencies," Valen said, not meeting his eyes. "Every operative on the strike teams carries one."

"But–"

"Look, Ironheart," Valen snapped irritably. "I know it doesn't seem worth much. But, well, it's not exactly for the type of emergency you're thinking. It's for more…desperate eventualities."

"*What?*"

"Trust me; you don't want to be taken alive by the empire for questioning," Valen said grimly. "It's your responsibility as much as saving yourself from torture. We can't have anyone revealing the location of this base or any of our other secrets, like the location of the portal mirrors. Besides," she shuddered visibly. "It's better to be

199

dead than go through Imperial interrogation. I'm sure you've heard the stories. Brutality doesn't have a...gentle reputation."

Right. Suicide.

"Oh," Valen seemed to think of something as they reached the landing. "And be careful with those grenades. They're faulty little bastards. They're as likely to just sit there forever or blow up in your face as go off when you need them to."

"I know," Jack said wistfully. "We used them in the gangs. They never worked quite as well as I'd have liked."

Valen grunted in agreement as they entered the command center.

Everyone else was already there, situated at various places around the large oaken table. Jack didn't think they were late, however; the others were just chatting together in groups. The meeting was made up of the members that Jack was beginning to recognize as the leaders, including the new arrival, Tempest. Freedom, Sentinel, Hero, Champion, and Justice sat with her on the far side of the table. Rook, Bannen, Valen, Devalere, and himself seemed to be the human participants, though he noted that Devalere sat apart from the others. Perhaps he wasn't involved with the strike teams. Morthal was also present, which Jack found curious provided his lack of involvement in fieldwork. Apparently, many of the room's occupants had not been informed of his inclusion in the operation, and they looked surprised at his attendance. Justice was scowling thunderously.

Jack ignored him, focusing instead on the large three-dimensional model of a city spread across the tabletop. He noted the incredible detail put into the tall spires and massive domes. A map of the Celestial City.

Freedom stood up from her seat just as Jack was settling into his. Her voice called everyone to order.

"You all know why we're here," Freedom's voice cut through the air like frozen crystal, icy and clear. "Greed, Order and Tyranny's Minister of the Treasury, may be the key to finding the Instrument of Fate. From the intelligence we've received from both Courage and Charm, this shouldn't be an incredibly risky operation. However, given the vital nature of our success in securing our objective, it is imperative that everyone treat this mission with the gravity it deserves." She stared around silently for a moment with hard eyes. "We only get one shot at this. This *shouldn't* be exceptionally difficult. The empire has no reason to suspect an offensive of this nature. They're still expecting us to hit military targets: weapons depots, high-ranking Primal enforcers or military officers, airship sabotage. But as soon as we make our intentions known, they will quickly allocate troops and resources to block us where we've hit. *We have one chance.*"

Jack nodded with the rest. He wondered if they were suddenly as nervous as he was. Freedom seemed satisfied, and she turned to look at Devalere.

The young aristocrat picked up on her queue immediately. "The intel from both Charm and Courage indicates the same thing." The young lord seemed perfectly comfortable with all eyes on him, and Jack realized the man's role here was likely operations, as well as Primal and aristocratic intelligence. His styled hair and straight-backed bearing only added to the sense of poise and competence he exuded while fulfilling his task. "Greed is most vulnerable when returning home from the Treasury building in the Imperial District of the Celestial City. He has a five-kilometer flight back to his mansion, and, more importantly, he takes the same route every day. The entire flight takes little more than ten minutes, but that's when he's feeling leisurely. This operation must be time efficient, especially considering how close we'll be operating to the Imperial District. Primal enforcers could arrive within minutes."

"Why can't we hit his mansion at night?" Rook asked gruffly. "We'll have a slower response time by enforcement, a greater distance from the Imperial District, and it won't be *the middle of the steamblown day*. Snatching Greed as he flies home will be bloody difficult if there are other Primals around."

"For one," Devalere raised a finger, "we've struck inside the city enough times that they know we have a secure way into the city. It's almost certain that the emperors suspect we possess a pair of mirrors. This has caused most Primals to increase their private security." Devalere raised a second finger, as if checking off a mental checklist. He'd clearly been prepared for this question. "Two, Greed is both fabulously wealthy and extremely paranoid. You wouldn't believe the security he has in place at his mansion to protect it. Three, the portal mirror is an even greater distance from his mansion than it is from the ambush location en route. Four–"

"Fine," Rook cut him off, chuckling. "I get it. A night strike on the mansion is a bad idea."

Jack spoke up hesitantly. "Rook raises a good point, though." He almost ducked his head as all eyes turned on him. "Won't there be Primals all over the city?"

"The Celestial City is largely vacant, Jack," Hero explained from across the table. "It's large enough to house hundreds of thousands Primals, but only ten thousand or so exist."

Jack was stunned. The city had seemed largely uninhabited when he'd been there, but he hadn't been in a position to think much about the emptiness. It was strange to think about so much wasted space in such a beautiful place.

"The Primals pick the largest, grandest, plushest mansions for themselves," Hero was continuing with his explanation. "Generally everyone picks a dwelling far from other inhabited structures, since it doesn't take long for a Primal to fly anywhere in the city." He smiled with amusement. "And, of course, they must have plenty of room to house their servants." He chuckled. "Ironic, isn't it? The Celestial Realm is "reserved" only for Primals, but in reality, with all the servants, troopers, and enforcers stationed there, its population is predominantly Myrmidon."

"Besides," Devalere pointed out, bringing the discussion back to the objective. "Greed often works longer than the majority of the Imperial Primals. We can expect him to fly home virtually alone."

Champion held up a hand at that, stopping him. "Virtually?"

Freedom rounded the table, unfolding a collapsible rod. She pointed to several buildings on the Celestial City model. "As Devalere stated earlier, Greed is extraordinarily paranoid, and that extends to his person." Her rod pointed to the highest towers in the city's center. "When he leaves the Imperial District, he'll be under the watchful eye of the district's security. Not until he reaches this point along his route," she indicated a building several kilometers from the city's center, "does he definitively go beyond their sight. Of course, that's where his own security picks up the slack." She traced a line of buildings, each separated by a few blocks. "He has pairs of rocketeer bodyguards set up at incremental stations along his route." She lowered her rod. "Luckily, they're all private security, so no Primals."

"Why?" Jack asked quizzically.

"Primals can take anything they want," Justice answered him brusquely. "So we have no use for money as a society. Working for the empire is considered a civic duty. It is done as the emperor's command, but working for any monetary reason is unnecessary."

"This is where we strike." Freedom indicated a set of three tall spires that formed a triangular zone in between. "It's close to midway between his mansion and the Imperial District, giving us the optimal amount of time to capture Greed and extract. Hero, Champion, and Justice will be responsible for quietly incapacitating the sentries stationed here, here, and here," she pointed at each of the three spires in turn. The three Primals nodded mutely. "That will give us a nice area devoid of watching eyes to spring the trap."

Three Primals versus six human bodyguards? Jack thought. *Sounds easy. So far.*

"The rest of the strike team will set up a perimeter in a circle around the target area," Freedom said. "Rook to the northeast, Bannen to the south, and Valen here," she indicated a high tower with a flat-topped roof," to the northwest." She looked straight at Jack. "Mr. Booker will be stationed there with her, as will Sentinel. Tempest will provide support from Bannen's position."

Jack wasn't surprised, but he still felt his stomach drop with disappointment. They were keeping him well out of the fight, it seemed.

"Why so many at Valen's position?" Sentinel asked. "We could spread out more."

"It's the closest point that leads back toward the Imperial District," Freedom said impassively. Her voice was almost too calm. "If we fail to capture Greed quickly, the last place we want him running is the city's center of security."

Sentinel nodded. "That leaves you, ma'am. I suppose you'll be close to the center to spring the trap?"

"Correct," Freedom confirmed. "I'll be at ground-level in the center of the perimeter. When Greed enters, I'll fly up, engage, and incapacitate him. Champion, Justice, Hero – you'll converge in the middle and help me as you are able. Your priority is to block off any escape routes he might take." She glanced over at Sentinel and Tempest. "You two are the reserves here. Both of you are free to observe and act where you are needed."

Freedom looked at everyone in turn. "*Keep him contained*. He's a weak fighter; I can easily incapacitate him if I can get him cornered. Whatever happens, *do not* kill him. It is vital that we take him alive. Does everyone understand?"

"Yes, ma'am," Sentinel answered. Jack nodded along with the rest.

"Good," Freedom said. "Extraction will be here." Jack assumed the building she indicated was the same that held the portal mirror he'd entered before. "Primals will airlift out all Myrmidon members. If for any reason you don't have time to extract, we have a safehouse here." She pointed to a low building a few blocks away." If you can enter the building unseen, there is a furnished area hidden beneath the first story staircase that can be opened by pulling the second rail that supports the banister. Stay put until we can send someone to help you leave the city unseen."

Freedom collapsed her rod, and then cocked her head sideways, looking straight at him. Jack shifted uncomfortably.

"Mr. Booker needs an alias," Freedom said.

Jack was surprised. "Why?"

"We use codenames while in the field to protect the identity of our human members," Sentinel answered. "It also serves to keep the empire guessing our numbers. If all our fighters are referred to by Primal sounding names, it is more difficult for the empire to discern the number of Primals at our disposal."

"He already has an alias," Valen piped up, giving Jack a malicious grin.

"*No*, I don't–" Jack insisted frantically.

"Good," Freedom said, cutting him off. "Ironheart will work fine."

Jack resisted the urge to slam his forehead on the table.

"Dismissed," Freedom said to the room at large. "We move out in two days' time."

A great scraping of chairs went up as everyone rose.

"Oh, and Mr. Booker," Freedom called across the room. "If you are to fully benefit us, I suggest you start training with a jetpack, and quickly. We'll need another strike member able to go airborne if need be." Her eyes seemed to glimmer, and Jack thought he could see the hint of a smile on her lips. It was as if she could sense his excitement at the order. "Morthal and Bannen will be assigned to bring you up to speed with all possible haste. Good luck."

***

"He will betray us as soon as he escapes these confines," Justice warned. The briefing had ended a few minutes before. Only Justice and Sentinel had remained with her. "He is a criminal. He will turn on us for his own profit, and you've given him the perfect chance!"

"I've made my decision," Freedom said firmly. She resisted the urge to rub her temples. She was growing tired of this. "I believe Mr. Booker's skills will prove to be invaluable to us."

"And if they prove to be our undoing?" Justice demanded. "He knows everything, from the location of this base to where our portal mirrors are placed. He even knows the resources and numbers at our disposal! We are offering the empire victory on a silver platter!"

"That is why you are to kill him if you sense the slightest hint of treachery," Freedom said softly. Sentinel's head perked up at that. She'd thought it might get his attention. "If he makes any move that looks even vaguely like an escape attempt, you are to eliminate him." She stared hard at Sentinel. "*Both* of you. Understand?"

Justice nodded, seeming mollified. He left the command center without another word.

"I need you to know that you understand and will carry out the order I just issued, Sentinel," Freedom said.

"He won't run," Sentinel insisted.

"Sentinel–"

The weathered Primal was silent. Then, he sighed heavily and nodded.

Freedom rubbed a hand across her brow.

"I'll be leaving soon. It's almost time."

Sentinel inclined his head in understanding.

"We'll capture Greed as soon as I return," she commanded. She rose from her chair. "Then, we will find the Instrument."

"Yes, ma'am."

Chapter 30

"I foresee that the jetpack will be remembered as the defining military invention of the century. The possibilities for large numbers of highly mobile airborne units in combat are virtually endless, especially in urban warfare."

– Excerpt from an annual report to the Emperors by Victory, Supreme Commander of the Imperial Armed Forces

"This jetpack weighs a ton," Jack noted. He shrugged his shoulders to relieve some pressure.

"You're carrying several liters of water both for steam conversion and cooling purposes," Bannen chuckled. He continued to fiddle with the straps encircling Jack's waist. "That's in addition to the machinery itself."

Bannen was the only human Resistance leader with whom Jack was largely unfamiliar. He was a nondescript man of average height, average build, and, seemingly, average everything else. He didn't appear to be a genius, like Morthal. Jack had heard nothing exceptional about the soft-spoken man's marksmanship skills or combat ability. He was just always there, standing quietly in the background and helping move things along.

"What do you do here?" Jack asked curiously. "Morthal's the doctor and scientist. Rook's the weapons specialist and leader of the human Resistance military forces. Valen is long-range support. Devalere handles intelligence from the Primals and human elite. Other humans are here that don't fill such specific roles, but none of them sit in on councils with Freedom. What do you do?"

Bannen didn't stop tightening the jetpack straps, so all Jack could see was the man's thin brown hair as he started laughing.

"I'm the putty," Bannen's voice answered with amusement. "Have you ever laid brick before?"

"No."

"Well, when you lay brick you have to slather each one with mortar so that your wall is solid. That's what I do here. I fill in the cracks."

Jack nodded, considering the man. "You're dependable."

Bannen chuckled lightly. He seemed to do that a lot.

"If you say so," he shrugged. "I just do whatever I'm told, and I do it as well as I can." He tugged one last time on a strap, testing its tension. "There we go. How does it feel?"

Jack moved his arms, jumped in place, and took a few experimental steps. The jetpack didn't restrict his movement much except to pull across his shoulders and chest. It felt like running around with a bag of rocks strapped to his back.

"A little strange," he admitted.

"You'll get used to the weight," Morthal assured him absently from where he sat at a table beside Sentinel, tinkering with a whirring machine. Even when not giving something his full attention the man's words flew from his mouth at twice the speed of normal dialogue. "Valen, Bannen, Rook – everyone we've trained to use these has become proficient, given time. Mostly learning to compensate for the additional load."

Bannen nodded in agreement. "It's all about balance."

Jack moved tentatively, jogging a few paces back and forth. They had set up in the Crypt for practice, since it was the only place available with the required height. Morthal, Bannen, and Sentinel had cleared away most of the tables, explaining that they didn't want them to get "damaged." That didn't sound promising.

"Now," Bannen said as Jack came to a halt. "The first thing you've got to understand is what a jetpack is for. Right, Doc?"

"Correct."

"Jetpacks don't provide the skills of a Primal," Bannen explained. "They aren't really for sustained airtime. They're for short bursts of flight."

"That's why Freedom carried Valen instead of letting her fly on the day you picked me up," Jack said to Sentinel.

The weathered Primal nodded. "They're useful contraptions, but in a race with a Primal, you'll lose every time. We can fly much faster and significantly further."

"Don't expect to have the agility of a Primal in flight either," Bannen warned. "A Primal's wings are part of their bodies. Their use is instinctual, the same as you use your hands. The jetpack will be difficult to master fully, and once you do it's still a machine, with all the limitations that entails."

"But they're still brilliant," Morthal noted absentmindedly.

"They're still brilliant," Bannen agreed with a laugh. "Sorry, Doc. No offense meant."

"None taken," Morthal said. He stood from the table and walked to Jack's side. "This is what you use to control your flight." He indicated a box about the size of a brick attached to Jack's left shoulder. Tubes that were a thumb-width in diameter connected to the sides of this box, curled under Jack's left arm, and attached to the body of the jetpack itself. What looked to be a small switch protruded from its center.

"What does it do?"

"Regulates flow of built-up pressure in the jetpack caused by steam," Morthal answered delightedly. "By pushing down on the lever in the center of your regulator, you release some of that pressure out of the exhaust ports, causing you to rise into the air. The harder you push, the more pressure is released, and consequently, the higher and faster you fly.

"The lever is also how you steer," Morthal continued, never slowing down. "By pushing the lever in any direction, you allocate more pressure to be released from a particular exhaust port, which allows you to turn, bank, or even rotate sharply."

Jack nodded. He was a bit overwhelmed, but he thought he'd caught the majority of Morthal's lightning explanation.

"The regulator is affixed to your left shoulder so you can tuck in your arm and control the lever with your left hand," Bannen explained. "That leaves your right hand open for use. That's why it's best to carry single-handed weapons when equipped with a jetpack. If you're going to carry a rifle, you're going to need a strap that allows you to fly with your hands free. Valen uses a belt sling that lets her drop her Sharps and rocket away. The rifle hangs in front of her chest during flight." He shrugged. "Cumbersome, but effective."

"Rook and Bannen prefer to have a strap attached to their rifles," Sentinel called from the table. "They sling their rifles over a shoulder during flight and pull out their pistols. It makes flying a little less awkward."

"Come on," Banned urged. He stepped back several paces. "Why don't you give it a try?"

"Remember," Morthal babbled quickly as he stepped away as well. "Start out slow. Push in *very lightly* on the lever. Rise a few feet. Hover for a moment. Drop back to the ground."

Jack clenched his teeth. A mixture of excitement and nerves coursed through his veins. *Stay calm*, he reminded himself. He was about to *fly*.

He pushed down on the lever.

Jack exploded into the air, rising several meters about the Crypt floor at an alarming speed. He immediately released the lever to stop his ascent and plummeted back toward the ground. His hand slammed back on the lever again in a panic, which only served to send him rocketing upward again. He released the lever frantically, and crashed into the dirt.

Jack groaned

Unbridled laughter filled the Crypt. Morthal's quick tittering, Bannen's infectious chuckling, Sentinel's amused gasps – and the snide sniggering of the most irritating person in all the Realms. Jack spat out a bitter mouthful of dust. "There are a few things that bring me great pleasure in life," Valen called. "One of them is watching you flop around in the dirt, Ironheart. I'll be savoring that memory for a while. Can you imagine if I'd have missed it?"

"Don't take it too hard," Bannen was still chuckling as he and Sentinel helped Jack to his feet. "Call it a rite of passage. Everyone does that the first time."

"It was actually quite impressive," Sentinel laughed. "You didn't go veering off some random direction. You stayed vertical."

"Don't listen to Valen," Morthal said amiably. "She nearly broke her nose running into the wall on her first day."

Valen was grinning from a few feet away. "Good times."

Jack found himself smiling as he found his feet. The thought of her smashing into The Crypt wall at high speed brought him no end of joy.

"Why are you smiling like an idiot, Ironheart?"

Jack grunted vaguely.

The next time, he pressed very, *very* lightly on the lever. He kept his hand steady, and he rose into the air. Dampening his elation, he let his hand loosen up, barely putting any pressure on the switch. The jetpack leveled out with a low hum, leaving him hovering a few feet in the air. Morthal, Bannen, and Sentinel were whooping with excitement, and even Valen's lips were twitching upward a bit.

"Well done, Jack!" Morthal called. "A natural! Normally takes hours to gain such control."

Jack felt himself begin to waver dangerously, so he let off the lever and dropped back to floor with a solid *thud*. His smile was so wide that he felt his face might split open.

"I believe that's the first true smile I've seen from our gangster," Sentinel joked. He pushed on Jack's shoulder and nearly knocked him back to the ground. "Looks kind of painful, eh?"

Jack wanted to scowl at him, but his lips wouldn't comply. He could feel his cheeks growing sore, using muscles he had not put to use in some time.

Valen grinned and gave him a thumbs-up. Jack scuffed his boot against the floor and studied the impression. His face had grown inexplicably warm.

A few hours later, Jack was still practicing doggedly. He'd gotten to the point that he could even traverse the room in an unsteady, wobbly kind of way, sometimes without losing or gaining more than a few feet of altitude as he lurched along.

Morthal, Valen, and Bannen had left some time ago to tend to other duties, determining him to be proficient enough to practice without their supervision. Sentinel had stayed, however. The Primal alternated between trying to knock him out of the air and providing distractions for him to deal with as he wavered around the edges of the room.

Jack gritted his teeth with singular concentration, pressing on the lever and sending himself into a shaky left turn. He successfully traversed the northern wall of The Crypt and rotated in time to see a shape blurring towards him.

Sentinel crashed into his shoulder, and Jack drifted back to hit the wall, nearly losing his tenuous control. He righted himself hurriedly, saving himself from an unceremonious, and rather long, drop to the ground.

"Keep an eye on your surroundings," Sentinel chided cheerfully. He laughed as he swept by. "You're steadily gaining altitude."

Jack glanced around. He *had* nearly risen to the base of The Crypt's high dome. "It would be easier to master without all the distractions," he replied.

"Distractions?" Sentinel asked with mock surprise. "You mean like this?" The Primal swooped in beside him on green wings, grasped the collar of his coat, and flew. Jack was dragged in a circle around The Crypt's perimeter. He meant to growl at Sentinel in irritation, but his scolding turned into a whoop of laughter as the Primal picked up speed and let go of his collar. Jack spun through the air. He tapped intermittently on the regulator of his jetpack, righting himself from his midair cartwheels and slowing his descent. He grinned triumphantly at Sentinel, who was looking at him in astonishment. "Well done, Jack." Sentinel smiled. He nodded with satisfaction. "Impressive recovery."

Jack leaned forward. "You'll find I'm full of surprises." He pushed down hard on the lever and shot forward unsteadily, but his aim was true. Sentinel's eyes widened as Jack barreled straight toward him at high speed.

Suddenly, the Primal wasn't there. Jack let up on the regulator, trying to stop and turn about. Instead, he smacked into the wall with his shoulder. He groaned ruefully.

"Did you miss me?" Sentinel floated in front of him, sporting a roguish grin. Jack would never have believed the Primal could dodge that quickly.

"No," he grunted. "I was aiming for the wall."

"Well, you got it," Sentinel mused. "Good job."

Jack pushed off, carefully keeping enough pressure on the regulator to stay level.

"Why don't you keep trying that?" Sentinel suggested. "It will help you learn how to control your direction. Try to fly by me and hit my hand without slowing down."

Jack nodded and flew toward the other end of The Crypt at a steady pace. He turned, sized up the distance, and shot forward, but he missed Sentinel's outstretched hand by a hair's breadth. "Close," Sentinel said with encouragement. "You managed to slow down and about-face much quicker that time."

It took a while, but after the first few misses, Jack was able to slap the Primal's extended hand with consistency. Sentinel was looking very pleased. "Sentinel," Jack asked, as he zoomed by again, slapping away the hand in front of him. "Why are we waiting so long to go after Greed? Freedom's not waiting on me to learn how to use this, is she?"

The weathered Primal shook his head. "No. It will be nice if you can use the jetpack in an emergency, but it's not technically needed for the capture. All the human strike members will have to be extracted by Primal flight anyway, or hide out in one of our safe-houses until they can escape through the portal mirror."

"Then what is she waiting for? This plan could be executed on any normal day."

Sentinel grimaced slightly as Jack slapped his hand as hard as he could. "Freedom had to leave for a few days. There was something she had to take care of first."

"Something more important than finding the Instrument?" Jack asked in confusion. "I thought that was all she cared about."

"Not more important," Sentinel admitted. "More pressing, though. It's not uncommon for High Primals to be unavailable at inconvenient times."

Jack sped by again. He almost missed Sentinel's hand with his attention on the conversation. "High Primals?"

"As you're no doubt aware, some Primals are more powerful than others," Sentinel explained. "Much like your Myrmidon class system. Except our hierarchy of prestige is based on an individual's power, not on wealth or social standing." Jack nodded his comprehension. "The most powerful Primals are referred to as High Primals," Sentinel continued. "They are rare, but significantly more powerful than the rest of us."

"And Freedom is a High Primal?"

"Yes. You know two, actually," Sentinel said. "Justice is a High Primal as well."

"Are there many others?" Jack asked curiously.

"Oh, yes," Sentinel nodded. He moved his hand abruptly, but Jack had expected him to try something tricky soon. He changed course just enough to snag Sentinel's fingertips. "It's an elite group, and they aren't plentiful. You'd only know of a few by name, such as Tyranny, Order, and Chaos."

"So where do they go?"

"What?"

"You know," Jack said. He came to a hovering stop in front of Sentinel. "You said they were 'unavailable at inconvenient times'."

Sentinel gave him a disarming smile. Jack had begun to realize that was a normal occurrence when the Primal was about to give an evasive answer. "Let's just say that such extraordinary power often comes with…complications."

"What sort of complications?" Jack pressed, trying to keep his voice disinterested.

"The sort that is kept secret except on a need-to-know basis," Sentinel said, smiling. "And I'm afraid you don't need."

Jack shrugged. It was refreshing to get a straightforward answer for once, even if it wasn't the answer he wanted.

"Come on," Sentinel said, waving him back toward The Crypt floor. "That's enough for one day. You made great strides. In fact, I've never seen anyone pick up the basics so quickly."

Jack nodded, and let his hold on the regulator lessen. He dropped slowly to the ground.

"It won't be too long until I'm knocking *you* out of the air," he said as innocently he could. It was always a challenge to get the unflappable Primal agitated.

"Two weeks in the Resistance and he already thinks he's a big shot," Sentinel shook his head, muttering with sarcastic ruefulness. "Flying circles around you is going to continue to be my great joy, Booker."

Chapter 31

"Even the best laid plans do not survive first contact with the enemy."
— Victory, Supreme Commander of the Imperial Armed Forces

"Say something," Valen muttered. "It's like I'm sitting with a rock."

Jack glanced at her. "We've got a job to do."

"Do you not see me doing it?" Valen asked as she peered through the scope of her Sharps. "It's called multitasking."

Jack shrugged. "I do better when I focus on one thing at a time," he explained simply.

Valen snorted. He could practically feel her rolling her eyes beneath her helmet. "Figures."

It was three days after the briefing. A somewhat haggard Freedom had finally returned. They were set up and prepared to capture Greed. Jack and Valen were lying face down side by side on the southwest corner of a flat-topped tower. Fortunately, there were plenty of decorative statues and carved facades to conceal their observation post. The building had likely been picked for that particular reason. Primals had extraordinary eyesight; it would be imperative on any mission to first find locations that neutralized their heightened senses.

The Celestial Realm was just as radiant and beautiful as Jack remembered, perhaps more because he could actually appreciate it. He was not weak from hunger and thirst and no gallows awaited him after this trip. Probably.

He had been slack-jawed for a time after exiting the portal mirror through the wardrobe. Valen, Rook, and Bannen didn't seem as distracted by the splendor as he was, but he still had a hard time wrapping his mind around the fact that he was in the physical realm of paradise.

Jack shook his head and forced himself to ignore the view of the remarkable city and the diamond sea he could glimpse in the distance. He shifted to pull at the neckline of his combat suit. It was hot, but he reckoned he'd never felt safer going out on a job. The suit was made of lightweight fabric that allowed him to move freely. It didn't restrict his joints in any way, but it was also layered on his chest, back, thighs, shins, lower and upper arms, and neck with heavy woven fabric that Morthal assured him would slow traditional bullets. Thin strips of Celestial Steel were fitted under the weaves for added protection. It wasn't the head to toe defense of a Primal's Celestial Steel plate, but the protection to weight ratio was phenomenal.

Valen peered alternately through her scope at the trap location and toward the Imperial District from where Greed would arrive. Jack sat and observed with his Lee-Enfield Carbine held loosely in both hands. He could feel his double Ranger shotguns in their holsters where they pressed against his thighs. His Webley revolver rested against the small of his back. Even the weight of his jetpack was becoming somewhat familiar.

Sentinel had been uncharacteristically somber today, as if a great weight had settled on his mind. He was hidden behind a large spire, which thrust from the center of the tower ten to fifteen paces to their rear. Jack thought he'd caught the weathered Primal eyeing him several times, but every time Jack returned his gaze, Sentinel would smile uncomfortably, and then look away with an ill-concealed grimace.

"Looks like Hero and Champion are now in position," Valen. "No difficulties in neutralizing the sentries that I can see. Justice has been in place for some time now. Everyone is good to go." Jack gave a grim nod. She lapsed back into silence.

After a time, Valen's stillness grew somewhat oppressive, even to Jack. She had a way of making him feel uncomfortable simply by the way she held herself. If she didn't like how something was going, he was sure to know about it, even if she never uttered a word.

Jack sighed but couldn't think of anything to say. He decided he'd try to get her to do the talking instead. "So...where are you, uh, from?"

Valen glanced at him, but with the helmet shielding her features he wasn't sure if it was in surprise, amusement, or irritation. "Did you finally tire of impersonating a stone?" she asked. "And what do you mean?"

Jack shifted uneasily as he considered his next words. "Well, you're not like any other girl I've ever met. You don't talk or act like the tavern girls or any of the common folk in the city. You're too entitled to be from The Narrows. Most of your time is spent with Devalere, who is an aristocrat, but you *definitely* don't act like the noble ladies – all prim and proper and made up. Plus, you can *shoot and run and fight*." Jack cocked his head. "I just can't fit you anywhere."

Valen was very still. *"Too entitled?"*

Jack sighed again. He'd be in trouble for that, but he didn't know how else he was supposed to say it. "Look," Jack explained. "What I mean is that you're strong-willed and opinionated, but I can't even imagine you in one of those fancy dresses..." Her body was stiffening noticeably. Jack cut off. What had he said this time?

"Never mind," he mumbled.

Steamblown woman. *This* was why he kept his mouth shut and his mind on the mission.

There was a tense silence.

"I'm a bastard," Valen muttered.

Jack glanced at her. "What?"

"I'm a bastard," she repeated. "And before you make any stupid comments, I mean the kind born out of wedlock."

"So?" Jack asked in confusion. "Most of the people I knew growing up were bastards."

"Idiot," Valen growled, shaking her helmed head. "Half the people living in The Narrows were born in a whorehouse. I'm a *noble* bastard. My father was a lord."

Oh.

"And I'm not saying I'm better than other people," she snapped when he didn't answer. "I'm just explaining why I don't seem to fit anywhere. I'm half-common, half-nobility. I don't know what it's like to live like the common folk of Victorian, but I've never been acceptable to the aristocrats either."

"So, you were raised among the nobility?" That would explain a lot.

"Sort of," she said, fidgeting. The conversation seemed to make her distinctly uncomfortable. "My father was well known among the aristocracy for his...unfaithful ways. To his credit, though, whenever he discovered any of his illegitimate children he always claimed them."

"Any of...? How many?"

"I was raised with twelve other illegitimate half-brothers and sisters," Valen said bluntly. "Those were just the ones he knew about. It is likely that many others exist. And before you start leaping to conclusions about a pampered upbringing of balls and parties," Valen continued vehemently. "I wasn't raised in Victorian. All of the bastard children were kept outside the city at my father's hunting manor to be raised separately from his heirs."

Jack grunted dryly. "I'm sure it was difficult for you to eat your fill and learn your letters." He could almost see her blushing under her helmet.

"I'm not saying I had a hard life," she muttered. "I just had different kinds of problems, like figuring out where I fit in to the world. Noble bastards are shunned by everyone. The commoners regard you as just another noble. They wouldn't dare treat you as anything but an aristocrat even if they recognized you weren't quite the same as the others. The aristocrats, on the other hand, treat you like some second-class citizen, never as an equal. You've got noble blood, but it's tainted. In their minds that's almost worse than being purely common."

Jack didn't really understand why their acceptance mattered, so long as there was plenty of food. He didn't say that, however. *Wiser to keep your thoughts to yourself.*

"You think I'm shallow," Valen's accusatory voice broke through his thoughts. He realized he'd never answered her last statements.

Jack opened his mouth to deny the accusation, and then sighed. She wouldn't appreciate dishonesty, and she would know he was lying anyway. "Why did you care about any of that? You lived in a *manor.*"

"Just because you have the emotional range of a thimble doesn't mean the rest of us do," Valen spat. "*Normal* people consider friendship and acceptance to be a basic need."

Jack felt his face harden. A basic need was not starving to death in an alleyway. A basic need was not watching your brothers die because you were just orphans and nobody cared what happened to you. A basic need was winning a filthy scrap of cloth in a fight with another beggar so you didn't freeze in the winter. He didn't want to hear a lecture about basic needs from this girl.

It didn't matter if she understood. So he didn't answer.

"Sorry, Ironheart," Valen said after a moment. Her voice sounded strange, as if the words physically pained her. "That was...unfair." She was quiet for a few seconds.

"But you really do show about as much emotion as a block of wood," she added.

Jack grunted. The bloody girl was trying, at least. "So where did you learn to shoot?" he growled. "I don't imagine they teach highborn girls much in the way of martial skills, even bastard ones."

Valen laughed quietly, still peering through her scope. "No, they don't," she agreed. "It's all manners and etiquette and musical instruments."

"You can play music?"

Valen pointedly ignored the question and hurried on. "I was the youngest of the children at the manor and a bit of a tomboy. My father was...getting on in age; he let me get away with some scandalous pastimes because, put simply, he was just too old to care anymore. Also, I was father's favorite, and he indulged my every wish."

"*He* taught you how to shoot?"

She nodded. "Complete breach of propriety, but it was unlikely anyone would know with us living far outside the city. He took me hunting with him often. The governess there was absolutely mortified."

"How does someone like you end up fighting for the IAL?"

"Devalere," she answered simply. "I first met him when my father brought him and his father out for a hunting expedition. I wasn't allowed to go hunting when others were there, obviously, but Devalere was different than most of the aristocrats I'd met. He was kind and accepting where others had been cold and aloof; they hadn't wanted to mix with bastards."

"Why is Devalere different?"

"There is a sect of the nobility, mostly made up of young men, who consider themselves to be advocates of human enlightenment. They have radical ideas, many of which are similar to Freedom's own views on equality and liberty. As you can imagine, their views aren't popular, and they have to be careful to keep their meetings a secret. This group believes the empire to be immoral; Devalere was one of them. He was also the first to put his views into action. He left behind his old life to join Freedom's resistance while the rest just

218

talked about change. His family has disowned him, but they've still fallen out of favor with the Primals."

Jack grimaced. He'd thought very little of the high-class dandy when he'd arrived at the IAL base. Perhaps he had underestimated the man.

"So the short answer," Valen, concluded. "Is that Devalere visited the manor frequently, often under the pretext of hunting with my father. We grew to be friends, and he eventually began to confide in me about his controversial views. When he resolved to contact and join the Resistance, I followed."

Jack grunted. "That must have been difficult."

"They don't exactly recruit on the street corner," Valen agreed. "It took several months to find a way to get in contact and much longer to get them to trust our intentions."

Jack lapsed back into silence. He was unsure what to say. Despite himself, he was impressed with her nerve. Both she and Devalere had left behind a life of comfort and privilege to do what they thought was right. That would take great courage of a sort different to what he normally experienced.

"All right, here we go," Valen said suddenly. She was staring through her scope towards the north. Her voice had risen noticeably; Jack recognized the beginnings of an adrenaline rush. He shifted to loosen his stiff limbs. "He's winging towards us." Valen provided a running commentary of what she could see. "If he keeps to his present course, he'll pass not a hundred paces from our location." Jack could almost hear the smile in her voice. "Perfect. *Bloody* brilliant.

"He's just about at the range that Freedom and the others will be able to see him." Valen continued. "Make sure you keep your head down and stay still, Ironheart. The last thing we need now is for Greed to spot some sort of movement that spooks him…" Valen trailed off suddenly. Jack felt his stomach drop.

"What happened?"

"He's swinging around behind us," Valen said. Her voice was void of all emotion. "Flying on a southeastern trajectory. It will take him well outside the trap zone. Why in the steaming hells is he breaking his routine *today*?"

Jack could now see the small silhouette of the target with his naked eye, moving well away from the expected course. He waited calmly; he had been expecting this. One thing he'd learned in Fist's gang was that jobs never went as intended. The best plans were solid, but always fluid and able to change with the circumstances.

"Is Freedom seeing this?" Sentinel's composed voice came from behind Jack. The green and gold armored Primal crouched over them.

Valen nodded. "As long as the buildings don't break her line of sight from the street, she ought to be aware of his change in course." She glanced back at Sentinel. "Will she call it off?"

Sentinel hesitated, and then shook his head firmly. "Under normal circumstances I'd say yes. But this is about the Instrument. She's going to let this play itself out. Be prepared to do some improvising."

"I've got Freedom in sight," Valen confirmed. "She's moving covertly through the street, trying to reset the trap to the southeast." She cursed. "Hero and Champion are going to have to get on the other side of Greed to stop him from fleeing to the south. There's no way they're going to be able to do that unobserved."

"I see them," Sentinel agreed. "Some of Greed's sentries to the southeast are going to see something is wrong any moment now."

Jack peered over the lip of the tower. Greed was not far away. He was a small figure in the air to the southeast of their position. This was going badly, and quickly. Rook would now be well out of position to help from his post to the northwest; Bannen and Tempest would be scrambling to relocate to the other side of their target. Hero, Champion, and Justice would be similarly pressed to reposition the nucleus of the trap around Greed. It was looking like Freedom might have to corner the target on her own.

"He's aware of our presence," Jack warned. He saw Greed come to a halt in the air, hesitating. "One of his sentries must have spotted someone." As if to punctuate his words, a gunshot rang out across the city. Greed immediately fled back toward the Imperial District – straight at their position.

Sentinel sprang up and his wings unfurled into brilliant waves of green behind him. "Valkyrie," he barked. "Locate Greed's support and provide cover fire. That gunshot wasn't from one of ours. Ironheart, watch her back. Imperial reinforcements are going to be here soon."

Sentinel launched off the roof.

The air was alive in the distance. Jack could see Freedom, Hero, Justice, Champion, and Tempest rise up and pursue the fleeing Primal. At Sentinel's appearance, Greed came to an abrupt halt and spun, searching for an escape route. Several shots echoed to the south, and Sentinel jerked as the subsequent projectiles smacked into his armor.

"*There* you are," Valen muttered after the reports. Jack covered his ears just as the air exploded to his right. Valen's Sharps sent a bullet screaming into a tower several hundred yards distant. "One down," she informed him dispassionately. She ejected the bullet casing and inserted a fresh round into the barrel breach. "The other is keeping his head down. Smart man."

In the brief time Jack was distracted, Greed had flown vertical, attempting to fly up and over the circle closing around him. Hero had mirrored the action to cut him off. Sentinel closed up the gap in the ring. He was flying slower than he had been before. Freedom shot straight for the target as the others constricted the circle. Greed dodged her. His flight was growing increasingly erratic and panicky.

"We've got a problem," Jack observed. "Two Primals approaching from the north. They'll be on Sentinel within seconds."

Valen swore loudly. "That was fast." She kept her face pressed close to her scope. Her Sharps released another deafening BOOM. Jack's ears rang after the shot, but he still managed to hear her following question.

"Does Sentinel see them?" It sounded like she was talking to him from inside a metal box.

"Yes," Jack answered. He shook his head in an effort to clear the buzzing from his ears. "He's spun around to engage."

Sentinel met the first Primal in the air. His opponent wore the navy blue armor of a Primal enforcer and was borne on silver wings. He smashed at full speed into Sentinel's shield, taking the tip of the green-winged Primal's spear across the right shoulder. They became a tangled, grappling blur in the air.

The other Primal ignored the pair's struggle and shot directly for Freedom. She was barely an arm's length behind Greed, but she was forced to break off pursuit and take on the incoming enforcer. They collided heavily.

Greed saw his chance. He shot for the opening created by Sentinel's preoccupation and headed for the heart of the city.

Jack leapt to his feet.

"What are you doing?" Valen snapped.

"He's going to get away." Jack observed. He slung his Lee-Enfield over his shoulder to free his hands.

"You're going to take on a Primal by yourself *in the air?*" Valen's voice was incredulous. "You can't even control your jetpack yet!"

"No time to argue," Jack said. "Shoot Greed."

"*What?*"

"Shoot Greed," he commanded. "Slow him down for me."

"If I hit him with this it might kill him!"

"I'll take that chance!" Jack shouted over his shoulder. He ran toward the tower's edge before he could think about what he was doing.

"Steamblown idiot– Ironheart, wait!"

Jack leapt off the tower into the air.

Then, he made a mistake. He looked straight down.

A drop of over fifty stories greeted him. Jack slammed a hand on his regulator, propelling him erratically upward. He gritted his teeth, and lessened his hold, leveling out somewhat into a wavering hover. He leaned forward and flew unsteadily at the Primal ahead.

Greed's headlong flight had brought him very close to Jack, close enough that he could see the Primal's eyes widen in incredulous surprise at his approach. The target didn't slow, and Jack wondered in a detached way if Greed would dodge around or simply crash through him.

Another earsplitting shot came from behind, slamming into Greed's right shoulder. The .50 caliber Celestial Steel bullet – in no way hampered by the fashionable suit the target was wearing – stopped the Greed cold in the air, spun him in a complete circle, and caused his wings to flicker dangerously. A look of dazed disbelief settled on the Primal's immaculate face. This was Jack's chance.

He propelled himself forward as fast as he dared, attempting to capitalize on Greed's disorientation. He nearly missed. Wavering in the air, he stretched out his hand. He snagged Greed by the ankle of his left boot.

In the midst of such a bizarre moment, Jack irrationally noticed the flawless, fine-tooled leather of the boot from which he hung. Greed looked down, appearing more bewildered by the situation than

222

angry or scared. Jack's weight, in addition to the Primal's injured shoulder, was serving to drag them toward the ground in erratic jerks as the Primal's wings struggled to keep them aloft.

Greed's eyes hardened. A gleaming dagger appeared in his left hand. He slashed down awkwardly at Jack's face.

Jack released the Primal's boot, going into freefall. He felt the tip of the dagger swish through the air his nose had just occupied. He slammed the regulator with his left hand and drew a Ranger in his right.

The act propelled him up beside Greed and over his head. On the way up, Jack raised his shotgun and fired a slug of pure, Celestial Steel buckshot into Greed's unarmored chest at point blank range.

Jack heard the gasp of shock from the Primal but couldn't exploit his advantage. He struggled to bring his jetpack under control, and he eventually managed to bring his flight to a hovering halt. He looked down.

Greed was plummeting towards the ground, halted sporadically by the briefest flicker of wings. Jack looked to the north. Blurry, indistinct shapes filled the sky in the distance. There wasn't much time. He allowed himself to fall, keeping just enough pressure on the regulator to control his descent.

He landed harder than intended upon the glittering, diamond-pressed street. The force of the impact sent jarring pain up his legs. Greed was on his knees in front of him. His perfect face sagged, silver blood oozed through the tattered remains of his waistcoat, and his wings flickered in fitful bursts. Jack popped open his Ranger and replaced the spent casings with new shells. He pointed the barrels at Greed's face.

It was incredibly difficult not to pull the trigger. Freedom needed this one alive, but Jack had never had a Primal's life within his power before. The face in front of him was different than that of the glowing Primal on the docks years ago, but the perfection was the same, as was the sneering superiority behind the eyes. Jack stared at Greed, and Greed stared back. Even in defeat the Primal brimmed with contempt for what he was: a Myrmidon. The face before Jack was round and soft whereas the murderer's had been slim and sharp, but all he could see was the cold look of disdain on the golden Primal's face as he snapped Morgan's neck.

A sudden *whoosh* sounded overhead, and Justice smashed to the ground. He stood from his landing and delivered a blow with his armored elbow to Greed's head. The target crumpled to the ground.

Justice's huge executioner's sword was still in his hands, and a strange light shone from the ebony Primal's eyes. The golden irises never wavered from Jack's face. The sword rose slightly in his grip.

"Justice!" Sentinel barked, landing heavily beside him. Two neat holes were punched through his breastplate.

Justice didn't answer, but he turned away at Sentinel's arrival. His sword disappeared, and he bent to gather up Greed's unconscious form.

"Well done, Ironheart," Sentinel smiled. He grabbed Jack by the waist. His eyes flickered toward Justice as the other Primal launched into the air bearing their prize.

"Where is Freedom?" Jack asked. He holstered his shotgun quickly.

"Gathering the others for a *very* speedy extraction," Sentinel answered, flaring his wings. "Imperial reinforcements are nearly on us. It's time to get out of here."

Chapter 32

"Do the ends ever justify the means? A righteous person would say never. But a practical individual is more discerning."

– Freedom, Primal Leader of the Independent Army of Liberty

Freedom strode through the corridors impatiently.

"I would never have believed you were capable of such a thing." Sentinel's tone was frigid.

"Capable of what, exactly?" Justice was equally cold. His voice was dangerously soft and deep. "Protecting our cause?"

"There is no justice in murder!" Sentinel spat. Freedom listened with an inattentive ear to the two Primals following behind her. She had never before heard Sentinel this upset.

"Murder? I *considered* following explicit orders!" Justice barked in return. "He was given clear instructions to observe and support; there was no way of knowing his true intentions."

"Greed would have escaped without Jack's intervention," Sentinel growled.

"We *nearly lost* Greed by his intervention," Justice replied. "The Myrmidon was about to finish him when I arrived."

"He had just *captured a Primal*, for steam's sake! He was holding him–"

"That was not victory in his eyes when I arrived," Justice snarled. "It was vengeance!"

"But he didn't–"

"Because I arrived and stopped him," Justice cut him off. "He would have killed Greed, thus depriving us of our most vital objective, and then escaped to the empire to tell all he knows. We would be utterly exposed and ruined."

"You can't *possibly* believe that," Sentinel's voice was venomous and scathing. "Look past the flaws of others for once to see the good beneath!"

"Freedom, surely you see can that–"

"Your judgmental paranoia is–"

"ENOUGH!" Freedom roared, spinning on the pair of them. "*I do not care.* Do the two of you understand me? We've just acquired the most strategically important asset of this war. Greed can point me to the Instrument, and there's a good chance he will soon die on us." She glared hard at Sentinel. "If Greed *does* die before we can acquire that information, I may execute Jack Booker myself."

Sentinel's face was stunned.

"And if Greed survives," Freedom rounded on Justice, "you *will stop* your witch hunt and smile through your teeth while I pin steamblown medals on the boy's chest. Despite nearly killing him, Mr. Booker is the only reason we have Greed in our custody."

Freedom turned on her heel, not waiting for or expecting a reply from either of them. She pushed open the door to the medical ward.

Inside, the room was a flurry of activity.

"Get me more fluids!" Morthal snapped from where he was bent over Greed's prostrate form.

Sara scurried to the bedside with one of Morthal's whirring machines. She set it down carefully, and then rushed to grab a large bag of clear, silvery liquid. Morthal snatched it from her and hung it from a small rack. He jabbed a needle into Greed's arm and connected the syringe to the bag with a long tube.

"Left lung punctured," Morthal was muttering at an incredible speed. "Right shredded. Multiple ribs cracked from force of fall. Internal and external bleeding from buckshot. Without Primal fortitude and regeneration..." His head whipped back up from the mangled chest. "Need those clamps now!"

Freedom leaned back and settled her shoulders against the wall. She glanced at Justice and Sentinel. "There's nothing we can do now but wait to see if Morthal can work a miracle."

***

Jack tried to catch his breath.

They had hardly escaped through the portal mirror, ensuring no one had followed them, before Jack was standing nearly alone again. Justice had immediately handed Greed off to Tempest, who had sped from the room. Freedom had stayed long enough to get a head count before striding out herself, closely followed by Sentinel and Justice, both of whom were glaring at each other with hard expressions.

"Hero," Champion said. "Let's go." He was looking after Freedom worriedly. "Well done, Booker." He left without another word. Hero gave Jack a strangely guarded look and followed his brother out.

Jack was left standing with Valen, Bannen, and Rook.

"Is it true you captured Greed *by yourself*?" Bannen's voice sounded awed.

Jack shrugged with embarrassment. "Mostly I just tried not to die. Valen shot him through the shoulder."

"He was hanging on to a flying Primal's foot," Valen told Bannen, shaking her head. "The most ridiculous thing I've ever seen."

"Wow," Bannen looked at him with no small bit of awe.

"It was steaming incredible," Rook growled. "I was headed toward the fight as fast as I could. All of a sudden Jack leaps off the tower and flies straight at Greed, who's about to escape. He catches Greed's foot, swinging fifty stories in the air, and holds on for dear life." He chuckled roughly. "Bloody brilliant, it was."

"It looked absolutely absurd," Valen said dryly, but Jack detected something else in her voice. He couldn't pin it down.

"Look me in the eye and tell me you weren't impressed, Valkyrie," Rook demanded. "That was the most unbelievable thing I've ever seen." He turned to Jack. "Especially when you let go of him in midair and dodged his attack!" He spun back toward Bannen. "Then, he shot upward, drew his shotgun, and just, BOOM!" He mimed pulling the trigger. "Blasted that bastard right in the chest on his way up and over."

"Wow," Bannen repeated, grinning infectiously. The man looked speechless at Rook's lively rendition.

Jack cleared his throat in embarrassment. "What do we do now?" he asked to stop the conversation before it went any further. Rook looked like he was about to launch into a much more in-depth interpretation.

"Normally I'd say we'd have a debriefing," Valen frowned. "But I rarely see Freedom all wound up like this. She's usually so calm."

Jack frowned. "So what are you saying?"

"Well, we've got plenty of time to go get cleaned up, for one," Valen said wryly. "We probably won't have another meeting until Freedom gets her answers."

"Go have a bath, Ironheart!" Rook laughed. "Then, stop by The Crypt. You'll be the hero of the hour once this story gets out."

Jack groaned.

***

"There he is!"

"It's Booker!"

"Ironheart!"

Jack carried his plate of food to a seat at the long tables beside Rook.

It was the first time he had ventured from his room since returning from the mission yesterday. He was utterly bewildered. Every person he'd yet seen had either whispered as he passed, waved at him enthusiastically, or approached to shake his hand. As soon as he'd entered The Crypt, he'd become the undivided center of attention.

It was downright baffling.

Jack nodded to those who called out to him, which seemed to be enough. He considered going straight back to his quarters and holing up for the next year, or at least until whatever this was blew over. What in the three Realms was going on?

"What did you *do*?" Jack glared at Rook.

"What did I do?" Rook repeated blankly. His gruff face was puzzled. "I ate a bread loaf a few minutes ago."

"Why are all these people staring?" Jack asked through clenched teeth. "They're all talking about me and waving at me and trying to get my attention. *What did you do?*"

"Well done, Ironheart," a man said as he walked past, clapping him on the back. Jack struggled to remember his name. James, perhaps? "Most amazing thing I've heard in all my years. A human fighting a Primal head-on? Extraordinary!" Jack did what he'd learned to do by rote in the last several minutes: he nodded weakly. The man grinned, gave him one more pat on the back, and walked away. Jack turned an intense glower on Rook.

"Ohhhh," Rook said innocently. "What did I do to cause *that*? Very little, really. This kind of stuff tends to spread like wildfire on its own."

Jack stared at him, unblinking.

228

"I might have told the tale of you bringing down Greed, alone, in the air, with nothing but a shotgun and killer one-liners," Rook admitted. "Nothing extravagant. One or two renditions with appropriate dramatic embellishment."

"*Appropriate dramatic embellishment?*"

"He told the story about fifty times, not two," Valen corrected suddenly. She collapsed into a chair on the other side of the table. "The details became more colorful and implausible with every retelling."

"All the best war stories have an added touch of exaggeration," Rook stated. "Trust me. I've been in a lot of wars, and I've told a lot of stories. Do it right, and stories make steamblown legends out of people."

Jack dropped his head into his hands.

"It's a soldier's responsibility to brag about his exploits," Rook insisted. "You were doing your broody loner act somewhere, so I had to cover for you."

"The man of the hour!" Jack raised his head as yet another hand descended on his shoulders. Devalere sat down next to him. "Ironheart! The invincible Primal-hunter!" Jack stared at him, open-mouthed.

"Well," Devalere chuckled. He winked at Valen with a twinkle in his eye. "That's what they're saying all over the base, at any rate."

By the bloody, steaming Abyss. Jack laid his head down on his arms in defeat. *It's happening again.* He hoped Dasher hadn't heard any of this.

"Stop moping about being a hero and eat your food," Rook said, "or I'll eat it for you."

Jack tucked into the platter reluctantly. He'd lost his appetite, but he still found it difficult not to hoard every scrap of food he could find. The chicken and vegetables were piping hot and savory, but he hardly tasted any of it.

"Any word from Freedom yet?" Jack grunted.

Valen shook her head worriedly. "She's just sitting in the medical ward; hasn't come out since the mission. I don't think she's even taken off her armor yet."

"And Greed?"

She shrugged. "I've not heard anything. He's not dead, that's certain. Otherwise, Freedom would have already strangled you."

Jack shifted apprehensively. "I didn't have much choice," he muttered, trying to suppress the memory of Greed before him. He'd wanted nothing more than to blow the Primal's head off.

"I know," Valen sniffed. "And so does Freedom, but you can bet that won't make her more accepting of the fact that she's lost her chance at the Instrument if he dies."

"Freedom knows you're the reason Greed is even here," Devalere assured him. "Primals heal very quickly. I bet he'll wake up any time now, and she will get her answers."

Jack shrugged uneasily and took another bite of chicken. He tried not to think about *how* Freedom might get those answers.

***

"Is everything ready?" Freedom asked with a calm she did not feel. The eager anticipation in her gut threatened to overwhelm her cool exterior, but she crushed it vehemently. She'd been waiting to find the Instrument for a long time. To ruin her chances from impatience at this stage would be the epitome of foolishness.

"He is stable," Morthal nodded. The sluggishness of his words was a testament to how weary he must be. He actually spoke at the speed of a normal person. "He's *been* stable for the last several hours, and I believe the danger of losing him is past." He eyed her accusingly. "Though excessive pressure may push him back to the edge."

"He is awake?"

"Yes," Morthal replied, "and astonishingly responsive. Primal fortitude and regenerative capabilities never cease to surprise me."

"Good." Freedom was utterly deadpan. She turned to Tempest, who waited silently by her side. She'd sent the others away. Most of them were uncomfortable with non-combative violence. "No one is to disturb me, Tempest," she commanded. "Am I clear?"

Tempest's shifting eyes sparkled wildly. Her smile had become almost feral. She nodded.

Morthal looked about to object, but Tempest positioned herself between the doctor and the medical ward. "Thank you, Morthal," Freedom said quietly. "I'll take it from here." She opened the door.

Greed was stretched out on a bed with his back propped up on a mound of pillows. He was abnormally round-faced and soft-looking

230

for a Primal. His green eyes widened at Freedom's entrance, but a stubborn expression flickered across his features. The steamblown fool was going to be obstinate.

Freedom sighed grimly. She would soon change that.

She slowly circled the bed. "Do you see these machines?" she said casually, indicating the whirring contraptions at the bedside. She kept her voice quiet and serious to make him strain to hear every word. "I don't know what any of them do, really, but I know they're keeping you alive." She shut one off with a flick of her finger.

Greed's eyes bulged at her.

"Now," Freedom smiled coldly, finger poised over the next machine. "Let's talk about the Instrument of Fate."

Chapter 33

"Perseverance, not strength, is the key to success."

– Helmi, Philosopher

Freedom stared down at her hands.

Was she surprised? Not really. The Instrument of Fate was her Holy Grail. It seemed destined to remain forever just beyond her reach. Freedom laughed quietly to herself. Just beyond reach? No. That was the kind of delusion that kept her chasing false leads. Eternally out of sight was more appropriate.

Still, the knowledge she'd gained today was not entirely worthless.

"Freedom?" Hero's voice was hesitant. She broke out of her brooding reverie. Faces peered at her with consternation. She'd almost forgotten they were there.

The command center was completely still. The Primal and Myrmidon leaders were looking to her in expectation. Freedom realized she'd been standing in front of them, silent, for a very long time.

"Greed," she said in a slow, detached voice, "is unaware of the location of our prize." The statement was not greeted with an audible response. Some faces registered disappointment. The gangster remained a blank slate. "The Instrument of Fate," Freedom summarized. "Is not in the Empire's hands." There was continued silence. Everyone appeared to be processing the new information. Freedom felt a sense of guilt and shame, as if she had let them down. She had been so sure this time. They would finally have a direction, a purpose, a path to pursue. Every time she tried to move the Resistance past petty skirmishing, she found herself back where she'd started.

"Perhaps I simply have not grasped something everyone else has realized." The gangster's voice was solid and heavy. It broke the stillness like a cobblestone shattering a windowpane. "But is this not good news? The Empire *does not have* the Instrument. If this artifact is so powerful and valuable, should we not be pleased that it has not fallen under Imperial control?

"It's *bad*," Valen snapped at him from across the table, "because we now have no direction. We don't have the slightest idea of where to look."

"Neither does the Empire," Booker pointed out calmly. He did not rise to match her antagonistic tone. "Besides, even if it had been discovered that the Empire controlled the Instrument, would it not be somewhere we could never hope to recover it? Surely the Instrument would be surrounded by every kind of security imaginable. We would either break ourselves in the recovery attempt or be forced to leave it in Imperial hands. It seems clear to me that this is the better of the two answers we could have been given."

Valen looked like she might reply, but then closed her mouth with a snap. Freedom found herself thoughtful at the gangster's statements as well. The stocky young man noticed her unwavering gaze and stared back impassively.

"In part, the situation is bad because we've been using this idea as a crutch," a new voice broke in. Calm. Steady. Sentinel addressed the room with careful words. "When we believed the Empire was in control of the Instrument, we could rationalize our failure to make headway. The Instrument was a scapegoat. Its power was somehow keeping our efforts suppressed. Myrmidon's do not flock to our cause, Imperial forces are barely even hampered by our guerrilla strikes, and we've achieved little of substance for decades. The only thing we *can* claim is that we have kept a struggle alive against the Empire for a very long time, and this is common knowledge to the Myrmidon masses."

Booker inclined his head at the Primal in understanding. Freedom just looked at Sentinel flatly. He shrugged at her in return. Trust Sentinel to bring the concern they did not want to confront into the light. It was an issue Freedom had not yet allowed herself to consider.

"So why not achieve something of substance?" Booker asked bluntly. "Forget this Instrument. I don't know anything about the future or mysticism or fate, but it's a prophecy, right? If it is meant to be found, it will be found. All we can do is what we are here to do."

"And what are we here to do?" Rook growled.

"I'm here to bring down the Empire," Booker replied simply.

Justice's laughter was loud and cruel. "Your ignorance is telling. You have just arrived as a newcomer amidst a struggle of decades. What, then, do you think we have been doing? We have been committed to this fight since long before your birth."

"The Instrument is a means to an end, yes?" Booker demanded. "It is not *the* end. Its purpose, in our hands, would be to bring down the Empire. We cannot find it. Let us instead work directly toward the final goal."

"I've been saying this for years," Hero quipped. He winked at Booker. "Nobody listens to the smart ones."

"I will tell you the same thing I've told Hero many times before," Freedom addressed the gangster. "We have tried rousing the population. It does not work. They are apathetic. They are broken. And they are daily bombarded by propaganda that we are the enemy." She nodded at him indicatively. "Your attitude towards us upon your arrival should be proof enough to convince you of that. To most, we are nothing more than another cult. The Illuminati has convinced the bulk of the population that our professed goals are not just immoral, but little more than a power grab at the Imperial throne."

"The Instrument is no longer an option," Morthal answered. "We don't know where to look. Quite simply, that means the only course left to us is what Jack is suggesting."

"Mr. Booker is not suggesting anything," Champion spoke up finally. "He is only reiterating our goal as an organization. That is not a plan. There is no solution provided."

Morthal raised a finger. "We find ourselves for the first time in years in the position of possessing a goal, but no plan. Jack is saying that we are back at the beginning. The first order of business is to formulate a plan. Only after that is in place can we proceed."

"*Do* you have a plan, then?" Justice addressed Booker in a hard voice. "Or is it merely your intention to tell us what we already know?"

The gangster shifted uncomfortably under the group's gaze.

"Portal mirrors."

Hero laughed upon hearing the gangster's proposal and grinned at Freedom. "He catches on quick."

"From all I've been told, the Empire relies on its portal mirrors." Booker said. "They are indispensable for governing an Empire on two different Realms."

"Any war is about mobility," Rook agreed gruffly. He looked pleased. "This war, in particular, is about instantaneous mobility. Whoever controls the most portal mirrors has an incalculable advantage. That can be seen by our struggle. The Empire controls dozens. We control one pair. Thus, all of our efforts are marginalized."

"You came up with a concept that took us some time to realize," Hero congratulated Booker. "But that is a course we've explored and discarded. The emperors are cunning; they are careful to keep the locations of their mirrors hidden from us."

"And the sites where we can reasonably infer a portal mirror might be located, such as Enforcement Headquarters, are far too heavily guarded," Sentinel added.

Champion shot Freedom a strange look. She stared at him quizzically.

And suddenly, she understood.

"Of course," Champion smiled, a rare occurrence indeed. "Now we have inside information. Greed may yet prove useful."

Chapter 34

"Legend is the only true form of immortality."

– Helmi, Philosopher

"Jack!"

Jack was walking through The Crypt with Rook on his way to the armory, but he turned when he heard an excitable voice call his name.

Dasher was hobbling toward them. A smile stretched across his face, and his eyes danced with enthusiasm.

Jack hid a grin. "Dash," he greeted him gruffly, "good to see you up and about, boy." Dasher slammed into him and wrapped his arms around him in a hug. Jack stood frozen, utterly stunned. He ruffled the boy's hair uncomfortably.

"Careful, lad," Rook chuckled. "Doc's going to be irritable if he has to patch you up because you overexerted yourself."

Dasher pulled back and peered up with bright eyes. "I knew you would do it, Jack," he said fiercely. "I knew you would help them. You always do what's right in the end."

Jack could not respond to that.

"I knew you would be what they needed," Dasher continued. "I told everybody! Then, you caught Greed singlehandedly! I *told* them you were unstoppable. If anyone could help Freedom take down the Primals, it was you."

Jack felt like he was falling. "Dasher," he said. "What have you been saying to people?" At least the boy had the grace to look a little embarrassed.

"I, uh, I told them about our time in the gang. I told them about all the stuff you did, and–"

"Dasher," Jack interrupted sternly. "Tell me you did not start that ridiculous rumor again–"

"All right!" Dasher garbled with guilt. "Yes, I told them you were invincible. But, really, after they heard all the stories, they agreed. *Nobody* could live through that stuff."

Rook was laughing with his gravelly voice, but Jack just felt cold.

"Did you tell them about..." He clenched his teeth and struggled, forcing himself to say the name. "Morgan?"

The boy could tell he was angry, but he just shook his head. "No."

Dasher likely wasn't lying to him, but Jack very much doubted that the entirety of that particular story had been omitted.

"You told them I've fought a Primal before, didn't you?" he asked bluntly.

Dasher looked down at his feet. He nodded.

Jack sighed heavily, but relented, resting a hand on the lad's shoulder. Dasher looked up at him in shame. "It's fine, Dash," he said, "but you need to understand something." He held the boy's eyes with his own. "*I am just a man*. I've lived a hard life, and I've had to do some terrible things, but that does not change what I am: mortal, fallible, and human."

Dasher's features were thoughtful for a long time. When he spoke, his answer took Jack by surprise. "Maybe you are all those things," he said slowly. His young face was serious. "Maybe you are just human. Maybe you're not invincible. But it doesn't change what has happened, Jack. It doesn't matter what you are. You're *special*."

Jack stared at him. He kept his face deadpan. The boy's faith was misplaced, and it was infuriating, but he couldn't help but feel a tinge of contentment at Dasher's conviction. This boy believed in him. Not because of what he could do *for* him, like Fist or Freedom. Not out of fear of what he could do *to* him, like the other gangsters.

Simply because he was Jack Booker, and he was Dasher's friend.

"Come on," Jack grunted. "You want to see the greatest place in the world?"

Dasher hobbled along beside him as they left The Crypt. He looked up eagerly. "Is it the armory?"

"How did you know?"

The boy shrugged. "You like guns."

Rook bellowed out a laugh.

***

237

There it was again.

Invincible.

An uncommon word for daily use, but one bandied about with peculiar regularity around the gangster.

Freedom watched the trio's backs as they retreated from The Crypt and out of earshot. Jack Booker's broad shoulders, thick arms, and brooding countenance remained in her mind long after the last glimpse of the man himself faded from view.

A seed of suspicion took root in Freedom's mind.

It was less than a seed, less than the shadow of a coherent thought. But it took hold quickly and wrapped around her mind with an iron grip, refusing to be ignored no matter how she tried to push it away. It grew with surprising swiftness, blossoming and sending out tendrils like the Realm's most explosive vegetation.

She immediately commandeered the first people she saw and sent them to fetch Heb. Then, she settled into a seat in the command center.

She wasn't waiting long.

Heb was a short, furtive-looking man who had been born and bred in Victorian's underbelly. His time on the streets had left him with a remarkable number of underground contacts and shady friends. Freedom had put him and his resources to use the second he had joined the IAL.

"You are the Resistance's intelligence expert in Victorian's criminal underworld," Freedom said, almost to herself, as the man entered.

The thin, oily man's face cracked into a smile. He doffed his bowler. "I am, milady."

"A few weeks ago," Freedom said carefully. "I asked you to look into Jack Booker's past. I requested that you discover everything, every scrap of fact and hearsay." She raised an eyebrow. "Have you?"

This time Heb swept off his hat in a full bow. "Just as you commanded, milady.

"And?"

"Rumors and rumors," Heb professed as he fitted his bowler over his greasy hair. "You know how gangsters are. Every single one tries to have the fiercest reputation, to cultivate the greatest legend. They want people to fear them."

Freedom cocked her head. "But Jack Booker is different, isn't he?"

"He is," Heb admitted. "The whispers and tales pop up around him like buds in the spring, but not a one can I trace back to him."

"Which of these tales is most numerous?"

Heb grinned and took a seat. "Why, milady, surely you know. It's said that he's *invincible*." The man's eyes sparkled; there was much more to be learned.

"Martially, Greed is the weakest of Primals," Freedom muttered in an attempt to organize her thoughts. "Yet he is still a Primal. Jack Booker faced him, alone, and still survives."

Heb looked at her quizzically. "Milady?"

She settled back in her chair. The seed had sprouted into a garden. One that could be torn up by the roots at any moment, but if she was correct...

Freedom folded her hands on the table in front of her.

"I want to hear everything," she said softly.

Chapter 35

Jack hunched up his shoulders.

After all this time hiding underground, walking about Victorian in the middle of the day was decidedly strange. It had been months since he had roamed the city streets of The Narrows, and to do so in such casual fashion now struck him as bizarre.

The clothes didn't help either.

His raiment was still a far cry from the waistcoats and top hats worn by the nobility, but since his arrival at the IAL base Jack had grown accustomed to the quality of the clothing provided for him. Now, striding down the alleys of his old abode reminded how dramatically his life had changed. He fiddled with his coat every time he passed other pedestrians on the street. They wore the same rough, filthy woolens that he had possessed for the majority of his life. It was disconcerting now to walk among his fellows dressed so presumptuously.

And the sun! It was strange to see the golden sphere hanging in the sky. Jack had almost forgotten what it felt like for its light to warm his skin. The Celestial Realm's alien glow had become more familiar in the past weeks. He had several operations under his belt now, enough that Rook was calling him a veteran, but most of their assignments took place during the dark of night or in the Celestial Realm. As strange and discomfiting as it felt to rejoin Victorian in fine garb, it felt right to wander beneath the sun again.

At least it isn't cloudy. Jack breathed deeply. He'd been afraid that the one chance he'd had in ages to leave the base would be a typical Victorian day: overcast and dreary.

Jack glanced sidelong at Valen.

She'd insisted on coming along, though he had wanted to spend some time in the city alone before meeting up with Bannen and the others. The girl seemed utterly uncomfortable.

Jack had to admit that she *looked* out of place in The Narrows. Everything about her was peculiar in such a setting. He had seen her stare down attacking enforcers and enemy Primals without batting an eye, but the crowd of sour, unwashed laborers and hawkers seemed to terrify her. She twitched and jerked every time a passerby brushed past with a gruff mutter of pardon. It didn't help that she received so many inquisitive looks. Pretty, clean women weren't the most numerous of people in The Narrows. Before Valen, he had certainly never seen a woman on Victorian's streets wearing anything but a dress of either roughspun wool or lace petticoats, depending on their station. That a woman would wear breeches in public caused almost as many looks as the way the shape of her legs and body were emphasized by such clothing.

Valen jumped, startled and uneasy, when a dockworker stumbled by, but the man's eyes grew interested and lingered hungrily when he took notice of her. Jack felt a twinge of annoyance at the man's clumsiness and glared at him until he hurried away.

"You look like you're about to be sick," Jack grunted. He placed Valen's hand on his arm so he could steer her around a boisterous group of drunks. She shied away from them timidly. What was wrong with her? She was completely helpless out here. Valen was *never* helpless.

"I'm just not used to…this," she gestured timorously. "It's so squalid and vulgar and appalling. It's like an entire city full of you, except they actually talk," she finished, regaining some of her normal personality as she threw in a jab at Jack. "It's an entire population living at the end of their rope."

"These are rough people," Jack agreed. "You don't survive long in The Narrows without some jagged edges."

"I grew up in the country," Valen continued. "On the occasions my siblings and I came to Victorian, we only saw the nice parts of town. Sometimes father would take us shopping in the Diamond District, or, when he really wanted to treat us, we'd attend parties with the other nobles. I hated those parties. Everyone was so fake, and they all hated us because of what we were. But this–" she nodded again at the scene around them. "This is a whole different type of horrible. It's nasty, but it's raw and genuine, not a pretentious charade like the life I detested before."

"That awful, eh?" Jack muttered. Strangely, he felt a little offended by her obvious dislike of his old home.

"Look," she answered, catching the meaning of his tone. "It's the fact that this is normal for the people that live in The Narrows. That's what is horrible, not the location itself."

"And that's what you can't understand," Jack answered dispassionately. "I know you think you're not the same as the other nobles, but the way you were raised blinded you to many things. This *is* normal. The Narrows is exceptionally bad, yes. But the majority of the city lives in a similar reality, not far off from this desperation. Believe me, I've seen it."

Valen was frowning in a pensive manner.

"I respect both you and Devalere for leaving your lives behind to fight for your ideals," Jack continued. "But that's all that they are: ideas and concepts. Equality, fairness, justice – ideas don't matter to these people. They just want to survive a little while longer. If we can topple the empire, everyone here will have a chance to drag themselves out of this life. That's why I'm fighting, to give everyone that chance."

Valen didn't snap at him, for which he was grateful. In fact, she seemed to be giving his words a fair amount of thought. That was a first. "This place is very important to you, isn't it?" she asked after a long time. For once, there didn't seem to be any scorn or sarcasm in her voice.

Jack looked at her flatly. He meant to remain silent, but he surprised himself by answering after a moment. "Right there," he said. He pointed to a corner of the street not ten paces from where they stood. "I remember like it was yesterday. I nicked ten shillings off a drunken man in that very spot eight years ago. Morgan and I thought we were rich. We ate for three weeks off that take." Jack spun and pointed to the west. "And there," he continued, so caught up in the memories he didn't even realize how strange it was that he was sharing them. "Three blocks over in a dingy little alley was the first place I was shot. The bullet shattered one of my ribs, but I killed the man who fired it. I was fourteen years old."

The Narrows around him – the alleys, the grimy pubs, the filthy, downtrodden inhabitants – poured recollections into him. Thoughts of the past came from everywhere, threatening to wash him away in a flood. "Just a little further to the south there's a rundown plaza

242

called Maturin Square, I drove off two men who tried to take the tattered blanket Morgan and I shared with a broken shovel handle and a cobblestone. They thought two boys would be easy prey, but they were wrong." Jack was sliding further and further into the past with every reflection that leapt out at him from the cobbled streets and decrepit shanties. He couldn't have stopped his recitation even if he'd realized he was sharing raw, buried memories. "A tavern wench used to work just there," he indicated. "Sometimes she'd throw out the scraps, and we'd eat our fill on what she'd tossed in the alley. I'm certain, now, that she knew we came by. Sometimes the food was a little too plentiful and fresh to be garbage." His eyes flashed toward the airdocks in the distance. "Morgan loved to watch the airships. We could have spent years just staring at them as they cruised to the horizons. We'd fantasize about sailing away on one of them someday. To a place of our own. That's what we were doing the day that Primal...the day he–" Jack cut off in confusion. He shied away from that memory. The pain it brought snapped him out of the strange reverie in which he'd been entranced.

"I–I'm sorry," Jack muttered, shaking his head. What was he *doing*? Those were private, painful memories. He'd just been spouting about his past like an idiot. "I didn't mean to– I only meant...I'm sorry," he repeated dumbly. His face was flushed with embarrassment. He glanced at Valen.

She was staring at him. For a moment – a brief moment that was gone so fast Jack was sure he imagined it – there were tears in her eyes. But he ducked his head, humiliated by his outburst, and when he looked back up her eyes were clear.

Just a trick of the light.

Valen took his arm again, hesitantly. They walked in silence for a long time.

Jack felt like a fool. He never let anything get the better of him, especially not his memories or emotions. Valen was probably laughing inside, waiting to go back to base and share about the little boy she'd seen return while they were in The Narrows.

He sighed. There was nothing he could do about it now. He'd given her a whole arsenal with which to mock him. He'd just have to weather it as he had all her other contemptuous assaults.

"Where are we meeting the others?" Valen asked quietly as they neared the airdocks.

"In front of the old fountain at the intersection of Lee and Bots," Jack reminded her. "We'll hit the docks before taking Lee back into The Narrows."

"Why not cut straight across to the east?"

"That's Fist's old turf," Jack grunted. "I don't know who has taken over the area since we were busted, but I don't want to risk anyone recognizing me."

They reached the airdocks and turned east, following the line of quays. Jack regarded the airships as they sat in port. The rigging and high prows towered over the water. When one prepared to depart the hot air balloon would fill, the steam engine in the boiler room would chug to life, and the entire ship would rise with a great groan into the sky.

Jack led Valen out of the middle of the street as a chevaline trotted past with its pistons whirring and steam releasing intermittently from its mechanical nostrils. The noble who rode the contraption wore his top hat at a jaunty angle and his coattails fluttered behind him. He didn't slow for anyone to step aside.

"I love chevalines," Valen noted. "Father used to ride them while hunting."

"Really?" Jack asked in surprise. It had never occurred to him that she might have ridden such an extraordinary, expensive apparatus. "Why not use regular horses?"

"Real horses have minds of their own. Chevaline are more reliable. They don't spook, and they only do what you want them to do."

"Strange."

She shrugged. "All the nobles have chevaline if they can afford them. They're kind of a status symbol for aristocrats. Show up to a ball on the finest pureblood stallion, and you'll still get shown up by the next lord to step off a chevaline."

"Jetpacks would be even better," Jack noted, though he had to admit the idea of galloping in on a mechanical horse was very appealing.

"Sure," Valen agreed. "They let you fly, after all. But remember, the emperors have restricted jetpack use to their military and enforcement. The only reason we have them is because we, um, requisition them from Imperial depots. Chevaline are legal for consumer purchase, though. They're just really, *really* expensive."

Jack nodded, but didn't answer. He enjoyed their walk in silence for a time.

"What is this all about, Ironheart?" Valen asked suddenly. She was raising her eyebrows at the bowler he wore over his curly hair.

Jack glanced at her. "Should you call me that out here?"

She frowned at him but relented. "You're probably right." She looked thoughtful for a moment. "What am I supposed to call you, then? Jack?" She cringed. "Absolutely not. *Way* too weird. Booker? Better, I suppose, but still kind of bizarre. Maybe if I just add an underlying tone of disdain it will fit better."

Jack shook his head and sighed. "Just say it the same sarcastic way you say the other name and everything will seem normal."

"So are you going to answer me, Booker?" Her mouth twisted strangely at the name.

"What?"

"What's with the hat?"

"It's a bowler," Jack corrected. He shrugged. "Liberty overheard me telling Sentinel I missed my old one. I found it in my room the next day."

"Should we be saying *those* names out here either?" Valen said innocently.

Jack frowned with irritation, but sighed. "I suppose not."

"How are your reading lessons going with her?" Valen asked. Her voice was strangely casual, deadpan, as if she were entirely uninterested in the conversation.

"Good," Jack said. He grimaced. "I think. Reading is *hard*."

"What does that sign say?" Valen pointed.

"Wilshire Street."

She glanced at him, surprised. "That was fast. You really are learning."

Jack chuckled. "I know this city like the back of my hand. I know what all the street signs say, even if I can't *read* them."

Valen scowled. "Then I'll give you a real test later with a book. That way you can't cheat."

Jack took a left on Lee, pulling Valen along. They left the docks behind.

"Well, it suits you," Valen muttered grudgingly.

"What does?"

"The hat," Valen repeated. The words were strange and awkward as if she struggled to force them out. "The bowler. Whatever. It suits you."

A compliment from Valen. "Uh, thanks?" Jack said doubtfully. They lapsed into silence.

What was that *all about?*

The meeting place looked like it had been hit by a comet. "What happened here?" Jack gasped as he stared, wide-eyed, at the destruction. He noted where the old fountain used to be. He had slept next to its edge once, with Morgan curled up beside him. There was nothing left but crumbled stones and jagged rubble.

"You hadn't heard?" Bannen asked when Jack approached. His cheery face was uncharacteristically somber. "Chaos and his boys had a massive engagement with enforcement several weeks ago, just before we captured Greed."

"This isn't the work of human weaponry," Jack shook his head. The devastation appeared to stretch over a five-block radius in almost every direction. Most of the flats in the area were demolished. He shuddered to think what had happened to those who had lived here, trapped in the middle of a bloody clash between the coppers and Chaos.

"Rumor has it that Chaos himself made an appearance," Bannen agreed. "And there are confirmed sightings of Brutality personally directing his enforcers in the area. If both of them were present, it would certainly explain this," he waved vaguely around him.

"Two Primals did all this?" Valen asked incredulously. "It all seems too excessive for a one-on-one fight."

"This *is* Chaos and Brutality we're talking about," Bannen reminded her. "Excessive would be the word I would use to describe their personalities. But you're right. There were Primals, both mobsters and enforcers, crawling all over this place. Chaos arrived after the fighting got *really* out of hand. Then, it obviously got worse. Heb told me from what he'd gathered from his contacts, it's possible that as many as twelve squads of enforcers were involved. That's over a dozen Primals and a couple hundred human coppers."

"Damn," Jack muttered. "Chaos must have been out in force to escape that."

"He had his entire gang out here," Bannen agreed. "Anarchy, Riot, Turmoil, Turbulence – almost every Primal at his command was present."

"There's not been a clash like this since..." Jack shrugged. "Since before I was alive, probably. Chaos is always blowing stuff up and killing enforcers, but I don't remember anything like this happening before."

"Why now?" Valen demanded. "It seems like a random time to decide to challenge Brutality head-on."

Bannen chuckled, getting back some of his humor. "Who knows with Chaos? There was probably a fly in his drink or something, so he decided to wreck half The Narrows. Brutality was happy to oblige."

"I'm glad Tempest wasn't here to see this," Valen muttered. Bannen nodded solemnly.

"What?" Jack asked.

Valen's smile was grim. "Did you think you were the only gangster to join the Resistance?"

"Tempest used to work for *Chaos*?"

She nodded. "Long time ago, a century or so. She and Chaos go way back. Old friends or something."

"That's why she's gone most of the time," Bannen explained, speaking for Jack's ears alone. "She's undercover."

"But," Jack protested. "Surely she's been spotted working for Freedom?"

"Perhaps 'undercover' is the wrong word," Bannen admitted. "Chaos allows her to come and go as she pleases. He knows she works for Freedom. Freedom "knows" she works for Chaos. It's how the two keep tabs on each other. Neither seems to mind so long as one doesn't get an edge over the other."

Jack was utterly taken aback. "Freedom *cannot* approve of Chaos knowing her plans."

"Tempest doesn't actually tell Chaos our plans, dull stone," Valen said dryly. "She gives him false information that appears relevant to our current actions. He just *thinks* he knows what's going on in the IAL. She's on our side." Valen gave him a hard look. "And before you start with your trust issues again, just remember that Tempest has been with the Resistance a lot longer than you."

Bannen chuckled, but clapped them both on the shoulder. "Enough chitchat. We're here to help with the recovery of the area. We'll clear some debris and help get this neighborhood back to some semblance of normal." He grinned at Jack. "Not opposed to doing some honest, hard labor, are you, Booker?"

"Of course not," Jack said simply. He removed his coat, and rolled up his shirtsleeves in preparation. "I wasn't aware the Resistance did stuff like this."

Bannen nodded. "This neighborhood's Elder – unofficial spokesman and leader – is one of our contacts. He requested our aid in this matter." He raised an eyebrow at their surroundings and grunted. "With good reason. Freedom likes to keep her people happy. Most of the city won't know of our part in the recovery efforts, but it's still important to cultivate some goodwill for the IAL with the city's inhabitants." He smiled lightly. "Oh, *and* I hear that it's good to help people."

Jack grunted, then pointed to the nearest wrecked building. "Let's get started then. Where do you want us to shift this rubble?"

Chapter 36

"Trust me. When you've earned the gods' favor, you'll know."
– Gaius III, Victorian Illuminati Pontifex and Radical Primaphile

Jack and Sentinel were perched on a cliff face two hours east of Victorian. It was Jack's first time outside the city. He couldn't *believe* the plant growth. There were trees and grass everywhere. He'd heard stories, of course, about what it was like in the country, but he never imagined he would see so much vegetation. It was utterly foreign to the brick and chimneys and streets of Victorian. And so much space! There simply weren't any people out here. Which was why, he supposed, this location had been chosen for the ambush.

"I cannot believe Rook agreed to this," Jack muttered. "It's suicide!"

"I think he was rather excited by the whole notion," Sentinel answered.

Jack grunted. He clutched his Lee-Enfield Carbine in both hands and peered into the sky. He didn't know why he bothered. Sentinel would spot the airship long before his human eyes.

"I just wouldn't have pegged Rook for the undercover type, that's all." Jack grumbled.

"Oh, he's not," Sentinel agreed with amusement. "He hates spying and sneaking – says he prefers a straight-up fight any day."

Jack chuckled. That did sound like the Talon Rook he knew. "What's different about today then?"

"He wouldn't admit it, but I think he was eager to put back on his dress blues," Sentinel said with a smile. "He's the perfect choice for getting someone inside that vessel."

"Are the troopers and the navy that similar?" Jack frowned. "He's from the Fusiliers, not the Marines or the Navy. If they have different protocols, Rook could get caught."

"He knows what he's doing," Sentinel answered in a soothing tone. "Don't worry about him. In all likelihood, he's gleefully berating some poor recruit right now."

Jack snorted. "I hope not. He'd better be providing a distraction. This could get ugly in a hurry if we're spotted too soon."

Greed had proven to be an invaluable, if unwilling, asset. Luckily, he'd shown himself to be a coward willing to do anything if it would save his own life, though he continued to insist that the Emperors would soon find and crush them. The latest information that Freedom had forced from the craven Primal was the best lead yet. And the riskiest.

The Empire was transporting a pair of portal mirrors from the Celestial Realm to Victorian aboard the HMS Ironsides, a heavily armed ship-of-the-line of the Imperial Navy. The whole voyage was top secret, but Greed had discerned the purpose behind its passage from irregular expenditures surrounding its submitted flight plan. Or, at least, that's what he maintained. It seemed a lot to discern from a bunch of numbers. Jack never trusted Greed's information, but Freedom insisted that it was genuine. He supposed the prisoner hadn't led them into a trap yet. Greed was too spineless to risk his captor's wrath.

Jack had wondered why the empire didn't just move the pair of portal mirrors through another set of portal mirrors. It would be far more secure than to risk them being captured in transit, as they were planning to do. When he'd voiced the question, however, Morthal had given him an incredulous look. Apparently, anyone but a simpleton knew that a hole in time and space couldn't be moved through *another* hole in time and space. Jack had nodded sagely. Of course not.

The doctor's answer still didn't make sense to him, but then, very little of what Morthal said ever did.

"How did we get Rook planted on such an important assignment?" Jack wondered aloud.

"By calling in a lot of favors and pulling a lot of strings," Sentinel replied absently. His tone grew more serious. "Courage had to pull out all the stops to get Rook assigned to the Ironsides. If we keep asking too much of him, his cover is going to get blown."

"Courage is one of Freedom's Primal agents?"

Sentinel nodded, still keeping an eye on the sky. "Our most important one. Courage is one of the Imperial military's senior generals. He's outranked only by Victory herself."

"*Second-in-command*? That's quite an advantage."

"He's not second-in-command of the entire armed forces," Sentinel pointed out. "He's one of the Imperial Army's Corps Commanders. The Seventh Corps, I believe."

"Still…"

"He's also in the most danger," Sentinel continued. "He risks much more than our other agents, mostly because we request more from him than anyone else. His position provides us with an unimaginable resource. Can you imagine what Tyranny would do if he discovered one of his highest ranking military officers was a traitor?"

Jack grunted. "I guess he's called Courage for a reason."

"Quite right."

Several hours passed, and the morning had turned into late afternoon by the time Sentinel spotted the ship sailing through the clouds.

"Gear up, Ironheart," he said calmly, slipping into operational jargon. "It's almost time."

Jack shouldered his jetpack dutifully. "Are you sure it's necessary to seize the ship?" he asked doubtfully.

"Perhaps not," Sentinel said as he helped him with the straps. "But Freedom's right; we're going to need a lot of people to take the Ironsides. That means shuttling up too many humans to extract easily through flight, especially with a portal mirror in tow. Our only option is taking control of the ship."

"What are we going to do with a warship? Surely the empire will be able to find such a huge vessel."

Sentinel chuckled. "Always thinking ahead, aren't you? That's good, Ironheart. But don't worry. We've got a hidden port a few days outside the city, and if need be, we can sail the Ironsides all the way beyond Jackson. We've got another large base there, with its own secret harbor. Quite large, too. That's where we base most of our privateer vessels that harass Imperial ships."

"You have people *attacking* Imperial ships?"

"Not Man O' Wars," Sentinel replied while finishing with the last strap. "Just small supply frigates and such.

"Now," he said, peering to the north. "Freedom is headed up. Can't see the others yet, but it's time to move out. Tempest is already headed up with Damon, I hope, since she's shuttling the rest of our human forces to the Ironsides. I'll answer all the rest of your questions once this operation is over." He grasped Jack firmly. "Ready?"

"Let's do this." Jack grinned grimly at his friend, and then almost dropped his carbine when such an odd word crossed his mind.

Sentinel *was* his friend. The thought of having friends was strange; the idea of one such person being a Primal was even stranger. But it was true.

So much had changed.

"Here's hoping Rook has the crew distracted," Sentinel said cheerfully. His green wings burst out behind him, and he launched into the air.

The ground receded below them with incredible speed. Jack stared down until the trees began to look like bunches of broccoli, and then he turned his eyes to the sky before he could think about the distance to the ground. It *had* been a gorgeous view – the gold of the undulating grassland covered sporadically by stands of green timber – but he needed to keep his mind on the mission. Besides, the thought of a fall from this height made him queasy.

The Ironsides was no more than a dot at first. As Sentinel pushed higher and higher, the massive hull grew in Jack's vision until he could discern an enormous navy warship cruising along at over three thousand feet. The only ship Jack had seen to compare was the Titanfall. He shivered. That ship had been crawling with Imperial Marines; the fact that the Ironsides would be comparable made the task before them seem even more daunting.

"Do you see that?" Sentinel shouted over the sound of the wind. His tone was somewhat worried.

"What?" Jack yelled back.

But then he saw.

Smoke was rising from the Ironsides, drifting up into the air from the gun ports.

"That crazy bastard *set a fire inside the ship*?"

"Well," Sentinel replied nervously. "We *did* tell him to provide a good distraction."

They reached the bottom of the Ironsides' hull and skirted along the keel until they reached the stern. "Hero will eliminate the lookouts in the crow's nest if there's anyone still there," Sentinel said. "Then, he'll drop Valen for sniper cover from the high point.

We're going to take the poop deck to ensure we have a foothold onboard to push forward."

"It's not called the poop deck," Jack scowled. "You're all just having a go at me. As soon as I call it that, everyone will start laughing at your funny joke."

"It *is* really called the poop deck," Sentinel insisted with exasperation. "Promise."

"Whatever," Jack grunted.

Sentinel flew up the edge of the stern, making his way past the large windows of the captain's cabin. One of them was smashed, and Jack saw Freedom prowling inside with Bannen before they drifted further up.

"Freedom's inside," Jack muttered. "No captain, though. The fire must have drawn him out. Is she going to fly up and join us on the rear deck?"

"On the poop deck," Sentinel reminded him. "No. She'll secure the captain's cabin with Bannen so that we have a footing on two levels." His head popped up above the rail of the stern. He lifted Jack high enough to peer over as well.

Imperial sailors in white uniforms and Marines in red scurried over the decks like a kicked anthill. There was a distinctly frenzied appearance to the situation. The shouting and cursing was centered on the smoke pouring out of the lower decks. All seemed intent on the task of not letting the fire reach the boiler room or the armory. A mustached man not ten feet from the rail in a resplendent blue officer's uniform – the captain, Jack assumed – was shouting at the helmsman and every other sailor in sight. Most of those surrounding him appeared to be officers as well. Jack smiled grimly. *Cut off the head…*

Sentinel sank back below the rail. Jack glanced down.

Champion was approaching from a few hundred feet below. James was held in his arms.

"We'll have backup soon," Sentinel observed calmly. "Let's clear a staging area on the deck. Ready?"

Jack slung his Lee-Enfield over his shoulder and drew his Rangers in both hands.

Sentinel grinned. "I'll take that as a yes."

The Primal launched over the rail. He dropped Jack to the deck and landed beside him. His long spear and blocky shield materialized his hands. In the light of the sun, his gold and green armor shined with a resplendent glow. Jack raised both shotguns.

The offices turned with shouts of alarm. Even the captain's eyes widened. The helmsman gaped at them in open-mouthed amazement.

"Good afternoon, gentlemen," Sentinel said pleasantly. "Stay calm, if it please you. Captain, kindly order your men to put out the fire and surrender their arms. We are taking over this vessel."

The Captain recovered from his shock with admirable speed. "An Imperial Captain never surrenders his ship!" The man barked. He waved a hand at the officers surrounding him. "Drive these–"

Jack pulled the trigger of both Rangers simultaneously. Smoke rolled from the barrels and a thunderous blast split the air. The officers went down under a wide wave of buckshot.

"Brings a whole new meaning to 'clear the deck'," Sentinel muttered. Every eye on the ship was suddenly turned on them. "We'll take out resistance on the upper decks while they're still disorganized," he shouted, lifting into the air beside Champion.

The silver and red armored Primal released James and joined Sentinel. "Hold this deck, Ironheart." Jack crouched down beside the rail in answer, covering the stairs on the portside. He waved James to cover the starboard stairs, and the man rushed to comply.

"Where is Tempest?" Jack shouted as he reloaded his Rangers.

"Delayed," James yelled. He had his Lee-Metford propped up on the rail. He fired into the milling sailors on the quarterdeck below and cycled the bolt. "She'll be here soon."

Sentinel, Hero, and Champion were swooping over the decks, slashing or stabbing at the exposed Marines. Hero grabbed an officer by his collar and threw him over the side. His scream faded away slowly.

A magnificent explosion covered over the man's plummeting shriek. Jack's eyes flicked to the crow's nest, where Valen was sending suppressing fire into the forecastle with her Sharps. Jack holstered his shotguns and brought around his Lee-Enfield Carbine. He worked the bolt to feed a round into the chamber, and then rose above the rail to shoot a Marine through the forehead.

Between their fire and the Primals sweeping the ship, the forecastle, quarterdeck, and upper gun deck quickly cleared of enemies. Some fell beneath the steady hail of bullets or to the

254

Primal's searching blades, but most scrambled for the safety of the hatches. A small few ran for the captain's cabin. Jack almost felt sorry for them. He knew what was waiting in there: an indomitable Primal called Freedom.

Boots thumped to the deck behind him. Jack glanced aft in time to see Tempest rocket back toward the ground below. Justice launched away to join the other Primal's harrying the upper decks, while Damon and Tad rushed to join them at the rail.

"Orders, sir?" Damon asked. He unslung his carbine.

Jack was slowly getting used to questions like that, though he'd had little choice in the matter. After the capture of Greed and his unofficial addition to the council with Freedom and the other leaders, he had found himself receiving salutes from the men. Apparently, as a member of the strike teams, he had precedence over the other IAL fighters. He suspected that Rook's stories weren't helping. Most of the men seemed to look at him with the same awe as they did the Primals. "Keep this deck secure at all costs," Jack bellowed above the roar of discharging firearms. "We have control of the upper decks, but their Primals will respond any moment now. This area *must stay secure* for Tempest to drop-off reinforcements."

"Yes sir, Ironheart."

"Where will you be, sir?" James shouted.

"Wherever I'm needed," Jack responded. "First, I'll see if I can extract Rook. Keep a look out for him and watch friendly fire. He might still be in Imperial unif–"

The hatch below the forecastle smashed open. Primal Enforcers poured out, and armed Imperial Marines were right behind them.

"Suppressing fire!" Jack roared, firing round after round into the hatch opening. "Keep them bottled up at the hatch! Don't let them get a foothold topside!"

"What about their Enforcers, sir?"

"Let me and the Primals worry about the Enforcers," Jack commanded. "Just keep the Marines pinned below deck."

"Yes sir!"

The Primal Enforcers had broken from the lower decks in force. Most flew to engage the Resistance Primals in the air. Deadly, graceful duels broke out as the Primals parried and struck through the masts and rigging. The hot air balloon above it all cast a shadow over the aerial combat and the gunfire on the decks below.

With Valen covering from above and those at Jack's position pouring on heavy fire, Marine casualties mounted. They scrambled back out of view, leaving the hatch choked with bodies in red uniforms. "Keep up your fire!" Jack shouted. "They'll try for another push!"

An Imperial Primal in armor he didn't recognize burst from the hatch, scattering the bodies in his way, and made directly for the stern. Jack dropped his carbine and drew his Rangers. The others focused their fire on the incoming Primal, but to no avail. He was flying too fast, barreling straight for them. Jack raised his guns grimly.

Just before the Primal smashed into him, a green and gold blur descended from the top of the mizzenmast, driving a foot-long spear blade between the incoming Enforcer's shoulders, pinning him to the deck. The Primal writhed, spurting silver blood along the length of the spear haft in his death throes. Sentinel yanked his weapon free and brought it back down.

Jack scooped up his carbine and scrambled to force the Marines back.

It was too late.

In the respite caused by their preoccupation with the Primal, the Marines had stormed onto the upper gun deck. They fired in disciplined bursts, keeping Jack and the others pinned down behind the rail. Splinters rained on Jack's head as the bullets smacked into the wood. He heard the report of Valen's Sharps before she ducked to take cover from return fire.

Jack glanced back to see Devalere deposited on deck and Tempest leaving for more troops. The aristocrat looked decidedly out of his element with weapons in hand and garbed in an IAL uniform. He appeared to be in shock, staring at the bodies littering the decks. Jack quickly seized him by the sleeve and dragged him behind the rail.

A loud smack sounded beside Jack, and Damon fell, cursing over and over. Blood oozed from his right shoulder. "Devalere!" Jack slapped him in the face. The man looked at him with surprise. "Put pressure on his shoulder. Do you hear me?" Devalere nodded dumbly and bent, putting his hands in Damon's blood with a strange look on his face.

"Stay down!" Jack ordered Damon when the man struggled to pick up his rifle. "Draw your pistol and put a bullet in any Marines who make it up these stairs." He moved back to the rail and leaned out to take a shot. Freedom emerged from the captain's cabin.

The silver Primal swept across the gun deck like a furious whirlwind. Her blue wings flashed. Marines were scattered by her passage and dispatched by her sweeping blade. The decks exploded into true chaos.

The Marines were spread in confusion throughout the innards of the ship and exposed on the forecastle and upper gun deck. The Primal battle above would be the deciding factor now. Whichever side controlled the air and the rigging above would be able to sweep down and destroy the enemy on deck with ease. Jack peered upward.

Sentinel was grappling, midflight, with an Enforcer in vivid orange armor. Freedom engaged two other Primals just above the forecastle. He couldn't see Justice or Champion amidst the intervening rigging and aerial combat. Hero slashed and hacked ferociously at Villain as they spun around the mainmast's topgallant. Jack's mouth twisted. It figured that the black-masked Primal would be here.

Jack heard another report from Valen's Sharps, and he raised his eyes to the crow's nest. She was no longer aiming at the Marines.

A Primal in venomous green Celestial Steel plate was swooping in on her. Spite. The dripping fangs on his breastplate were distinctive. Valen drew her revolver and fired several rounds, but Spite was flying swiftly and avoided them with ease.

Jack stood. "You've got the deck!" he bellowed at James, and then rocketed into the airborne battle above. He slung his Lee-Enfield and drew a Ranger in his right hand, pushing his jetpack for more speed. Spite crashed into the crow's nest just as Valen leapt from its confines, igniting her jetpack on the way down. The Imperial enforcer flipped in the air and shot straight toward her – an easy target while drifting toward the deck.

Jack pushed hard on his regulator, initiating a burst for more momentum. He intercepted Spite a few feet from Valen's exposed back, ramming into the Primal's solid plate. The brunt of the collision was taken by his shoulders, and he gasped as a sharp pain lanced through his back. He tumbled through the air, inextricably tangled with his enemy, until they crashed into the deck. He landed on his jetpack, and all breath vacated his lungs.

Spite stood with surprise, and then looked down. The astonishment turned to intense anger, and he pinned Jack by his shoulder, holding him with a massive, armored fist.

Jack struggled vainly beneath the Primal's unrelenting grip. "The nerve of you, Myrmidon filth," Spite spat. "You *dare* to struggle with gods?" Jack writhed in panic. Spite raised his fist. It smashed into the center of Jack's chest. He felt several ribs crack at the impact.

Spite stood and turned, allowing his wings to release in waves of sickly green.

Jack stared dumbly at his own body.

He wasn't dead. A blow like that should have crushed every bone in his torso and punched through to the deck. His breaths came in short, sharp bursts. He could feel the fractured ribs pressing against his skin.

But something was happening. An uncomfortable writhing sensation twisted in his breast. His whole body tingled strangely, as if tiny ants scurried over the numb nerves of his body. *Am I going into shock?*

One of his ribs moved with an audible *crack*. He grunted at the pain and fumbled at his chest. It was a little sore, but otherwise normal. All of his ribs appeared to be whole again.

Suddenly, Jack realized Spite was advancing on Valen, treading with heavy steps across the deck. The girl stood still, not looking at the incoming Primal, but staring at him where he was stretched on the deck. The eyes behind her helmet were wide with horror. She didn't seem to notice when Spite summoned a black trident into his hands.

Jack struggled to his feet. He felt odd. It was as if some alien energy coursed along his limbs. He ignored the feeling. Now was not the time. He picked up his Ranger that had fallen to the deck and hit the regulator on his jetpack. He shot forward in a fifteen-pace leap and landed just behind Spite.

The Primal heard the thump of his boots on the wooden planks and spun. Jack pulled the trigger. Spite stumbled as the double slugs of Celestial Steel collapsed his breastplate where the dripping fangs used to be. Jack drew his other Ranger and unloaded that as well.

The wings on Spite's back extinguished, and he collapsed to a knee. He swiped with his trident in a fit of anger and pain. Jack hit his regulator, dodging out of range of the weapon. Spite staggered back to his feet and took a step toward him with clear fury in his eyes.

Jack holstered his Rangers and drew his Webley. Two gunshots followed from his left and right sides simultaneously. Valen's revolver was raised, and smoke rose from the barrel. Rook stood on his other side with a standard issue Imperial Navy carbine raised to his shoulder. Spite collapsed to his knees.

Sentinel screamed from the air and drove his spear into the Primal's back. Spite twitched twice and was still. "Are you all right?" Sentinel demanded, just before an Enforcer followed from the rigging. They crashed together mid-deck.

At the same moment, another squad of Marines burst from a nearby hatch. Jack raised his pistol and fired until it clicked. Valen and Rook emulated him.

The gunshots put down several of the Marines; the rest milled in confusion for a moment. Then, they charged, firing across the deck as they came.

Jack holstered his Webley and waited with bare hands. All of his handguns were empty, and the Lee-Enfield would be more hindrance than help in a close-quarters fight. A bullet whistled past his left ear. Beside him, Rook stumbled with a strained grunt.

Jack met the first Marine, dodging the bayonet thrust at his midriff. He smashed his elbow into the man's face and drew his knife in his left hand, plunging it up and into the Marine's stomach. Hot blood washed over his wrists, and a strangled, choking sound came from his victim's mouth. Jack allowed him to fall and slid his blade free. He searched for a new opponent.

Valen was struggling with another Marine. He attempted to grab her revolver, but she pulled the trigger and a bullet smashed into his thigh. He collapsed with a scream.

Sentinel was still locked in an intense duel with the Enforcer, and Rook was struggling with a third Marine over a single carbine. Blood seeped steadily from the blunt veteran's chest. As he watched, they careened toward the rail. Jack stepped forward anxiously. "Rook!"

259

Both teetered for a moment next to the edge, and then toppled over the side. Jack raced for the rail. "Ironheart!" he heard Sentinel bellow. From the corner of his eye, he could see his friend parrying furiously with his shield in a frantic struggle to disengage. "*No! Wait!*"

Jack didn't think about the fact that they were sailing at three thousand feet. He didn't think about the fact that jetpacks weren't built for skydiving. He just leapt over the edge.

Wind screamed in his ears as he plummeted to the ground. Rook was a small dot tumbling over and over below. Jack straightened his body and allowed himself to arrow toward the ground. He was catching up slowly. He slammed a hand to his regulator for more speed.

The whole world loomed before him, approaching at an alarming rate. The stands of trees grew in size from tiny clumps to miniature bushes. Jack couldn't hear anything over the air wailing and the thumping of blood in his ears. Rook was plummeting just ahead.

A bit further…

Jack reached out and snagged his comrade. He wrapped him in close to his chest. They were falling at a disorienting speed. The trees were full-sized in his confused vision. Jack struggled to get his bearings. He glimpsed a meadow fast approaching below. Too fast.

Jack smashed his hand to his regulator desperately. Their breakneck speed reduced.

Not enough.

He thought he could hear someone shouting his name. The meadow rushed up to meet him, and he screamed.

Chapter 37

"The Instrument of Fate will come, and the Realms will shake at the arrival."
– Excerpt from the Prophecy of Fate, uttered by Omen

Morgan was here.

It was a strange place of cracked cobblestones and benches, like one of the dilapidated courtyards in The Narrows. But ghostly trees with vaporous, white bark thrust from the ground despite the lack of soil. They were shifting, changing; whispering in voices he struggled to understand.

Jack approached the crumbling fountain in the center that was shaded by a stand of the ethereal trees. Morgan was waiting for him there, seated on the deteriorating stone edge.

"Jack."

A voice whispered behind him. He turned slowly. His every movement was sluggish. Measured. No one was there.

"Jack."

He recognized the voice this time, though he could not find its speaker.

Fist.

"Don't let them get you, Jack. Invincible–" He strained his ears. "Don't let them get you, Jack. Don't let them get you. Invincible–"

Another voice echoed to his left. "I should've known you'd survive. Invincible and all. I wonder if it will kill you when they stretch our necks? Or will you just flop forever on the end of the rope?"

Jack spun again. Slowly. Like moving through syrup. "Goldi?"

The whispers flooded over him. Some he recognized, others he didn't. A few echoed strangely in his mind. Jack eyed Morgan and ignored the whispers after a time. He never caught a face to accompany them, just the shifting trees. He stepped forward deliberately.

Morgan didn't move when Jack stood over him. The boy hadn't aged a day. His bright eyes studied his long, thin fingers. Jack remembered how deft those fingers had been. Light as a feather.

"INVINCIBLE."

Jack looked at Morgan with a start. His younger brother was glaring at him now. It was an expression he'd never seen in life. Fire rose from those eyes. Anger. Pain.

The voice was deep and guttural. He stumbled back at the sound.

Suddenly, the incessant whispering around him stopped. Morgan's relentless stare fell, and his voice took on another tone not his own. "Don't know. Found nothing to suggest anything different. Anatomy is of a normal, if extraordinarily healthy, human male." Jack's eyebrows drew down. It could not be Morgan who spoke. The voice was quick. Choppy. Words flew at an absurd speed. He felt he should know that voice.

The shadowy trees began to fade. The courtyard of stone melted into a grayish haze. Morgan's face remained clear, but it morphed slightly. The eyebrows and cheekbones became less sharp, the nose a bit shorter, and the ears grew in size to poke from beneath thin, black hair.

Dasher?

"He's awake!" A voice said sharply.

Jack felt his eyelids flutter as his pupils adjusted to the light. The haze drifted away. Several faces surrounded him, but he knew them all.

He swallowed reflexively and coughed. His throat was very dry. A glass of water was raised to his lips, and he took a long, grateful drink. He watched Valen carefully as she tipped the liquid into his mouth. She avoided his gaze, but the look on her slim face was soft. It was good to see her. After he had finished, she removed the cup from his lips and stepped back.

"Jack." Sentinel's voice came from his right. The weathered Primal's face was equal parts stern and cheerful. "Don't jump off of airships. I know people say to do that all the time, but it's only an expression."

Jack grunted and laid his head back on his pillow. "Go jump off a steaming airship, Sentinel," he croaked. "You don't tell me what to do."

Sentinel chuckled dryly. "Well, we know the fall didn't damage him any worse than normal." He said with a jovial grin. "He's the same stubborn fool as before."

262

Morthal, Valen, Sentinel, Dasher, and, oddly, Justice were arrayed around his bed in the medical ward. Jack still struggled to put together his thoughts.

"I *told* them you would be fine," Dasher said with authority. "I've seen you recover lots of times before."

"The bothersome child was exceptionally anxious when you were brought back," Justice frowned. "So much so that Morthal had to sedate him for a time. He lies to you now to display bravado."

"Thanks, Justice," Dasher scowled.

The huge, bald Primal shrugged. He gave Jack a strange nod, and then strode for the door. As it closed behind him, Jack noticed a large number of people peering in from the corridor.

"I thought you were dead," Valen said softly. She still wouldn't look directly at him.

"Me too," Jack grunted. "Sorry. I know you were looking forward to it, but I guess you'll have to put up with me a bit longer. What about Rook? Did he–?"

"You cushioned the fall for him," Sentinel said. "He's in worse shape, though. Doc says he'll pull through."

"You broke more bones between the two of you..." Morthal muttered.

"I have broken bones?" Jack asked. All of his limbs seemed to be working correctly, and he didn't feel anything particularly excruciating in his torso. "What happened?"

The room grew very quiet. Valen, Sentinel, and Morthal exchanged glances. All of them became fascinated with their feet. Dasher, it seemed, was the only other person interested in an answer.

Jack opened his mouth, but the door opened to admit Freedom before he could press them further. The crowd outside looked to have grown considerably, and a steady buzz of voices drifted into the room even after the Primal leader shut the door behind her. "Leave us," she said curtly to the others. They did so without question. Even Morthal. Jack regarded the silver-haired Primal with surprise.

Her face was completely serious, which was an expression he had come to recognize as normal. She stood at the foot of the bed. Freedom was not as tall or broad or physically daunting as Justice or Champion, but she seemed to loom over him with a distinctive imposing air.

"How are you feeling?" Freedom asked quietly.

"Not bad," Jack admitted with surprise. "Considering I didn't think I would be feeling anything at all."

She didn't smile. "What do you remember?"

"Falling," he said.

"No, tell me everything. Not just the fall. What do you remember?"

Jack searched his still sluggish mind. Recollection flickered back to him in intermittent flashes. "We were fighting on the Ironsides. Damon was hit, but you cleared the deck again. Valen was trying to fend off Spite..." He grimaced. "I– I tried to help, but Spite pinned me to the deck. He crushed my chest..." Was that right? Jack frowned, looking down at his bandaged torso. It wasn't shattered to pieces. He thought he remembered what happened, but clearly the fall had somehow disrupted his memory.

"Go on, Mr. Booker," Freedom encouraged him. There was a strange look in her eye. "Spite crushed your chest. Then what?"

"I don't know," Jack said simply. He shook his head. "It should have killed me. I thought some of my ribs had been shattered, but–" He was now thoroughly confused. "It must not have hurt me as badly as I thought, because I was able to get back up and reengage."

Freedom's eyes were hard. "Don't lie to me, Booker. You *were* injured. You're holding something back."

Jack scowled at her. "Look, *I don't know*. I'm not lying. I felt strange. Something...some kind of energy started working under my skin. It hurt, but my ribs were back in place." He settled against his pillow with a sigh, closing his eyes. "It's just some kind of hallucination. Probably something I was dreaming about when I was out. I'm sorry. You're not going to get the real answer from me. Whatever actually happened, that's all I can remember. After that, I jumped off the Ironsides to catch Rook."

"I believe you, Mr. Booker." Freedom said. Her voice was filled with satisfaction. "I just wanted to hear you say it out loud so that you would better accept what you're about to hear."

Jack cracked open his eyes warily. "What am I about to hear?"

"It *wasn't* a hallucination," Freedom answered him. She leaned forward over his bed. If he didn't know better, he would have said she was holding back a display of enthusiasm. "Everything you said actually happened. Spite intended to crush you. You should have died from such a blow. Somehow, you survived." Jack's eyes

264

narrowed, and he opened his mouth to answer. Freedom continued over his interruption. "Still, the blow left you seriously injured, but you were able to leap up and continue the fight. Your body *healed* itself with incredible speed. That's what you felt: regenerative healing like that seen only among the most powerful of Primal abilities."

Jack stared. "What?"

"Valen saw it all," Freedom explained. "As did Sentinel. You're shattered chest was real; they saw everything. Suddenly your injuries were gone, and you were back on your feet."

His head hurt. He rubbed his temples lightly. "Look, Freedom, stop playing games with me. What you're saying isn't possible."

"You remember it yourself."

"But it doesn't–" Jack had never been this perplexed in his life. "What do you mean? What are you trying to tell me?"

Freedom revealed one of her rare smiles. Her face had never been more determined or beautiful. A radiant aura almost seemed to burst from her skin. He knew he wasn't going to like what came next.

"What I'm trying to tell you, Mr. Booker, is that *you* are the Instrument of Fate."

Chapter 38

"Conviction is more useful than righteousness."
 – Freedom, Primal Leader of the Independent Army of Liberty

"*What*?" Jack repeated.

Freedom visibly struggled to control herself. Her excitement faded back into her normal, emotionless expression. "I believe that you are the Instrument of Fate," she said again, this time much more calmly.

Jack couldn't say anything for some time. Nothing came to him. When he finally did speak, he uttered the only words going through his stunned mind.

"You're crazy."

Freedom considered him impassively. "Am I? Your entire life, those who you've known have recognized something different about you. They cannot correctly express what they sense, and so they fall back on superstitions to explain the anomaly." She cocked her head to the side, causing her shining, silver hair to spill over one shoulder. "Does the term "invincible" jog your memory?"

"This is a ridiculous conversation," Jack said flatly, "and I'm not having it. You see the Instrument everywhere, Freedom. You're obsessed. You know it. I know it. Everyone here knows it. I'm not going to be the next fixation of your mania because you can't accept that the Instrument is beyond your grasp."

Freedom's brilliant blue eyes flared with cold anger, but her next words were measured and composed. "There are only a few living beings left who have heard the prophecy, and I am one of them. If you think anyone is better qualified to determine what or," she looked meaningfully at Jack, "*who* the Instrument may be, then, please, enlighten me."

Jack gritted his teeth. "You're grasping at straws."

"On this, I am not," Freedom said in light voice. She perched on the edge of his bed. "I have suspected for some time now, and I have done what I could to ascertain the truth. The events on the Ironsides only further confirmed my suspicions."

"And what might those be?"

"That you are something the world has never seen," Freedom said softly. "A revelation that will shake the Realms." Her eyes were almost hungry. "A hybrid. Half Myrmidon, half Primal."

Jack barked out a laugh. "You'll have to do better than that. My mother and father were two poor sods from The Narrows. Distinctly *human*. I can remember them both."

Freedom's smile was triumphant, but strangely cautious. "I told you I have been thorough. I've been looking into your past, Mr. Booker, and I believe I can share things with you about your family that you've never known."

Jack stiffened. His eyes narrowed. She'd been digging into his past?

"Tell me about your brothers," Freedom said suddenly. "What did they look like?"

He considered not answering. He was done with this farce. But Freedom would not let this go. When it came to the Instrument, she never did.

"Both were thin and gangly," Jack sighed. He closed his eyes, remembering. "Harv was very young when he died. Morgan had fine, black hair, the most vivid green eyes I've ever seen, and a slim face with sharp cheekbones. By the time he was twelve he was already as tall as I was."

"And your mother?"

"Slim and willowy. She had brown hair, like mine, and a kind smile. Morgan was always beaming, but she smiled rarely. When she did, though, it was the same smile I could see on Morgan's lips"

"Your father?"

"Is there a point to this, Freedom?" Jack demanded.

"Indulge me."

"Black hair, soot covered, and dead before I was five," he growled. "*Human*."

"A tall, gangly man from all accounts we've uncovered," Freedom said quietly. "Green eyes."

"So?" Jack was nearly snarling.

"Then we have you," Freedom said, voice soft. Her fingertips stretched out and stroked his cheek lightly. He flinched away from the odd gesture. "Brown hair, like your mother, but everything else..." She peered down at him. "Muscular, stocky body, a bold chin, iron jaw, and prominent brow. Dark eyes." He realized what she was saying, but clenched his mouth shut stubbornly. "What did you inherit from you father, Mr. Booker?"

Jack hesitated.

"Nothing," she supplied for him. "Because you were born several months before your mother met your father."

He fumed. "I don't believe you."

"The truth does not require your belief," Freedom said in answer. "It simply is."

Jack said nothing. He had no more to say.

"Even without this," Freedom continued at his silence. She was suddenly vehement. "You cannot deny what you've seen with your own eyes. What you've felt on the inside. You've taken tremendous blows that should have killed you. You've felt your own power healing you from inside. Others can see a difference, even when you choose ignore it. Time and again you're renown has grown, despite your best efforts to hide from what you are. Your very nature reveals itself."

"Until the airship attack, I've never exhibited any signs of supernatural ability." Jack protested. "And I'm still not certain what that was anyway. Everything I've survived before was luck and simple determination."

"You are nineteen years old now, correct? I believe that physical maturity was needed for your powers to fully manifest and start exhibiting themselves," Freedom said calmly. "You are now entering the prime of your life, thus, your powers have fully developed. Besides, it's possible your abilities have been keeping you alive over the years. They had not completely evolved, but they were able to nudge you away from death and allowed you to take more punishment than a purely Myrmidon body should have been able to handle. It was subtle, but always there beneath the surface."

"Stop twisting everything!" Jack snarled, lunging up in his bed. He ignored the sharp pains that accompanied the motion. "I don't know what happened, but I'm *human*. Nothing more!"

"How do you think you survived the fall?" Freedom blazed suddenly. He resisted the urge to shy from her torrid anger. "If you had been human we would be scraping bits of you out of that meadow."

"Rook survived too," Jack muttered.

"Because you absorbed most of the impact for him!" Freedom answered. The pale blue anger roaring from her eyes didn't waver. "You've seen your power for yourself. You know something is different." She jabbed a finger at his damaged chest. "Now that you have that knowledge, can you really still keep to the shadows? You must rise to the potential within. You can help so many others by becoming what you were born to be: a symbol, a *leader*. That's what your people need. I cannot be that. I am a Primal. You are still recognizable to them. You're something different, perhaps, but still perceptibly human, still a hero they can follow. You have the power to light a fire beneath the Myrmidons that Tyranny cannot suppress."

"I don't want to be a leader," he snapped, growling bitterly. "I've never wanted it."

"Selfish thoughts," Freedom spat. She loomed over him. Her angelic face was inches from his own, somehow unmarred by the fury twisting her features. "By accepting this, you will be doing what is *right*. By becoming the Instrument you will be protecting hundreds of thousands from Tyranny's oppression. Can you truly turn your back on that and still be the man you claim to be?"

"What do I claim to be?" Jack said. "I've never claimed to be anything."

The intense anger bled slowly from her face. Calculated calm settled over her icy gaze, hiding the coldness from view. "Your actions proclaim that you are a good man." She stood suddenly and strode for the door. "Are you?"

Chapter 39

"On the verdict of the Instrument shall fate fall, for by such judgment is destiny ruled."

– Excerpt from the Prophecy of Fate, uttered by Omen

"From minder to bodyguard," Jack grunted as he fumbled his way along the corridor. "Quite the joke of a journey. Does Freedom delight in making you suffer?"

"What about your journey?" Sentinel answered with mock seriousness on his weathered face. "From distrusted prisoner to the warrior of destiny."

Jack groaned. "Don't ever call me the 'warrior of destiny' again. I think I might be sick."

"What?" Sentinel said. Mischievous innocence played across his face. "You don't like it better than 'Ironheart?' I thought it had a ring to it."

Jack was traversing the corridors of the base in an attempt to get used to being back on his feet. He tried not to think about *how* he was back on his feet just five days after taking a three thousand foot plunge. Maybe Freedom had a point after all.

But he wasn't the steamblown Instrument of bloody Fate.

Sentinel was walking along beside him with his hands clasped behind his back. Since Jack was suddenly Freedom's most valued asset, the solid Primal had been appointed as his bodyguard. It sounded like a boring job to him, but Sentinel had taken to it with as much enthusiasm as he did everything. Nothing, it seemed, was too mundane to elicit disappointment.

"Tell me something, Sentinel," Jack growled. He propped himself up for a moment against the wall. "You don't actually believe this nonsense, do you? That I'm the Instrument of Fate?"

Sentinel pursed his lips thoughtfully. "Why? Do I have to stop making jokes about you if I say yes?"

"Because you're my friend," Jack said, feeling foolish for saying the word out loud. He hurried on. "You know me. I'm not the fulfillment of some mystical prophecy."

"You forget that I've seen you do some extraordinary things with my own eyes," Sentinel pointed out. The steaming Primal was

270

laughing. "It's a bit hard to convince yourself everything is normal when you see a man's shattered chest pop back in place or watch him survive a suicide skydive."

"Look, I don't know what happened there," Jack muttered as he continued on his walk, "but it doesn't mean I'm the Instrument or half Primal."

"Do you have another explanation?"

"No," he admitted.

"Then don't dismiss Freedom's theory out of hand," Sentinel advised. He shrugged. "At least she has a theory. I just thought you were a freak."

"Thanks."

"The short answer is yes," Sentinel said more seriously. "I do believe you're Fate's Instrument."

Jack turned, surprised. Of anyone, he'd thought his level-headed companion would see the truth of the matter. "So you think my destiny is set?"

"Of course not," Sentinel smiled. "We always have choices. Nothing is certain, but you're *potential* to be the Instrument is there. Everyone is subject to fate, Jack, right down to the humblest peasant. You just get a fancy title. That doesn't mean, however, that you can't decide to be something else. If you left this base behind forever, I don't think you would be the Instrument anymore. The choice would have broken that bond. But I know you, and you won't abandon the duties you've accepted or the people you protect. So fate really does decide after all, because you choose to allow it."

Jack shook his head. This was all too much. "Sometimes you make less sense than Morthal."

"I'm three centuries older than that hyperactive lunatic. I ought to be able to baffle someone every once in a while."

"Come on," he insisted. "I'm ready to go back to my room."

Sentinel fell into step beside him. "At this rate," he said. "You'll be back to full strength in a day."

"Don't remind me."

"You don't like your newfound healing ability?"

"Bloody useful," Jack grunted. "But steaming disconcerting too." He looked down at his legs. They should have been unusable for weeks. Maybe months. Hell, he should have been dead and buried. But here he was, walking circles around the base after a few

271

days recovery. He tried to think of anything else. "Let's avoid The Crypt," he scowled. "I don't want to see everyone again."

"But they want to see you," Sentinel said with amusement. "Besides, I don't think there's a way to get to your room from here without going through The Crypt."

"Great," Jack muttered. "Just bloody fantastic."

"Think of it as a chance to sharpen your PR skills," Sentinel joked. "Steam knows you need practice in that department."

"I hate you."

"See?"

Unfortunately, The Crypt was full to bursting when they arrived. They had inadvertently timed their entrance right before evening mess. Jack cursed his luck, but focused on limping across the wide expanse as quickly as possible. He would just have some food delivered to his rooms later.

"There he is!"

"Ironheart!"

Jack tried to ignore the whispers and the many eyes on him. It wasn't easy. Heads craned toward him from every direction.

"Acknowledge them," Sentinel whispered through clenched teeth.

Jack raised a hand to the room at large. He tried to paste a smile across his face.

"Do you know that when you smile," Sentinel stated in a conversational tone. "You look like you're grimacing at something revolting?"

Apparently, it didn't matter how his smile looked, because at his attention large groups moved to intercept his path. Jack slowed to meet them with reluctance. "See what happens when I do things your way?" he snapped.

"Just smile and wave, boy," Sentinel laughed. "Shake a few hands. Show everyone you care about them. Some of these people have been searching for the Instrument with Freedom their entire lives. To have finally found it, and discovered that it is, in fact, a hero, is a dream come true for them."

"No pressure," Jack muttered.

They crowded around him. He shook their proffered hands and, as politely as he could manage, declined invitations to eat. Oliver

Winsley ran around him in circles. He awkwardly ruffled the boy's hair, to which Sentinel nodded his head in approval.

In the distance, Jack saw Hero get up from a table and leave The Crypt. Just before he revealed his wings to float to the alcoves, the brilliant Primal shot him a cold stare. Jack was taken aback. Hero had always been friendlier than many of the other Primals. What had changed?

After a time, the people began to drift away, giving him final handshakes, smiles, or salutes. Jack breathed in relief. He continued to limp toward his rooms.

Another man stood from his place at a table to intercept him. His right arm hung in a sling, and he wore the uniform of one of the IAL regulars. Jack stopped to let him catch up.

The man came to a stop in front of him and saluted awkwardly with his left hand. "Damon," Jack acknowledged. He returned the salute. "Good to see you back on your feet."

"You as well, sir. We were afraid you and Rook were gone for good."

"He's not out of the woods yet," he said, pointedly not addressing the question in the man's statement.

But Damon, it seemed, was as much an adherent to the indirect approach as Jack.

"Is it true what they're saying, sir?" The wounded man asked bluntly. "That you are the Instrument of Fate?"

He gave a sour grunt. "What do you think?"

"With all due respect, sir," Damon answered, keeping his eyes fixed over Jack's left shoulder. "I don't care what you are."

Jack shifted in surprised at the answer. "Really? Why?"

"Because of what you've done for us, for The Resistance, sir," Damon replied. His face remained resolutely professional. "I don't care if you're the Instrument of Fate, an ordinary man posing as an immortal, or a deluded lunatic. Your actions have proven your intentions, sir. You're a man worth following, and I'll go where you lead."

The answer was unexpected and disturbing. Jack shuffled his feet uneasily. He'd done nothing to deserve this man's devotion. It seemed alien and unmerited. He found he didn't like the idea of having followers. Despite his disquiet, however, he nodded his head. "Thank you, Damon."

"Ironheart," the man replied, snapping another salute with his good arm. He spun on a heel and walked back to his seat.

Jack stood for a moment to watch Damon's retreat. Sentinel laid a hand on his shoulder.

"I don't like any of this, Sentinel," he muttered. "I'm not a leader. I'm not a hero. And I'm certainly not the Instrument of Fate."

"I don't like being this muscular and handsome," Sentinel shrugged. "We've all got our burdens to bear."

Jack chuckled despite his mood.

"You'll be all right, Jack," Sentinel assured him. "In time, I think you'll find that you are all of those things."

Chapter 40

"Men are haunted by the vastness of their ignorance. Religion, science, philosophy, and ambition are little more than futile attempts to compensate for the infinite expanse that is all we do not know."

— Helmi, Philosopher

Jack shot toward The Crypt's dome. When he neared the apex Jack slowed his momentum and allowed himself to fall. He tapped lightly on the regulator, shifting his weight forward at the same time. He flipped in the air and straightened out, coming into a light hover far above The Crypt floor.

He was getting good with the jetpack. Even Rook said he was a better flyer than anyone he'd ever seen, and the gruff soldier had been trained long ago in the Imperial military. It all had to do with weight compensation. The more he practiced, the more he discovered how his body weight affected his movement, especially while attempting aerial maneuvers. It was exhilarating to weave through the air, high above the ground. It had been slow going at first, but now every movement felt natural.

A figure dressed in the standard blue IAL uniform appeared on an alcove balcony below. Jack started to descend, but brilliant blue wings grew from her back and she rose up to meet him.

"Trouble sleeping?" Freedom asked as she matched his height.

He nodded. "It appears that we now have similar problems."

"One of the burdens of leadership, I'm afraid."

"Well, thanks for sharing that with me."

Freedom continued staring at him with a thoughtful expression.

"Checking up on your prophecy boy?" Jack grunted sarcastically when she did not speak.

The angelic Primal's head cocked sideways. "I see you've accepted your destiny."

"I've accepted nothing," he corrected firmly. "But my protests convince few. I assume I have you to thank for that."

Freedom inclined her head in an almost regal gesture. "Of course. Many of our comrades have searched for the Instrument for decades. They have the right to know their efforts were not in vain."

"And what about the city of Victorian?" Jack questioned coolly. "Does it have the right to know? I've been told that a rumor has been sweeping over the city like wildfire. A human savior, long prophesied, has entered the city. Victorian's lunatics are already crying his inevitable triumph over our Primal overlords on the street corners."

Freedom watched him expressionlessly for a moment. "You knew that when I found the Instrument I would use it against the Empire."

"I'm just another pawn, eh, Freedom?" Jack growled. "Another tool."

"Don't act surprised," she reprimanded. "You were not ignorant of my resolve when you joined this fight. This is war, and I will use every means at my disposal to attain victory."

"And you say you're different from Tyranny," he sneered.

"Don't presume to judge me, boy," Freedom snarled in sudden anger. Her eyes blazed. "I've never forced you or anyone else to do anything."

"No," Jack agreed bitterly. "But you twist events to allow for no other choice."

"There is always a choice."

"Don't mince words with me, Freedom," he spat. "The ultimatums you provide can hardly be called choices."

Freedom glared. Her eyes burned with cold, blue fury. "Do you wish to leave? No one will stop you. But you *are* the Instrument; one way or another, you will help decide the fate of this struggle. If you leave this place, Tyranny will either imprison you or offer you more than you ever dreamed existed."

Jack sighed wearily. He was tired of this same argument. Tired of struggling with himself inside his own mind. "You know I won't leave," he growled. "And that is why you give me the option."

Jack pressed on his regulator and swooped toward The Crypt floor before she could answer. He didn't want to see Freedom right now. He didn't want to listen to more of her talk of destiny or choice or reason. When he landed, Jack didn't stop to remove his jetpack. He continued out of The Crypt and into the halls, not even knowing the destination of his cold march until he reached the stairs. He climbed them two at a time and pressed his fist to the hidden lever.

The sandstone altar lifted up, and he exited into the ruins of Blackgate Cathedral.

It was the dead of night, but with the glow of Victorian's gas lamps and the crumbling remains of the cathedral's old, vaulted ceiling above it was difficult to see the stars. Jack began the ascent up the crumbling bell tower stairs to its summit. By the time he reached the top, he was panting with exertion, but his breath caught in his throat when he realized someone was already there.

It was Valen. Jack noted the combat suit fitting tightly over her body. He cursed his luck. He should have remembered there would be a watch posted, but he hadn't been expecting *her*.

Valen had been noticeably cold toward him for weeks. She'd come to see him only once since his awakening, and even after recovery she had avoided him or remained pointedly silent when he saw her. It wasn't the sarcastic, disdainful iciness to which he had grown used. It was something different. Something deeper.

"What are you doing here?" she demanded at his appearance. She sat with her back against the brick and her legs stretched comfortably before her. Her Sharps rested on her lap. Jack climbed out of the stairwell and collapsed across from her, emulating her posture.

"Couldn't sleep."

"So the combat suit and jetpack are to help you count sheep?"

"Practicing," he grunted. "In The Crypt. Freedom showed up."

She snorted. "Got into another argument, huh?"

"Yes," Jack confirmed. He laid his head back against the wall and closed his eyes. "And I'm not looking for another, so could we, please, just not get into it right now?"

Valen scowled. He sighed to himself.

Now you've done it.

"Why would we get into an argument, Ironheart?"

"You've been avoiding me," Jack said bluntly. "And looking at me like I've been eating babies. I don't know what the problem is, but I'm exhausted and I can't sleep and everyone thinks I'm some steamblown prophesied savior and *I don't bloody want to get into it right now.*"

Surprisingly, she did as he asked and remained silent. He almost thought he saw a regretful grimace pass over her face before she

277

went back to looking out over the twinkling lights of the city. A few minutes later, she spoke up again.

"I'm sorry," she muttered.

He squinted at her suspiciously. "Why?"

"For being so standoffish," Valen said. "I just– I don't understand anything going on anymore."

"You and me both," Jack mumbled.

"Everything is confused around you," she said. "I had you pegged when you first arrived. You were human. You were something I could understand. Humans are saints and jerks and everything in between." She grinned one of the nasty smiles Jack was all too used to receiving. "You were more toward the jerk end of the scale. But then we put your head on straight, and you joined us. Grew a little bit as a person."

Jack only grunted, wisely choosing not to address the jab.

"But then, all this happened," Valen waved a hand vaguely in the air. "All of a sudden, you're not human anymore. Freedom says you're the *Instrument of Fate*. Some Primal-human hybrid. How am I supposed to wrap my head around that? How could you, *you*, possibly be some hero out of prophecy?"

He shrugged helplessly and answered with the only response he had. "I don't know."

"I mean, you *can't* be half Primal or a legendary savior or any of that," she protested. "It's insanity. You're...well, you're...you're *Ironheart*."

Jack watched her for a moment. She looked back toward the city. Confusion and something...different painted her face. He couldn't decide what it was, but the whole issue seemed to be causing her great distress.

"Do you think I'm the Instrument?" he asked. He just wanted one person to tell him no. One person to say everyone else was crazy. That *he* was crazy. He wanted her to say he'd been imagining the rapid healing and the death-defying resilience.

"I don't know," she whispered instead. "I've always believed Freedom. Always. And I saw it, Booker. I saw it with my own eyes. Spite should have killed you, but he couldn't. And then you were up and running like nothing had even happened. But I *saw* it. It did happen."

Jack collapsed glumly into silence. He would get no consolation here. No answers.

"Wait," Valen said, abruptly alert.

"What?"

"Tempest," she answered, looking in the distance. "See her? She was running a reconnaissance flight over the city, but she's back way too early."

Jack squinted to see a small winged shape approaching in the dim light provided by the city's lamps. It grew swiftly in his vision until Tempest alighted on the landing beside them.

"Raids by the enforcers," she said curtly. Her hair and eyes were shifting at an abnormally rapid speed. "All across the city." She grabbed them each by a shoulder. Her expression was urgent. "Valen, go gather the troops. Jack will come with me. We've got to stop this madness."

Chapter 41

"Poet! Make certain to write this down."

– Hero, Famous IAL Warrior

"I hope you're really invincible," Tempest said as they winged over the city. "Otherwise we're going to have a tough time stalling the enforcers until the others arrive."

"Why is Brutality doing this now?" Jack asked as he pulled out his pistol and checked to make certain it was loaded and ready for use. It was the only gun on him. He hoped Valen remembered to grab some of his others. "Why raid a bunch of random houses throughout Victorian?"

"The coppers are hitting dwellings occupied by our informants," Tempest answered through clenched teeth. She looked recklessly angry, her hair phasing from black to blazing red. "They have likely been sitting on that information, wherever they got it, for some time now. Waiting for the opportune moment to strike. It's a good bet that gossip about you has reached the ears of the Emperors. They're determined to crush the Resistance's will early, while the rumors are still fledgling whispers. Tyranny has always been obsessed with the Instrument. Even the slightest hint that we might have it would provoke him to instant action."

Fires were blazing below them. Screams rent the night. Sporadic gunfire punctuated the pandemonium. "Right there!" Jack pointed urgently. "Look! The coppers are dragging people out of that building." A gunshot cracked. He gaped. "Steaming hell, they're executing people in the streets! We've got to get down there!"

"Those aren't our people," Tempest said curtly. "We'll help later if we can, but the Resistance comes first. Besides, Freedom and the others will expect to meet up with us where the nearest informants reside."

Jack clenched his teeth as the wails faded behind them and new ones rose to take their place. The whole of The Narrows was a hotbed of milling confusion. More muffled gunfire reached his ears. "Some of the gangs are putting up a fight," he grunted. "At least that's something." A thought pushed into his mind. "Chaos is sure to

280

take advantage of this confusion, right? Surely we can expect him to be harassing the enforcers in the midst of all this."

"Chaos is indisposed at present," Tempest replied shortly. "So don't count on anything. It's likely that his gang will be out in force though. All of these coppers roaming the city in squads will likely draw out a healthy opposition from Anarchy and some of the others."

"I don't know if that's good or bad."

Tempest didn't reply to his statement. "There's our destination." She pointed to an alley below. Coppers were pulling a family into the street and forcing them to their knees. Most of the neighborhood was gathered around – either watching or shouting at the enforcers – but none interfered. If they did, they would be next.

"There's another informant under our protection two blocks to the north," Tempest continued. She was looking ahead with her extraordinary Primal vision. "She's about to be executed too."

"Drop me," Jack said, "and go save her. I'll handle this squad."

"Are you sure?" Tempest asked dubiously. "You've got one revolver against a squad of ten, and as soon as you ignite your jetpack they'll see you coming."

"I'm not going to ignite it," Jack explained impatiently. "I'm going to test out these so called abilities."

"We don't even know that—"

"No time to argue," he said firmly. "Drop me and save the next informant."

"If you insist."

Tempest swooped toward the street. The scene grew in his vision. The prisoners were leaned over the alley gutter with hands on bowed heads. The enforcers pointed Webleys at the backs of their skulls. The crowd around them shouted and spat, but the coppers ignored it all.

"Now!" Jack said urgently.

"Two-story drop, coming right up," Tempest muttered. She released him.

He fell toward the cobblestones with his pistol in hand and legs braced. The ground was approaching very fast, and his nerve gave out just before he reached the ground. He pushed on his regulator at the last moment.

It was a good thing he did.

Jack hit the bricks hard. Even the last second ignition had done little to slow his plunge. Pain lanced up his shins and knees, and he gasped at the pain. There was no time for his aching legs, however. The coppers turned with surprise when his jetpack ignited. He forced himself to rise from his landing crouch, ignoring the excruciating objection of his knees. He raised his revolver and fired. The bullet entered the forehead of the nearest copper, a mere pace from his smoking barrel, and blew through the back of his skull. His second shot quickly followed the first, and another copper fell.

Jack leaned forward and slammed a hand on his regulator as the coppers recovered from their surprise. He plowed into the nearest group, scattering them with the blunt force of his flying body. Then, he twisted and tapped his regulator, allowing him to flip behind an enforcer and grab his coat collar as he landed. He pulled the unfortunate man in front of him as the other coppers fired. Bullets smacked into the human screen. He held the body up in front of him as a shield and raised the revolver in his right hand to return fire.

The street around him was pandemonium. The crowd was screaming and scattering for cover as bullets flew and ricocheted off The Narrow's brick walls. The terrified family was crouching in the gutter, still frozen by terror.

Jack fired until he heard the click of his revolver. Six shots expended, four coppers down on the street, and one falling apart in his hands. He dropped his weapon to the cobblestones and ripped the enforcement baton from his shield's belt. He shot forward again, dropping the dead man, and laid about with the club.

The coppers tried to follow him with their revolvers, but Jack spun through them on light feet that were supplemented by quick bursts of his jetpack. He cracked on wrists and skulls, desperately dodging the enforcers' frenzied gunfire.

And he was alone. His baton was raised over a dazed copper. The rest were stretched, unmoving, across the alley floor. The man's eyes refocused, settling on his face.

Jack brought the club down.

A sharp pain lanced through his torso at the movement. He glanced down to see blood oozing from a bullet hole in his combat suit just below his rib cage. He ignored it. It didn't appear to be a deep puncture; Morthal's combat armor seemed to work as he had said it would.

Jack turned to the family. Faces watched from windows, and most of the dispersed crowd hesitantly returned. He noticed with chagrin that some few bodies lying in the street were bystanders, caught in the crossfire as the coppers had tried to kill him.

The informant, Jack assumed, was the man draped protectively over the woman and two girls. They peered fearfully up at him from under the man's arm.

"It's all right," Jack said gruffly. He held a hand out to them. "I'm with the IAL. Everything is going to be–"

Something hit him with the force of a train. He was smashed against the alley wall by a heavy metal bludgeon. A Primal enforcer in full Celestial Steel plate pinned him down. Red wings fanned behind him.

Jack noted with some amazement that he wasn't dead. His body seemed fully functional, despite the small crater he had made in the brick at impact. The bullet wound had stopped bleeding. A small tinkling sound echoed in his ears, and he realized with shock that the metal bullet had been pushed from his healing body.

The Primal's eyes had a look of astonishment behind the helmet. Apparently, the fact that his prey was still breathing had flustered the enforcer as much as everyone else in the now silent street. Jack struggled to free himself from the iron grip, but the Primal's grasp grew harder. An armored fist rose, and a sword appeared in its grip.

"Jack!"

The Primal looked up just as he did. Sentinel swooped in on green wings, and something fell from his hands. Jack reflexively caught it.

One of his Rangers.

The sword began to fall, descending to remove his head from his shoulders. He pressed the double barrels to the blue gorget that covered the Primals neck and fired.

The enforcer was thrown to the other side of the street. He sputtered and choked on the silver blood washing over the shattered metal. Sentinel landed beside Jack and offered his other Ranger.

Jack took it and finished the job.

"What were you thinking?" Sentinel demanded as soon as it was done. He ignored the other occupants of the street. All were hushed in stunned shock at the turn of events. "I'm your bodyguard now, Ironheart. I should always, *always* be by your side."

"It's all right, Sentinel," Jack replied. He rarely saw the unflappable Primal this agitated. "My new abilities weren't working at first as they should have been, but all of sudden, when I was in serious danger, they popped up again. Did you see that Primal smash me into the wall? I should have shattered into a thousand pieces!"

"I'm supposed to protect you," Sentinel snapped. "I can't do that if I'm not *with* you."

"Fine," Jack soothed impatiently. "You didn't used to be tasked with protecting me. I think you're taking this bodyguard thing a bit seriously."

"Freedom gave me a responsibility," Sentinel growled. "One that aligns with who I am, I might add. So, yes, I take it seriously." Some of his humor abruptly returned. "And I happen to like you a little, so I don't want you to get decapitated any time soon."

Jack felt a smile twitch at the corners of his mouth. "Well, thanks for the shotguns. I wasn't looking forward to decapitation myself." He walked over to retrieve his revolver and put it back in his belt. "Did you bring any extra ammunition?" Sentinel tossed him a bag of shotgun shells and extra rounds for his revolver. "That'll do for now," Jack said as he reloaded his weapons. "Where are Freedom and the others?"

"Dispersing to protect the citizens," Sentinel replied. "It's steaming chaos throughout the city, Ironheart. Enforcers are kicking in doors everywhere. We've got every available man mobilized. It's all just a messy, citywide firefight. Chaos' men are adding to the confusion as well: blowing up buildings, shooting at coppers, shooting at civilians, shooting at *us*. Mostly they're staying focused on slaughtering squads of enforcers, though."

Before Jack could reply, he realized the street's occupants had gathered closer and closer. They were in a circle; nearly close enough to touch him. Most kept crowded well away from Sentinel. "What are you?" a dirty man in a coal-caked jacket whispered. His voice carried a hint of awe. Eyes kept flickering to Sentinel's brilliant green wings, but they inevitably came back to Jack, wide with wonder.

Jack realized everyone in the street was looking at him. He shifted uncomfortably.

"He's that freedom fighter everyone's been talking about!" A man in a flat-topped cap shouted from further back in the crowd.

"They say he's destined to bring down the Primals." A hush fell over the crowd, and the man nodded his head triumphantly. "The Ironheart."

A frenzy of babbling murmurs engulfed the crowd. Jack tried shaking his head, but the people began to mill about excitedly. Some shouted his name and others cursed him.

"There is no human hero!" a female voice wailed over the noise. "That is foolishness. The Primals cannot be defeated!" This only increased the noise, and the physical nature of the mob grew more turbulent.

"You heard the Primal!" Another man shouted over the din. "He called him Ironheart. We've all heard the rumors of a human who will destroy the Emperors." Everyone in the crowd was shouting at once.

"Destroy the Emperors? Listen to yourself, you madman!"

"The Ironheart will crush–"

"The gods will surely punish us for such sacrilege!"

"ENOUGH!" Sentinel's voice roared over the ruckus. He stood amongst the squalid crowd, radiating glory over their destitution. His armor shone green and gold in the sparkling light of his majestic wings. The mob cowered down in fear. "Get up," Sentinel commanded. His voice was deep and terrible and ironically filled with authority. The crowd struggled back to their feet. "You will not bow to me. You will not bow to any Primal. The time of your deliverance is nigh."

Jack watched, as thunderstruck as any of those around him, as Sentinel pointed an armored finger at him. The motion was striking.

"Ironheart stands before you. The very Instrument of Fate. Do not worship him. Do not worship me. We do not wish it." Sentinel strode through the stunned crowd with his long spear held in a one-handed grip. He pointed it dramatically at the filthy, stunned faces around him and held their eyes with his own. "You are humans, not Myrmidons. A people proud and powerful! The Primal Empire's oppression holds no sway over you. Rise up! Your leader stands before you. One of your own! Follow Ironheart to victory and liberty! Spread the word to your comrades! Spread the word to every human with a proud heart and a thirst for freedom! Primals will no longer be your masters. Rise up and seize your independence! Rise up!"

A roar washed over Jack as the crowd surged forward, reveling in the illumination of Sentinel's blazing wings. They pushed in on Jack, struggling to touch him, to speak to him. He grabbed their proffered hands and listened to their thanks and saw the tears streaming down their cheeks. He could no more speak than he could understand what had just happened.

"The Ironheart!"

"Ironheart for freedom! Ironheart for freedom!"

Their cries surrounded him. Pierced him. Jack nearly shrank away from the adoration and the fervor in their voices.

"Down with the Emperors!"

"For The Ironheart!"

Sentinel strode through the mob. They parted without question to let him pass. He laid an armored hand on Jack's shoulder.

"Come, Ironheart," he said gently. "We still have a city to save."

Chapter 42

"Pacifism has no place in the struggle for liberty. There is no such thing as a peaceful revolution."
— Freedom, Primal Leader of the Independent Army of Liberty

"What the hell was that, Sentinel?" Jack demanded. He collapsed to the ground in exhaustion.

The whole of Victorian was in uproar. The raids had been carried out across the width and breadth of the city. Human coppers and Primal enforcers had clashed with the IAL in the first truly large-scale engagement for decades. Portions of the city were aflame. The dead – Imperial enforcers, IAL freedom fighters, gang members, and civilians alike – littered the streets. Jack was unsure what had happened tonight, but he knew one thing for certain. Nothing would ever be the same.

"I gave the humans something to believe in," Sentinel answered calmly. He sounded weary, and he slid to the ground to rest beside Jack. A line of silvery blood trickled down the side of his face from a gash near his temple.

The night had been spent flying from one scrape into another: fighting off coppers, dodging Primal enforcers, and engaging them when need be. Sentinel had repeated his passionate speech to every group of citizens they had rescued or encountered. With the raids providing stark evidence of the Empire's brutality and the message of the Resistance providing a counterpoint, riots had erupted throughout the city before the raids had ended.

"Something to believe in?" Jack said incredulously. "You offered me up as some kind of symbol. What you gave them to believe in was *me*. I can't be a savior for these people!"

"That is how it must be," Sentinel replied, unperturbed at his distress. "You are the Instrument of Fate. Did you think you could still fight in the shadows?"

He couldn't believe this. "I'm no prophesied hero, Sentinel. I'm not the Instrument!"

"You are," Sentinel contradicted him. "And for better or worse, the entire city now knows it. Make your peace with that knowledge, Jack, and soon. We are now past the point of no return. Become the man you were meant to be, or we will be destroyed by the power of the Empire."

Jack rested his head against the wall. He was *not* the Instrument. He knew it in his bones, but he found he was too tired to argue. The fate of an empire, of his race, of his entire world now rested upon his shoulders thanks to Freedom and her delusions.

He was something different. He knew that now, after what he'd seen tonight. But he refused to give in to this madness. Jack knew the truth: this would be the downfall of his people. Their faith was given to a false champion.

Jack wasn't exceptional.

He wasn't special.

Chapter 43

"I don't want to watch the world burn. I want to dance inside an inferno while the Realms are reduced to ashes around me. Why, you ask? Because everything is better when it's on fire!"

— Chaos, Legendary Primal Mob Boss

"Tell me we're not considering this," Jack demanded.

Freedom did not answer.

"The fact that you allow your Myrmidons to speak to you in such a manner is disturbing," Anarchy drawled. "Particularly this "hero" of yours."

Riot bellowed out a raucous laugh. Jack's face hardened, and he crossed his arms to stop himself from reaching for his Rangers.

Twilight was beginning to descend on Victorian. The meeting between Freedom and Chaos had been arranged to take place in a warehouse near the airdocks, but still close to The Narrows. With the increased patrols of Imperial forces, setting up this meeting had been dangerous, difficult and, to his mind, completely unnecessary. But Freedom wanted to hear what the god of mayhem had to say, and she wanted Jack to come along. So, here he was.

Directly following the night of the enforcement's raids across the city, Victorian had been in turmoil. Enraged by the opposition the enforcers had encountered from the IAL and Chaos' fanatics alike, the emperors had ordered a full military occupation of the Grounded Realm's capital city. Two entire corps of the Imperial Army had been sent in to aid Brutality's considerable, but stretched, enforcement service in putting down resistance and restoring order. Now, the masses of Victorian lived under martial law, a measure that had not been taken by the emperors for decades. Many humans cursed the IAL and all the "rebel gods" for their predicament, but no small portion of the city's population was in uproar over the occupation. They were spurred on by the IAL's calls for revolution and the spreading fervor of belief in "The Ironheart," a human savior who was destined to destroy their divine overlords.

Jack clenched his teeth in frustration at the thought.

He could not argue with Freedom's success, however. He had never felt Victorian this close to its breaking point. For his entire life, the human masses had simply accepted submission to the gods. It was the way things were supposed to be; Primals rule and humans serve. Now, the city was torn between those who believed in Freedom's declarations of liberty and those who thought the empire was not to be resisted, led by members of the powerful Illuminati church. There was no room for apathy or middle ground. Everyone in the city had been forced to choose a side.

There was a third option, of course: throw caution, life, and sanity to the wind, join Chaos' camp of lunatics, and refuse to acknowledge anything. Nothing really mattered. Primals, empires, liberty, emancipation, right, wrong, philosophy, religion – Chaos denied the importance of all, and, to those who found the new state of the city too much for their overstrained minds, it was an appealing alternative.

Jack had grown up on the streets of Victorian. He knew Chaos and his ilk. They were maniacs with no goals, no morals, no rules, and no regard for the sanctity of anything. So when Tempest brought news that Chaos wished to meet to discuss the possibility of a tentative alliance, he had openly scoffed.

Somehow, he still found himself here, listening to this preposterous proposition.

"The Empire will crush your little rebellion soon," Anarchy continued his slow, oddly intimidating drawl. It wasn't the way the words were uttered that made Jack uneasy; it was the hints of volatility beneath the measured calm. "The emperors will raze this city to the ground before allowing this *revolution*," he spat the word like a bitter taste from his tongue and his mouth twisted with amusement, "to grow powerful enough to challenge them."

Jack's lip curled.

Anarchy was a disconcerting Primal. Chaos' second was tall and thin, with snarled, reddish hair that hung to his shoulders and a face that was somehow equal parts wild and vacant. But the most disconcerting feature was his eyes. They pierced their target with a remarkable passion that didn't seem to register behind the blank light of his nearly colorless irises. It was a chilling juxtaposition of infatuation and neglect, made all the more disturbing by the sheer, deadpan sense of psychosis he exuded. Jack suspected that beneath the calm exterior, the Primal was exceptionally insane.

Riot was different. He was still clearly mad, but in a more predictable way. The hulking creature was a massive specimen of Primal power: broad, thick, and brutal. Dark stubble covered his brutish features, and his severely crooked nose was quashed on his face beneath gleeful, frenetic eyes. His round skull was shaved but for a broad strip of black hair that ran from his forehead to the back of his burly neck.

Freedom still didn't answer, but Jack had had enough. "We don't want or need the help of homicidal psychopaths," he growled.

Riot's grin following the statement was oddly proud, but Anarchy only glanced at him for a brief moment. "This city is aflame because of him," he said. The slightest nod of his head was the only hint that he was referring to Jack. He kept his gaze firmly fixed on Freedom's stoic face. "The Myrmidons are in an adorable tizzy about the rumors of this *Ironheart*." When he said the name, Anarchy's lips twisted again with bizarre amusement. "But you and I both know that a bunch of fervent Myrmidons aren't going to accomplish anything against Tyranny."

"Give us a chance," Jack snarled. "We might surprise you." Sentinel laid a soothing hand on his shoulder, and he subsided into silence again.

"We are natural allies," Anarchy went on while studiously ignoring Jack's interjection. "You need us and we need you. Tyranny will crush your pathetic attempts at rebellion. You need more Primal support; we've got some of the numbers you need."

Finally, Freedom spoke.

"And what's in this for you?" Her voice was quiet, as it always was when she was very serious. Jack nearly interrupted again in protest. Surely Freedom would not ally with the likes of these?

"The destruction of Order has always been Chaos' great passion," Anarchy answered, laughing. "The Empire is the will of Order incarnate. It forces everyone to live by neat little rules." His smile was feral. "The only way to live is without rules, Freedom. If the empire is destroyed, we get what we always wanted: a world without rules. A place where mayhem, change, and lawlessness are the norm." Anarchy sighed theatrically. "Steamblown paradise, my dear."

Freedom was quiet again, and Jack held his tongue, though he wanted to snap that Chaos could take a long leap off an airship.

Sentinel stood calmly beside him. Jack took a few deep breaths and followed his lead as best he could.

"We'll consider it," Freedom said bluntly.

"*What?*" Jack exploded.

"That's all we ask," Anarchy replied in a humble voice that didn't suit him. He smiled; it didn't reach his colorless eyes. "Of course, we also ask that, once you *have* considered, you make the correct choice." Riot bellowed another raucous laugh. "You would do well to remember that Chaos is not known for his patience."

"I am well aware of Chaos' temperaments," Freedom replied with neutral calm.

"Yes," Anarchy's smile was telling. "I imagine you are." He turned and strode for the opposite exit of the warehouse.

"I look forward to seeing what you can do," Riot's grin was utterly manic. His eyes flitted sneeringly over Jack's face. "Never met a Myrmidon who thought he could take on a Primal before." Jack glowered at him, which the hulking Primal seemed to find enormously entertaining. At his continued silence, however, he followed Anarchy from the building.

As soon as the warehouse was empty but for Freedom, Sentinel, and himself, Jack furiously rounded on his angelic leader. "How is this even an option?" he demanded.

"The end of this empire is the objective," Freedom replied, refusing to rise to his anger. "I can only deal with one goal at a time, Mr. Booker. If Chaos helps us to reach that goal, everything else is secondary. Whatever might happen after liberation is not my current affair."

"This isn't about your objective," Jack snapped. "It's about what is right!"

"You're awfully self-righteous about your allegiances now," Freedom pointed out. The beginnings of an icy tone were creeping into her voice. "Did you not do what you had to do as a gangster? Did you not fraternize with some questionable individuals to survive?"

Jack clenched his teeth and cast about with his mind for an answer. He found none. "This is different," he answered lamely.

"It's no different," Freedom countered. Her tone was brusque and final. "Besides, I've not yet agreed to anything."

"Jack has a point," Sentinel spoke up softly from where he'd been listening. "In addition to the moral implications of allying with Chaos, there are other things to consider." He raised an indicative, armored finger. "For one, many people, humans and Primals alike, have been aggrieved by Chaos as much as the empire. We could drive away large numbers of supporters interested in aiding our cause by collaborating with an organization that is often considered to be worse than the empire. Also, though we will gain many veteran human fighters and powerful Primals, they will be decidedly unpredictable partners. All of Chaos' men will be difficult to control, especially the Primals. We would have an army of loose cannons on our hands."

"All true," Freedom agreed. "But Anarchy's analysis of the situation is not incorrect. Without plentiful reinforcements, and soon, Tyranny will destroy our fighting forces and end the current unrest by putting down insurrection in the most brutal way possible. We have our reserves coming from Jackson, as well as a number of airships to comprise a weak navy, but it's not going to be enough."

Jack tried to interject, but she continued over his objections stoically.

"With Chaos' Primals and gangsters, we have a fighting chance if we must meet a sizeable Imperial force in an open engagement," Freedom pointed out. "Besides, an enemy of an enemy is my friend, and Chaos is as likely to target us as the empire if we spurn this offer. Accepting may be necessary to keep from having to watch our backs. I say, let Tyranny deal with Chaos' volatility."

"It just feels wrong," Jack grumbled. "None of this makes up for the fact that Chaos is a maniac that murders and destroys on a whim."

"I've not yet even accepted the proposal," Freedom snapped. "What do you want me to say? I would be lying if I said I wasn't considering it, and these are my reasons."

Jack folded his arms stubbornly and braced himself for further argument.

"The sooner we're back at the base, the better," Sentinel interrupted the brewing quarrel swiftly. "It's well past dusk. Imperial patrols will be out enforcing curfew. We're going to have a long and arduous time getting back unseen as it is, so we'd best get started.

Otherwise, Champion's going to get anxious at the delay and send out a rescue party."

"You're right," Freedom agreed in a serene voice, but Jack noticed she still shot him an irritated glance.

He nodded his agreement to Sentinel as well, but turned to his silver-haired leader. "This isn't over, Freedom," he growled.

Freedom shook her head wearily, but a hint of a smile flitted across her lips. "I think I preferred when you were just a new recruit: talented, suspicious, and accustomed to following my orders. Now, you're the key to everything we are trying to accomplish. It has changed you, Mr. Booker. You're becoming the leader you were meant to be."

Jack grunted sourly, but didn't protest.

***

Jack stretched out his legs from his seat at the long tables. Sentinel emulated him wearily. The last weeks since the fateful night of the raids had been long and relentless, with little time for rest. Everyone was tired, but Sentinel seemed abnormally so.

Their trek back from the meet with Anarchy had been long and tedious, as they had been forced to dodge patrols of Imperial soldiers in blood red uniforms. The skies above Victorian were full with the watchful eyes of Primal enforcers and rocketeers, so a quick flight had not been an option. It had taken nearly four hours to slip back to base unseen.

Jack laid his head down on the table.

Freedom had left them the moment they returned. She was likely as tired of their disagreements as Jack. The closer this city came to its breaking point, the more distance he felt between himself and the IAL leader. It wasn't just his new position of quasi-command, and it certainly wasn't the fighting. The harsher Tyranny and Order became, the harder Freedom resisted in response. Jack was beginning to sense more than a desire for liberty. There was something personal, primeval, and unforgiving here. He would not have thought it possible, but Freedom had become yet more ruthless as her rebellion had picked up steam.

"Do you think we may have gotten in over our heads?" Jack wondered aloud. He turned to look at Sentinel. The weathered Primal arched an eyebrow at him.

"All the time," Sentinel answered jokingly, but a hint of seriousness was beneath his amused sarcasm. "I suppose I knew once the stone started rolling it would be difficult to stop."

Jack grunted and shrugged his shoulders. "Primals are freakish strong. You should have no trouble stopping a rolling boulder."

"I'm exhausted," Sentinel pointed out cheerfully. "If I tried, I'd be smashed into a green and gold pancake."

"What are you two still doing awake?"

Jack craned his neck toward the deep, reverberating voice. The bald head and armored body of Justice greeted him. His face was customarily somber and hard, but it was no longer filled with the dislike he had seen in the past. Strangely, after the taking of the Ironsides the golden Primal had been, not warm toward him, perhaps, but decidedly less cold. In fact, he was now friendlier toward Jack than nearly anyone besides Champion and Sentinel. It was a bizarre change, and Jack was unsure what had brought it about. "You need rest." Justice's voice was almost chiding. He scowled at them.

"Couldn't sleep, Justice," Jack explained. "There's too much on our minds. We figured we would stay on call in case there was another emergency."

Sentinel laughed. "Which is steaming likely. There has been a riot nearly every night this week."

"Worried about an alliance with Chaos?" Justice asked perceptively. He moved to the table to join them. The benches rattled as the huge High Primal sat.

"Stop reading me," Jack protested. "It's creepy."

"It is part of who I am," Justice shrugged. "I do it unconsciously. Besides, I don't need to read either of you to see you weren't thrilled with the meeting's conclusion."

Jack grunted and gave a grudging nod. "Surely you can't believe an alliance would be acceptable? You know better than anyone what Chaos is like."

"I cannot say I relish the thought of working with him or any of his lackeys," Justice admitted. "It is better to be defeated than compromise who we are for victory. But everyone has their failings;

at least Chaos and his people have the guts to recognize their own depravity. Most people deny that they have transgressions."

"Must be nice to know what your crimes are and just not give a damn," Sentinel chuckled.

"Don't worry about Freedom," Justice assured them. "She's hard, and I have always seen a thirst for vengeance alongside the hope for freedom and justice. But, in the end, she does what is right for the Resistance and the Myrmidons." A small smile played on his dark lips. "Sometimes she cares too much for them. The Myrmidons deserved to be cut loose a long time ago."

"Is all that from a reading?" Jack asked. "Or a regular observation?"

"Both," Justice smiled. "Freedom can be as complex as she is one-dimensional. Not all Primals are like that. Some never take a step past their base nature."

Jack gave the words silent contemplation. The three sat this way until the scuffling of feet in passage outside The Crypt declared someone's approach.

"There's another riot in The Narrows," Bannen announced. He was breathing heavily after having hurried to report. "Some of the other scouts and I caught wind of it not ten minutes ago."

Jack jumped up anxiously with the others. "How bad?"

"It's a big one," Bannen confirmed. "The mobs have already clashed with a few curfew patrols."

Jack looked at Justice and Sentinel. Sentinel smiled at him, but his eyes displayed a worrying level of exhaustion. Justice gave him a nod. "Alert Freedom and gather the men we have available," Jack commanded. "Imperial troops and Primals will be there shortly, I imagine. If we don't get a response team on site to counter the crackdown the streets are going to be swimming in blood."

"I'll go ahead to scout the situation," Justice responded. "You, Bannen, and Sentinel come along with the backup as soon as you can."

Jack nodded and gave the golden-armored Primal a tired slap on the back. "It never seems to end," he sighed wearily. "See you up top."

Chapter 44

"All that is required for oppression to prevail is the apathy of good men."

– Excerpt from *Freedom's Progress* by Lady Liberty (pseudonym),
blacklisted author

"*Slouch*," Jack demanded. "Justice, you have to slouch."

The dark-skinned Primal's shoulders slumped a mere fraction of an inch.

Jack sighed. "Better," he said, giving up. It was likely the best Justice could do.

Justice didn't make a good human any more than Jack did a half-Primal. The golden-eyed giant was too straight-backed. Too perfect. The most regal human lord couldn't come close to comparing with the force of will he possessed, nor could they hope to emulate the impeccable poise with which he held himself. Asking Justice to realistically impersonate a human was like asking Jack to pass himself off as a dog.

The Primal was posing as a wealthy merchant from the southern isles so as to pass through the daytime streets of Victorian "undetected." Jack supposed if every Victorian citizen was blind such a plan might actually work. Justice wore the well-cut merchant's suit with the same aggressive self-confidence with which he wore his gleaming golden plate.

Jack shrugged the sack he was carrying high up on his shoulders and tugged on the brim of his bowler, muttering a gruff pardon for his master to the passersby who stared. He shook his head. It was like trying to hide a lion in a steamblown fishbowl.

"Sentinel will be irate when he wakes to find you gone," Justice said as he strode past a cluster of gossiping housewives near a bakery. Every eye followed as they passed. Jack bobbed his head at them and doffed his bowler anxiously.

"Everyone's exhausted, Justice," he pointed out. "And Sentinel seems more so than most. Freedom must have him working on even the few occasions I can get some shuteye. It's good we let him sleep."

"He's right," Valen agreed from her place on Justice's arm, where she played the part of the wealthy merchant's mistress. "Sentinel's looked awful for weeks now."

"Just because he needs the sleep doesn't mean he's going to like you leaving the base without him," Justice replied. A heavy carriage rumbled toward them on the street, but the huge Primal let it swerve around him rather than make room. Jack shook his head in disbelief. The carriage's driver looked equally stunned at his own compliance.

"Justice, it will be *fine*," Jack assured him. *If you don't alert the entire city to our presence.* "I'm hardly defenseless without my bodyguard. Invincible, remember? Besides, you're here. How much safer could I be than with a High Primal?"

Justice growled. "I'm just warning you that he's not going to like it. You know how he is about you going anywhere without him."

"I know," Jack soothed. "But somebody needs to attend and observe this assembly, and we're available. Freedom is gone to make certain the arrival of the men from Jackson goes smoothly. Champion's in charge at the base while Freedom is gone. Tempest is watching Chaos. And Hero and Bannen were on duty all night; we're stretched thin right now."

"What are the Emperors up to?" Valen wondered aloud. "Why have a gathering in the Imperial Square? It could be a propaganda rally."

"Maybe," Jack agreed. "Attendance is 'mandatory' for Victorian's citizens; imperial troops and enforcement have been out all morning rousting people from their homes and workplaces to herd them to the square."

"I don't like it." Justice scowled so impressively that several other pedestrians nearby turned on their heels and ran away. "Whatever it is, Tyranny wants everyone to see it. It's going to be big."

"And big news for Tyranny isn't likely to be good news for us," Valen finished.

Justice nodded.

The nearer they came to the square, the busier the streets became. Flocks of people streamed toward the gigantic courtyard in the heart of Victorian. Beggars and laborers from The Narrows, nobles in carriages from the Diamond District, dockworkers from the shipyards, urchins scampering between gaps in the crowd – all ushered onward by roving bands of coppers and regiments of Imperial troops in resplendent red uniforms.

"They can't fit the whole of Victorian's population in the Imperial Square," Valen scoffed.

"That's not the point," Justice replied gruffly. "Tyranny wants as large an audience as possible for his display. The larger the audience, the faster his message is dispersed to the whole of the populace."

As the flow of people continued to press them onward, Jack began to look for a good vantage point. "We need to get up high. It will make it easier to see."

"And easier to escape if we're discovered," Valen muttered.

"Agreed," Justice said. He turned against the stream of pedestrians and easily pushed through the throng. Jack followed in his wake, lugging his heavy sack.

They waited for the nearest group of coppers to look the other way, and then slipped into the nearest alley. A group of furtive-looking teenagers occupied the alley as well. They were probably trying to avoid attending Tyranny's assembly, but one look at Justice's hulking form sent them scampering away. Jack handed his sack to the Primal, who looked to either side before releasing his wings and floating hurriedly to the roof of the nearest building. Valen and Jack followed him up a nearby drainpipe.

The Imperial Square was less than a block to the north. Jack could hear the loud buzz in the air that only comes from a gathering of thousands of people. Justice led the way north across the rooftops. He prudently did not use his wings. Platoons of rocketeer troops occasionally swooped by as they patrolled the skies. Jack, Valen, and Justice carefully kept out of sight, using Victorian's sloped roofs and plentiful chimneys for cover.

The buildings that bordered the square were government buildings: tall, pillared, authoritative constructs that displayed the power of the Primal Empire. Jack crouched furtively on the roof of the Victorian Municipal Assembly Hall and peered into the gigantic courtyard.

The Imperial Square covered a wide area with a spire thrusting up from its center. The image of Victory, the Empire's greatest general, was affixed with raised sword on its tip. So large and dense was the crowd that he could discern not a single cobblestone beneath the carpet of human flesh that milled and babbled below. Tens of thousands of Victorian's population murmured about the strange assembly, creating a steady hum so loud it threatened to overload his ears.

Directly across the expanse was Enforcement Headquarters, a blocky, imposing structure of dark brick and few windows. It appeared more of a fortress than a government building. Beneath the bastion's wide shadow was a raised, wooden platform. A Primal in glaring, golden plate stood at the platform's head, and a platoon of Imperial Fusiliers stood at attention behind him. Jack could discern nothing else from such a distance. The Primal was little more than a gleaming man-shaped ant no bigger than his thumb. Justice could surely make out the details, but he offered no insights and was characteristically silent.

"I don't like this," Valen said suddenly. Her tone was filled with unease. "It's not like Tyranny to waste time on a rally while there are enemies to crush. This assembly has to be a trap or serve some other purpose."

"I must agree," Justice's deep voice rumbled quietly from behind them. "But Order does occasionally get her way. It could be her hand in this."

"We'll see soon enough," Jack grunted. "Justice, do you still have our jetpacks? We may have to leave in a hurry."

The Primal patted the burlap sack by his side. "Let's hope you don't have to use them."

Jack fidgeted restlessly. "What's the time?"

Justice pulled a pocket watch on a chain from his merchant's outfit. "A minute to five." His eyes crinkled as he peered toward the platform. "It will begin any moment now. Order is nothing if not punctual."

"What could this be about?" Valen muttered. "A propaganda rally would make sense, but, even in the Imperial Square, the emperors can't expect anyone past the first hundred paces to hear what is being said."

That sounded ominous to Jack. "Perhaps it's not a message they need to hear," he said slowly. "Perhaps it's a message best shown…"

He fell silent as small figures in drab, colorless rags began to shuffle on to the platform.

300

The resplendent Primal below did not move as the line of humans, burdened with chains, shuffled to the platform's edge. He watched silently as the Fusiliers lined up across from the prisoners.

A great roar went up from the crowd as the Imperial firing squad drew their rifles to their shoulders. Jack knew not if it was in outrage, fear, or exhilaration. The weapons' reports were drowned out by the shouts of the multitude; the prisoners crumpled like rag dolls.

"And so the message becomes clear," Justice's voice rang over the overwhelming shouts. "It is an example. It is a warning for all who would defy the Empire."

A second group of prisoners was prodded up to the platform.

Again, Jack scarcely heard the discharge of the weapons, so great were the screams of the spectators. Smoke billowed from barrels, and humans collapsed in bloody heaps.

The line of prisoners continued, unabated. They were marched from the bowels of Brutality's great fortress in a ceaseless stream. The bodies fell from the platform to the ground opposite the crowd, creating a gruesome mound.

Jack had lost count of those executed, and still the bloody spectacle continued. The crowd had slowly lost its volume, and they fell gradually into a sickened silence. The air was pregnant with quiet horror. Each volley from the barrels of the executioners fell on the ears like a vicious blow.

The Primal below did not stir.

"This…" Valen whispered at his side. Her voice was horrorstruck, but Jack could not bring himself to tear his eyes from the grisly scene. "This is…"

Her voice faded away. Whatever it was, it was beyond expression.

Eventually, the endless line of victims did subside. There was no fanfare. The last were simply forced into position. Their heads were bowed; their spirits crushed. The last, crashing notes were sent from the firing squad's weapons like a grand finale.

And then there was silence. Tens of thousands of people shocked into utter stillness.

The Primal finally stirred. His armored hand rose deliberately. Pointing toward the crowd.

"NO…" Justice growled.

301

Suddenly, Jack found himself on his feet.

The humans below realized what was happening when Imperial soldiers pushed into the crowd, seeking those indicated by the golden-armored Primal. A collective cry of dismay engulfed the square as those individuals were dragged on the stage and summarily shot.

The Primal repeated the process.

Panic flooded the crowd as the realization hit home. The Primal was selecting people at random to be executed.

The message was clear: You are Myrmidon subjects of the Primal Empire, and your lives are forfeit to our whims.

No particular person was spared. A young child was ripped from her mother's arms in the second group, a panicked, protesting aristocrat was forced to the platform in the third, even an Illuminati priest in the fourth. Laymen, dockworkers, merchants, and housewives were subjected to arbitrary execution. Men, women, children, the old, and the young – all were identified as the Emperors' property. To be disposed of or kept alive at Primal leisure.

The crowd swayed violently, and terror-stricken groups moved to rush from the enormous plaza. They were confronted by Imperial troops in tight formation, filling the streets that led away from the square. Most of the citizens slowed in the face of Imperial military regiments. Some did not.

The troops poured volleys into the onrushing mob.

Slowly, the masses accepted the inevitable and huddled together in the square, leaving their fellows dying upon the cobblestones. Better to hazard the random selection of the firing squad than be shot down in droves.

Beneath the mounting horror at what he was observing, Jack felt a hot, tense rush of rage in his breast. He'd chosen to fight to protect people. How was he to protect them from pure evil such as this?

Jack felt a cautionary hand on his shoulder. He realized he was tense as a stretched wire, leaning out over the roof's edge. He attempted to wipe the enraged snarl from his face and turned to face his companions. "I'm going to stop this." The calmness of his voice surprised him. Inside, his fury threatened to overwhelm his sanity.

"Ironheart, no, you can't," Valen protested immediately. "There are only *three* of us, and–"

"You're right."

Valen cut off in shock, and Jack unclenched his fists in confusion. He had expected to have to wrestle his jetpack away from Justice.

"This is not justice," the huge Primal continued. There was a light in his golden eyes Jack had never before seen. The deep voice he had grown used to hearing filled with disdain was brimming with anger and authority. "I can no more stand by and watch this happen than I could hold up the heavens." Justice nodded at Jack. It was a gesture imbued with respect. "No matter the outcome, we must contest this injustice. If we do not, then who shall? I am with you, Ironheart."

Jack couldn't speak. He simply nodded in return. Justice seemed to understand.

"But, Justice," Valen protested, "you *despise* Myrmidons. Why do you suddenly wish to champion their plight?"

"Dislike is no excuse to let evil prevail," Justice stated. "Nor can prudence be allowed to become a screen for apathy. Besides," his voice fell to an uncertain mutter completely alien to his normal confidence. "I was, perhaps, wrong about the Myr– the humans." His eyes flickered from Jack to Valen and back. "There is great strength and honor that I had refused to see. And even if only the potential is there, then humans should be given the chance to show it."

Jack held out his hand, and clasped Justice's forearm. "Thank you," he said fiercely. Justice nodded, and his brow drew down with determination. Another crackle of rifle fire ripped through the air. Jack flinched as if he'd been slapped. "We need a plan."

"We fly down and stop this," Justice said simply.

"We'll have no chance," Jack countered. "There are Imperial troops everywhere. Justice, you move the fastest. Fly back and bring every available man that you can."

"You two won't last a minute down there alone," Justice protested. "With a Primal–"

"We'd be taken almost as quickly," Jack cut him off. "Valen and I can't fly as fast as you can. It's got to be you. Without help, there is no way we can stop this."

Justice looked like he was about to refuse. Then, surprisingly, he bowed his head in acceptance. Another volley from the firing squad split through the wails of fear rising from the masses. "This is a

303

trap," Valen said with exasperation as Jack dug around in the burlap sack for his jetpack. "A blind man could see it!"

Jack nodded his agreement. "Yes, it is."

"If we go down there," Valen replied. "We'll be doing exactly what they want. This is set for you, or Freedom, or–"

"You're not going with me," he interrupted.

"*Excuse me*?" Valen's eyes narrowed dangerously. "If you're going out there, then I'm going with you. There's no way I'm sending the face of the Resistance out there alone!"

"You'll be more useful doing what you do best," Jack pulled his Lee-Enfield Carbine from the sack and tossed it to her. "You know I'm right."

She looked like she might cry. "Ironheart, this is crazy…"

Jack turned away uncomfortably from her pained expression. He clapped Justice on the shoulder. The Primal helped him strap on his jetpack over his coat.

"You have your combat suit on underneath you clothes?" Justice asked.

Jack nodded. "Does anyone have any other suggestions?"

"She's right," Justice whispered in his ear. "This is a trap, and you won't last until reinforcements arrive."

Jack smiled with forced bravado. "I'm invincible. Remember?"

Justice nodded slowly, and he could tell the Primal knew he was lying.

"I'll just stall them," Jack said. "Now get out of here."

Justice looked at him with clear eyes. "I was wrong about you, Jack Booker."

The next moment, he was gone. His golden wings released, and he shot into the air, soaring south with great speed.

Jack tightened the last strap on his jetpack just as the execution squad fired again. He stood, strapped on the holsters containing his double Rangers, and slipped his Webley revolver into the holster on the small of his back. He met Valen's eyes. The look on her face was as stubborn as ever. "Wait until Justice arrives with help," she commanded.

"The longer I wait to intervene, the more people die," Jack said simply.

"But–"

"We can do this," Jack said fiercely.

He was going to his death. He knew it. She knew it. But it felt good to say. He walked to the roof's edge.

"Jack!"

He turned, stunned as much by the use of his name as the fear in her voice.

"Jack, you can't go down there!"

"We can't watch this and do nothing," he countered brusquely. "I'm going."

"You're not invincible!" she shouted, but her voice broke and a small sob escaped her lips. He was astounded to see tears on her face. "I don't care what Freedom says. You *can't* go down there. They'll kill you."

Jack stood rooted to the spot, utterly lost for words. It was the first time anyone had reminded him of his mortality in a long time, and Valen's fear shocked him to the core. "You're right," he admitted, taking her hands in an awkward attempt to console her. Strangely, he could think of little besides how beautiful she was, even with tears streaming down her cheeks. "I don't know if I'm the fulfillment of some prophecy or a freak of nature or some pawn that's been fooled. It doesn't matter. I don't think I'm invincible. But I know one thing with absolute certainty. I'm going down there. It's who I am."

"I...we can't lose you," Valen whispered. "The Resistance *needs* you. You're our figurehead. Our Ironheart."

Jack smiled. "Despite what Freedom says, I'm nothing special. I've always known that. I'm not important." He glanced toward the square below. "But I have to go down there. You know I do."

She looked into his eyes, and then nodded slowly. He let go of her hands and turned away. Her voice stopped him short at the building's edge. "You're wrong about one thing, Jack Booker," her voice called out clearly. "You *are* special. Don't ever forget that."

Jack smiled and leapt from the roof, plummeting toward the square below. He didn't believe her. But he appreciated her saying it anyway.

Chapter 45

"The greatest enemy of man is not evil or sin, but the loss of all hope."

– Helmi, Philosopher

Jack ignited his jetpack after a brief fall and steered himself over the crowd. Gasps from below told him that the host had noticed his presence, and a sea of faces turned from the appalling massacre before them to watch his descent. A single, solitary voice – the high and hopeful cry of a small child – broke the sudden hush that enveloped the square.

"It's The Ironheart!"

A thunderous roar swept over the multitude.

Jack was nearly deafened by the clamor of voices. At first it was an amorphous rush of sound, swirling and chaotic, a frantic cry of desperation and hope. But it altered slowly, melding into a mantra of fervor. Men, women, and children screamed his name in frenzied shouts of fear and conviction that grew into a rousing chant.

"Ironheart! Ironheart! Ironheart!"

The Primal on the platform turned to face the wild cries with a look of bewildered incomprehension. Then, his head tilted up to observe Jack's approach to the courtyard's forefront, and he became utterly still.

Jack landed on the platform's edge, dropping to a knee to brace his fall. He stood slowly from the crouch. The riotous chant shattered once again into an unruly, unrecognizable roar.

After he had risen, he nearly collapsed back on his knees.

It was The Primal.

Jack had dwelled on that face for so many years that its presence lent a sense of familiarity to the situation. The same sharp, flawless features, sunburst eyes, and sneering lips were a duplicate to the face he saw in his nightmares. Morgan's face appeared unbidden in his staggered mind.

The Killer.

"Pathetic," Pride said calmly. "Aren't they?" He turned his bright golden eyes to Jack. A contemptuous smile played across his perfect lips.

Jack took a stumbling step backwards. The cries of the crowd had been suppressed in his ears to a hollow buzz.

"They are aimless," Pride continued without waiting for an answer. "Meaningless. An entire race whose lives are so mired in insignificance that they must search for purpose in something greater than themselves. It's no wonder they choose to worship us." His eyes betrayed an emotionless disregard. He pondered a question that was at the same time both puzzling and of no consequence to him. "Primals are everything they are not: powerful, certain of ourselves, and, above all, equipped inherently with meaning. With a purpose."

Jack was silent.

"But you," Pride pointed a golden finger at him in a flippant, musing sort of way. "You're different. You're one of them," he waved his arm at the masses. "But you've taken your lack of meaning and twisted it to suit your own ends. It's repulsive that you would wish to steal their devotion from us, but the very concept of usurping their worship…" He paused pensively. "The scheme has a certain *audacity* to it.

"Despite my abhorrence of your wretched race, you would think that such boldness would engender a low sort of respect." Pride's arched eyebrows drew down. "Indeed, it would take nothing less than an extraordinary effort to engender even a modicum of positive feeling toward a Myrmidon in me. But, instead, I find myself even further revolted." Finally, the Primal's face dropped its facade and twisted into the visage Jack remembered from years before: a cold, contemptuous sneer. "Respect is something I thought I could never give to such hollow beings, but, in a way, I find that I have some small measure of respect for these other cretins." This time, Pride didn't even bother to indicate the objects of his disdain. His golden eyes held the whole of the Realms' hatred as they bored into Jack's own. "Because, despite their numerous faults, *they know their place.*"

Jack drew a Ranger in his right hand. When he spoke, the deadpan sound of his voice surprised even him. "I've seen this moment in my dreams."

"Have you?" Pride asked with amusement. The Fusiliers behind him had trained their weapons on Jack, and hundreds of troops were pouring into the square. The Primal waved them all down indifferently. "Tell me, *Ironheart.*" The name was released from his lips alongside a smirk, a token of his disdain. "Do you know why I am here?"

Jack took a step forward.

"I am here because of a legend," Pride informed him. "A silly little tale about a Myrmidon who thought he was *invincible*. This Myrmidon fought a High Primal, it was said, and survived. I thought it preposterous, when I heard the story. A fanciful dream of the rabble. But do you know what happened next?"

Jack took a second step.

"*My* name began to appear in the legend." Pride snorted with laughter. "Can you imagine that, Ironheart? The very idea that I would deign to fight a lowly creature like a Myrmidon? Ridiculous! I've killed hundreds of your kind, of course, for offending their betters with their presence, but I would surely remember *fighting* with one of you."

"You killed my brother," Jack growled. Fury was finally beginning to leak into his voice.

"Did I?" Pride asked with apparent glee. "Delightful! Strange that I have no recollection of that. But we have come full circle to the original question. Do you know why I am here?"

"No," Jack snarled and crouched to spring.

Pride's features twisted as he snarled back in kind. "I am here to prove that no Myrmidon can defy the Primals. I am here to restore the natural order of things. And I am here so that I might clear my name forever from this slanderous fable!"

Jack bellowed and shot into the air, directly at Pride. The crowd roared, rising in intensity. Morgan's face receded from his mind. It was unexpected, and it was strange. But it was welcome. For so long, he had wanted to kill this Primal, to make him pay for what he had done. Now, he was surprised to find that it didn't matter. He would stall this Primal, and then he would defeat him – for the humans who had witnessed the grisly scenes in this courtyard, for all the citizens of a city lost in oppression, for Dasher and Rook and Valen, even for Sentinel and Champion and the other Primals.

Jack closed on Pride, and the screams of the masses crested into a storm of anticipation and fear. He raised his Ranger.

Pride waited with disappointing calm. Light flickered in his armored right hand, and a golden flail appeared. It snapped out with unbelievable speed.

Jack tried to dodge, but the shining tendrils wrapped around his waist with ease. Pride swung his arm in a vicious stroke, and Jack found himself being slung through the air.

He slammed into the platform with incredible force. The boards beneath him nearly snapped at the impact.

Jack gasped at the pain that bloomed from his body. The right side of his face felt like it was on fire. He touched his cheek with a trembling hand. His face was a mottled mess of torn flesh and deep splinters. He didn't think his right arm was working properly either.

Jack reached out with his left hand to grasp his Ranger where it had fallen beside him. Pride approached as he struggled to his feet. In only moments, the crowd had gone deathly silent. Jack could almost feel their horror. "I fail to see anything divine in you," Pride sneered dismissively. "*This* is what seeks to usurp the supremacy of the Primal?"

Jack raised his Ranger and pulled the trigger.

Pride moved faster than Jack had thought possible, slapping away his hand with enough force that he heard his wrist crack. The shotgun clattered to the platform's wooden planks.

Cradling his arm to his chest, Jack attempted to leap back and reach for his other Ranger with his right hand, ignoring the sharp shot of pain that lanced through his shoulder at the motion. Pride followed. He stepped forward with a nonchalant air and shoved Jack lightly on the chest.

Jack was thrown back ten paces to land on his jetpack. All breath departed from his lungs.

What is happening?

His wrist was not mending. The ragged flesh of his face refused to recuperate. The slightest effort by Pride was enough to deal him grievous injury.

It was as if he were simply human.

Jack had long professed it, but he had not realized the extent to which he'd come to rely on his toughness and healing.

Pride was strolling toward him.

Jack struggled to his feet. He sucked in desperate breaths to refill his vacant lungs. There was no time to ponder his power's betrayal. He awkwardly managed to maneuver his second Ranger from its holster on his left thigh into his right hand.

Pride casually dodged aside as Jack fired – the recoil sent a wave of pain up his injured arm – but a flash of terrible anger crossed the Primal's features when a portion of the buckshot smacked into his breastplate at close range. He snarled and leapt forward, borne on brilliant wings that burst from his back, and smashed down on Jack's left knee with an armored fist.

Several of the bones in Jack's leg snapped audibly, and he cried out at the pain. He crumpled. Pride caught him by the coat collar before he reached the ground, lifted him above his head with one hand, and hurled him from the stage to the cobblestones.

Jack's shoulder shattered at the impact. His head cracked on the courtyard stones. The world shifted woozily for several moments before restabilizing. Pride floated to the ground to stand over him, and the crowd jostled against each other in an attempt to stay clear of their golden executioner.

"They don't believe it now, Ironheart," Pride said smugly. He gestured out at the horrified people surrounding him. "They thought they could believe in you and your fairytale. *Invincible*. For a short while, you gave them hope that they were more than the feeble, worthless beings that they are. They're quickly learning otherwise. You should have known better than to test your delusional prowess against a god."

No. NO. Why now? Why, of all times, did his newfound power abandon him? He had never needed it like he did today. This was the day he had lived for all his life, and it all deserted him *now*? He refused to accept it. Jack rose to his knees.

Pride snarled, apparently no longer amused by his doomed persistence. His armored hand blazed toward Jack's face in a disdainful slap that would have no doubt removed his head from his shoulders, but he managed to lurch away just enough that the Primal's hand fell on his battered body.

Jack crashed back to the ground.

He could no longer feel anything. The cobbles beneath him, the searing pain, the warmth of the sun. Everything was gone. He felt as if he were floating. Darkness was pushing into the edges of his vision, and the view he had of Pride standing over him was hazy and indistinct. A stifled sound came to his ears from somewhere near. A subdued sobbing.

The sound of shattered dreams. The sound of crushed hope.

Pride sneered down at him, and his perfect mouth formed words that he could no longer hear.

Morgan appeared before him. That constant grin was spread across his cheery cheeks. Dark hair spilled over his forehead. His green eyes sparkled in some unknown light. It wasn't a memory. It was a vision.

Jack smiled, and closed his tired eyes.

Chapter 46

"Blood can only be repaid with blood."

— Vengeance

Far away, a muffled gunshot echoed in his receding consciousness.

A familiar vibrancy crawled along his limbs, followed by the slow, painful *pop* of a resetting bone.

Jack opened his eyes. Pride was staring up at the rooftops with an enraged expression on his face. His golden breastplate was heavily dented near his right shoulder.

The alien, yet recognizable, tingling continued to course through Jack's body. The jagged puncture in his skull began to mend. The torn flesh reformed across his marred face. Something had changed, but it was happening too slowly. He struggled futilely in his mind, straining in an attempt to hasten the regeneration.

On the cobblestones at the Primal's feet, Jack's broken body stirred. Pride grabbed him by the back of his coat collar, and he thought everything was over. Pride would finish him. But the Primal didn't appear to have noticed that he was recovering. Jack hung limply from the god's grasp.

Pride rose to settle back on top of the platform and dumped him unceremoniously to the planks. Jack willed his recuperation onward. The shattered bones of his right shoulder were regenerating painfully beneath the skin when he realized that Pride was not even paying attention to him. The Primal was following something through the air with amused eyes.

Heavy armored boots, green and trimmed with gold, slammed onto the platform near Jack's head.

"Sentinel," Pride greeted the newcomer. "Sporting of you to make an appearance, but if you've come to save your Myrmidon puppet, I'm afraid you'll find you are too late. He has been irreversibly damaged."

"I am certainly late," Sentinel replied calmly, "but I think you'll find you are mistaken about Jack Booker."

Pride opened his mouth to reply, but his eyes flickered down at Jack. What he saw must have given him pause, because a frown replaced the eternal smirk on his immaculate face.

Jack could feel the strength beginning to pump back into his damaged muscles. He struggled to climb to his feet and failed. He peered up at his friend while he tried to rise. Sentinel had placed himself at Jack's side. His aegis was raised, his spear poised, and his unshakable weathered face was set in a determined stare that grimly defied the High Primal before them.

But Jack had never seen his friend so weary.

The eyes behind the gold and green helm were hollow and deep set, and, despite his resolute bearing, Jack recognized severe fatigue in the slight sag of Sentinel's shoulders. The man was clearly exhausted. He placed the butt of his spear on the planks and leaned on it casually, as if he wasn't worried about the current situation at all, but Jack realized that his friend needed the weapon's support to remain standing.

Jack recognized a new surge of strength and raised himself to a knee.

Pride's eyes flickered at him in bewilderment. His golden flail appeared in hand. "As touching as your rescue is," the High Primal stated, still addressing Sentinel. "I don't have time for any more of this. I have shown the masses that this Ironheart is no match for a god, and I will kill him to finish the task Tyranny set for me. It is time we wrapped this up."

Pride's hand rose and fell in a peculiar gesture. A signal.

Jack realized what was happening too late.

The Imperial troops arrayed around the platform raised their weapons and fired in synchronized volleys.

"NO!" Jack screamed.

Celestial steel bullets slammed into Sentinel from all sides, punching through the beautiful armor at short range. His friend jerked over and over, stumbling under the hail of flying shot as the storm of metal continued.

It was over in moments. Ringing remained in Jack's ears after the final volley. Sentinel slumped to the ground. Silver blood flowed from countless punctures in his armor. It pooled on the boards, dripped steadily over the edges and through the cracks to the courtyard.

Jack roared in anger and stumbled to his feet, ignoring his unhealed injuries. Pride gave him a contemptuous glance before leaping forward on golden wings. The Primal snatched up Sentinel's fallen spear and thrust it through his stomach.

Jack's cry of anger turned into a choking gasp. He clutched at the spear shaft protruding from his abdomen and coughed up a spray of crimson blood. Pride shoved mercilessly on the spear, driving him back to the platform and pinning him to the planks.

Another gunshot echoed from far away.

The round smacked into Pride's shoulder, deflecting off the metal and leaving another sizeable dent. The Primal ignored it, but motioned absently toward the rooftops. Despite the sizeable hole in his stomach, Jack's mind flickered to Valen. Rocketeer troops would now be coming for her too.

And he was powerless to stop it.

Jack could feel life slipping away from him again. He tried to stand, but Sentinel's spear remained a deadly anchor. He could see a stream of red spilling from his guts and spreading on the platform. It joined with Sentinel's silver blood in a large pool, swirling together in sluggish tendrils. He knew he was going into shock, but somewhere, deep within the heart of his lethargic mind, Jack thought the mixture was the most beautiful thing he'd ever seen.

Pride stood above him. A golden sword was in his hand.

Sentinel stirred.

For a moment, he almost didn't believe his eyes. A ruined body, covered by shattered green and gold, dragged itself to its knees. The Imperial soldiers around the platform appeared as surprised as Jack; several moments passed before the troops belatedly raised their weapons.

Sentinel staggered to his feet. Pride continued to stare down at Jack with utmost loathing. His golden sword rose for a killing blow. Jack met Sentinel's eyes just as his friend and guardian tottered forward on broken legs. Beneath the pain and the weariness, Jack saw a familiar determination. Then, he knew he was hallucinating. Sentinel was *glowing*.

Pride's weapon descended.

Jack struggled against the inevitable in vain. Sentinel lurched between Jack and the blade with a desperate cry that seemed to shake the heavens. The sword arched downward, and clove through his outstretched body.

Sentinel exploded into a wave of green light. Pride, the soldiers, the watching crowd, Jack – all stared at the tiny motes of light that drifted on the breeze. The last vestige of what had been a living being only moments before. The crack of the explosion had been deafening, but complete silence now hung over the square. Pride and Jack locked eyes in dumbfounded consternation.

Jack was filled with a vast, terrible energy. He thought he had felt power before. But he was wrong. This was the light of a star in his breast. It was the fire of an inferno, the force of a raging hurricane. The small buzz of regeneration that had run along his veins in the past now felt like a trickling stream when compared to the furious flood that washed over him. The energy of the cosmos was at his command.

Jack ripped the spear free of his body, ignoring any further damage he might cause. As the weapon was removed, his wounds closed instantaneously. He rose to his feet and snatched up Sentinel's fallen shield, slipping it on to his left forearm.

Pride stared at him in mystified shock. The crowd was shouting in wonder. Jack thrust powerfully at his adversary with Sentinel's spear, and Pride leapt back to avoid the searching blade. "What..." The Primal's face was twisted in incomprehension, wonder, and disgust. "What are you?"

Boundless anger pulsed through his mind. Infinite vigor raced through his veins. Jack had never felt this alive. He sucked in a deep gasp of the most refreshing air he'd ever breathed, and roared his exultation at his enemy.

"*I AM IRONHEART!*"

Jack slammed his left hand to his regulator, blazing toward his adversary. He couched Sentinel's spear under his right arm, its tip aimed at the golden breastplate.

Pride dodged to the side, narrowly avoiding the leaf-bladed spear. Jack executed an airborne about-face and kept up the pressure, jabbing and thrusting to keep the High Primal off balance. Pride's flail was in one hand and his golden sword in the other, but Jack was always moving. He spun through the air and danced on the platform's planks, taking off from the ground in short bursts and landing for quick jabs. He was a flurry of motion. He was an untouchable skirmisher. Pride growled with aggravation as the searching tendrils of his flail wrapped around nothing. Jack pivoted behind him and scored a hit on the Primal's hip, then took back to the sky. Pride released his wings and followed.

Jack led him on a winding course around the platform, swooping to scoop up one of his fallen Rangers. But in the air, Pride was his better. Jack returned to the stage, reversing the hit-and-run from moments before. His adversary dove and dipped on golden wings, swinging with flail and sword time and again. Jack waited patiently before igniting his jetpack, taking to the air in short hops that avoided the strokes.

Pride was clearly becoming frustrated.

The Primal sneered and feinted, as if coming around for another pass. Then, he broke off and signaled with a waving flail.

But Jack knew what was coming.

He took off in a dizzying spiral, flickering first this way, then that. The Imperial riflemen in the square below tracked his airborne progress with difficulty. Most of the shots went wide. Two found their mark, piercing his leg and shoulder. Jack ignored the wounds; the raging torrent of power within him made the punctures seem like no more than the bothersome bites of a fly. In moments the bullets were pushed from his skin and the muscles beneath fully regenerated.

The crowd had become a screaming, unruly beast while viewing the spectacle. As Jack gathered himself for another round of evasive maneuvers, the mob charged the soldiers arrayed around the platform. Focused on their airborne target, the troops did not realize what was happening until it was too late. It cost them the advantage of their rifles. The mob rolled over them, and the courtyard descended into a roiling mass of struggling bodies. Troops in red uniforms struggled to hold off an enormous mass of citizens armed with pried-up cobblestones in a brutal hand-to-hand struggle.

Pride continued to signal frantically. Rocketeer troopers descended from the rooftop of Enforcement Headquarters in droves, led by two Primal enforcers.

Several squads of rocketeers and three Primals would have convinced Jack he was doomed in the past, but he was not the same anymore. Righteous fury pumped through his veins at the death of Sentinel, and the power to move mountains seemed to burn in his chest. He flew at the incoming Primals head-on, screaming as he came.

Both of the Primal enforcers were clearly not expecting this. They halted in midair, and then tried to get out of the way of his flying rush. The first was too slow, and Jack's spear drove through the gorget of his armor and into his throat.

Most of the rocketeers had broken off to engage the mob in an attempt to relieve their beleaguered comrades, but the last squad closed in on him, following the remaining Primal enforcer's lead.

Jack tore across the courtyard like a hurricane. The rocketeers could not stand against him. He executed a deadly ballet in midair, spinning around his adversaries with consummate control. The Primal's searching blade missed over and over; Jack weaved in and out, always keeping an enemy between himself and the remainder of his adversaries. At first they held their fire to keep from hitting their comrades, but as he dispatched them with his flickering spear, they began to fire wildly in desperation.

It did them little good. Jack was untouchable. Jack was *invincible*.

Soon, he was alone in the air but for a crippled Primal, and something happened that Jack thought he would never see.

A Primal fled from him.

The enforcer's wings were flickering from his injuries. The Primal descended toward Pride in an attempt to force Jack to take them on two-on-one.

Jack pursued the Primal and ran him through the back. Then, he alighted on the platform, spear at the ready. Pride glared at him with wonder and hate. The High Primal's eyes flickered to the crowd, who had largely overwhelmed the Imperial troops. The mob looked poised to storm Enforcement Headquarters itself with their captured firearms, but they had paused, watching and waiting as he faced the golden god of Pride.

The Primal readied his weapons, flicking his flail in resolute anticipation.

Jack charged. The flail flickered out to capture him, but he was ready for it this time. He rolled under its grasping tendrils, came to his feet and launched into the air, feinting with his spear. Pride took the bait.

The Primal moved to counter the thrust. Jack released his jetpack's regulator and fell toward the ground, drawing his Ranger. His left hand came up, pointed the shotgun at Pride's breastplate, and pulled the trigger.

The High Primal's armor caved under the close-range, Celestial Steel firepower. The god stumbled, and his golden wings gave a telltale flicker. Jack dropped the Ranger and threw the spear to keep his enemy off balance. Pride dodged the weapon, but it gave him time to draw his revolver. The Primal recovered from his evasion to find himself staring into the barrel of a Webley Mark IV. Jack emptied the chambers of Celestial Steel.

Pride slumped slowly to the ground. His wings flickered fitfully...and were extinguished. Jack took his time replacing the spent cartridges in his Webley. After the last chamber was filled, he cocked the hammer.

The crowd didn't seem to know if they should roar in exultation or watch the execution in reverent silence.

"Stop." Pride's voice was weak, but somehow still filled with arrogance despite the blood pooling around his body. "You have no right," he snarled feebly. "Myrmidon filth – I am a god!"

Jack shot him in the head.

"Gods," he whispered, "don't bleed."

Chapter 47

A great roar went up from the crowd as Pride slumped at his feet. Jack lowered his pistol.

The cry of the masses was deafening. They were chanting his name. *Ironheart, Ironheart, Ironheart*... He stared in weary apathy. The force within him was still there, but Pride's defeat had taken the drive to use it from him. He looked over the blood-soaked courtyard listlessly.

Sentinel...

The crowd had not stopped its rhythmic chant. Jack peered out at them. The recent display of brutality and defiance had transformed them from a fearful gathering of subjects into a feral mob. But they had joined him in the fight, and they were with him now.

Jack raised a grateful fist. The response was overwhelming. A wave of sound rolled over him. The individuals at the fore waved their captured weapons or fired them into the air. He could see regiments of Imperial troopers trying to push through the crowd from the back of the courtyard to see what was happening.

It was time to leave. He had accomplished what was necessary. He had finished what he had come here to do. The executions had been halted. But he was looking out at the vanguard of a rebellion. Something had changed with the events of this day. This mob... It was the forerunner of a new age. The previous weeks' opposition seemed petty in light of the fervor before him. No longer was this a city of riots and insurrection. This was revolution!

Suddenly, the sun disappeared.

It was not actually gone. Jack could still feel its warm rays on his face and see the bright ball in the sky. But in his heart, a dark cloud covered everything beautiful and lovely. This city, this realm, these people – his fellow humans – were doomed because of what he had done here today. Jack realized the crowd had gone silent. They clutched each other fearfully and cast down their weapons in dread.

Two angelic forms descended from the sky and landed at his side. He greeted them with a despondent nod of his head. Justice was

319

resplendent in his golden armor. His executioner's sword was held in his armored hands. Freedom's eyes flickered over the courtyard's grisly scene.

"We need to leave," she said curtly. "*Now*. Tyranny is here. I can feel his presence."

Imperial troops flooded the courtyard. Rocketeers in the hundreds encircled the Imperial Square from the rooftops. Entire, fresh regiments of foot and elite Fusiliers poured out of Enforcement Headquarters. Coppers filled in the spaces between the military regiments, shotguns and revolvers at the ready. Dozens of Primals in gleaming plate alighted on the lip of the headquarters' roof. Brutality himself – a massive juggernaut of Celestial Steel – was at their head. Villain smirked down at Jack from the enforcement commander's side.

The Emperor floated to the platform from above.

Tyranny's hair was black as night and appeared to drink in the sun. His flawless face bore an expression of regal nobility, and Jack had never seen such piercing eyes. Wings of white lightening crackled from his shoulders, and a purple cape fluttered from armor of the most beautiful silvery white, like the color of Freedom's hair.

This was what majesty looked like. This was the incarnation of power and supremacy. The authority he radiated blocked out every other thought. This was a being born to rule.

The Emperor alighted regally on the platform's surface. He was mere feet away. Freedom and Justice, the most striking beings Jack had ever encountered, paled in comparison to the imposing sovereign. Tyranny considered them with a serious gaze.

"My old enemy," the Emperor addressed Freedom. His voice was like thunder in the mountains. It was a deep, rolling reverberation that exuded command even when his words were nothing more than a peculiar greeting.

"Tyranny," Freedom hissed. Her beautiful eyes had narrowed to mere slits, and her nostrils flared with deep-seated rage.

"I am disappointed in you, my love," Tyranny chided. He displayed an easy smile, and his tone was strangely warm. "I will admit, your stubborn insistence had me intrigued by your pet, but then you allowed him to appear where I could observe him for myself." The Emperor shook his head with disappointment. "You cannot hide the Instrument from me, Freedom, no matter what form you choose to claim it wears. I am not easily deceived."

Freedom had locked eyes with her enemy. Her posture was wary. Instead of answering, she grasped Jack's hand. He braced himself for a harrowing and futile attempt to escape the trap that had been sprung.

"Pride had his faults," Tyranny pointed out when he noticed Freedom's preparation for flight. He indicated the corpse of the former High Primal. "He wallowed too long in his triumph, savoring the moment until it had time to recover and snatch away victory. I will not make the same mistake."

Tyranny raised a hand to his troops. Justice stepped forward in front of Jack and Freedom. "Go," he growled to them. The golden Primal did not turn away from the Emperor. "I will do what I can. The two of you must escape. Revolution is hollow without the dream of Freedom, and any struggle will fail without an Ironheart to lead it."

"Justice..." Jack began.

"Justice has always seen more clearly than most," Freedom said quietly. "He's right. We must go."

Tyranny did not look inclined to let them. "Capture them alive, if possible," he commanded his troops. "If not, dead is just as good."

"Who dares?" Justice roared at his enemies, cutting in before the Emperor could finish his order. His two-handed executioner's sword was held before him like the judgment of a true god. "I am Justice itself!" His sword point swung to aim, unwavering, at Tyranny. "Who can challenge me on this madman's orders and claim still that he is righteous?"

The power in the question was potent, just compelling enough that a wave of uncertainty swept through the Imperial ranks.

They hesitated for a brief moment. Jack and Freedom had their chance.

Jack slammed a hand to his regulator as Freedom rose up beside him. He had expected a shower of Celestial Steel bullets to follow them; he had not anticipated cries of alarm to sweep the courtyard.

Every eye was trained on the sky, but not where they hung suspended in the air by wing and steam. Jack rotated.

A fleet of airships filled the air above the rooftops of Victorian.

Most were small schooners or light frigates, able to hold only a few cannon, but they were great in number, a small armada of repurposed trading vessels and transport ships. The captured Man O' War, the HMS *Ironsides*, was at their head. A half-healed Rook saluted him from the prow, where the veteran manned a mounted Gatling. IAL rocketeers gathered on the rooftops of the Imperial Square's periphery. Ropes dropped from the sides of the nearest ships, and squads of Resistance fighters shimmied down to take positions on the rooftops and in the courtyard. Primals in red and black armor mingled with those in white, silver, and blue, filling the air around the ships. Jack recognized Champion and Hero in the vanguard. A maniacal-looking Riot was at their side. Anarchy and the Primals of Chaos had come.

With no Imperial troops to oppose their escape, the masses in the square began a frenzied flight, pushing and trampling each other in an attempt to flee the impending battle. They streamed away through the now unobstructed streets and alleys.

Tyranny's voice had become something terrifying. No longer were his words pleasant and calm. The sound of his wrath boomed out over the courtyard. "Destroy these traitors! Crush the rebels! Show them what it means to defy the Primal Empire! Above all, do not let Freedom and the Ironheart escape!"

Every Imperial answered the order, and the square exploded with gunfire and motion. The IAL responded in kind. Jack and Freedom shot backwards, avoiding the worst of the volleys. The air to the north was filled with a wave of charging Primals led by Brutality and his enforcers. Champion responded by leading the Resistance Primals and the forces of Chaos in a screaming countercharge. The rocketeers of each side joined them. The airborne lines smashed together with the harsh screech of metal on metal. Rifle fire crackled from the IAL forces congregating on the rooftops and in the courtyard. Cannon boomed from the broadsides of airships targeting the Imperial troops below. Rhythmic, persistent shots punctuated the mayhem; Rook had finally gotten to open up with his Gatling.

Jack gathered himself to join his friends. He readied Sentinel's spear and shield, but Freedom stopped him with a hand on his shoulder.

"No! We need to go!" she commanded urgently. "This cannot become a pitched battle. We *must* withdraw!"

"We have them, Freedom!" Jack argued. "We have Primals, air superiority, and the numeric advantage for once. We can't give up this chance!" Below, Jack saw Tyranny try to follow them, but Justice blocked his path. The Emperor engaged him.

"Do not underestimate Tyranny," Freedom shouted. "He may have been caught off guard, but we are fighting on ground of his choosing! Ships of the Imperial Navy will be lifting off from the airdocks to join this battle as we speak, and he has nearby portal mirrors in Enforcement Headquarters that he can use to summon thousands of reinforcements in moments!"

Jack contemplated this for a few precious seconds. The clash of Celestial Steel rang in the air, the discharge of firearms added to the din and wreathed the square in disorienting smoke, and the screams of dying men tore at his ears.

Justice was fighting a desperate duel with a power-crazed god so they could escape.

"You've done all you could here today, Jack," Freedom urged. "There is a time to fight, and a time to regroup."

Jack hesitated for a moment. Then, he nodded reluctantly.

"Go!" Freedom commanded. She sounded relieved he had listened to her. "I need to organize a rearguard and a withdrawal. I'll be close behind you. Go!"

Jack turned his back on his enemies and departed.

Chapter 48

"When it comes to controlling Myrmidons, there is no better tool than lies. You see, at our core, Primals believe only in who we are, but the Myrmidons live by arbitrary beliefs. They believe in love and fear and joy, good and evil and nothingness. Somewhere in humanity can be found the belief in almost anything, and belief can be manipulated."

– Deceit, Imperial Ambassador

A green shield trimmed with gold rested on the bed, and a long, leaf-bladed spear lay atop it. Jack considered the weapons somberly.

He hadn't expected to lose anyone close to him today, but he found he wasn't surprised. It was the way of the world. Jack, it seemed, would always be doomed to watch those close to him depart. He had been bitter in the past. Those he tried to protect were always taken from him while he lived on. But *Sentinel* had tried to protect *him*. By rights, if events had been true to the pattern, he should be dead while Sentinel despaired at the futility of safeguarding others. Perhaps it was destiny's idea of a cruel joke that the roles had been reversed at this moment, leaving Jack alive and alone once again.

Sentinel was not the only one that had died today. The battle had raged for only a few short minutes in the Imperial Square before Freedom had formed an effective rearguard and withdrew most of her troops in good order. The fleet had broken up and scattered to confuse the Imperial Armada that had assembled in response. Some of the ships had successfully anchored at the Resistance's secret port outside the city. Some had made the long voyage back to Jackson. Nearly a dozen had been run down and shot from the sky by pursuing Imperial flotillas.

The city itself was still a battleground. Imperial troops had pressed on the heels of the retreating IAL forces until reaching The Narrows, where they had run into heavy resistance and been forced to fall back. Citizens throughout The Narrows and the southeastern section of the city had entered into open rebellion, throwing up barricades in the streets and alleys. A third of Victorian was effectively under the control of the IAL.

Justice had remained locked in combat with Tyranny to prevent him pressing a strong attack while Champion and the other Primals of the rearguard withdrew. He had not returned.

Justice, Sentinel, and who knew how many others were dead. Jack touched the shield with a pensive hand. He could have saved them.

Jack could feel the power coursing through him even now, buried just beneath the surface. It was always there. Always constant. It had not been so before. Though his power had revealed itself when he needed it in the past, it had never been a constant presence. And it had occasionally failed him, refusing to show itself even when he was in great need.

As it had today. He could have saved them.

If only he could have summoned it sooner, before Sentinel arrived...

Jack froze.

His numb mind hammered back through the events of the past several weeks. The times when his power had failed him: that was what he needed to see. He coldly analyzed the memories one by one.

You cannot hide the Instrument from me, Freedom. No matter what form you choose to claim it wears. I am not so easily deceived.

Jack leapt from his chair. He marched through the halls of the base. Most of the Resistance members he encountered watched him stride by without comment, staring in a sort of quiet awe, but he did not slow even when he was addressed. Groups of bewildered faces were left in his wake.

Jack found Freedom in the command center. It had transformed into a true intelligence hub since the prior events of the day. Reports from lookouts all over the city were piled into an ever-growing stack. Lists of supplies, weapons, ammunition, and other essentials for a long fight were also spread about; they would need a true quartermaster soon. Rook's part time duties for supply would no longer be sufficient. Casualty reports were still flowing in from all over Victorian. Maps, both of the city and of the entire Grounded Realm, were spread haphazardly across the large round table. They were covered with small markers of different colors and shapes.

It was with one of these maps that Freedom was occupied. She had yet to remove her armor. Jack noted the mingled remnants of silver and red gore that covered portions of the armor like splattered paint.

Champion was with her, pointing to the map with a concerned frown. Hero stood on her opposite side. He was nodding his head and looking distinctly irritated about something. Devalere was reading aloud from a pile of dispatches when Jack entered. He did not stop his report.

"News is pouring in that insurrection is rampant throughout the Grounded Realm," Devalere was saying. "The entire city of Jackson is in open revolt. When the garrison of IAL members there heard of the executions, they led the citizens in an unsanctioned attack on the Imperial garrison and on government officials, slaughtering anyone in the city even slightly connected to the Empire."

"Freedom," Jack called firmly. He surprised even himself with the brazen anger in his voice. "We need to talk. Now." Champion raised an incredulous eyebrow at the clear order. Hero's eyes narrowed, and Devalere looked at Freedom with surprise.

Freedom simply looked up from her maps, and when she saw his face she nodded. A sort of tired resignation rested on her beautiful features. Clearly, she had been expecting this. "Leave us," she commanded the others.

Devalere scurried to comply. Champion inclined his head and strode from the room, but he gave Jack a strange look as he left. The glare Hero shot him was cold, almost openly hostile, but he left without a word. Jack wondered once again what he had done in the past weeks to anger Hero. The golden-haired Primal was the friendliest person he'd ever met, and somehow he'd managed to alienate him.

But Jack would not be distracted. Right now he needed answers, and Freedom *would* deliver. He waited only until the door had closed behind Hero before addressing her coldly. "You lied to me."

Freedom was quiet for an eternity. Her angelic face was expressionless.

"Yes," she said at last. The sheer, candid simplicity of her answer took Jack by surprise, but he refused to be put off guard.

"How long have you known that I am not the Instrument?" he demanded harshly. Freedom was again silent for a time. The everlasting pauses before her answers were becoming unbearable.

"From the beginning," she admitted finally. "When first I told you that you were the Instrument, it was a lie. But it was a necessary one."

A necessary one? Jack was so angry he could hardly speak. It took several tense moments for him to gain enough control to utter a single, strangled word. "*Why?*"

Again that intolerable silence.

"Answer!" Jack barked. He shocked himself with both the enmity and authority in his tone. Freedom complied.

"The Instrument was beyond my grasp," Freedom explained carefully. "It still is. But I was tired of waiting for it to reveal itself. So, I saw an opportunity, and I seized upon it."

"An opportunity?"

"You," she explained. "It was all perfect. Your arrival here, the reputation you had created throughout Victorian's underworld, even the morale of our forces – it all fit. My people were weary and disheartened by our lack of progress. They were ready to see a success and willing to believe in it when I supplied them with one. I knew the power the idea of the Instrument held over our forces; I knew how badly this city yearned for a savior from Primal oppression. All I needed was a suitable, believable focus for their faith and the cooperation of Sentinel."

"So I was the focus for their faith," Jack growled through gritted teeth. She nodded in confirmation. He'd been used. Again. "Why did you need Sentinel?" he asked.

"Tell me," Freedom countered. "Have you ever wondered what Sentinel's Primal ability was? Didn't you ever think it odd that he never openly used it?"

"Yes," Jack admitted. "I asked him about it once, but he avoided the question. He said it was of no use to him."

"That's because it is of no use to him," she said. Her face fell so slightly that Jack almost didn't notice the sorrow in her features. For Freedom, it was close to a display of raw emotion. "*Was* of no use to him. Sentinel's power was the ability to safeguard another with a protective aura. It granted the target increased toughness, so that he or she could take punishing damage with relatively little injury. When injury did occur, the body would regenerate rapidly."

Jack stared, unable to utter a word. She was describing him. His power. It had been Sentinel all along. Once again his mind flitted back to the moments his power had failed him. Sentinel had been absent every time, and he had regained his abilities only when Sentinel had arrived. His friend had always been unreasonably angry at being left behind.

"But," Jack still struggled to order his thoughts. "Why hadn't Sentinel been using his powers before? He could have protected hundreds of others before me."

Freedom shook her head. "It doesn't work like that. Sentinel's power drew energy from his own body. Every time a target under his protection became injured, *Sentinel's* body took the brunt of the damage. Every time a target regenerated, it sapped energy from Sentinel himself to perform the act."

Sentinel's face flashed through his mind. Tired eyes looked out from a worn but smiling face. No wonder his friend had been so exhausted. He had been physically crumbling beneath the punishment Jack had put him through.

"It's also an ability that takes extreme concentration," Freedom had continued on with her explanation. "Sentinel couldn't switch the target at will every time someone was hurt. In order for the aura to work properly, he had to focus solely on one target for days at a time to initiate the ability, and then it was a constant process of deliberate attention to keep it working. It was a difficult and draining ability, and in the end, we had decided that it was more beneficial to have another fully-capable, unhindered Primal on our side than one that was always partially distracted and vulnerable." She hesitated. "Until you arrived, that is."

"When you needed Sentinel to confer 'supernatural' powers on a Myrmidon," Jack finished for her harshly.

Freedom did not answer, but she still held his eyes. Jack gritted his teeth. Of course *Freedom* would never admit feeling guilt over her actions. She was too bloody proud for that.

"Is any of it true?" he demanded. "My father?"

"Was not a Primal," Freedom answered. "Though your past is muddled enough that I could easily imply such an origin. However, it *is* true that you look nothing like the descriptions of your father and that you were probably conceived before your parents met."

Jack didn't even blink. Nothing surprised him anymore. He'd been lied to enough that he wasn't sure what he believed anyway.

328

Something was still wrong with her explanation, however. Jack drew a knife from his belt and slashed carelessly at his forearm, scoring a deep gash. Freedom started with surprise at the motion.

"What are you doing?" she demanded.

The wound was already closing up. Jack could feel a slight buzzing running along his arm, and the skin began to regenerate before blood had time to well out of the cut.

"Sentinel is dead," Jack said emotionlessly, though he felt a violent surge of sorrow at the words. "He is gone. I saw him explode into a million motes of dust. Yet his aura remains, stronger than ever it was in life. Why?"

Freedom nodded. "Valen told me what happened." She eyed him carefully. "I believe that when Sentinel died, he conferred the aura to you. In fact, I don't think it was Pride's blade that killed him at all. Blades do not kill by explosion." Jack snorted, conceding the point. "Sentinel sacrificed himself for you," she continued. "Just before the blade struck, he thrust every modicum of energy he had at you in the form of his aura. He even used the energy of his..." she waved vaguely around in the air, searching for the correct term, "his life force. I believe that this bestowed a long-lasting aura on you, possibly even a permanent one, though, with Sentinel gone, I have no idea where the ability now draws its energy. Perhaps... well, I've nothing but speculation. I have never heard of anything like this. Only time will tell."

Jack beheld his now flawless forearm. No trace of the wound remained. Freedom was watching him with guarded, unrevealing eyes. She seemed to be waiting for something.

"It was all a lie," he growled bitterly.

"Of course not," Freedom answered. Her tone became slightly angry. "Nothing is ever entirely unambiguous. Sentinel *believed* in you. Who you are. What you stand for. He knew you for a friend and a hero. No one will ever hold you in such high regard as he."

Despite his resolve to be bitter at Sentinel for the ruse, Jack felt grateful warmth in his chest at the words. He was determined not to show it to Freedom, however. This betrayal could not be forgiven. "Why, Freedom?" Her explanations had not eased his disquiet at the deception. In fact, he felt little toward her but resentment. "Why not tell me your plan instead of deceiving me and thousands of others?"

She returned his hurt stare with one that was somehow both unapologetic and filled with pity. "Because I needed you to *believe*," she said simply. "You're not an actor, Mr. Booker, and you would never have agreed to such a plan. I needed your belief to make it work. Others were already willing to accept the lie, but they needed to see your own conviction to follow without reservation. It took you a while to accept it, but you did today in the Imperial Square. We have a revolution in this city as a result."

Jack was finished with her games. "I'm leaving," he said bluntly. "Congratulations. You have your revolution. I'm through with you and your plots."

"You would abandon these people *now*?" Freedom demanded. "Where, then, will you go? The entirety of the Empire is looking for you. If—"

"I don't care!" Jack roared. "I have been deceived and used my entire life. I am finished with all of it! Find yourself a new puppet for your strings." He turned to walk out.

"Jack," Freedom said quietly. For the second time that day, he stopped out of sheer surprise at the use of his name. "I will not apologize for doing what is necessary, but it is true that I have abused your confidence and the trust of my people. That is why I am turning over command of the IAL to you."

Jack started walking again without turning back. He didn't answer her offer, and Freedom didn't try to stop him.

Epilogue

"You're just letting him desert?" Hero asked incredulously.

"He has every right to leave," Freedom replied in a calm voice, though a hot feeling of guilt had settled in her stomach. Hero's face was a mask of displeasure, but she had seen the brief flash of relief before it settled into frustration.

"You were serious, then? You planned to turn over command to that untested boy?"

"That 'untested boy' just killed one of the greatest Primals in all the Realms," Champion interjected dryly.

"It is imperative that both this city and this organization see him as the figurehead of the revolution." Freedom said. "The only way to ensure that will happen is to let him *be* the leader. No new lies. No more deceptions." Hero threw up his hands.

"Without that boy, everything that's been started here will fall apart," Champion warned. Freedom was mute, but she nodded in understanding. She had made her choices. Now it was time for Jack Booker to make his. She only hoped he was the man she had come to believe him to be. "The question is," Champion asked. "Will he really leave?"

Freedom rested her hands on the table and looked for the answers in the carved wood. "I don't know."

"You have fallen for your own creation," Hero accused. "You've come to believe in your own lie."

Freedom was silent for several seconds. "Perhaps."

Hero growled, clearly unsatisfied. He turned on his heel and marched out of the door.

"Booker won't abandon the people, Freedom," Champion assured her. "But what will become of the rebellion without your leadership?"

"The rebellion is over," Freedom corrected him. Her voice was harsh. "The revolution has begun."

***

Jack wasn't exceptional. He knew that. Somehow he'd always known. Freedom's insistence, the city's disturbing admiration, even the newfound powers – Jack had known even then.

And yet…despite Freedom's treachery, despite every instinct telling him otherwise, despite everything this pitiless world had taught him, he found that he'd been wrong all along.

He was exceptional. He was not the Instrument, but he was in a unique position. They *believed* in him out there. That he could protect them. That he would fight for them.

Jack knew that he always would.

A gust of air howled around the cathedral's bell tower. Jack absently closed his coat against the wind and reached up to pull his bowler down tighter on his curly hair. It was dark. The city had settled into an uneasy stillness. The two portions of the city – the area still occupied by Imperial forces and the remainder in open rebellion – were uncannily quiet. It was the calm before a violent storm.

Valen sat at the tower's pinnacle beside him. She was as quiet as he, but it was a comfortable silence. Scuffling footsteps echoed behind them, and he turned to see Dasher clamber out of the stairwell. "Jack?" The boy queried, his eyes adjusting to the dark of the night. Jack noted the lad's resemblance to Morgan for the thousandth occasion, but it was different this time. The hair wasn't quite the same, the nose and cheeks slightly less sharp. There was a resemblance, but he wasn't an exact copy. Not a portal into the past. Morgan was dead, and Jack missed him terribly. This was his friend, Dasher, and Jack was glad to see him.

"What is it, Dasher?" he asked.

The boy paused for a moment at his serene tone, but sat beside him when he made more room. "Freedom is looking for you, Jack. She seems…worried."

Jack shifted uncomfortably. She needn't be. He had felt a fool after his stormy withdrawal. He'd been betrayed. He'd been used again. But it didn't matter. This was bigger than Freedom and her lies. It was bigger than Jack and his hurt. He would stay and fight for his people, and nothing Freedom ever did would change that.

"I'll go see her soon," Jack assured him quietly. "But for now, I just want to savor this moment of peace with the two of you." He put his arm around Dasher, and the boy looked up at him happily. Valen's hand was in his own, but it didn't seem strange.

"Everything is going to change, isn't it?" Valen whispered.

He looked out over the lights of Victorian. He could feel the tension hanging over the streets like a heavy shroud.

"Yes," Jack answered.

If Ironheart blew your socks off (or even if it just didn't annoy you), check out my other works on Amazon!

Try my epic fantasy

The Arrival

Or if spaceships are more your style, pick up my science fiction novella

The Shrike Chronicles: Goddess

If you enjoy my books, please leave a review on Amazon. I love to hear feedback from my readers, and every review counts.

Acknowledgments

Look, I'm just the writer. I put in the hours to get this story on the page (or the screen, depending on your preference), but it wouldn't be worth the paper it's printed on if it weren't for the aid and support of a multitude of wonderful people.

My editor, Cate Baum, was equal parts supportive and stern with my original manuscript, which is exactly the combo every serious writer is looking for in an editor. Her aid in polishing the mistake-ridden first draft was indescribably helpful, and she displayed admirable patience in dealing with my stubborn eccentricities.

The staff at Kwill Publishing deserves my gratitude as well for their dedication to delivering a high-quality product. They were responsible for the cover design, formatting, publication, and much of the launch promotion. If anyone can be directly credited with *Ironheart*'s new-book shine, it's Cate and the team from Kwill.

As always, my family members were my biggest supporters. My mother and sisters have cheered for every work I've ever written, whether those stories have deserved applause or not. My dad and brother have always been my foundation. As I said in the opening pages, *Ironheart* is dedicated to the paladins in my life. Dad has always been there for my family as a father and husband, and he's been there for many others over the years during his service as a law enforcement officer. My brother, Kaleb, has had my back since our days fighting through the Oklahoma brush with our cap guns, cowboy hats, and plastic bandoliers. He has been my companion and best friend my entire life, and he's carried on the thankless tradition of the protector to this day, serving as a Sentinel to society as an Oklahoma State Trooper.

My alpha readers were as important to the refining process as ever. In no particular order, they are Kaleb, Kaitlin, Steve, and Angie Kemp, David Schoenhals, and Victoria Gaydosik. They provided insight that only discerning readers can supply. In addition to providing their opinions on plot, character development, and dialogue, they managed to catch roughly five hundred grammatical errors. I'm indebted to every single one of them.

In addition to those individuals who aided me with this particular novel, there are those who deserve my thanks for their influence on my writing career. Stephanie White and Dr. Victoria Gaydosik (Dr. G) have had a huge impact on me as an author. Mrs. White encouraged my passion for writing back in my more formative years, and I've never kicked the bug. Dr. G has been instrumental in making me strive to be the best writer I can be. She's been quietly supporting my books for several years now, and I would still be floundering if not for her guidance.

Finally, as with all my endeavors, the greatest appreciation goes to my readers. I am grateful for your patience in allowing me take a trip to the corner of Steampunk Street and Allegory Avenue. You wonderful people keep giving my books chances they don't deserve, and that means more than anything else.